DECLAN REEDE: THE UNTOLD STORY
(BOOK 3)

MICHELLE IRWIN

COPYRIGHT

DEDICATION

To the bloggers who have thrown their love behind Declan. Alison, from Alison S Parkins Book Reviews, Jennifer from The Power of Three Readers, Belinda from Hopelessly Devoted 2 Books, Siobhan from Diary of a Book Addict, Cryssy and Angie from United Indie Book Blog, Clare from Clare's Mad About Books, VDub from Romance Between the Sheets, Donna from Rebels & Angels Book Blog, Maari from Maari Loves Her Indies, and so many, many more. Thank you all for your faith.
For signing up to help share Declan at every opportunity.
And for loving this potentially unloveable man.

To the Chicken Soup girls—thank you for keeping me sane.

To Jenny C., I could thank you for all that you've done with Declan, but I'd rather thank Declan for bringing you into my life.

To those wanting anxious to find out what might become of Declan with Alyssa gone, I give you Decipher.

DECLAN REEDE:
THE UNTOLD STORY

CONTENTS:

GLOSSARY:

Note: This book is set in Australia, as such it uses Australian/UK spelling and some Australian slang. Although you should be able to understand the novel without a glossary, there is always fun to be had in learning new words. Temperatures are in Celsius, weight is in kilograms, and distance is (generally) in kilometres (although we still have some slang which uses miles).

Arse: Ass.

Bench: Counter.

Bitumen: Asphalt.

Bonnet: Hood.

Boot: Trunk.

Bottle-o: Bottle shop/liquor store.

Buggery: Multiple meanings. Technically bugger/buggery is sodomy/anal sex, but in Australia, the use is more varied. Bugger is a common expression of disbelief/disapproval.

Came down in the last shower (Do you think I): Born yesterday

Cherry (Drag racing): Red light indicating that you "red-lighted"/jumped the start.

Cock-ups: Fuck-ups/mistakes.

Diamante: Rhinestone.

Dipper: See S Bends below.

Do (Charity Do): Function/event.

Doona: Blanket/comforter.

Face Washer: Face cloth.

Fairy-Floss: Cotton candy.

Fillies: Girls.

Footpath: Sidewalk.

Formal: Prom.

Fours: Cars with a four-cylinder engine.

Gobful: Mouthful

Hydralyte: Hydrating formula (electrolytes).

Loo: Toilet.

Message bank: Voicemail.

Mirena: An IUD that contains and releases a small amount of a progesterone hormone directly into the uterus.

Mozzies: Mosquitoes.

Necked: Drank from.

Newsagency: A shop which sells newspapers/magazines/lotto tickets. Similar to a convenience store, but without the food.

Off my face: Drunk/under the influence (including of drugs).

Pap: Paparazzi.

Panadol/Paracetamol: Active ingredient in pain-relievers like Tylenol and Panadol.

Pavlova: Meringue-based desert, usually served covered with fresh cream and seasonal fruits (aka: sugar heaven).

Phone/Mobile Phone/Mobile Number: Cell/cell phone/cell number.

Real Estate: All-inclusive term meaning real estate agency/property management firm.

Rego: Registration (general); cost of vehicle licence.

Ricer: Someone who drives a hotted up four-cylinder (usually imported) car, and makes modifications to make it (and make it look) faster.

Rugby League: One of the codes of football played in Australia.

S bends (and into the dipper): Part of the racetrack shaped into an S shape. On Bathurst track, the dipper is the biggest of the S bends, so called because there used to be a dip in the road there before track resurfacing made it safer.

Sandwich with the lot: Sandwich with the works.

Schoolies: Week-long (or more) celebration for year twelves graduating school. Similar to spring break. The Gold Coast is a popular destination for school leavers from all around the country, and they usually have a number of organised events, including alcohol-free events as a percentage of school leavers are usually under eighteen (the legal drinking age in Australia).

Scrag: Whore/slut.

Shout (referring to drinks or food): Buy for someone. "Get the tab."

Silly Season: Off season in sports. Primarily where most of the trades happen (e.g. driver's moving teams, sponsorship changes etc).

Slicks: A special type of racing tyre with no tread. They're designed to get the maximum amount of surface on the road at all times. Wet weather tyres have chunky tread to displace the water from the track.

Skulled: (can also be spelled sculled and skolled) Chugged/Drank everything in the bottle/glass.

Stiff Shit: Tough shit/too bad.

Sunnies: Sunglasses.

Tassie: Tasmania (in the same way Aussie = Australia)

Taxi: Cab.

Thrummed: Hummed/vibrated.

Titbit: Tidbit.

Tossers: Pricks/assholes/jerks.

Tyres: Tires.

Year Twelve: Senior.

Wag: Ditch school.

Wank: Masturbate

Wankers: Tossers/Jerk-offs.

Weet-Bix: Breakfast cereal brand.

Whinge: Whine/complain.

Uni: University/college.

CHAPTER ONE

AN END IS A NEW BEGINNING

ALYSSA IS GONE.

The words repeated in my mind on an endless loop until they were hollow.

Meaningless.

Empty.

Like me.

Like my life.

The thoughts whipped through my mind until they filled the void the words had created, replacing everything I was with an agony that crushed my lungs and stopped my heart. The truth in it all raced through me, the pain ripping through my heart and soul. It clawed through my chest, tearing my heart into a thousand pieces that scattered like dust in the wind.

How had I gone from having everything to having nothing? All gone because of one stupid article, filled with a bunch of bullshit.

After dropping the phone handset and sinking to the floor, my mind tortured me with an endless loop of everything I'd lost.

My career.

My future with Alyssa.

My daughter, Phoebe.

The life I'd hoped I might deserve one day.

The words Ruth, Alyssa's mother, had said before ending our phone call moments earlier raced through me over and over. *"She called here a little over an hour ago, frantically shouting about a magazine or something. I couldn't get a straight answer out of her—except that she was leaving town."*

Even though Ruth hadn't known what magazine Alyssa was talking about, I did.

The damn fucking magazine that had fucked up so much for me already. It was the latest issue of *Gossip Weekly*—an article filled with little more than a fucking stack of half-truths and lies. They'd printed a series of compromising photos teamed with innuendo and bullshit as "facts." It had already destroyed my career after an early copy had been sent to Danny Sinclair, the owner of Sinclair Racing, my *former* employer.

After rushing down to Sydney to see him at his request, all of my dreams had gone up in smoke in a matter of minutes.

All of my dreams, including my new one. The one I'd barely started to have; barely dared to imagine. A life with my girls: Alyssa and Phoebe.

But now Alyssa was gone, and she'd taken Phoebe with her.

Every time I closed my eyes, I saw the bitter disappointment and heartbreak in Alyssa's honey-gold eyes. I'd seen it—caused it— often enough and this was obviously one step too far.

How could I come back from this when I'd been on my last chance as it was? The evidence that I was having an affair with Eden, my former teammate and friend, was compelling in print. The truth was that I was no more attracted to her than I was to the other subject of the article, Alyssa's sister-in-law, Ruby.

If I'd had a chance to explain, maybe I could have fixed things. I couldn't though.

Because my Alyssa was gone.

The knowledge that she'd run after seeing the article clawed at every happy memory I had from our time together since my suspension. Made me question every word I'd said. Every kiss we'd shared. Had I given her reason to doubt me? Had I not told her enough that I was ready to stand up and be the man she needed me to be? Or had I left her so broken over the years that any happiness we'd shared was weak enough to shatter at the first test?

The doubt, the fear, and the loss all pulled at the recollection of each smile. Every memory was torn to pieces like old photographs until I was nothing more than a shell filled with my bad memories and four years of regret.

One thing was clear. Whatever Alyssa believed because of that article was my fault. I'd given the gossip magazine so much ammunition, and not just in recent months. She'd had the image of me with other women shoved down her throat over and over. During my life in Sydney, I'd become the poster child for the bad-boy image. For so long, I'd thought I loved it. I'd fed it, encouraged it, and watched my notoriety grow. It'd left women lined up at my door, scrambling for a piece of the great Declan Reede. Every woman but the one I'd really wanted, even if I'd denied it at the time.

Now, that life—those choices—had come back to bite my arse big time. Even without the magazine in front of me, without my own face, turquoise eyes, and auburn hair staring back at me from the pages, I could recall each damning picture and every spiteful word.

With the thoughts of everything I'd lost, everything I'd thrown away before I ever really had it, racing through my mind, I sat on the floor and cradled my head in my hands. The pressure growing in my chest, stealing my breath, and throbbing against my skull made it impossible to move. I was unable to do anything but give in, and unwilling to even try to resist.

My fingers fumbled in my pocket to draw out the small box I'd brought with me from Brisbane. I'd slipped it into my pocket at the last second, not wanting to leave it at home just in case someone else stumbled across it. Plus, I'd thought it'd be a good luck charm.

Good fucking luck indeed.

I flicked open the lid and looked at the ring inside. Thousands of dollars I'd invested in a future that had looked to shine as brightly as the diamonds inside the white gold band, but was now as empty as the hole in the middle. Unable to look at the symbol of my shattered dreams any longer, I snapped the lid shut and shoved the ring back in my pocket.

My mind cried out, begging for relief. For a sweet tonic to salve the agony. There were plenty of options nearby. A fully stocked wet bar sat just metres away, waiting to be tapped.

Blissful oblivion hid at the bottom of each bottle.

Damn, was it fucking tempting.

My tongue slicked my lips at the thought of the liquor burning down my throat. Of it razing away the layers of doubt and remorse until they faded into the blur of hazy memories. God, I wanted that. Nothingness more complete and numbing than the blistering ache that scorched my skin with the imprint of Alyssa's touch.

I wanted a drink.

I wanted freedom from the agony of remembering.

More than anything, I wanted to drown the pain that threatened to tear apart my chest.

It's not like it would take much. A bottle. Two. Then I wouldn't have to worry about magazines or Alyssa, anything. For a few hours, I would be numb.

Unfeeling.

Uncaring.

Blissfully unaware.

It was almost too easy. I was at the bar before I had even decided to move. Just the sight of the bottle of whiskey front and centre on the shelf was like a punch to the gut.

I snatched the bottle off the shelf and sank to the ground, nursing it against my chest. One hand was already on the lid, unscrewing the top as my throat ached with the need to burn.

Alyssa's rules rushed through my head as a warning.

If I did it, if I resorted to using alcohol as a salve, I would lose her forever.

But what did it matter when she was gone anyway?

When everything was gone.

What was the point of anything?

It wasn't just the loss of the life I'd thought I might be able to have, it was the fact that I'd lost everything. I didn't even have the small victories my job had provided to hide behind any more.

I had nothing.

I *was* nothing.

Without my girls, I was less than nothing.

The bottle slipped from my hands and I let it fall into my lap. Reaching up, I clawed at my hair, fisting it. More than anything, I longed for the chance to explain myself to Alyssa. If I could convince her to grant me that tiny concession, maybe I could prove to her what she meant to me. I wanted to tell her that I hadn't meant to hurt her. That I'd *never* cheated on her. Never even felt the smallest desire to try.

From the moment I'd set foot back home in Browns Plains, every piece of me had belonged to her.

Even the broken parts.

I'd hoped that love and desire would be enough to piece us back together. I'd been wrong. So wrong, about so many things. And I'd left things in a bigger mess than when I'd arrived.

If only she'd let me explain that all I'd ever done was love her, even if my love wasn't enough to save *us*.

All my love had done was hurt her more.

Sinking into the foetal position, I found the blinding truth of it all. I should have trusted my first instincts and stayed the fuck away from her. I should have listened to her father, Curtis, and brother, Josh, when they'd tried to warn me away. To the voice in my head that had whispered that Phoebe didn't deserve a fuck-up like me as a father.

I couldn't even imagine the pain Alyssa must have been in at that very moment. She'd told me, and shown me, so often how much it hurt her to trust me. How frightened she'd been of me.

And every one of her fears had been proven right with one fucking magazine article.

I'd caused enough pain to force her to leave. To make her feel that running away without even allowing me the chance to tell my side was the only option. All because of the crap I'd brought into her life and dropped onto her lap. How much of the eight-page article had she believed? Did she think I was sleeping with my friend and teammate, Eden? Had she been poisoned against me by the bitter words of her enemy, Darcy, and my father's little whore, Hayley?

If only there was a way I could take away some of the pain. Both hers and mine.

I knew from my experience in London that if she wanted to disappear it would be impossible for me to contact her. She'd been as stubborn about being contacted then as I had once been. That didn't mean I couldn't get her a message somehow though.

There was one way I knew of to do it.

The thought gave me a small sense of purpose. It was weak, and I didn't know how long it would last, but it was enough to force me to set the bottle of whiskey beside me, climb to my feet, and get to my study.

After stumbling across the room, I yanked open the drawers. With one hand leaning on the wood to support myself, I rifled through the shit in my desk to find what I wanted.

Without letting myself stop and think about what I was doing, I slammed the pen and piece of paper onto the desk and sat my arse on the chair. In that moment, I knew it was vital that I tell her what she meant to me, even if she never believed a word of it. I would write her a fucking letter and I would make her read it.

Somehow.

If I had to, I would mail a copy of it to anyone whose life she'd ever touched. Hopefully at least one of them would be able to convince her to read my honest words.

Alyssa,

I've made so many mistakes over the years when it comes to you. To us. So many that it would be impossible to even try to list them all.

The first, and biggest, was letting you go.

I can never fix the wounds inflicted by that one action, or change what happened next. There is nothing I can do to wipe away the consequences of that decision. I've hurt you in ways I can't even imagine.

Because of all the ways I've fucked up, I know I don't deserve anything from you, least of all your understanding or acceptance. But I still want you to know what you mean to me. The time I spent with you in Brisbane was so fucking perfect. I might never be able to find the words to tell you exactly how special it was. All I can say is that rediscovering you was the best thing that could have ever happened to me. Despite what happened after it.

I promise that no matter what anyone else says, I was completely and utterly faithful to you for every second I was with you. You're the only woman I want for the rest of my life, but I get why you ran. I've screwed up so utterly and completely that you may never be able to find it in your heart to forgive me.

Just know that for those few weeks I was happy, genuinely fucking happy, for the first time in I don't know how long. Ever since I moved to Sydney, there's been a void in my life. An absence that I've tried to fill. But I've never been able to. That's why I turned to drugs. To other women. Even to alcohol. I tried it all to see me through when all I really needed was something much more wholesome and pure.

You.

I can see that now. You are by far the best thing that has ever happened to me. The best thing that ever could happen to me, save for Phoebe.

Our little miracle.

I'd never expected fatherhood to be like this, to feel like this. I would lay my life on the line if it would guarantee her safety and happiness. I've only known her for a few short weeks, but I can't imagine ever forgetting the impact she's had on my life.

That is why I have to beg you, even if you can't find it in your heart to forgive me, please don't take Phoebe from my life as well. Please allow me to continue to be her father. It pains me to think that I've lost you, but if I were to lose her as well . . . it would kill me.

If you can't offer me that, then please can you at least make sure she always knows she was made by love, even if things got a little broken along the way?

With the way things are right now, I don't expect anything more from you. I hope in time, you'll recognise the honesty in my words. Maybe you could even find some small degree of forgiveness in your heart. Regardless, I need you to understand that you will always be my only true love. You will always be the last one on my mind when I go to sleep and the first one I think of when I wake up in the morning.

I love you, Lys. I always have and that will never, ever stop, even if the reverse isn't true.

Yours forever,

Declan.

Once I was happy with the words, I rewrote the letter a number of times. I didn't care how many tears I shed over the pages. When I was done, I folded each of the copies up and placed them in envelopes ready to send to any address with even the loosest connection to Alyssa. I didn't know if it would be enough to get her to understand, but I had to try something. I couldn't just let her go without some fight, however pathetic it might be.

With that task done, and the purpose it had instilled in me burned out, I made a fresh move toward the alcohol. Plucking the bottle from the floor, I balanced it in the crook of my elbow. Then, reaching into my liquor cabinet above the wet bar, and the bar fridge below, I gathered up every bottle. Without letting myself think about what I was doing, or feel guilty for what came next, I carried them upstairs.

The mere sight of the drinks tempted me, calling to me like a mistress and begging me to give in.

Just a little bit.

The bottom of each bottle held the promise of oblivion and a temporary peace. Not long ago, I wouldn't have even paused before draining every single drop in a desperate attempt to find that momentary forgetfulness.

Even as the thought of the numbness I could achieve entered my mind, Alyssa's words from the day we made our agreement replaced it. They ran through my mind as the bottles clinked together in my arms. *"This is what I fucking mean about trust. One thing goes wrong and you fucking drink yourself into oblivion and end up in hospital. I mean Christ, what if I'd left for the night or didn't hear that bottle smash. You could have been fucking dead. How would I explain that to Phoebe? How could I tell her that her father died in a fucking alcohol binge session because one thing didn't go his fucking way?"*

As much as I wanted to drink it—all of it—I couldn't.

I couldn't do it to Alyssa or Phoebe.

I couldn't do it to *myself.*

When I reached the top of the stairs, I headed for the bathroom and lined the bottles up in a row on the floor. The longer they were in the house, the stronger their siren call would become. I had just enough reason left to be certain I wasn't strong enough to resist for long.

Even as I stared at the bottles, there was a small voice in the back of my head that whispered to me, working to convince me to keep just one bottle aside. To drink just a little. Whispering that I could stop after one.

A little bit wouldn't hurt. One glass. One sip.

Something.

Anything.

Tuning out the voice as best as I could, I shifted so that I was standing next to the line-up of booze. One by one, I picked up the bottles and hurled them into the bathtub. I flinched away as the bottle exploded on impact, sending shards of glasses flying around the tub.

The sound of the glass crashing and the liquid glugging down the drain filled me with a sick sense of purpose. Each smash brought back another memory of Alyssa, or of Phoebe. Of things that I'd done in the precious time that I'd had with them. Such a minute amount of time out of my whole twenty-two years, and I'd lost it again already.

The images raced on repeat.

Our family trip to McDonalds. *Smash.*

My date nights with Alyssa. *Crash.*

The trip to the track where I was able to show Alyssa the reason for my passion toward V8s, and thought she'd finally understood.

The last thought stopped me cold. Mid-throw, I held on to the bottle of vodka. That trip to the track was the one *Gossip Weekly* had featured in their exposé. The private moment Alyssa and I had shared, on display for the whole of Australia to fucking see. My hands shook as the happy memory burned at the edges. The bottle in my hand weighed more and more with every passing second.

The voice in my head screamed that it would be a lighter load if I just pressed the neck to my lips. If I drank down a draught—just a shot—of the clear liquid, it would make things better. It would ease the pain that surged through my body. Lessen the ache in my heart. Shake the memories from my head.

It would be one tiny step toward oblivion.

Toward peace.

It was so fucking tempting it was ridiculous.

One. Just one sip. Now.

Do it!

Sucking in a deep breath, I tossed the bottle across the bathroom just like I had all the rest. It landed higher than the others had, smashing into the tiles on the wall behind the tub. When it broke, I fell to my knees on the cold tiles and buried my face in my hands.

What have I done?

The voice in my mind cried a lament for the loss of my salvation and kicked off the chain reaction that threatened to drive off the last of my sanity. My chest constricted, my heart sped, and I couldn't focus on anything but the rising panic clawing at my throat—the beast the alcohol would have appeased. Closing my eyes, I ran my affirming mantra through my head. *I can get through this; I've had one before and I made it through then. I can get through this; I've had one before and I made it through then.*

It barely worked, but barely was enough. After another couple of calming breaths, I stood. Without another glance, I turned my back on the alcohol-stained, glass-filled tub to drag myself into my bedroom.

I'd intended to cocoon myself under my blankets, but simply stepping foot into that room filled the space with inescapable memories. Ghosts of the past rose up to surround me, boxing me in with my own regret. The gasps and wanton cries of so many random screws flooded the space around me. Although I preferred my conquests far away from my private areas, there were still plenty that had made it through the door. Who'd given themselves to the great Declan Reede to do with as he pleased.

Fuck.

It was no wonder Alyssa was gone. No wonder she didn't want to put up with my shit anymore. I was poison of the worst kind. Even though I hadn't cheated on her while we'd been together, I'd done it so often in the time we were apart. Each time I'd bedded a new woman, it was always a way to stave away visions of Alyssa for just one more night. Even when I hadn't admitted it to myself, I loved her. And yet, I'd fucked them all.

Fucking arse!

Needing a place as dark as I was inside, I squeezed into a tight corner in the back of my wardrobe, shutting out both light and life. It hid me from the ghosts and the demons that haunted my bedroom and quietened the cacophony of remembered moans in my mind.

Safely tucked away, I let the pain take me. Every tear I'd ever held in. Every curse I'd ever bitten back. Every bit of pain and agony that I'd ever suppressed came to the surface. A wave of remorse so powerful it threatened to wipe away every piece of me rose up, and I curled in on myself, letting it sweep me into the abyss.

Four years of wasted life ripped into my chest like a monster from a childhood nightmare, tearing me apart at the seams.

My throat was dry and ached with my need for a drink. My lips were parched and no matter how many times I wet them, they ached. Only booze would soothe the fire, but I'd smashed every bottle and lost every drop.

Fucking idiot! How could you be so stupid?

The pounding in my head crashed against my skull so hard that it rattled my mind and left me breathless.

Flashes of the life I'd missed with Phoebe rushed through me. The mistrust Alyssa had shown me—the look in her eyes whenever she didn't believe my promise that I wouldn't leave again—raced through my mind. Thoughts of my son, Emmanuel, and the fact I'd never hold him in my arms like I might have been able to if I'd been at Alyssa's side through it all. Rage at the unfairness that he'd never grow up burned my soul before razing through me like a bushfire.

Instead of being there for Alyssa, for Phoebe, and for Emmanuel, I'd been in Sydney with a revolving bedroom door.

The thoughts were stolen away when I gave in to the chest-wracking sobs that struck me. Each sob was so painful, I was certain it would be my last. It was beyond me to fight the beast back, so I gave up and let it consume me.

I longed for the bliss of unconsciousness and cursed that I had nothing to speed me into the darkness. A few tablets, a shot, anything.

At some point, someone knocked on my front door, as if trying to draw me back from the ledge. At first, I could barely hear it, but then whoever it was banged against it harder than before. The sound offered tiny distractions from my destructive darkness, but I couldn't find it in myself to move. Nor could I give the pounding anything more than a moment's attention.

I couldn't even raise my head to acknowledge the noise. There was no way I would be able to climb to my feet, trudge down the stairs, and answer it. Ultimately, it didn't matter who it was because nothing mattered anymore.

Everything important to me was gone.

My career, which had once flown so high, had sunk to depths so low that I couldn't see any way for it to be salvaged. It was in the trash somewhere in Danny's office, hidden among the pages of a glossy magazine.

By far the worst loss I had endured though was the love and family that I'd barely admitted I wanted. They'd been cruelly ripped from my life far too soon, just when I was finding hope for a different future. I would give back everything I'd ever achieved on the track for another day with Alyssa. For just a single hour more with Phoebe.

After some time, the banging stopped, and I was alone again. I didn't know minutes from hours, or hours from days. I could have been hiding in the back of my wardrobe for any length of time. I had no idea, nor any inclination to care.

The blackness in my heart and surrounding my eyes was too absolute. I was happy to reside in that pit for the rest of eternity. I deserved it for the darkness I'd bestowed on those who'd done nothing but offer me their love.

Thoughts of Alyssa crept into my mind again, invading all my senses. Reckless hope that she might one day see the article was a fabrication created a devastating cocktail when mixed with unending despair that she never would. Together the hope and fear twisted through my insides, forming knots that might never be undone.

Eventually, my mind cracked, and I heard the voice of an angel call my name.

For a moment, the beautiful sound held me in place as my heart began to beat once more—whole and undamaged at just the imagined sound of my name in that perfect voice. When it called again, it compelled me to rise from the ground. It was enough to pull me from my hiding space and send me hurtling out of my bedroom. Especially as it continued to call my name on a desperate loop, sounding more concerned with each repeat.

Racing down the hallway, I tried to work out where the sound was coming from.

When I reached the stairs, the sight waiting for me at the bottom stopped me dead in my tracks as my heart all but exploded in my chest.

CHAPTER TWO

THE DREAM

ALYSSA WAITED ON the ground floor. At the sight of her, I said a silent thank you to whatever god had granted my prayers.

She was dressed in the same clothing she'd worn when she'd left me at the airport. Her hair was up in a ponytail, but little strands of chestnut poked out at random intervals as if she'd been rubbing at her head repeatedly. Tears streaked her face, and it looked like she had just endured the worst twenty-four hours of her life.

In that moment though, it didn't matter. Because she was there.

I didn't know if she was getting ready to scream and shout at me for the stupid things the magazine had accused me of doing, but I didn't care. She was *there*.

"Lys," I sobbed.

At the exact same time, she glanced up at me and whispered, "Dec."

I threw myself down the stairs with no regard for my own safety. I took them two at a time, screaming toward the bottom as fast as I could. My only goal—my one objective—was to get to Alyssa. I needed to hold her and know that she was really there, that it wasn't some sick joke my mind had invented to torture me.

My heart beat against my throat, each painful thump evidence that this was real.

As soon as I hit solid ground, Alyssa's warm body smashed against mine. Her hands grasped my face, guiding my lips to their home. My tongue pushed forward without waiting for invitation, attempting to imprint the memory of her taste on itself just in case this was the last time she would ever allow me the opportunity.

My hands gripped her waist and I pulled her against me, not allowing even an inch of space between us. Despite that, I couldn't get nearly close enough. I had to prove to myself that it wasn't a dream. Even though I could see, feel, and taste her, I still couldn't believe she was actually there.

After releasing her mouth, I planted continuous small kisses on her lips and cheek. Her name left me again and again as a reverent prayer. With each passing second, the light of her presence penetrated further into the darkness that had welled up inside me.

Finally, I laughed in spite of myself.

The joy I felt at having her close again pushed aside any concerns that it wouldn't be for long.

"I can't believe you're really here." I chuckled again as I rested my forehead against hers. I kept the questions of how and why suppressed because I didn't want to break the spell that was keeping her in my arms.

"Are you all right?" she asked.

I shook my head and gently clasped her face between my hands as I continued to pepper her with kisses. "It doesn't matter how I am. I don't matter. You're here. You're really here."

But for how long?

"Dec," she started, but I stopped her.

"I need to talk to you. About the magazine. About Eden . . ." I trailed off as I braced myself for the worst. When I thought about the fucking magazine, about how guilty it all made me appear, I wasn't sure how exactly to form the words I needed to say without risking losing her.

"It's too late," she said. "I already know about your relationship."

I froze. Her words confirmed my worst fears. My body sagged against her, and I pulled her closer to me, fearing the moment she would speak the words that would finish me off. Terrified of the moment she would leave. It was too late.

"Please don't take Phoebe away from me," I whispered. "I couldn't bear it if you did. I need her in my life. I need *both* of you in my life. *Please . . . don't . . . leave.*"

"I'm not going anywhere." Her voice was breathy but reassuring as her hand brushed across my cheek.

"But the magazine . . . the story. *Eden.*"

She offered me a small, knowing smile. "I know."

The calm she exuded confused me. "Don't you think I cheated on you?"

With her honey-brown gaze locked on me, she said, "What did I tell you, Dec? I *wanted* to trust you. Somewhere along the line, I think I genuinely started to. If I'd seen that filth a few weeks ago, I probably would have believed every damn word. But now? After everything you've done? With the way you reacted to finding out about your father? I just don't believe it. I can't. You might have done some shitty things over the years, but you're not a bad person. And you're not a hypocrite."

I could have argued her last two points, but I didn't want to stop her perfect words.

"Unless of course you're trying to tell me that you really did have an affair with your co-worker."

I shook my head. "Edie's just a friend. That's all. There's nothing else between us."

"I thought so."

"But why?" I frowned as confusion bubbled within me. "Why do you believe me?"

Her brows pinched together and a breathy chuckle left her. "Would you prefer that I didn't?"

I held her tighter still, squeezing her against my chest. "No."

"I stopped to get bread and milk on the way home from the airport. Because I was at work, I popped into the back room and saw the magazine. At first, I *was* shocked and prepared for the worse. Then I decided to ignore it and see what you had to say about it when I saw you next. But I couldn't help myself; I had to know what they'd said. I've been buying everything with you on the cover for as long as I can remember." When Alyssa spoke, she rubbed the back of my neck, just above my still-fresh tattoo. "Even as I read the article, I saw a number of things that didn't make sense."

"Like?" The hope that maybe things weren't permanently damaged between us took root as a tiny ember in my heart and warmed me from the inside out.

"Well, for starters, I know for a fact that nothing's going on between you and Ruby, even though the article insinuated there was." Amusement lit her voice, and I understood why. Ruby had hardly been my biggest ally over the years. Even if she'd softened slightly toward me after our little chat the night before I took Alyssa to the track, she would hardly be willing to jump into bed with me—nor me with her. "Second, you might not remember, but you sent me a text the night you were out with Eden. You told me about the great time you were having with your friend and that you missed me. You went on about how you wished I could meet her. I really don't think you would have texted me if you were sleeping with her.

"Finally, and most importantly, when I got back home, magazine in hand, I found your phone. I was worried someone might try to contact you about the article, so I turned it on. I thought I could at least tell them to contact you on your home number if they had it. It lit up instantly with about twenty missed calls, all from one number."

"Eden," I whispered.

"Eden," she confirmed with a smile. "Not long after I'd turned the phone on, it rang again. Because I assumed it had to have been important for her to call so often, I answered it. She didn't even stop for breath as she told me what Danny was doing, and checked whether I knew about the article. She made sure I knew it was all BS."

"I'm sorry, Lys," I said as I recalled the things the article had said about her. "I didn't mean to drag you into my shit. Maybe it would have been better if I'd never come back into your life."

"Don't say that. Don't you *ever* say that!" Her words were spoken so vehemently that I tugged her closer again to give her some comfort. The undercurrent of pain, the doubt and fear that I'd worked to wash away, existed once more in her impassioned cry. I wondered whether she was as scared of me running as I was of her pushing me away.

With her in my arms, a sense of sanity returned to me and I could think properly again. I turned the article over in my mind.

"I just don't understand why they would attack me like that," I murmured. "And why they would attack you at all?"

"To sell magazines?" she offered.

I shook my head. That would have been part of it, for sure. A cover with a scandal almost guaranteed a greater circulation, but a one-page article hinting at a relationship with Eden would have done that. Even the revelation of Phoebe's existence would have been enough to bump up sales. The article was too long to be just about numbers. There was something else happening. There were too many coincidences. Too many times that a photographer was close at hand and ready to capture my mistakes.

"It feels like there's more to it than that. It's almost like it's connected somehow—"

"Like *everything's* connected," Alyssa finished my sentence.

"Exactly." The more I thought about it, the more it made sense. It was no coincidence that the photographers were at the benefit, and someone had to have been following me to have gotten the photos of Eden and me, as well as the photos with Ruby in the one tiny moment we'd embraced. They had to have been waiting for that shot.

Even the fight with Dad had been over too fast for a random pap to have stumbled across us—unless they were already in the area.

"Alex," Alyssa whispered.

"What?" I pulled away, shocked. My own mind drifted toward the one woman who seemed to be around each time things had gone to shit. And that was a certain redhead from a nightclub, not Alex, the PR representative for my former employer's rival.

"Alex," she repeated louder. "She mentioned something to me, at the benefit, about hearing something around Wood Racing. While you were in the bathroom, she pulled me aside and warned me that Paige was not above using dirty tactics to get to you. That's why I wasn't there when you came out to find me. She wouldn't say anything more though."

"You think all of this might be a fucking recruitment campaign to get me to go to Wood Racing?"

"I don't know," she said. "Maybe it's not what she meant. Maybe it's not related. But if it is, well, it's worked hasn't it? I mean . . ."

I closed my eyes to block out the unfinished part of her statement. Yes, I was sacked. She knew it and I knew it, but neither of us could use the word. "No, it didn't."

"What?" she asked.

"I might be out of Sinclair Racing, but there is no way in hell I would race for that fucking lunatic Wood. Especially if she's orchestrated this. I'd rather stay unemployed."

"You know you'll probably never know for sure whether she did or didn't."

"I know. But regardless, it would mean moving to Brisbane when you're moving down here." I cupped her cheek with my hand and met her gaze. "I'm not going to choose a job over you again, Lys. Not again. That's a mistake I'm not going to make twice."

She kissed me softly in response.

I closed my eyes and rested my head on her forehead. "Not that I am complaining, but what the hell *are* you doing here? And where's Phoebe?"

"After I spoke to Eden, and she told me what Mr. Sinclair was doing, I knew you'd take it badly. I know it was always your dream to race for them. I didn't even think about what I was doing. I just threw together a few basics for Phoebe and me, climbed into your car, and drove. Phoebe's outside right now. With Eden."

"Eden?" I asked. I was still amazed that this beautiful, understanding, loving woman was actually standing in front of me. But it was even more astounding that she trusted my judgement enough to put our daughter's care in the hands of one of my friends, especially one she'd never met.

"She was camped on the front doorstep when I arrived. She'd tried calling, but the phone must be off the hook or something. We weren't sure what state you'd be in, so we thought it might be better for me to come in alone. Just to be on the safe side."

"You mean just in case I was lying in a pool of my own vomit after passing out from a drinking binge?" I challenged, seeing the real reason she'd put her trust in Eden. It was the lesser of two evils. But I wondered whether she'd admit the direction of her thoughts out loud.

"Something like that," she said, stepping back and linking her fingers with mine. The shy apprehension on her face as she continued made it impossible for me to feel even slightly upset with her words. "I'm sorry. I tried to have faith, I really did, but . . . I couldn't be sure. And if something had happened, I didn't want Phoebe to see." She frowned, no doubt recalling the situation in London when I'd passed out and cut my arm badly enough to need stitches. "I didn't want her to have that memory seared into her mind."

I sighed. "I don't blame you. Not really. It was a close one, Lys. Even I wasn't sure I could resist."

"But you did?" She beamed at me, already guessing my answer.

With a smile lifting my lips because of her confidence—even if it was tentative—I shook my head. "I couldn't do it."

She brought our linked hands to her mouth and kissed mine softly.

"I love you," she whispered.

"I love you, too," I said, shifting my hands so my palms caressed her face. I met her gaze and refused to break our stare until

I knew she understood not only the truth in my words, but the depth of my love. "Now, let's go get Phoebe. I need to see her too."

Hope, happiness, and love filled the void I'd felt since climbing onto the plane to come back to Sydney. I refused to release Alyssa's hand as we walked to the front door. Together: the way we would be doing everything now.

"How did you get in anyway?" I asked.

"Have you forgotten already?" She laughed before holding up the three-hundred-dollar key ring I'd given to her with my house keys dangling from it.

I smiled in wonder at the amazing woman who'd blessed me with her love.

As I walked out the door, Phoebe threw herself at me. "Daddy!"

I let go of Alyssa's hands just in time to catch Phoebe. Alyssa wrapped her arm around my waist as I stood back up holding Phoebe.

"Is this your castle, Daddy?"

I looked back at my house and tried to see it through the eyes of a three-year-old. The two-and-a-half story building was huge, especially compared to the three-bedroom house she and Alyssa lived in. It was easy to indulge her. "It sure is, sweetie. And you know what? It'll be your castle too very soon."

It wasn't until after the words had left me that I wondered whether Alyssa might not want Phoebe to know that just yet, but it was too late to reel the statement back in.

"Declan." Eden's voice reminded me of her presence.

"Eden," I greeted semiformally. Despite the fact she'd tried to warn me and had helped Alyssa out, I wasn't sure where things stood between us. She was Sinclair through and through, even more than I'd ever been. Now that I'd been sacked, I worried she might consider it a reason to end our friendship.

"Wow, this"—she indicated Phoebe and Alyssa—"really suits you."

"Thanks." I couldn't meet her eye. She'd read the magazine. Considering we'd been linked as an item, she had to know it was mostly bullshit, but did she believe any of it?

She tickled the back of Phoebe's neck before resting her hand on my shoulder. "I'm sorry about Danny," she whispered. "I tried to convince him to let you stay, or to at least give you a chance to explain. I told him that there was a lot of BS in the article and the rest was probably a misunderstanding too, or flat-out lies, but he just wouldn't listen. You know him. He's so old-fashioned sometimes. Loyalty is the thing he values above all else. I guess he felt betrayed by the stuff with Wood."

"It's okay, Edie." It wasn't. I was putting on a brave face, but still there was some truth to my words because I had Alyssa and Phoebe. Nothing else mattered compared to that. "But why aren't you in Bahrain with everyone else?"

"I couldn't just go," she said. "Not after Danny told me what was going to happen. I'll be flying out to meet the team in the next few days."

With those words, it was clear that at least some of her loyalty still resided with me. She'd sacrificed so much, staying home and risking disciplinary action herself so that she could contact Alyssa and help me. "Thank you for your support."

Even as she nodded, she eyed the arm Alyssa had around my waist with a small grin. After a moment, she obviously felt she was intruding.

"I'm going to leave you in Alyssa's capable hands," she said, beaming as she looked at Phoebe again. "But I'll be back soon. I don't care if you're not with Sinclair Racing anymore. Don't think you can escape me that easily."

I just nodded, although inwardly I blew a sigh of relief that things between us could at least return to status quo.

She turned to Alyssa, grabbing her hand. "And you . . . I'm awed at how fast you've been able to domesticate him." She winked at Alyssa and they both chuckled. "Keep in touch, won't you?"

Alyssa nodded and gave her a small hug. My little family stood watching as Eden climbed into her Holden Cascada and drove off. I perched Phoebe on my hip and wrapped my arm around Alyssa's shoulders.

"Shall we go inside?"

"I get to look inside the castle?" Phoebe asked.

Alyssa met my eye and nodded. "Of course, sweetie. Daddy told you, it's going to be your castle soon too."

Phoebe clapped her hands. "Yay!"

I didn't care that it took Alyssa saying the words to make them real for Phoebe, because hearing them offered a sense of relief that I hadn't anticipated. I put Phoebe back onto the ground and reached for her hand. "Let's go then, princess."

Alyssa chuckled and I led them inside. The smile on my face was half a lie. Even though things seemed okay for the moment, I worried about what might come next. What could I offer them but my love? I'd lost everything except them. I was unemployed, with no skills, and with a sizeable mortgage hanging over my head.

"We'll be okay," Alyssa whispered, as if reading my thoughts.

All I could do was hope she was right.

CHAPTER THREE

FAMILY

AS SOON AS we were inside, I led Alyssa and Phoebe around the house, showing them from room to room, starting on the ground floor. Then I took them upstairs and continued the tour there. When we hit the bathroom, I paused at the door. Liquor stained the wall and the bathtub was full of glass.

"Daddy, your barftub's messy."

"Uh . . .," Alyssa started, but then trailed off before she asked any questions. Curiosity blazed in her eyes, though.

"It was a close one," I said, repeating my words from earlier as I hung my head.

"But you didn't," Alyssa whispered.

The reality of everything came crashing over me. There was so much on the tip of my tongue. So much I needed to say—that I wanted Alyssa to know. The letter I'd written her when I'd thought hope was lost sprang to mind. The longing I'd felt when I thought she was gone.

While Phoebe was otherwise occupied, I turned to Alyssa.

"Lys, I—"

She cut me off by pressing her finger against my mouth. "There's time for that later. Let's just enjoy being together tonight? Please?"

It was clear she was asking for herself as much as for me. Even though the day had no doubt been harrowing for her, just as it had been for me, she was there and willing to push it aside for a little longer just to be a family.

"Okay, but I think you need to call your mum," I said. "She was a little frantic when I spoke to her last."

"Which means she's probably talked to your mum."

Alyssa's words were a reminder that Mum was due to leave the country the following morning. "Shit, I better call Mum."

"Language," Alyssa said, nodding in Phoebe's direction.

"Sorry. Habit. I'll try to clean it up, I swear. After all, I have a reason to now."

I held out my arms for her, and she stepped inside. Phoebe wrapped herself around us, one arm around my leg and one around Alyssa's.

"Two reasons," I added, running my fingers through Phoebe's hair. She looked up at me with a grin and I couldn't resist picking her up and resting her on my hip.

"We should probably get the phone calls over with so we can enjoy our night," Alyssa said.

The next hour was a whirl of me entertaining Phoebe while Alyssa called her mum, and then the airline to book a return flight for her and Phoebe. Because she'd driven my car down to meet me, rather than waiting for me to fly back up to claim it, she needed to get back to Brisbane another way.

Once she'd done what she had to, we swapped so that I could call Mum to say goodbye before she left to jet-set around the globe.

"You're okay with this, aren't you, Declan?" Mum asked. "With me going away, I mean? I can cancel if you'd prefer. Maybe come to Sydney for a while instead."

"Mum, how long have you been dreaming about going overseas?"

"W-what are you talking about?" The innocence in her denial was almost comical.

"Well, clearly you've wanted this for a while. The decision to leave was too impulsive, too fast. Too . . . like me. Not like you at all. You've obviously wanted it for a while, and maybe even planned it out in your head."

"I—" The guilt in her voice was clear.

I cut her off with a laugh. "It's okay, I get it. Really, I do. With the shi—stuff Dad did, I'd be surprised if you hadn't been planning this escape for years. Who am I to tell you not to go?"

"You're my son, that's who. If you need me to stay until this magazine stuff blows over—and it *will* blow over—that's what I'll do."

Turning so that I could watch Alyssa and Phoebe, I smiled. "No. I think I'll be fine. After all, I've got Lys."

"If you're certain?"

"I'm positive, Mum. Go, live your life for you for a while. We'll all be here when you get back. Maybe you can spend some time with us in Sydney then?"

"I'd like that."

We chatted for a little while longer, in a way we hadn't ever done while I'd been at the peak of my career. Later, after I'd wished her a safe flight, I disconnected the call feeling lighter than I had since before flying in for the meeting with Danny.

After I'd finished the call, I sat on the floor with Phoebe and watched while she and Alyssa played with a doll Alyssa had obviously brought with her from Brisbane. Near the door was an overnight bag stuffed to a point just past full and looking ready to burst at the seams.

"So when are you going home?" I asked, even as the thought of them leaving caused a lump to grow in my throat.

"Wednesday." She frowned as she said the word. "I just booked our flights home. I'm sorry, Dec, I can't get any more time off work."

The mention of the *W* word reminded me that I no longer had to work. No longer had a job. Was unemployed and most likely unemployable. After all, what team would want a driver that has scandal follow him everywhere? My knowledge of sponsorships and the way they worked might not have been perfect, but it was enough to understand that I was a liability.

"Dec," Lys said. Her voice was soft as she drew me from my thoughts. "It'll work itself out. Somehow."

"I hope you're right."

"How about we put it out of our minds and see what's for dinner?"

I laughed.

When Alyssa tilted her head in confusion, it made me laugh harder, which caused Phoebe to giggle.

"I told you before, Lys. I don't do domestic. There's fu— nothing here."

"Well, I guess you get to show us your favourite restaurant."

"There's an awesome Chinese place just around the corner."

"Great. Let's go. And we can grab some bread and milk on the way back home."

We headed out for dinner, giving me the chance to get things right for a change.

I SAT bolt upright as a scream pierced the night.

"Mummy!"

My heart raced at the sound of Phoebe's terrified shriek.

The few days I'd stayed in Alyssa's house in Brisbane, when Phoebe had slept through the night without any issue, hadn't prepared me for the sleeplessness of an unsettled child. It was like an all-night bender, but without the booze buzz before we started.

It was worse than I'd expected it could be. Mostly because it'd been a hell of a night after such a shitty-arsed day. First the bathtub had needed to be completely cleaned and scrubbed before Phoebe could have her bath, which she apparently could not possibly go to sleep without—not even for one night. I'd done what I could to get rid of the glass, and used the sprayer to shift the bulk of the sticky liquid that coated the tub and tiles behind. After I'd finished, Alyssa had gone over my handiwork to make sure there was nothing left.

Then, when Phoebe was settled into the spare bed—the first time—I led Alyssa into my room. Once again, I was struck by regret that I'd brought my conquests there over the four years I'd been alone. My legs liquefied with each step and my hands grew clammy at the thought. I was such a fucking player. Any plan of a proper reunion with Alyssa flew from me. Each fresh glance around the room dragged another muddied memory through my mind.

The bed, most of the bedroom, was tainted with the history of things I now regretted. Tying a blonde to the frame there. Being pinned against the headboard there while redheaded twins fought over my cock. Holding on to the bedpost there while the chick with black curls and huge boobs rode me. A rotation of faces, bodies, and positions. My stomach churned as they assaulted my mind.

I buried my face in my hands. Any one of the nights would probably have been enough to fill most men's spank banks for life, but it was never enough for me.

Each empty encounter only made me long for something more.

For Alyssa. I understood that now.

If only I hadn't been such a stubborn arse and refused to take her phone calls, I could have avoided all the twisting aches that had taken up a permanent home in my gut each time I even glanced at my king-sized bed.

As regret sank deep into me, I'd argued that we should find somewhere else to sleep—that she didn't belong in the room filled with the ghosts of the past. Only, there weren't many options. Either we had to squeeze into the double in the spare room with Phoebe or crash on the fold-out sofa in the other spare room. There wasn't anywhere else. I'd relented to Alyssa's need to sleep even though it made me feel like shit doing so.

Before Phoebe's frightened cry had died away, Alyssa was already halfway out of bed.

I put my hand on her shoulder and stopped her. "Don't. I'll get her."

"It's my—"

Certain that her sentence was going to end with the word responsibility, I cut her off. After all, Phoebe was as much my responsibility as she was Alyssa's.

"Lys, you've spent the better part of the day on the road." Even as I said the words, I climbed out of bed.

"But—"

"And you've got up to her three times already," I added as I walked to the door. The more we argued over who should go, the longer Phoebe's sobs would continue. "Let me go."

Right before I left the room, I turned to say to Alyssa that I'd have to get used to it anyway, but she was already lying back down and her eyes were closed. The rise and fall of her chest was too rhythmic for her to not be well on her way back to sleep.

Her exhaustion had to be almost complete, but I couldn't blame her. I knew from experience how dreadful the almost twelve-hour drive was when it was vital to reach the end destination. She'd had a long couple of weeks. We all had.

So much had changed. There were things I'd learned that I'd never forget. People who'd become so important,

I'd discovered children I'd never thought I wanted. Experienced heartbreak I'd never anticipated. Phoebe had gained the father she'd always imagined. Alyssa had claimed her rightful place in my life and won my heart in return.

I couldn't help feeling like she got the short end of the deal.

"Hey, princess," I said to Phoebe as I walked into the spare room—the room that would be hers when they moved in permanently. "What's up?"

I hoped I would be enough to quieten her fears on my own, but I was still a practical stranger really. The thought that I wouldn't be enough for her terrified me, but it wasn't enough to stop me from trying.

"D-Daddy?"

I sat on the edge of her bed and stifled a yawn. "Did you get scared again?"

She nodded, her loose brunette curls bouncing around her head. "I woked up and no one's there." She crossed her arms and pouted at me.

Through the darkness, I could see the accusation in her turquoise eyes. I reached out and cupped her face. "We're here. Just up the hall, remember? Like I showed you before bed."

"I don't like this room." Impossibly, her pout deepened. "It's scary."

"Why's it scary?"

"It's dark. And there's monsters."

"Where?"

She pointed to the window. "Out there."

Following the line her finger made, I walked to window and made a show of peering out into the darkness. "There's no monsters, just trees. Wanna come see?"

She shook her head and whimpered. "Scary."

"It's okay, no monsters will come near the window while I'm with you," I promised. "You know how I know?"

The only response I got was another shake of her head.

"Because they wouldn't dare mess with your daddy. Not in his castle."

A glimmer of a smile crossed her lips but she still didn't move.

I pretended to rub my chin in thought. "You know what? I think you're right. I think this room is a little scary. But do you know what I think the problem is?"

"What?"

"The walls." I ran my hand over the beige surface. It was the first time I'd really noticed that the house was just a building with my stuff in it. There was no personality. No *life*. Everything was architecturally designed and set up for maximum resale value. It was all without any of my influence and every wall was beige. Just like my life had been without Alyssa and Phoebe in it. "They're not the right colour, are they?"

Phoebe shook her head.

"What colour would be the right one?"

"Umm, yellow?" When she said the word "yellow," her mouth stuck on the *Y* to make it sound almost like an *L*. The sound made my heart skip a beat. She was too fucking cute.

I nodded. "Yellow could work."

"Or purple?"

"Purple could work too. Maybe we can pick four colours and do one wall of each?"

She giggled. "Don't be silly."

"I'm not being silly." I crossed back over and sat on the edge of the bed again. "This'll be your room, so you get to choose whatever colour walls you want."

A grin lit her features.

"But you have to be able to sleep in here, or it can't be your room, can it? We'll have to pick a different one."

Her teeth captured her lip. "There's none closer to Mummy."

"Nope. This one is the closest. We're just down the hall, remember?"

She gave a small nod.

"So, are you happy with this room then?" I asked as I sat on her bed again.

"Can we leave the light on?"

"We can look at getting a night light for the hall if you like? Will that work?"

She gave me another little nod.

"Well, I guess that's settled then. When you and Mummy move in, we'll paint the room any colour you want."

"Daddy?" She looked up at me from beneath her lashes. It was a look Alyssa had perfected years earlier. One that made me willing to agree to almost anything. With little gestures like that, the resemblance between mother and daughter was uncanny. Except for the colour of Phoebe's eyes.

"Yeah?"

"Can I sleep with you? Just one night?"

There was no point even trying to resist. I had no idea how I would survive the two of them, but I also knew I couldn't survive without them. "Sure, sweetheart. Just for tonight though."

I picked her up and carried her back to my bedroom where Alyssa was fast asleep. The moment I placed Phoebe on the bed, she climbed next to Alyssa and snuggled against her shoulder. Even though I was tired as fuck, I had to take a moment just to watch and appreciate how much my life had changed. I'd experienced what my life would be like if I lost them; I never wanted to feel it again.

CHAPTER FOUR

RELEASE

WHAT FOLLOWED WAS a terrible night of sleep, made worse by the tiny foot shoved in my face for a while. Then kicked against the green-yellow bruises along my ribs. Then buried in my armpit. I'd never known anyone who fidgeted so damn much while they slept. Even after getting to sleep between Alyssa and me, Phoebe still woke at regular intervals.

I was torn from sleep by the sound of the phone in my study ringing. Although getting up was the last thing I wanted to do, I didn't want the noise to wake up Alyssa or Phoebe. I raced downstairs to answer it.

Even before I said hello, I'd guessed who it might be. The international beeps only strengthened my suspicion. There were only a few people who would be calling me from overseas, and I didn't think Morgan would be calling while he was in race-preparation mode. If at all.

As soon as the caller spoke, my assumption was confirmed: Paige Wood, the owner of Wood Racing, and Sinclair Racing's rival.

The call wasn't exactly unexpected. Not after everything that happened and my conversation with Alyssa about the possible reasons for the in-depth and highly damning magazine coverage.

"I heard the unfortunate news," Paige said, almost sounding sincere. My sacking from Sinclair Racing had yet to be announced publicly, but she'd found out anyway. Most likely she'd heard it from one of the boys in Bahrain. Gossip spread fast through the pits, after all.

Or maybe she'd made an assumption based on her prior knowledge of what the magazine article would contain. Danny's expectation of loyalty wasn't exactly a state secret. It wouldn't have taken much to use it against me. A few tugged strings to get a photographer to snap a photo of me sitting at the Wood Racing table would do it. Added to the history I had with Paige—history I'd hoped hadn't made its way to Danny's ears but that Danny's wife, Hazel, had witnessed herself at Bathurst—it would have been far too easy for her to set me up.

"Yeah, well, these things happen, don't they?" I didn't feel like chatting idly on the phone with her. More than anything, I wanted to demand whether she'd been involved in the destruction of my reputation, but I couldn't accuse her of anything without proof.

"You do know that this setback need not be the end of your career, don't you?"

What's her game?

"I mean, I'm right in assuming you're free of your contract now?" Even down the telephone line, I could hear her Cheshire cat grin. It confirmed for me that she wasn't just lucky to be the one who'd been courting me prior to my unceremonious dumping.

"So what if I am?"

"Well, it leaves you free to discuss your options elsewhere, doesn't it? Like I said, it doesn't have to be the end. There are other teams willing to get behind you. Team owners who'd just love to have you."

"I'm not looking to race anywhere else, Paige." My voice was cool as I ignored the innuendo in her tone. When I said her first name, I said it with such contempt it had to show my complete lack of respect for her.

"You know you'll always have a position available under me. I can use a driver with your ... skills." The pathetic cougar was trying to lure me with techniques that might have worked six months ago, but had lost all of their power now that I was back with Alyssa.

I'd tried the softly-softly approach in telling her I wasn't interested in racing for her, but I couldn't do it any longer. There was only one way I could face the situation: head-on. Fuck the evidence, I'd call her out. There was no point just standing around and shooting the shit on the phone when there was no doubt left in me that even if she hadn't coordinated it somehow, she'd known about the article. "Did you have something to do with this?"

"With what, darling?"

"With the article."

She laughed, each of the shrill vibrations sounding less sincere than the last. "How would I have any influence over what goes to print at a gossip rag?"

The words and her tone made it sound like a lie. If I hadn't already been convinced, it would have been proof enough for me. "You turned me into a fucking liability."

Her throaty chuckle came down the line again and I wanted nothing more than to reach down the phone line and cram something into her mouth.

"I did no such thing, my dear. But you should know even the biggest liability can be turned into an asset, with the right amount of spin."

Sick of her voice, of her laugh, of everything about her, I decided to end the charade of polite conversation. "Why don't you go spin on it?"

"You're turning me down?" She seemed genuinely confused, as though everything had been a done deal. In her mind, it probably was.

I had no doubts left that she'd had it planned for a while. The timing might have been pure luck on her part, because I was in Brisbane at just the right moment with just the right reason to attend the fundraiser, but I was certain if it hadn't been then and there, some other fabricated bullshit would have caused my downfall. "Yeah, I'm turning you down. I'm a Sinclair man through and through."

"Sinclair is done with you, boy. They chewed you up and spat you out. No one else will want their leftovers."

I chuckled at the way she'd turned. Her true colours were definitely on display. "You obviously do."

"This position was an act of charity. A last-ditch effort to save your career before you pissed it down the toilet."

"Well, you can shove your charity up your fucking arse, Paige. I don't want it."

She blustered and muttered a few words I'd never heard from someone who pretended to be so refined before hanging up the phone. Good riddance. I'd rather never drive again than go work for her.

I headed back to bed, ready to enjoy a lie-in with my girls, but Alyssa stopped me halfway up the stairs.

She put her hand on my chest and gave me a wary smile—no doubt still coming to terms with everything that had unfolded in the last two days. I sure as shit knew I still was.

"Who was that?" she asked.

"Paige Wood."

The corners of her mouth twisted like she'd tasted something bad. "And?"

"And I'm pretty sure we're right that she's part of it. I just wish I knew how." The why seemed pretty fucking obvious after her phone call.

Alyssa lifted her hand and brushed her fingers through my hair. "We'll figure it out together. But first, let's get started on a game plan. She's asleep again for the moment," she said, indicating my room where Phoebe had obviously settled again.

With Alyssa at my side, we headed back to my study to dig out my contract with Sinclair Racing. While she wasn't looking, I slid the letters I'd written her into a drawer, embarrassed that I'd been such a pussy when I'd thought she was gone. Every word was the truth, but I didn't need her to see my weakness.

After an hour of studying every clause and paragraph, she declared there was nothing I could do to fight the dismissal. The contract was lopsided, with the power almost completely in Danny's court. I couldn't cancel early without penalties, but Danny had ultimate veto over the agreement and could cancel it at his own discretion. I kicked myself for not having someone more skilled than my fuckhead father go over it to ensure it was fair. Then again, Danny might never have signed me if he hadn't had an easy out. After all, I'd been young and stupid when he'd drafted me.

Dropping into my office chair, I buried my head in my hands. "What am I going to do, Lys? Racing's the only thing I know."

Even as the words came out, it struck me that it was an opening for a great big fucking *I told you* so if she was so inclined. If I'd gone to uni like she'd wanted me to, if I'd had a backup plan of any sort, I wouldn't be completely screwed. But I might not have ever had the chance to race either.

Instead of an *I told you so* though, she reached over and grabbed my hand in hers. "It's okay," she said. "We'll work something out. There are other teams. Maybe there's a way to get you onto one of them."

I stood and paced away from her. "Why would they take me though? It'd be a PR nightmare for them." I didn't add the bigger concern, that most other teams would mean moving away from Sydney. Neither did I admit that I wasn't sure whether I even wanted to race for anyone but Sinclair. They'd been my home for almost four years, and I knew what to expect. I knew the cars, the crew, and the inner workings. A new team would be an unknown entity.

"Not necessarily. People have been through worse scandals and come out with their careers intact."

"How?"

"It's all about how you handle the next few weeks."

I moved back to her side. "Okay. So what do you suggest?"

Even as the words left me, a sense of relief flowed over me that she was in my corner and fighting for me. I was certain if I had to face it alone, I'd have cracked and be somewhere at the bottom of a vodka bottle by now.

"I think we need to present a united front. Both of us in front of the media to prove there's no scandal."

"No. Absolutely not."

"Why not?"

"Because I'm not dragging you through the mud just to find a fucking job."

She rested her head on my shoulder and linked her fingers with mine. "You did read the article, didn't you? I've been dragged. This is about showing all of those people who tried to hurt us that we're stronger than that."

Her words meant more to me than I could ever express. "God, I love you, Lys. I—I don't know what I'd do without you." I kissed the top of her head. "Are you sure you're ready for this though?"

"No. But I'm ready for us, and that's enough for now."

What she didn't say was as clear as what she did. It was make or break time for my life. I had to stand up and be ready to claim what I wanted as soon as the opportunity arose, or I would risk missing out. She'd proven her faith in me, that I had her trust, and now I just had to keep it.

No more fuck-ups.

Not long after, Phoebe woke up in tears, sobbing because she'd woken alone and hadn't recognised her surroundings. Alyssa had raced to her side before bringing her down to the kitchen for some breakfast.

Guilt wracked me that I couldn't provide an environment to make my own fucking daughter feel safe. Feeling the familiar spiral of panic sinking into my stomach, I closed my eyes and took two deep breaths. Alyssa clearly picked up on my mood because she came up to me and grabbed my hand in hers. As it always seemed to, her touch instantly tugged me back from the edge.

"It'll take some time for her to settle in."

"Are you sure that's all it is? I want everything to be okay for her."

"Just wait until we've moved in properly, and all of our stuff is here. It'll make it easier."

"Really?" It was hard not to be insecure when it came to Phoebe's happiness. Or Alyssa's.

"She'll be drawing on the walls and running around like she owns the place before long."

"Drawing on the walls?" I swallowed down the swear words that rose to the tip of my tongue. I may have been happy to have her paint her room whatever fucking colour she wanted, but that was worlds away from vandalising the goddamned walls.

Alyssa leaned back and grinned at me. "Dec, she's three. It's inevitable."

"So what are you saying? That I should just let her get away with it?"

Alyssa's grin morphed into laughter. "No. She's three; she still needs discipline. I'm just trying to get you to understand the level of crazy that comes with having a live-in toddler."

Even as she said the words, Phoebe saw the two of us in an embrace and rushed to our side, once again mashing her face between our legs.

"There are benefits though," I said.

Alyssa just laughed.

"What?"

"Toddler. Remember?"

Wondering what the hell Alyssa was talking about, I glanced down. Fucking hell. Running from just behind my knee around to my shin was a huge smear of vegemite, butter, and crumbs from Phoebe's hands.

Alyssa picked Phoebe up to rest on her hip. "Are you finished with your breakfast?"

Phoebe nodded as she sucked on one of her vegemite-coated hands. Did any of it stay on the fucking toast?

"Do you mind getting the dishes while I do this?"

I flashed her a smile. "I'm sure I can manage that."

What I hadn't realised was that doing the dishes included wiping down the entire fucking table because somehow Phoebe had got vegemite over at least a third of it.

Fuck, kids were messy.

Messy, but worth it.

I SPENT the better part of my day with my girls, mostly running around the backyard and trying to push everything out of my mind. A little after five, Eden came to visit with a copy of a press release from Sinclair Racing. We set Phoebe up with a Wiggles DVD and sat at the dining table to chat.

With an apology on her lips, Eden passed the soon-to-be-issued document to me. The release announced my termination from the team. My heart shattered as I read the words ready to go to all major press agencies in the country. My termination in black and white. The devastation that swept through me made one thing clear: at least a part of me had been hoping for a last-minute reprieve. For Danny to call and say he'd made a mistake and had reconsidered.

It wasn't going to happen though. The release made that much clear, especially considering the second piece of information it contained.

I screwed my eyes shut to block out the words. My hand holding the offending paper dropped to the table so that I wouldn't reread the words printed on it over and over. A sigh that carried the last of my hope for another chance at my dream left my lips as I leaned my weight against the table and dropped my head.

"What is it, Dec?" Alyssa asked.

"He—he's already replaced me. He has a new driver starting in the new season."

"So soon? How? With who?"

I couldn't even form the words. How could Danny recruit the biggest lunatic on the track? Morgan and I could both be a little reckless, but neither of us took our personal vendettas onto the track. Not like—

"Hunter Blake," Eden answered when she saw I wasn't able to.

"Is he a good driver?" Alyssa asked.

"Does it fucking matter?" I shouted. "He's not me, is he? He's taking my fucking spot on the team!"

"He's with Wood Racing," Eden explained to Alyssa.

I pinched the bridge of my nose, wanting to block out the nightmare. Not only had I been replaced in a matter of days, it'd been by a psycho.

After a few deep breaths, I finally felt calm enough to join the conversation again.

"How did it happen so fast?" Alyssa asked. "Wouldn't he have been under contract?"

"Apparently Danny paid out the remaining years," Eden said. "Cost a small fortune. I don't understand it. It's not like he's the best driver out there. Top ten maybe, but his driving style doesn't really fit with Sinclair's strategy."

It was Eden's polite way of saying the dick was a lunatic on the track who was overly aggressive and often refused to listen to team instructions—usually to his own peril.

She didn't even know the worst of it. His behaviour was even worse off the track. There were things I'd learned about him that no one at Sinclair knew or would probably suspect. If Danny had known even a fraction of them, he'd never have signed up the bastard. He'd definitely never have paid extra for the fuckstick.

Now, it was too late for me to say anything. No one would accept my story as the truth. They'd assume it was just sour grapes on my part. I doubted even Eden would believe me if I told her how despicable he truly was.

All I could do was remind myself that it wasn't anything to do with me. Not anymore. I wasn't with Sinclair and any choices Danny made didn't affect me. Even if they did make me feel like I had a thousand eels churning in my gut.

My focus had to be my family, and trying to figure out what the hell I was going to do with the rest of my life. One thing still bugged me though.

Why Hunter? Why now?

"An eye for an eye," I murmured as the reason became apparent to me.

Both Alyssa's and Eden's heads whipped around to me. They'd

continued the conversation, but my words had silenced them in an instant.

"What?" Alyssa's voice prompted me to continue.

"It's Danny's version of an eye for an eye. Paige was trying to recruit one of his drivers—"

"So he recruited one of hers," Eden finished my sentence.

"Exactly." My voice lacked enthusiasm. Numbness had replaced the anger. "The question would be why Hunter would go from being number one at Wood team to playing second fiddle to Morg."

"You," Eden said. "It's because of you."

"What?"

"As if you don't know," Eden snapped. I felt like we were coming to the reason she'd come in person to deliver the press release. "I'd heard rumours, but I'd never believed that you . . . That you could . . ." Her expression twisted into something I'd never seen on her features before. I couldn't pin it down exactly. It wasn't anger, neither was it disappointment, but it seemed to be a bitter cousin of both.

"That I could what, Edie? What do you think it is I've done?"

"You were in talks with her, weren't you? This whole time, I've been sticking up for you and you've been planning on leaving the team as soon as you could. That's why Danny wouldn't listen to me. He's got other evidence about you and Paige."

I stood and paced away from the table. It was clear gossip had spread around the ranks of Sinclair long before the magazine came out. No wonder Danny was so fucking quick to believe it. My heart pounded in my throat. "It's not what you think."

"So she wasn't trying to recruit you?"

"No. I mean, yes, I mean, fuck." Maybe I should have told everyone at Sinclair sooner that Paige had made plenty of noise about wanting me to join her team. Maybe I should have made it crystal fucking clear that I'd turned her down every time. Maybe then Danny would've had less reason to doubt my loyalty when the article crossed his desk. My focus was on Eden as I looped back around with my hands trailing through my hair. With my gaze locked with hers, I admitted the truth. "She approached me, okay?"

Eden gave me her best bitch brow.

"A few times, actually. But each time, I told her the same thing."

"And that is?"

"That I'm Sinclair through and through, and always have been—even before Danny recruited me. That, well, that he gave me a shot at my dream, and I've never regretted saying yes."

In my periphery, I saw Alyssa's smile fall. Her brows pinched together slightly in pain, and the reason was immediately clear. Fuck! Would my big fucking mouth ever stop causing trouble? By trying to dodge one bullet, I'd stepped right into the path of another.

Without pausing, I strode straight to her and drew her into my arms. "I regret the way I handled some things," I murmured against her hair before looking back to Eden, "but I've never regretted the choice. Maybe I should've said something earlier, but Wood's offers just meant that little to me."

Eden assessed me for a moment, and then a smile took over her frown. She crossed to me and gave my shoulder a playful punch. "I knew it. Or at least I didn't think you'd be able to keep it from me if you were thinking about jumping ship. I can usually read you like a book."

"Why would I jump ship on the best fucking job I've ever had?" It might have been the only real job I'd had, but that was beside the fucking point. "But that still doesn't explain why Hunter left Wood."

"All I know is he's been running his mouth off around the track in Bahrain. Something about him not wanting to waste time with a team that'd put in so much effort to recruit a cockhead."

"Some fucking recruitment campaign," I said. "She's trying to ruin my fucking life."

Eden tilted her head in question.

"The magazine," Alyssa said. "We think she was behind the article."

"I don't think . . ." Eden trailed off. "I mean why would . . ."

She hummed in thought. "Okay, maybe, but how?"

"That's the mystery. But just think about it. Who stood to benefit the most from my contract being cancelled by Sinclair?"

"Why not wait though? Twelve months and your contract would have been up."

"Because I think she knows as well as anyone that I would've renewed with Sinclair if I'd been offered a place."

"But if that was the case, she'd have to know what's happened by now. Surely if she'd been trying to get you on her team, she'd have offered you a pos—" Eden cut off, no doubt seeing something in my expression. "Oh. She already has, hasn't she?"

"She rang this morning," Alyssa confirmed.

Eden's mouth twisted in distaste. "So she's won then? You'll be back on the track next year with her?"

"Fuck no."

Her eyes flared. "What?"

"What do you take me for, Edie? I'm not going to race for someone who's willing to pull those tricks to get me on her fucking team."

"But it might be your one chance to race again."

Lifting one shoulder, I gave a half-hearted shrug. "So? It's not worth it."

"Don't be noble if it costs you everything."

"I'm not being noble. I'm just not racing for a bitch. Especially if it means moving north while my family moves south."

"You know the worst part of it all?" Eden asked. "Hunter has been given the new car."

With everything happening, the news didn't really surprise me. Morgan had already confirmed he'd be running his car again because he was happy with the set-up. "Well, that was the one that was supposed to be mine, I guess."

"He's an arrogant arse!" Eden exclaimed. "He doesn't belong on our team."

The statement almost drew a grin from me, but only because there was a time she would have said the same thing about Morgan, and about me. My smile fell again because in Hunter's case, she was right.

"Apparently, he's done nothing but brag about everything he *thinks* he did at Wood Racing. If I was to believe everything he's told Morgan, he single-handedly built that team from the ground up."

"I don't know what to say, Edie. I think you're right. But I also think Hunter is dangerous. Just be careful around him, won't you?"

She rolled her eyes. "I'll be okay. I think I know a thing or two about how to handle jerk drivers." A half-smile lit her face when I raised my brow at her.

Phoebe came darting up to the table and the conversation stalled. "Wiggles gone," she said, pointing toward the TV where the DVD had reset to the start menu.

I'd seen her restart the DVD from there before—heck, the day I'd spent alone with her at Alyssa's house, she'd completely kicked off the DVD on her own—so I figured that she must have wanted to join in the conversation rather than actually being concerned about the DVD stopping.

"I think that means it's time to put this conversation to bed," Alyssa said, obviously understanding Phoebe's mood as well as I had—or more likely even better. "Unless there's anything else?"

Eden shook her head. "Only that the release is going out tomorrow morning."

"Shit."

Alyssa elbowed me in the ribs, clearly less tolerant of the swearing now that little ears were around and listening. When she caught the bruising that, although faded, still covered a good portion of my ribs, I winced. She gave me an apologetic look, but indicated Phoebe with her eyes—her silent way to tell me to lay off the fucking cuss words.

"Sorry," I said, rubbing the pain of Alyssa's wayward elbow away. "I was just hoping for a little more time before the vultures descend."

"They're already circling, Dec," Eden said. "At least this way it'll all be over at once."

It didn't even sound like her words had convinced her, but I nodded anyway to end the conversation.

"Would you like to stay for dinner, Eden?" Alyssa asked.

"As unique as a home-cooked meal in Declan Reede's house would be, I have to decline. Morgan's supposed to be calling me from Bahrain when he breaks for lunch. I don't want to miss the call. I just wanted to make sure you knew what was coming. I didn't think it was fair for it to be sprung on you without warning."

"Thanks, Edie. I appreciate it."

As I saw Eden out, she hugged me tightly. "Is Alyssa here for good?"

"No, just until Wednesday."

Eden's mouth mashed into an unhappy line.

"Why?"

"I'm leaving for Bahrain in the morning and I won't be back for a little over a week."

"So?"

"So, I don't think it's a great idea for you to be alone right now."

I scoffed at her insinuation. "I'm hardly going to top myself."

The look in her eye told me she didn't believe I could cope alone for a few fucking days. "I'll have my phone on roaming. If you need anything—and I mean anything—call me whenever. Any time. Day or night."

"Yeah, sure, Edie." I was done with the conversation. I'd managed without Alyssa before, I'd be able to do it again. Especially when it was only a temporary thing.

"I'm serious, Declan."

"I know."

After Eden left, Alyssa and I started to strategize on how we would present the united front Alyssa herself had suggested earlier in the day. It wouldn't be hard in some respects, like spending time together in public, but others would be more difficult, like keeping the vultures away from Phoebe. We both agreed though, that task had to be our number-one priority.

CHAPTER FIVE

VULTURES

IT DIDN'T TAKE long before I needed to put Alyssa's advice into play. Mere minutes after the press release was issued the following morning, I received my first phone call from the press.

After that first call the phone rang almost non-stop.

The media had a raft of questions, but mostly they boiled down to the two most vital ones. Who was I driving for now, and what was the reason behind the split from Sinclair Racing?

Following Alyssa's advice, I gave the same answer each time: "I'm not driving at the moment, and no comment."

Some of the more reputable organisations left it at that. Others weren't so professional. They'd gathered information about Alyssa, about Phoebe, and one or two had even found out about Emmanuel.

With an effort worthy of a fucking saint, I held my tongue as they tried to bait me to get a sound bite of me losing control. The one thing that helped me the most was to concentrate on Alyssa and Phoebe. Together, they did a fantastic job of distracting me from my worries over the whole situation between phone calls. After fielding the tenth call of the morning, I decided enough was e-fucking-nough and left the phone off the hook. I left the study with a snarl on my lips and Alyssa glanced over at me with a concerned look on her face.

"You know what? Let's blow this joint," I said. "How's a trip to the beach sound?"

Alyssa chuckled. "As much as I'd love to, I didn't exactly pack for the beach when we left."

"So, we'll go to the shops first then."

"You can't just spend money willy-nilly, Dec."

Not now that you're unemployed. Even though she hadn't said the words, they were as loud as the rest of her sentence in my head. A reminder that I had to start being more frugal. That I had to call my banker and work out my finances and see how long I could last without having to liquidate everything.

Fuck it. That could be tomorrow's problem. "Can we just have one more day without worrying about it?" I asked. "I know I'll have to start being careful soon, but not today. Okay?"

"If that's what you need."

"I need a day with my girls. A day without any stress. Most of all, I need a day away from that goddamned telephone before I give one of those leeches everything they deserve for their stupid-arse questions. Plus, you leave tomorrow."

Her gaze fell and she moved closer to me. "Don't remind me."

My lips twitched upward, knowing that it was as unpleasant a thought for her as it was for me.

Within ten minutes, we were in my Prado—it was at least a little more discreet than the Monaro—and headed for the local shops. Within an hour, we'd grabbed a basic swimsuit for each of them and were at Bondi Beach. The beach was busy enough to allow us to blend in, but not so busy that we couldn't find a quiet spot near the water. Hiding under my hat and sunnies, I was able to sit with Phoebe and help her make a sandcastle.

I pulled my shirt off to enjoy a little of the sun and to take Phoebe into the water to splash around in the shallow waves.

"Should you really go in there?" Alyssa asked, glancing at the ocean.

I gave her a questioning look, and she indicated her back.

"You know, with your tattoo."

"It'll be fine. I don't think I need to be up to my neck in the water with Phoebe."

"Okay, if you're sure."

"I'm positive." I turned to Phoebe. "You wanna go swim to wash off the sand?"

She nodded before taking off straight for the ocean. Unsure about how confident she was in the water, I rushed off behind her.

When I turned back to tell Alyssa to join us, I caught her gaze lingering on my back—on the tattoo celebrating Phoebe and commemorating Emmanuel. In the water up to my knees, I smirked at her to let her know she'd been caught staring. She just shrugged and gave me a look that said, "What do you expect?" before relaxing back against the towel.

I followed Phoebe a little further out, watching her like an eagle the whole time. She spun and danced in the ocean, jumping over some waves and diving under others. Each time a wave approached, she'd squeal and dance.

A couple of minutes later, a hand grabbed my arse. I twisted in place to give the molester a gobful, but the abuse stilled on my tongue when I saw it was Alyssa.

For a moment, I was completely stunned and it wasn't just the abusive words that died in my mouth. I couldn't even form a coherent thought, let alone make it into a sound.

It was probably a sign of how distracted I'd been that even though I'd caught a glimpse of the small black bikini at the shops as Alyssa had scanned it through the self-service checkout, I hadn't really imagined what it might look like on her. If I had, I don't think my imagination would have drummed up an image even half as hot as the one in front of me.

Black Lycra contrasted against her milky white skin. Her hair curled around her shoulders, the ends calling my attention downward. The ruffles along the top of the cups accentuated the perfect fullness of her boobs. The ties that were knotted at her hips hinted at just how easy the bottoms would be to remove. Without thought, I moved closer to her.

Alyssa's gaze shifted to Phoebe for a moment, checking that she was okay, before heading back to meet mine. On the way, her eyes trailed a smoking-hot path over my body.

"Don't look at me like that," I murmured to her as I captured her in my arms. I glanced quickly at Phoebe, playing not even an arm's length away, to ensure she was okay. "Or I can't be held responsible for what happens later," I murmured in her ear as I pulled her closer to me. Unable to resist her, I nibbled her neck.

Her breath came as a needy sigh before she chuckled. "Where's a babysitter when you need one, right?" Her eyes focused on Phoebe as she brushed her hair behind her ear, exposing more of her neck to me.

I moved us so that her back was against my front, my cock pressed between her arse cheeks. It was like heaven. Her words and the feel of her in my arms were sharp reminders that the previous night, for the second night in a row, Phoebe hadn't fallen asleep easily and had woken constantly. Between that, the stress of the situation, the fact I refused to make love to Alyssa in a bed where I'd seduced other women, and Alyssa's exhaustion when she'd first arrived, we hadn't exactly had the chance to reconnect properly. The need to take her was getting stronger with every passing second. I was dying for her.

"Hopefully she'll sleep better tonight," Alyssa murmured, leaning against my body. The heat in her eyes when she turned her head slightly to meet mine was too much. Need for her raced through my body and down to my cock, causing it to swell further and ache with need.

"Fuck, you really can't say things like that to me in public," I whispered against her neck.

"Why not?" Her voice was filled with false innocence. After checking Phoebe once more, she spun in my arms, put her hand on my chest, and whispered into my ear, "I guess I shouldn't tell you how badly I want you to fuck me." The last two words were nothing more than a breath against the shell of my ear.

I swallowed down the lump in my throat, but that didn't help the one growing in my boardies. "Fuck me," I murmured, a little louder than I'd intended.

"Maybe later," Alyssa said with a throaty chuckle as she moved away from me and closer to Phoebe. "If you watch your language." She turned and winked at me.

The lack of her warm body in my hold was instantly noticeable, but wasn't enough to deflate my raging hard-on. Knowing I needed to get myself under control considering we were on a beach filled with families, I checked Alyssa was close to Phoebe and then headed deeper into the tepid seawater.

"Where are you going?" Alyssa called after me, but I just raised my hand to tell her to give me a moment.

Looking out at the open ocean, I closed my eyes and breathed in the sea air as the water surrounded my lower half. The salty breeze whipped through my hair and around my face. After another deep breath, another lungful of the cleansing air, I turned back toward my girls. I watched for a moment without them knowing as Alyssa lifted Phoebe over a wave and then in a loose circle through the air. The wind carried their laughter to me. The moment was so fucking tender, it made my heart swell with pride that I was able to call them mine.

I was heading back over to join them when I saw someone standing on the beach. At first, I was almost willing to ignore the guy, but something about him demanded my attention. He was a young man—he couldn't have been more than eighteen. His camera was slightly too big to belong to a tourist—especially with the telephoto lens sticking out the front. My fingers curled into fists at the sight. A fucking paparazzo.

Did he know I was there? His camera certainly seemed trained in my direction.

A flood of other questions rushed through my mind. How long had he been there? Had he tipped off any others or was he a greedy arsehole who wanted a scoop? Had he seen me with Alyssa and Phoebe—had he gotten a photo of Alyssa and me? Of Phoebe?

I walked past where Phoebe and Alyssa were playing together, striding straight back toward the beach.

"Dec, what is—" Alyssa's question died on her lips, no doubt seeing the direction I was headed and making the connection. "Don't do anything stupid," she said. I heard her splashing behind me and figured she was following me.

I stopped midstride and spoke to her without meeting her eye. "Just wait here for a few minutes and then leave the beach. Pretend you don't know me and make your way back to the car. I'll deal with the vulture and meet you there."

"Dec . . ." Her voice trailed after me.

"No, Lys. I won't hurt him, and I won't do anything stupid, but I don't want him hassling Phoebe. She doesn't need it. Not yet. Just trust me, please?"

"Okay."

I was already walking again before I heard her confirmation that she'd follow my instructions.

The pap started to back away when he saw I was making a beeline for him.

You'd better run, fucker! I wanted so desperately to shout the words, but I bit back on them so that I didn't cause more problems for myself. The last thing I needed was yet another article about how I couldn't control my temper. But what type of sicko followed someone around on a family day to the beach, for fuck's sake?

By the time I was out of the water, the pap had turned his back completely and was heading up the sand away from the crowd. The fucker had the lead, but didn't count on the fact that I was fit and had plenty of stamina. More than some skinny-arsed dipshit photographer, at least. Despite the lingering injuries from my crashes, I was certain I could catch him. Especially because I wasn't willing to let the fuckwit get away with stalking my family. As soon as my feet hit the dry sand, I sprinted in his direction. Each time my bare feet hit the sand, a spray of sand kicked up behind me, no doubt hitting the tourists and sunbathers lying on the beach, but I didn't give a shit.

"Hey!" I shouted after him, hoping he'd turn and see that I was gaining ground. I wanted to see the blind panic in his eyes as he saw how close I was. "Hey you!"

People around us turned to look in my direction, no doubt wondering who the hell the crazy man running along Bondi Beach was, and why he was screaming at the man with a camera.

"You wanted a photo of Declan Reede, didn't you?" I shouted louder. "Well, take your fucking photo." I slowed my pace and held my arms out in invitation.

More heads whipped around in our direction. The crowd was more tourists than locals, so I didn't think they were paying attention to my name—just my shouting.

"Come on, you coward, turn and take my fucking picture now."

Even though I'd stopped running, by the time he reached the boardwalk, I was practically on top of him. I grabbed his shoulder and spun him around to face me. The kid was at least six inches shorter than me, and easily half my weight. It would almost be unfair to pummel him to dirt, but that was all I wanted to do. The only thing stopping me was the promise I'd made Alyssa.

"What's the matter?" I snapped, getting in his face to intimidate him. "Don't you want a fucking close-up? You'd rather take long-range photos like some sort of peeping fucking Tom, would you?"

"I—I'm just doing my job." He held his hands up in the air in surrender, his camera aloft and his face turned away as if he expected me to strike at any moment. A week ago, I probably would have, and even now it was damn tempting. If only he hadn't been quite so pathetic.

"Well, now your job needs to be taking happy-snaps of any-fucking-one else but me, do you understand that? If I see you around again, there will be issues."

"I just go where I'm told. I don't make the decisions."

I curled up my nose and laughed at the coward. "Well, how about you decide to grow a pair and say no for once."

"Why would I? It wouldn't make a difference."

"What do you mean?"

"If I refuse, she'll just send someone else."

"She?" My heart pounded against my ribcage at the word.

"What fucking she? Paige?"

"Who? What?"

"Did Paige Wood put you up to this?" I asked again. When he didn't respond straight away, I grabbed his collar. "Is she the one who sent you here?"

"The owner of Wood Racing?" His face twisted with confusion. "What's she got to do with anything?"

The hope that I'd stumbled onto someone who could provide evidence of a set-up fell as quickly as it had been inflated. I used the hold I had to push him away from me. "Which *she*, then?"

"T. My fucking boss, you lunatic."

"Well, you tell T from me that she and all of her lackeys can kindly back the fuck off, won't you?" I stepped back and the look of relief on the kid's face would have been comical in any other situation. He must have seen I would be behaving myself; or at least that his face wasn't in any immediate danger of an introduction to my fists. "If she dares send anyone after me or my family again, I'll fucking make her pay."

Clearly feeling safer than he had when I'd chased him down, he laughed as he turned away. "You really don't get how this works, do you?" He spun back around to glance at me once more. He raised another camera, one with a shorter lens, and snapped a few photos as he walked backward a few steps. "You don't have a choice in the matter. As long as the public are willing to read about the many and varied ways you fuck things up, someone will be there to document it in pictures. The sooner you accept that fact, the happier we all can be."

Even though I recognised the truth in his words, I refused to acknowledge it. I moved closer to him and held up my finger in warning. As much as I wanted to smack the smarm off his face, I forced my temper down. "Just stay the hell away from me."

"That's not gonna happen, and there's nothing you can do about it. Maybe next time, I'll focus on photos of that sweet, sweet arse that you're tapping. Or should I say, tapping for now."

Unable to control myself any longer, I charged after him. He whirled around and snapped another photo—one of my fist flying at his camera. Once he had the shot, he ducked to the side and narrowly avoided my punch.

Fuck. The whole running-scared act had clearly been a fucking set-up to try to get more incriminating photos. The smug expression he wore, with a wolfish grin and eyes set in challenge, confirmed it.

"There's the money shot." With a laugh, he turned his back on me. "See you tomorrow, Reede," he shot back over his shoulder. "Keep an eye out for your close-up in the magazines. Click click."

It took everything in me to walk away, and by the time I did, my breath came in short, sharp pants. As much as I hated to admit it, he was right. There would be no escape from the photographers so long as there was any public interest in me. They would bait me, just like the reporters with less class had tried to over the phone.

And in this case, I'd fallen for it. Not just hook, line, and sinker, but reel and fucking rod as well.

Fucking idiot! I kicked the tyre of the nearest car and let loose my irritation.

All I could think was thank fuck Alyssa and Phoebe were heading back home to Brisbane the following day. As much as I needed them with me, I wanted to spare them the humiliation of being front page features just to sell a magazine or two. I could only hope that returning home would keep them away from prying eyes—at least mostly.

CHAPTER SIX

LOCKED IN

I WAS STILL trying to calm myself when I met Alyssa back at the car. She already had Phoebe in her seat and was looking around anxiously for me.

"Fucking vultures," I muttered under my breath before forcing my mouth into a smile as I pulled the door open.

"What happened?" Alyssa asked.

My smile fell. "Nothing. I told him to piss off." To stop myself from uttering a hundred other curses that were on the tip of my tongue, I clenched my teeth together until my jaw ached.

"Are you okay?"

"Fan-fucking-tastic."

"Dec," Alyssa's voice held an admonishment, no doubt for my swearing.

I held up my hand just to ask for some time. I needed a moment in my own head, as dangerous a place as that could be.

"Daddy, where was you?"

The sound of Phoebe's voice should have calmed me, but it

didn't. It only reminded me of the fact that I'd have to contend with the fucking paparazzi for the foreseeable future. That they'd be trying to get photos of me fighting, in any compromising position at all, but the money shot—the ultimate prize—would no doubt be a clear photo of me and my daughter.

My mind travelled back to the days after I first learned of her existence, of looking into the mirror and trying to decide whether I should inflict my screwed-up life on her. Had I made the wrong decision? Not because I didn't want to be in her life, because I wanted that more than anything, and more than ever, but because being near me would see her caught up in the whirlwind of fuckery. I closed my eyes tightly and squeezed my hands around the steering wheel until my knuckles ached and protested holding on even a second more.

"Daddy just needs a minute, sweetie," Alyssa said.

My jaw clenched tighter. Their lives may not have been perfect before I came back, but at least they weren't hunted by the fucking media.

Alyssa's hand came to rest on my arm, causing my eyes to jolt open. With a frown pinching my brows together as all the reasons the two of them would be better off without me ran through my head, I turned to glance at her.

"Let's just go home, yeah?" Even as she said the words, her hand traced the length of my arm. When she reached the steering wheel, her fingers closed around mine. My traitorous body followed her lead and my grip on the steering wheel loosened until she was able to pry my hand away and hold it in her own.

"Lys, I—"

She met my gaze and shook her head. "No. I know what you're thinking—"

"I—" I wasn't even sure what I wanted to say, but I had to say something.

"I know, Dec. I can see it, and you're wrong. Just like you were wrong when you thought it in Brisbane." She leaned across the car and whispered in my ear, "She *needs* you. *I* need you."

The intensity that burned in her eyes when I met her gaze was too much for me to deal with on top of everything else. Without another word, I turned away from her and started the car. The drive home was tense. To try to alleviate some of the stifling silence in the car, Alyssa turned on the radio, but it wasn't enough to distract me from my thoughts or break the stilted atmosphere.

When I turned down my street, the first thing that caught my eye was the two cars parked in front of my house. The circular drive down to the garage was long enough that they wouldn't be able to see everything, but with their telephoto lenses, they'd be able to capture enough. I'd never wanted, or needed, a six-foot-high fence to enclose my front yard, but having to pull into my property and see just how open and vulnerable it was, I wanted one more than anything.

"Fucking vermin," I murmured as a camera lens poked out one window, confirming my suspicion about the purpose of the cars.

I drove down the drive and into the garage. After I'd killed the engine, I glanced in the rear-view mirror as the garage door rolled down.

It was when the door was completely closed that I noticed Phoebe was asleep in the back seat. I blew out a sigh of frustration. It should have been easy to pick her up and carry her the short distance to the house, but with the visitors I had camped outside the house waiting for the perfect shot, I couldn't risk it. I had to draw their attention onto me.

"You'll have to carry her," I said to Alyssa even as I shoved open my door and climbed out of the car. Without glancing back, I headed to the small side door to the detached garage and pushed through it.

My steps carried me away from the house and closer to the front of the property. One of the paps obviously saw me coming because a moment later, there was a small flurry of activity as cameras were pointed at me. I paced back and forth along a section of the circular drive, my hands fisted in my hair and a stream of filthy words just behind my lips ready to fly from me at any second.

The desire to curse out every pap, to scream and shout until they all just fucked off and left me alone, was so strong, but I couldn't. It would only make things worse.

It was almost fucking ironic that I'd spent four years boozing up and fucking almost anything with tits, but the paparazzi only became interested when I was settled down and living a calmer life. When I was trying to do the responsible thing.

Despite the lack of bars, I felt like a caged animal. A fucking zoo exhibit. Trapped within the confines of my own home.

Certain I'd distracted the photographers long enough for Alyssa to get Phoebe into the house, I turned and headed back inside—but not before flipping the bird at the cameras. Let that be their fucking money shot.

The first thing I did when I got inside was to ensure every set of blinds in the house was closed, that every curtain was drawn. I didn't want any of the fuckers getting a look inside my house. As I paced from room to room in my crazed state, I heard Alyssa singing to Phoebe, no doubt trying to get her back to sleep for an afternoon nap.

I was in the study, trying to see if I could see any of the fuckers on the street from the small window there, when Alyssa found me.

"Do you want to talk about before?" Her voice held no judgement. No anger. Just support.

It was enough to spur me into action. I crossed the room to her, drew her into my arms and claimed her lips. My tongue followed, probing at her mouth to demand entrance. She complied willingly, opening for me in every sense. I stepped between her legs and grabbed her arse to pull her closer to me.

All the fun and desire we'd shared in the water, the fun teasing, had gone—replaced by a craving deeper than any I could explain. I needed to give myself to her; needed her to take me in return. I had to surrender to her hold so that she could remove the doubt surging through me. The salt water lingered on her lips, adding a new dimension to her flavour I'd never tasted before. Each and every time I'd been with Alyssa was like a new experience—one I would never tire of.

All of the doubts that had been slowly twisting through my mind, taking root as dark thoughts and twisting into thick vines through every memory and emotion, were swept away by her touch.

She seemed to understand what I wanted. Seconds after I'd initiated the kiss, the sundress she was wearing came off over her head. Underneath was her still slightly damp bikini.

"Fuck." The word slipped from my lips at the fresh sight of the black against her skin. It was clear that visions of her wearing that outfit would be frequent visitors while she was back in Brisbane and I was stuck in Sydney.

I kissed my way down her neck, my fingers reaching for the ties on her hips. First one, then the other, and the bikini bottom fell away completely. Without stopping, my fingers explored her skin, pushing the cups of her bikini top down to expose her perfect nipples.

Matching sighs were on our lips as I took one breast in my mouth and rolled the other in my fingertips.

"I need you, Lys."

"I'm yours, Dec."

I wasn't sure if she realised I meant in general, and not only right then, but either way her answer pacified the need I had to tell her how I felt. Knowing that no further words were needed, I claimed her lips again as my hands explored her body.

Desperate for more, I guided her closer to my desk until her arse was pressed against the edge. I ground my hips against hers, desperate for more. I could feel her heat though the thin material of my boardies as my covered cock brushed against her wet and waiting pussy.

My lips pressed little kisses down her neck. "So fucking tasty," I whispered against her skin.

She pushed down my boardies and pulled out my cock. The feel of her palm against the engorged flesh was fucking superb. I was so hard it was painful. The relief her touch elicited merely hinted at what was to come.

Without any preamble, she lined me up at her entrance before stroking the head of my cock along her wet pussy. A hiss slipped past my lips at the pure bliss of the sensation. Barely a thought crossed my mind before I thrust hard into her, burying myself deep within her.

My lips and hands roamed and explored, touching and tasting every bit of her that they could. I was a hungry man desperate for a meal—possibly the last I'd enjoy for some time with her going home.

The thought was too much. I pulled away and sank to the floor, dragging her down with me. Taking the hint, she straddled over my hips and lowered herself onto my cock. Sitting up, I wrapped my arms around her waist as we moved together slowly. The dried salt on our skin moistened with the slickness of our sweat. Her breasts pressed against me; her hardened nipples tracing lines along my chest. The moment was messy. It was real. It was perfect.

In my lap, Alyssa was slowly coming apart. I could feel the tension coiling in her body, her pussy clamping tighter around me. I wanted to whisper to her to let go, but the sound of footsteps upstairs stole the moment from me.

"Fuck, Phoebe's awake," Alyssa said, climbing off me and instantly breaking the connection. She was dressed again and out of the room before I'd even finished the frustrated groan that left me.

My cock was stiff and sore, slick with the wetness of Alyssa's pussy. I needed release. Craved it.

Craved her.

But it would have to wait.

Fuck.

I slipped my boardies back up and tucked myself away. Taking a moment to promise my cock that he'd get another chance later, I called out to let Alyssa know I was going for a shower.

A fucking cold one.

AFTER I'D showered and changed, I felt a little more human. At least partly. I went in search of Phoebe and Alyssa. When I found Phoebe, she was alone in the living room playing with her dolls.

"Where's Mummy?"

"She had to maked a phone call."

A frown pulled at my brow as I wondered who she could be calling.

"I sorry I made you angry before, Daddy."

My gaze cut straight to Phoebe. Her eyes were round as saucers and her lip quivered. My frown deepened. She was fucking apologising to me? I sank to my knees and forced my mouth into a smile even though her words had been like daggers. "No, baby, you didn't. You and Mummy make me happy. Happier than I probably deserve to be."

Phoebe's mouth turned down and her eyes pinched together in confusion.

"Before I found you again, Daddy ... hurt some people. I didn't mean to, I just wasn't thinking. That's what made me angry. I was angry with me."

"Did you say sorry to dem?"

"What?"

"If you hurt someone you should say sorry." She placed her hands on her hips and gave me a withering stare. It was a look I'd gotten often from Alyssa, and the sight of it on her little doppelganger was enough to bring a genuine smile to my face.

"To some of them I have."

"Well, I guess that okay. But you should say sorry to the others."

"You're right. I should. I'll start now, shall I?"

She tilted her head in confusion.

"I'm sorry for all the times you had to go to bed not knowing where your daddy was, or even who he was. I'm sorry for every birthday, Christmas, and milestone I've missed. I can't ever make up for that lost time, but I'll do everything I can to make every day special from here on out. Deal?"

Her little arms wrapped around my neck and she planted a kiss on my cheek. "Love you, Daddy."

I cuddled her close to me. "I love you too, baby."

"Guess what?" She pulled away and grinned.

"What?"

"We're going on a plane tomorrow!"

Even though her words made my mood slip, I tried to keep a smile on my face so she didn't think I was upset with her again. "Are you excited?"

Her hair bounced around her face as she nodded. "I've only been on one twice before. When Mummy came to work and Nana and Josh came down. I didn't like it when Mummy went away."

"I can understand that. I'm not going to like it when you and Mummy leave tomorrow."

Her jaw fell slack and her eyes filled with horror. "You're not coming?"

"No. I've got to stay here."

"Why?"

"Because—" I had no reason for her. There wasn't really anything keeping me in Sydney, not until they moved down at least. "Because I don't have a plane ticket."

"Did Mummy forget to get you one?"

"No, baby, I told her not to."

"Don't you want to come?"

"I do. Very much."

"Then, why?"

It was impossible to explain the complex reasons why I couldn't just jump back on a plane to Brisbane. Especially with the paparazzi causing me grief. "I have a few people I need to see first, then maybe I can."

"When?"

"Soon. I promise." I drew a cross over my heart. "Maybe while I'm waiting I can paint your room?"

She grinned. "Yes, please!"

"Shall we pick a colour?" When she nodded, I led her into my study and booted up the computer. Phoebe climbed straight onto my lap and "helped" me with the computer. Even with her playing with the keyboard or the mouse every time I took my hand off them, I managed to pull up a paint chart.

We were halfway through the purples when Alyssa came to find us.

"Well, I've got some good news," she said.

I shifted Phoebe over to my other knee so I could talk to Alyssa better. "That's good, because I could sure as shi—could really use some."

"I just spoke to Mr. Kent—he'll be my supervisor at Pembletons—and he said that I'll be able to start work when they go back after their Christmas break rather than having to wait until after graduation."

Christmas. It was still over a month away. If Alyssa wasn't going to start her new job until after then, there was little hope that she'd be moving down sooner than that. I wanted to ask how that was *good* news.

"It'll mean I'll have to fly home to attend my graduation ceremony rather than staying for it, but at least we'll be able to move down almost two months sooner."

Two months sooner was something to fucking celebrate.

I could only hope I'd be able to shake the presence of the paparazzi by then, otherwise we'd never have a normal life.

CHAPTER SEVEN

EXORCISM

"WHAT ARE YOU going to do after we leave?" Alyssa ran her fingers through my hair as the question left her lips.

After getting Phoebe fed, bathed, and into bed, Alyssa and I had headed back downstairs to watch TV and try to find a moment together. Almost the second we sat on the couch, she'd curled her body around mine and seemed intent on touching me as much as possible. I wasn't going to complain, and in response, my fingertips dragged lazy trails over the thigh she rested in my lap.

I captured her hand in mine and brought it to my lips. "Don't talk about it."

"I have to know you're going to be okay tomorrow night."

Her insinuation and the concern in her voice made my teeth clench. After everything we'd been through, everything we'd battled, I thought she finally trusted me. With a simple statement, she's showed she didn't. Barely a day earlier, Eden had made similar comments.

It was like the two of them thought I would fall apart the

moment I was alone. Their lack of faith in me was un-fucking-believable. I dropped her hand and leaned away from her. "I'm sure I'll manage. After all, the keg's been ordered and cheerleaders are on speed dial. Maybe the sex tape can help pay the bills."

Even though my words had been barbed, I'd expected her to laugh, call me ridiculous or a jerk or some shit, and then make me feel better about the fact that she was leaving with her mouth, or her pussy. Instead, she twisted away from our embrace, stood, and then walked away without a word. Before she'd even left the room, a quiet sob left her lips.

Shock shook me as I watched her walk away. *Overreact much?*

"Lys?" I leapt off the couch and followed her. I caught up with her at the bottom of the stairs. Not wanting to let her walk away on such a sour note, especially when we wouldn't see each other until I could fulfil my promise to Phoebe to go back up to Brisbane, I coaxed her to turn around. "I was fucking joking. What happened to what you said about wanting to trust me? What happened to me not being a hypocrite or like my father?"

She refused to allow me to hold her, shrugging out of my arms. "I can't do this right now, Dec. I just need . . . I need a moment. Please?"

"No."

She spun around. Tears flooded her eyes, but her mouth was set in a hard line.

The emotions that swelled in her honey-gold irises were almost enough to drive me to my knees. The heartbreak and the pain echoing inside made me want to take back the words, even if I had no idea why they'd elicited such a strong reaction after she'd taken all the lies in the magazine article in stride. Almost as soon as she'd looked at me, she dropped her gaze again.

"Fuck, Lys, I was joking."

"You don't get it, do you?"

"How am I supposed to get anything, when I don't even know what the fuck I'm supposed to be getting?"

Her tear-stained eyes turned up to meet mine again. The corner of her mouth lifted in a smile that held nothing but sorrow and regret. I lifted my hand up to caress her cheek, thankful when she didn't pull away from me as I swiped her tears with my thumb.

"I told you all of this before. Why did you have to be drunk for it?" Her eyes sank closed as she leaned into my touch. "When you wouldn't answer your phone, after you first left home I mean, I tried sending you an email. I had no idea whether or not you'd get it, but I hoped that you would. I hoped it'd help you understand how desperately I needed to talk to you."

"Okay?" I had vague recollections of Mum mentioning something about Alyssa emailing me. At the same time, a flash of a conversation with Alyssa flittered through my thoughts, but the image was so fleeting it was hard to know if it was a drunken dream or born out of a desire to know why my words had hurt her so much. My brows dipped as I tried to grasp the elusive edges of the memory.

"When I opened your reply—"

"I wouldn't have replied." The words had left me before I could stop myself. They were enough to cause Alyssa to twitch away from my hold. In response, I shifted closer and moved my hand from her cheek into her hair to guide her gaze back to me. "I wouldn't have, because if I'd let myself have a conversation with you, it would have ended with me back in Brisbane. Trust me, I wouldn't have let myself reply."

"You replied all right," she said, tugging free of my hold again. Her sobs grew harder and it took everything in me to give her the space she so clearly wanted while her need for comfort was obvious. Only, it was equally clear she didn't want to find her solace in my hold. "You replied telling me to go fuck myself. That you were no longer interested in hearing from me. And then you attached photos and video of you fucking three other women for good measure."

Watching the pain in her movements made my heart ache for her. As much as I wanted to demand what her words had to do with why she'd walked off, I didn't want to insist on anything that might hurt her further.

"Three cheerleaders." The words were barely audible, but they struck my ears louder than thunder. My barbed, thoughtless statement had struck a nerve that was still raw and throbbing. Had clearly reminded her of one of the worst moments of her life. My knees quivered at the thought. No wonder she'd pulled away. It was probably a small miracle she was even allowing me to try to talk it out.

"Fuck, Lys, I—" I closed my eyes and rested my forehead against hers. She didn't pull away from me and I was so fucking grateful it hurt. "I can never apologise enough."

"The worst part was that I couldn't even force myself to stop watching. Even after I saw the photos, with them and their pom-poms all over you, I couldn't stop myself from pressing play. I was so pathetically desperate to hear your voice again, to see your face, that I couldn't help it."

I clung to her, hoping she'd keep me buoyed even as her words set me adrift on a sea of agony. She was the current dragging me away, and the life jacket holding me afloat. "I'm sorry, Lys. It meant nothing. They all meant nothing."

"I know—" Her voice was thick with tears, and it seemed like an effort for her to squeeze out any words. "That's what made it worse. I almost could have taken it if you'd moved on with someone else. If you'd found something meaningful. But to go from—" She choked back a sob. "From what we had, to a series of flings. To record them and share them. Seeing that video . . . it was the moment when I knew that the Declan I loved—the one who'd fathered the lives growing inside me—was gone. It shattered me, Dec."

Tears were in my own eyes as I considered her words. I tried to reverse the situation in my mind. How would I have coped with the knowledge that she was happily screwing half the town? I wrapped my arms tighter around her waist and pulled her body against mine.

"I'm so fucking sorry." My voice was hoarse as my throat held the words tighter than I'd wanted it to. "I can't even explain why I did it. All I know is that I'm a better person when I'm with you."

Even as the words left me, I could see the truth in them.

That was the real reason behind Alyssa's lack of faith. Being alone would leave me stuck in my own head. She knew as well as I did that I kept my demons in control better with her at my side. It wasn't that she didn't trust me to win the battle, but that she didn't want me to have to fight myself the whole time she was gone. And I'd accused her of lacking trust. Fucking arsehole.

"I'm going to miss you and Pheebs while you're gone, so fucking much, but I'll get through it because of the prize at the end. You're my first place, Lys, and I'm going to fight my way to it."

She rested her head on my chest. "I'm sorry I overreacted."

"No, you didn't. I'm sorry I made a crass joke without realising why it would hurt you. And I'm sorry for ever throwing away what we had and for making so much ammunition that would cause you pain."

I held her in my arms for a few moments more, unwilling to let her go or give her any reason to doubt the sincerity in my words.

"Let's head up to bed, shall we?" I said. "It's been a long day."

When she nodded, I swept her up into my arms.

"Put me down! I can walk." Her tears evaporated as she protested.

"Nope. Because tonight is my last night with you for a while, and I'm not letting you go until I absolutely have to."

She laughed. "You'll drop me!"

"Just because I did the last time I carried you like this, doesn't mean I will this time. After all, you're not wearing a ridiculously long dress this time."

"Dec, please?"

"And I'm stronger than I was then."

I glanced down at her and caught her staring at my shoulders, no doubt checking the truth in my words. Her breaths grew heavier and when her gaze met mine again, it carried a heat that I couldn't resist. Needing to touch her, to kiss her, and hold her close, I moved to claim her lips. As I did, I placed her back on the floor so I could run my fingers into her hair and hold her to me.

My lips moved against hers, our tongues danced a slow waltz—tasting and teasing during the back and forth. With the sensation of the kiss racing through my body, my cock leapt to attention—ready for a take two on the disastrous attempt that afternoon.

At the thought, flashes of the night with the cheerleaders flittered through the edges of my mind. I stepped away from Alyssa as my mind repeated the events that had led up to our kiss over and over. It wasn't fair to her to taint our last night in Sydney by making love while I had any thoughts of other women in my head. Even if the thoughts were ugly, grey, and tinged with regret.

"What's wrong?" Her breath was short and her chest heaved.

"I don't know if I should . . . If we should . . ." My frustration at being unable to articulate my thoughts slipped from me on the end of my breath. "I don't want to make love to you while I'm being haunted by thoughts of other girls."

Alyssa's eyebrows lifted at my words. They were poorly chosen, but accurate.

"I mean, we were just talking about the ways I hurt you, and now . . . well, I can't help thinking that I don't deserve it."

"Dec—"

I silenced her with a look. "I don't deserve you."

"You're right," she said.

My heart stopped. Was this it? The moment where she saw how strong my demons were and walked away?

She grabbed my hands and wrapped them around her neck. "The you that sent that email doesn't. But we both know that's not who you really are. The you in here," she put her hand over my heart, "deserves every bit of me. And you need to start believing that. I was upset at your words, at the reminder of what happened, but that doesn't mean I was upset with you."

"So you were pissed at me, but not actually pissed at me?" My mind refused to wrap around her words. "You know that makes no sense, right?"

She chuckled. "I'm a woman. We don't have to make sense."

"I'm going to shut my mouth, because anything I say now will probably just get me in trouble."

Her smile widened and her laughter hung in the air. "See,

you're learning already. Now c'mon." She held out her hand to me.

"Where are we going?" I asked as I wrapped my fingers around hers.

"Well, you said you were being haunted by ghosts and the demons of your past, right?"

"And?"

She pulled me toward the staircase. "And I think I've lived in their shadow long enough already."

"Okay?"

"So I'm going to perform an exorcism." When she turned back to glance at me, her gaze smouldered. Her tongue slicked across her lips in a way that made my cock twitch.

Fuck me.

"Besides," she continued. "I'm not going to leave you alone in Sydney in a house filled only with memories of other women. I'm claiming my territory and giving you something to remember me by while I'm gone."

Fuck, possessive Alyssa was fucking hot. Instead of letting her drag me up the stairs, I dashed ahead of her and pulled her along with me. Both of us were practically running by the time we hit the landing. We didn't even make it to the bedroom door before we crashed together in a meld of lips and limbs.

We tumbled into my bedroom together. Her hands tugged at my shirt; my fingers caressed her hair. Kicking my leg out behind me, I snagged the door and swung it shut. A huge bang echoed through the house.

"Fuck." The word left me between kisses and then I stopped and held my breath while I waited for the telltale scream that signalled the noise had woken Phoebe. When everything was still quiet after a couple of seconds, I renewed my attack on Alyssa.

Our clothes fell away as we kissed and performed our messy, uncoordinated dance to the bed. By the time we tumbled onto the mattress, all that was left were my boxers and Alyssa's underwear.

The moment we hit the bed, Alyssa climbed on top of me and straddled my hips. Her lips peppered hot kisses over my jaw and down my throat. The swell of her breasts pillowed against my ribcage. The sensation of her hips rocking over mine removed all thoughts of everything but what I was feeling.

My hands traced small circles over her hipbones, playing with the cotton resting over them. When Alyssa kissed me again, I pushed the material down over her hips. She lifted off me just far enough to give me room to maneuverer her panties over her thighs. Climbing backward off the bed, she pushed the scrap of material the rest of the way off.

"The bra too," I said, my voice hoarse with need.

With a smirk on her lips, she reached behind her and unclasped her bra. The weight of her breasts was released and I longed to hold them in my palms.

"Come here," I murmured.

She climbed back over the bed, one leg on either side of my body. When she reached my hips, she stopped.

I shook my head. "Higher."

She frowned in confusion, but moved further up my body, stopping around my stomach.

"Don't you know one of the staples of an exorcism?" I asked as I hooked my hands around her arse and forced her to move higher up still.

"What?" Her thighs were level with my waist when a nervous chuckle escaped her. All the bravado and possessiveness from downstairs was gone, and yet she was still just as hot.

"The poor sucker who's been possessed almost always ends up speaking in tongues." I waggled my eyebrow at her as I licked my lips. The lean muscles of her arse clenched at my words, or maybe it was the sight and promise of my tongue.

Without wasting any more time with words, I used my hold on her hips to slide down the bed so that my face was under her pussy. My tongue pressed forward and I kissed her clit with the same desperation I'd kissed her lips. Her body jolted with the shock of the connection and her hips surged forward to add more pressure to the mix.

One of my hands curled around her thigh and gripped her arse to guide her hips closer to me. The other lifted to follow the contours of her body. My gaze followed my fingers as they trailed over her stomach and up to her breasts.

With her breath coming in short, sharp bursts, she leaned her hands against the headboard and held on tight. Her head dropped downward and a tiny, desperate moan left her as I grazed her clit with my teeth. When her gaze met mine, I shifted my attention from her clit to the rest of her pussy. Meeting her eyes, I pressed my tongue against her entrance. My lips curled into a semi-smile at the way her eyes rolled back when I pushed my tongue into her, slow and steady so I could relish the taste as I prolonged the sensation for her.

Seeing she was clearly enjoying the attention, I closed my eyes again and turned myself over to my other senses. The taste of Alyssa's sweetness dancing on my tastebuds. The feel of her nipples tightening at my touch. The sound of the little moans escaping her with every thrust of my tongue or caress of her clit. Even though we'd joked about it being an exorcism, it was more like heaven.

Alyssa's body quivered above me as I continued to lavish my attention on her pussy.

Needing to taste her, to feel her, and to hear her as she shattered around me, I added a finger into the mix. Then two. Her thighs clamped around me as she dropped her forehead onto the headboard. Her hips thrust against my mouth in erratic jerks as her soft moans grew louder and louder.

With my tongue, I traced the letters of the words *I love you* against her clit. I was up to the *L* when she came apart, but I finished the letters as she rode out her orgasm. Her first for the night. The first of many, if I had anything to say about it.

While she was still boneless with a loopy grin on her face, I shifted her so that she was resting over my hips again. To my surprise, and extreme satisfaction, she leaned forward and kissed me hard. The taste of her filled my senses as our tongues danced together.

"Lys," I murmured as she shifted herself away from me. The movement left me bereft and wanting more.

"Relax, Dec," she whispered back. "I'm just getting rid of

these." Her fingers trailed into the waist of my boxers and she dragged them down my legs.

The instant my cock sprung free, I was reaching for her, pulling her back against me.

"Please, Lys. I need you." I guided her over me.

Taking the hint, she grabbed my dick in her hand and lined it up with her entrance.

"Fuck." The word squeezed through my clenched teeth as the feeling of Alyssa's body opening for me overtook every other sensation. It might have only been a few days since I'd last had the ability to fully experience her body, but even that was too long.

Lifting my hips, I bucked them against hers to bury myself as deep in her as I could. I wanted more. Everything. I wanted to take her in every possible way so that we could both have enough memories to carry us through until we were reunited. Maybe planning to keep her awake as long as I could was selfish, considering she'd be climbing on a plane with a three-year-old, but I couldn't care less. Not when I needed her so desperately.

"You're not getting any sleep tonight," I warned as I claimed her lips again.

CHAPTER EIGHT

NOT ALONE

MORNING CAME AROUND far too quickly and with it came the realisation that I would soon be completely alone. My family would be gone. I'd have no job to go to. I'd have nowhere important to be. Nothing to do at all.

Melancholy settled over me.

When Phoebe woke, I tried to force a smile on my face, but worried that I failed. We had breakfast as a family, and I tried to keep Phoebe entertained. The last thing I wanted was for her last hours with me for a while to be miserable ones. As I played with her, trying to give her some memories so that she wouldn't forget me, Alyssa repacked the overnight bag that had slowly been unpacked over the few days they'd been with me.

Barely an hour after we were awake, it was time to take them to the airport. I'd almost forgotten about the paparazzi until I was halfway up the drive and saw the cars from the night before were still stationed in front of my house.

My fingers gripped the steering wheel until my knuckles were white and my jaw clenched.

Alyssa's hand came to rest on my thigh. "They'll leave when they realise there is no story."

"I know," I said, more to pacify her than because I actually believed it.

The drive to the airport was quiet, stilted. Unlike when she'd dropped me off at Brisbane Airport for my flight down to Sydney, I didn't just drop them at the gate. I found a parking space and walked them in. I didn't want to leave them.

I didn't want them to leave me.

We found a secluded little corner, hidden away from prying eyes. Thankfully, the paps hadn't caught up with us before we found the quiet spot.

When the time came that I had to say goodbye, I picked Phoebe up and held her close against my chest. It was ridiculously impossible how readily she'd twisted her little self through my life and imprinted herself on my heart. In such a short time, she owned me completely. I buried my face in her hair and told her I loved her.

"Remember your promise," she said.

"I do."

Alyssa gave me a questioning look and I realised in all the stress of the previous evening, I hadn't mentioned to her what I'd promised to Phoebe. "That I'll come up to see you as soon as I can. If you'll have me, of course?"

"Don't be silly, of course I want you to come up. Maybe we can tie it up with our move? Then we can all come back home together."

The word "home" slipping so easily from her lips made my heart clench and a smile stretch across my lips. "I'd like that."

I pulled her into my arms and kissed her in a way that probably wasn't entirely appropriate. When we broke apart, I rested my forehead on hers for a few moments before closing my eyes and releasing a sigh.

When I couldn't delay any longer, I cupped both Alyssa's and Phoebe's cheeks with my hand and said another goodbye, ready for Alyssa to lead Phoebe through security. We'd already agreed I'd go first in case any of the paps from home had caught up with us, but I couldn't turn away from Phoebe and Alyssa until the last moment.

Once I'd left them behind me, my mood plummeted.

Why hadn't I insisted on going with them? I had shit to sort out at home, but that didn't seem like a good enough reason. Not anymore. Not without anyone at my side.

I'd barely gone a dozen steps away from the alcove when the vultures descended. I was thankful I was in Australia and only a race driver, not a rocker or movie star in the US. I couldn't imagine having to deal with the constant presence of the photographers. The pack around me was only six people. If I'd had to deal with more, I would have probably gone batshit crazy. Trying to ignore their catcalls and cries for attention, I paced back in the direction of the car park.

"Hey, Reede, did you see your pretty face on the *Gossip Weekly* site?" The voice was too familiar. I risked a glance in the direction it'd come from and spotted the pap from the beach.

My fingers curled into fists at my side.

"Captured the moment you viciously attacked me real well. If I do say so myself."

I blew out a breath through my nose, not trusting myself to unclench my teeth even to breathe.

Needing something to distract me, I turned on my mobile phone. It was the first time I'd turned it on since Alyssa had returned it to me, and it lit up with notifications. I sighed as I flicked through them all. There were at least a dozen text messages from various other drivers, mostly trying to get the lowdown on why I was out of Sinclair. Some of them I only spoke to at race meets, so I felt no obligation to call or message them back in any hurry.

Scattered throughout those messages were ones from Morgan. I knew I'd have to speak to him before too long, but I didn't know what I'd say. He'd gone from my hero to my friend during my time at Sinclair Racing, and I wasn't sure how to approach the situation now that I'd gone back to being a nothing. Would he even still want my friendship?

By the time I'd finished glancing over the text messages, I was at the short-term parking bay. With the small gaggle of photographers following my every step, I headed for my car. As soon as I was locked away inside the Monaro, I called message bank to listen to my messages on speaker as I headed home. I had no doubt that I'd have cars following me before long, but I was a better driver than any of the paps, so it didn't worry me too much.

As expected, there was a stack of messages from Eden, mostly ones trying to warn me about the magazine before I turned up at Danny's office.

How different would it have been if I'd known what I was walking into? I tried not to think about it. The worst thing I could do was start to turn over all the what-ifs in my head. After all, Danny had been set on his course. He'd set it up so that I would know exactly what was happening before he even had to say a word. I doubted me having any additional warning would have done much except given me something extra to stress over on the plane.

After Eden's frantic messages, there were a few relatively normal ones. Mum had called to ask whether Alyssa and I would be willing to come around for a dinner before Mum's flight overseas. I felt bad that I'd missed the message, and that I hadn't been able to see her off in person, but at least I had spoken to her before she went.

The last message was from Dr. Henrikson.

"Declan, I saw the *Gossip Weekly* article and the press release from Sinclair Racing. I think it is important that you call me as soon as you are able. Please, do not wait for our next appointment."

Checking the time, I decided to give him a call. After a short chat with Lucy, I was put straight through to the doc.

"Declan, I am glad you called."

"You did ask me to."

"Indeed. However, that didn't mean that you would."

A chuckle escaped me. "Ain't that the truth?"

"You sound like you're in a better mood than I would have expected under the circumstances."

"Circumstances? You mean having someone try to destroy my life with a magazine article and then getting the sack on top of it all?"

"Yes. Those circumstances. How are you coping?"

"The last few days have been better than I would have expected. I've been able to spend some time with Alyssa and Phoebe. I've just dropped them at the airport now."

"Is Alyssa aware of the article?"

"Yeah. That's why she was in Sydney. She was ... worried. About whether I'd have any issues."

"Did you?"

I chewed on the inside of my cheek and reminded myself that there was little to gain out of the sessions if I wasn't honest with him. And with myself. "It was close. I was so damn tempted to drink myself into oblivion—especially when I found out Alyssa was gone." I told him about the phone call with Alyssa's mum and the night that followed.

"I would like you to book in some face-to-face sessions as soon as you can."

"Uh, doc, I really don't know how I can afford it." The words tasted like poison in my mouth. It was the first time I'd admitted to anyone besides Alyssa that I had worries about my finances in the long term. "I don't have a job. I don't even know what I can do for a living. I mean, what transferable skills has being a driver given me? I don't—"

"Declan," he cut me off. "This is exactly the reason I would like you to come in. I know this situation is likely to set you into a long-term panic spiral. Especially with everything else that has occurred over the last few months. In regards to payment, you are entitled to ten sessions from Medicare. All you'll need to do is get a GP referral and consultation. Outside of those sessions, we can discuss a sliding scale payment system. I'm here to help, and I think it is important we don't lose any progress you have made in the last few weeks."

"Thanks, Doc."

He gave me the name of a GP. It might not have been my usual doctor, but she had a relationship with Dr Henrikson and would give me the referral to Henrikson on his word.

"Come see me on Friday afternoon; that'll give you time to see Dr Ling for the referral."

We set a time for my appointment, and I thanked him again.

The conversation left me feeling a little more in control. By the time it finished, I was almost back home. Letting my eyes slide past the cars gathered in front of my house and quickly trying to find parking along the street, I pushed the button to open my garage and drove straight inside.

I had no plans for the rest of the day, but I wanted to be in a familiar setting, around the new memories I'd made of my new family. As I headed into the house, I called the GP Dr. Henrikson had recommended, making an appointment for the following day. Then I called my finance broker's office to arrange a meeting to plan out my finances.

After I'd hung up from the broker's receptionist, I just found a seat at my dining table and rested my head in my hands. The words I'd said to the doc came back to me. What the fuck was I supposed to do with my life? I had some basic mechanical skills, some minor race management knowledge, a little bit of an idea of sponsorships. None of those had anything to do with anything outside of racing though. Even inside the racing world, none of my knowledge was complete enough to make it a new focus.

For a fraction of a second, I wondered whether maybe I should ring Paige Wood and take the position she'd offered. Without Hunter, she'd have no lead drivers ready to step into a ProV8 car. She'd be desperate and no doubt willing to offer anything I fucking wanted.

It wasn't worth it though.

Giving her what she wanted wouldn't make me happy. Yes, it'd be a job. Yes, I'd still be able to race, but at what cost? She'd have my balls in a vice and she'd fucking know it.

Alone, and lost in my own thoughts, it was easy to regret not listening to Alyssa when we were kids. If I'd followed her advice, if I'd taken my head out of my arse long enough to consider that maybe racing wouldn't be there for my entire life, I might have something else to do. Or at least a plan. It wasn't like life came with a built-in guidance counsellor, like school.

I hadn't realised how long I'd sat lost in thought until my

mobile rang. When I saw Alyssa's name on the screen, I leapt for the phone and had it at my ear in a second.

"We're home," she said. "There were no paps waiting for us, which is good. I think they're just targeting you at the moment."

It was something to celebrate, for sure. The last thing I wanted, or needed, was for Phoebe's life to be made into a living hell just because she'd been saddled with me as a father.

"I still need to get Phoebe down for a nap, but I wanted to call and see how you were."

"I'm as good as anyone can fucking expect, really." I told her about my conversation with the doc, and my meetings the next day. "I keep coming back to the same question though, Lys; what the fuck do I do now?"

"You've got a little time to think about it. Maybe jump onto one of those job sites and see what grabs your attention. You're not stupid, Dec, you can do anything you put your mind to."

"At least one of us has some faith," I muttered.

"When does Eden get back?"

I wasn't sure whether Alyssa hadn't heard my statement or if she was ignoring it. "Next week."

"Talk to her about it. She knows you better than anyone—"

"Except you."

"In some ways, she knows you better than I do. Especially about this. She might have some suggestions for jobs for you."

Life might not have a built-in guidance counsellor, but Alyssa was right. Eden knew me, knew my style, and knew the many positions that went into a race team. Maybe I'd have some way of staying around racing, even if I wasn't driving.

"I still don't know how I was lucky enough to get you back in my life."

"I wonder the same thing, Dec. I really am happy."

Her statement drew a chuckle from me. "Sure, an unemployed, drunken fuckhead with a pack of paparazzi on my tail; I'm a total catch."

"I happen to think you are, and no one will convince me otherwise. Not even you."

We spoke for a little longer before the sound of a key in my front door drew my attention. There was only one other person who had a key to my house. *Christina.*

"Shit, Lys, I've gotta go." I tossed out a quick, "Call you later," before hopping up from the dining table and heading to the door to meet Christina.

CHAPTER NINE

CLEANING UP

"HI."

WHEN I met Christina near the front door, she stopped in her tracks. Her green eyes widened at my greeting and her hands moved to play with her mousey-brown hair. She unknotted and retied the messy bun as she returned my hello.

After the initial greeting, I was uncertain where to start or how to approach her. Even though she came to my house every Thursday, we'd never really had much conversation. Usually, she'd be in and out without more than a handful of words shared between us. "We need to talk."

"Okay?" She blinked, clearly still uncertain about how to take my direct approach.

I led her over to the kitchen table.

Indicating a chair, I said, "Sit. Please."

Smoothing down her skirt, she sat. Then she folded her hands in front of her and watched me with uncertainty in her gaze.

"You know how easy you've made my life over the years, don't you?"

"Sorry?"

"Having you come and clean, do the washing, all of that shit. It's made my life so fucking easy."

"It's my job, Mr. Reede." Initially, I'd hired her mother, Susan, but when Susan had gotten sick, Christina had taken over all of the clients and we'd had a great working relationship ever since. Christina understood that I didn't want to be disturbed and kept to herself whenever she came. She'd handled everything to do with maintaining the house and keeping my closet stocked with clean clothes. She'd done it all silently and mostly in the background. She'd been fucking discreet about my ways and had earned a decent Christmas bonus off me every year because of it.

"Yeah, maybe, but you've done a good one. I want you to know that. I want you to know I've appreciated it even though I've never really said it."

"Okay. Sorry, but what's this about?"

"Do you read gossip magazines?"

Her eyes widened and she swallowed hard before squirming in her seat. The reaction was enough to confirm that even if she didn't make a habit of reading them, she knew the reason behind my question.

I found myself smiling in spite of the situation. "Obviously you've seen the one I'm talking about at least."

"I saw something, and I wasn't sure what to believe." With some of the things she'd seen and parties she'd had to clean up after, it didn't surprise me that she suspected some truth in the words. "But of course it's not my place to speculate."

Something told me that she had in fact speculated regardless of her assertions.

"I don't really give a flying fuck what anyone thinks about what was printed, but it's mostly bullshit."

She nodded, but I could see her mind working. No doubt she was trying to figure out the "mostly" part.

"After it was released though, Sinclair Racing released me from my contract." The words seemed almost too gentle for what had actually happened, but I couldn't bring myself to say anything worse. "Because of that, I'm going to have to start cutting costs."

"Oh." Her gaze met mine. "I understand."

"I'm sorry. If I could keep you on, I absolutely would. You know how domestic I am." I chuckled at the thought. Alyssa really didn't know what she was getting herself into. I didn't expect her to do everything, in fact unless I found a job I knew the bulk of it would likely fall on me, but that didn't mean I had a single fucking clue what I'd have to do.

"No, no. It's okay, I get it."

I felt bad to be giving her the shaft after close to two years. "Can you work through to Christmas? I'll probably be going away again soon, and I'd like to know there's someone looking after the house."

She smiled, her eyes softening and her posture relaxing. "Sure. At least, I'll stay until then unless I find another client to fill the gap."

"That works for me. Thank you, for everything you've done for me."

We made a little small talk around her mother's health. She said it was deteriorating less rapidly than it had been—which was the most anyone could hope for. After that, she set about doing her job and I headed into the study to find out just how bad the website article the paparazzo at the airport had mentioned was.

Only seconds after I'd clicked to load the website I saw how bad it was, but despite that I felt nothing but relief. The article painted me as a monster unable to control my temper, but I didn't care because there were no photos of Phoebe. It made me think Alyssa was right—they'd been told to target me. It was clear they were still trying to paint me in a negative light, and showing happy snaps of the family man I'd become wouldn't do that. It made me more certain than ever that there was something more behind it.

It was good and bad because it meant it would likely continue until I took Paige up on her offer. Or found some way to prove that she was behind the article.

If only I knew how to do that.

The need to figure out who was trying to ruin my life was strong. If it was Paige Wood, as I suspected, I needed a way to gather some evidence to prove it. Despite that, I decided to follow Alyssa's advice. I opened up the job search website and started scrolling through jobs in the area.

Three pages in, I still had no idea what exactly I wanted to do. No, I knew what I wanted—to race—but it was impossible. I grabbed my phone and texted some of the drivers who'd left messages about my dismissal from Sinclair Racing. I didn't say much, but quietly put my feelers to the ground for information about any roles available with their teams.

Once I'd done that, I returned to the list of jobs on my screen. Accountant. Lawyer. Panel beater. Data entry. Apprentice chef. Dish-hand. Everything either required a trade and experience, or sounded as boring as bat shit. It wasn't that I expected to come in at the top, just that nothing grabbed my attention. I was just contemplating giving up and getting off the computer to look for something for dinner when my phone rang.

It was Alyssa.

"Dec, they've done it again."

"Who's done what?"

"There's a new article about you up at *Gossip Weekly Online*."

"Yeah, I know," I said, letting her know I'd already seen it. "That fucking pap yesterday sure made me look like a violent arsehole."

"No, Dec. A new, new one. It seems someone is determined to keep you in front of the public, and maybe drive a wedge between us."

Fuck. I reopened the website. It loaded instantly and on the front page was a picture of Christina unlocking my front door. The headline screamed about cats being away and mice playing.

"Just hours after his love child and her mother left his luxury home, Declan Reede was spotted entertaining a mystery guest."

I couldn't read any more. "Fuck."

"What's going on?" Alyssa asked. Her voice didn't seem to hold any suspicion or doubt, so I didn't think the question was about the article, but I couldn't be certain. I didn't want to lose her over something as stupid as a fucking employee though.

"That's Christina, she's my housekeeper. Nothing—"

"I don't mean that. I mean why are they doing this? Why put up those pictures, and yet leave me and Phoebe alone? What's the game?"

I told her about my suspicion that it was all part of a plan to make me a villain. The words Paige had said to me on the phone played in my mind. That it was all about the spin. I wondered whether that was the plan—make me look as bad as possible and then use my family in an attempt to improve my image just as fast. Was that the reason the paparazzi had so far avoided the shots I had thought would've been the most valuable? Was that why I had such a small but seemingly dedicated group of paps following me?

Or maybe I was just being paranoid.

One thing was clear—I had to get to the bottom of it. And to do that, I had to figure out who the fuck T was and why her paps were following me.

CHAPTER TEN

CABIN FEVER

I PACED THE length of my living room. With each day I faced alone, I grew a little bit crazier.

The qualifying session for the Bahrain race played on my TV in the background but it wasn't doing much to calm or even distract me. Somehow, the weekend had already arrived and I felt like I was trapped in my own home. Technically I could go out. But where. And why?

I'd tried calling Alyssa, but she wasn't answering. I was stuck alone and unless I wanted to go outside and invite the handful of paparazzi doing a rotating shift in front of my house in for dinner, I had no one to entertain me.

Morgan's name on the TV drew my attention momentarily as he claimed the fastest lap of the session. My lips curled up in celebration before falling again as Hunter's car, decked out in the Wood Racing livery, flashed onto the screen, showing he was faster in the splits. I wondered whether the fact that he was nearing the end of his last season with Wood Racing would give him more or less incentive to win.

"Fucker!"

My pacing started again, heading from one end of the lounge to the other. As it did, the words of my finance broker played over and over in my mind. With my current expenses, I would probably have enough in liquid savings to last until Christmas, maybe the end of January.

Cashing out my longer-term investments would maybe get me another twelve months, even with getting rid of the cost of having Christina clean my house. After that, I was fucked unless I could get some income coming in. An income greater than I could earn flipping patties at the local burger joint. I had no idea how I was going to do it, especially when the costs of two extra people were factored in.

Why had I been so reckless with my money? All of the nights where I'd dropped a grand at the casino, a few hundred at a strip club, or God only knew how much in the VIP room of a nightclub. All of those stupid nights out that I could barely remember because of the free-flowing alcohol. If I'd stayed home for even half of them, I could have had enough money to last another few months. To go from not having to worry about what money was coming in because it was always more than I spent to having nothing was an adjustment I wasn't sure I could make.

The clawing sensation of icy fingers at my throat grew as I looped around in front of the couch again. My chest tightened and my breaths grew shorter—each breath shallower than the last. My fingers clenched and unclenched as my steps grew longer and faster, so each lap of the room took less time. The walls closed in on me and the sound from the TV seemed to come through a tunnel.

My throat ached, screaming for the delicious burn that only a shot could bring. I tried to roll my tongue around my mouth, but it felt sticky and swollen. As if it were three sizes too big and couldn't fit behind my teeth any longer.

On my next loop, I stumbled. My feet were moving too fast and I couldn't control them. The ceiling pressed downward and I fell to my knees to sink away from it. Curling into a ball, I gasped for air.

It was too much.

I needed . . . something.

I needed Alyssa. Only, she was a thousand Ks away.

Without her, only one thing could get me through. I needed a fucking drink.

Forcing myself to my feet, I staggered into the hall even as I gasped for air. I leaned against the wall and tried to catch my breath. When I reached the side table, I grabbed my Monaro keys and headed out to the garage.

I needed to get out of the house. There was a bottle-o up the road where I could find what I needed.

With my breath coming in sharp, painful pants, I forced myself to move to my car. After I climbed into the driver seat, I shoved the key in the ignition and pushed the button to lift the garage door.

Two seconds after the purr of the engine echoed around me, the radio kicked into life.

Blaring from the speakers was a CD we'd listened to on the way to the airport and that Alyssa had forgotten. A fucking CD full of stupid Aussie nursery rhymes and songs that Phoebe loved.

The icy claws of panic that had held my heart in a vice grip only seconds earlier disappeared at the sound of the beginning bars of "Teddy Bear's Picnic." A peal of laughter burst from me. Even though she was almost a thousand Ks away, Phoebe could warm my heart. I flicked the car into reverse as a plan for the rest of the day doing came into my mind. Instead of drowning myself in the bottom of a bottle of whiskey, I'd get started on a new project. After all, I'd promised my little girl I'd paint her room.

On the way to the hardware store I thought about the fact that I'd have to mention the renewed panic attack to Dr. Henrikson. My meeting with him the day before had been relatively uneventful. There was an initial layer of awkwardness being face-to-face with him again. Of being able to see his reactions to my admissions rather than making them into the impersonal speaker of a phone.

Despite that, we hadn't really covered too much that we hadn't spoken about earlier. He once again expressed concern that Alyssa and I were perhaps moving things too fast with her moving into my house, but he countered the statement with his delight that her influence on me was so positive.

By the end of the session, we'd done little more than set a structure in place that would allow my continued visits for as little money as possible. After he'd finished laying out his plans, I almost had to take back all the cracks I'd made over the years about him being opportunistic. They were true at the time, and if I was still raking in the big bucks he probably still would have charged top dollar. But with my chips down, he showed he did care about more than just the bucks in his bank account.

I wondered what he'd have thought about my little project to paint Phoebe's room. No doubt he'd have some warning about how dangerous it was to make big life decisions in a time of crisis, but fuck him. Paint colours were hardly life-altering, and if it made Phoebe's life that little more comfortable when she returned to our house, that was all that mattered.

An hour later, I returned home with all the essentials to paint and redecorate her room, including tins of paint the precise shade of purple that Phoebe had selected on the computer, rollers, and drop sheets.

Walking past the TV I'd left on in my haste to get out the door, I saw that Morgan had claimed pole over that fucker Hunter, which put a smile on my face. Sometimes good things did happen.

The rest of the afternoon was a meld of physical labour and painting. First I stripped the bedroom out, then I laid the drop sheets. As I used the rollers to paint the walls, I discovered I had no idea what I was really doing. The paint went in every direction, coating some areas darker than others. Even though it threatened to overwhelm me, I took a deep breath and started again.

I was halfway through my second coat when I wondered whether maybe I should paint the whole house. Maybe it would get rid of the ghosts of the past. Before I could get that far, I shut down the idea. One thing was clear: I had too much time on my hands. Before long, I'd be tearing down the walls just for the sake of it.

"HEY, DEC." Alyssa's voice was a welcome change from the monotony of silence I'd been surrounded with all day. "You want to see me and Phoebe again as soon as possible, right?"

Her voice was ringing with excitement—she was planning something. "Uh, yeah."

"Are you free next weekend?"

"Unless a job miraculously falls into my lap, I'll be free for the rest of my fucking life. Why?"

"Well, Flynn came over for dinner tonight—"

I clenched my jaw at the mention of his name. Even though I'd agreed to try with him for Alyssa's sake, that didn't mean I had to like the smug arsehole, or the way he spoke to me. He always seemed so fucking happy about my misery that it wouldn't have surprised me if he was laughing it up big time after the Gossip Weekly article and subsequent online stories. Fucker probably thought it was all my just desserts or something.

"—and he had a really good idea."

"Uh huh." I couldn't manage to form any other words or I risked saying something I'd regret.

"He suggested we have a mini-break. Just you and me."

I wasn't sure I'd heard her right, but it didn't seem like she needed a response from me anyway.

"He thought it could be a good chance to get everything out in the open. You know, a weekend where nothing is off limits. Where every question we ask each other has to be answered, regardless of how bad the answer might be."

Fucker! There wasn't a doubt in my mind that he was trying to set me up for a fall. And what about Phoebe? Where the fuck was she supposed to go while we had this weekend away?

"And the more I think about it, the more I think it's a great idea."

"Where?" It wasn't what I wanted to ask, but I wasn't sure what else I could say. Even though I wanted to say no, I couldn't. If I argued against it, she'd only think I had something to hide. Even though the words, "Fuck Flynn and his fucking idea," were on the tip of my tongue, I couldn't let them go.

After all, Dr. Henrikson had made a similar, albeit less outright, suggestion. In my session, he'd advocated getting everything between Alyssa and me out in the open. Especially with the paparazzi breathing down my neck, seemingly desperate for a scandal. At least if Alyssa knew everything, anything they dug up that could threaten the happiness we had would be meaningless. Or at least, she'd be aware of it long before it could become an issue. On the doc's advice, I'd already decided I was going to share any details she wanted, but I'd hoped it would be at our own pace and not all at once. And certainly not to a timeframe dictated by her fucking friend.

Obviously my discomfort over the idea was evident in my question because when Alyssa answered, it was with less confidence than before. "We don't have to do it. I mean, if you don't want to, I'm not going to force you to. It has to be something we both agree on or it'll be pointless anyway."

"It's okay. It might be good for us." My jaw was still tightly clenched so I had to force the words out between my teeth.

"Can you pick us up at the airport on Friday and drop us back the next Monday?"

"Airport?"

"Yeah, I, uh, I've already booked a weekend up at a motel near Bondi. It was a last-minute special and I . . . well, I really think it's worth us going there for our weekend of truth. I mean, I booked it hoping you would agree, but figured the deal was worth it even if I just had to use it for some time away. I could take Mum and Phoebe for a girls' weekend or something instead, if you'd rather."

There was no way Alyssa was going to come to Sydney and not spend time with me. "No, it's okay. I can pick you up."

"Great. Mum's going to come with me to watch Phoebe for the night. Did you want her to book a hotel?"

A weekend of letting Alyssa sort through my dirty past and having to see Ruth again for the first time since the magazine shit went down. Fucking great.

"Dec?"

A silent sigh slipped from my lips. "No, of course not. She can stay here. Hopefully Phoebe will be a little more comfortable than if she's at a hotel."

I found out all the details before disconnecting the call. The excitement that overtook her voice for the rest of the conversation almost made everything I'd agreed to worth it. Almost.

Placing my phone down on the counter, I closed my eyes and said a silent prayer for strength. And for Alyssa. There was so much I needed to tell her, and I could only hope my demons wouldn't chase her away.

As if to stave away the panic, the memory of the ring I'd purchased before our do-over date at the Suncrest Hotel flittered through my mind. Needing to have it in my hands again, to confirm that I was doing the right thing—that we were heading in the right direction—I headed straight to my bedroom. Digging through the top drawer of my dresser, I shoved aside my boxers and stray socks to find the little velvet box I'd hidden there shortly after Alyssa arrived on my doorstep.

Flicking open the black lid, I looked at the ring. The diamond was bigger than I remembered. I was fucking grateful I'd purchased it before I'd lost my job or I never would have splashed out on something so extravagant.

I gently plucked the white gold ring from the stand inside the box and held it between my fingers. It was the perfect ring for Alyssa. Slender enough to be feminine, but still packed with enough diamonds to shine like her inner beauty. The one-carat princess-cut diamond in the centre was set in a twist at a forty-five degree angle to the rest of the stones. I'd picked that setting because the rotation of the main stone represented the twists we'd faced on our way back to each other.

Cradling the ring between my fingers, the words Alyssa had spoken the night before she'd left Sydney floated back to me. Of wanting to chase away the ghosts and exorcise the demons from my past. That's what the weekend was about. If we were strong, the weekend would purely be a continuation of that process. My cock grew hard at the thought, because it would be two days and a night of nothing but Alyssa.

Besides, she knew most of the shit, and she was still there for me. Still willing to give me her trust despite the campaign Gossip Weekly seemed to be running against me.

I drew a deep breath, and forced away the negative thoughts. The positives were growing. Day by day they were gaining strength. I needed to focus on them, that was all. It was easier with Alyssa at my side, but it wasn't impossible to do it alone. After all, I'd done what I'd set out to do: I'd regained her trust. I'd earned it back despite the odds and the shit we'd faced since.

For a moment, I debated giving Alyssa the ring over the weekend, but it didn't feel right. The process was supposed to be about getting everything out into the open. Even if there was a positive outcome, the admissions I would make weren't the sort of things I wanted to associate with the day I asked her to be mine forever.

With one more glance at the ring, I put it back in its box. One day, when the time was right, I would offer it to her. In the meantime, all I could offer was my love. That would be enough; it had to be. It was all she'd asked for, after all.

As the positives that could come from the weekend solidified in my mind, I felt the stress rush from my body. Alyssa trusted me. She loved me. Those truths were all I needed. All I ever would need. I thought back to the moment Ruth had told me she'd left and wanted to laugh at myself for thinking she could be going anywhere but back to my side. How could I ever have doubted her? How could I have thought she'd leave over something as stupid as a few photos and a bunch of bullshit?

I slid the drawer shu I PACED THE length of my living room. With each day I faced alone, I grew a little bit crazier.

The qualifying session for the Bahrain race played on my TV in the background but it wasn't doing much to calm or even distract me. Somehow, the weekend had already arrived and I felt like I was trapped in my own home. Technically I could go out. But where. And why?

I'd tried calling Alyssa, but she wasn't answering. I was stuck alone and unless I wanted to go outside and invite the handful of paparazzi doing a rotating shift in front of my house in for dinner, I had no one to entertain me.

Morgan's name on the TV drew my attention momentarily as he claimed the fastest lap of the session. My lips curled up in celebration before falling again as Hunter's car, decked out in the Wood Racing livery, flashed onto the screen, showing he was faster in the splits. I wondered whether the fact that he was nearing the end of his last season with Wood Racing would give him more or less incentive to win.

"Fucker!"

My pacing started again, heading from one end of the lounge to the other. As it did, the words of my finance broker played over and over in my mind. With my current expenses, I would probably have enough in liquid savings to last until Christmas, maybe the end of January.

Cashing out my longer-term investments would maybe get me another twelve months, even with getting rid of the cost of having Christina clean my house. After that, I was fucked unless I could get some income coming in. An income greater than I could earn flipping patties at the local burger joint. I had no idea how I was going to do it, especially when the costs of two extra people were factored in.

Why had I been so reckless with my money? All of the nights where I'd dropped a grand at the casino, a few hundred at a strip club, or God only knew how much in the VIP room of a nightclub. All of those stupid nights out that I could barely remember because of the free-flowing alcohol. If I'd stayed home for even half of them, I could have had enough money to last another few months. To go from not having to worry about what money was coming in because it was always more than I spent to having nothing was an adjustment I wasn't sure I could make.

The clawing sensation of icy fingers at my throat grew as I looped around in front of the couch again. My chest tightened and my breaths grew shorter—each breath shallower than the last. My fingers clenched and unclenched as my steps grew longer and faster, so each lap of the room took less time. The walls closed in on me and the sound from the TV seemed to come through a tunnel.

My throat ached, screaming for the delicious burn that only a shot could bring. I tried to roll my tongue around my mouth, but it felt sticky and swollen. As if it were three sizes too big and couldn't fit behind my teeth any longer.

On my next loop, I stumbled. My feet were moving too fast and I couldn't control them. The ceiling pressed downward and I fell to my knees to sink away from it. Curling into a ball, I gasped for air. It was too much.

I needed . . . something.

I needed Alyssa. Only, she was a thousand Ks away.

Without her, only one thing could get me through. I needed a fucking drink.

Forcing myself to my feet, I staggered into the hall even as I gasped for air. I leaned against the wall and tried to catch my breath. When I reached the side table, I grabbed my Monaro keys and headed out to the garage.

I needed to get out of the house. There was a bottle-o up the road where I could find what I needed.

With my breath coming in sharp, painful pants, I forced myself to move to my car. After I climbed into the driver seat, I shoved the key in the ignition and pushed the button to lift the garage door.

Two seconds after the purr of the engine echoed around me, the radio kicked into life.

Blaring from the speakers was a CD we'd listened to on the way to the airport and that Alyssa had forgotten. A fucking CD full of stupid Aussie nursery rhymes and songs that Phoebe loved.

The icy claws of panic that had held my heart in a vice grip only seconds earlier disappeared at the sound of the beginning bars of "Teddy Bear's Picnic." A peal of laughter burst from me. Even though she was almost a thousand Ks away, Phoebe could warm my heart. I flicked the car into reverse as a plan for the rest of the day doing came into my mind. Instead of drowning myself in the bottom of a bottle of whiskey, I'd get started on a new project. After all, I'd promised my little girl I'd paint her room.

On the way to the hardware store I thought about the fact that

I'd have to mention the renewed panic attack to Dr. Henrikson. My meeting with him the day before had been relatively uneventful. There was an initial layer of awkwardness being face-to-face with him again. Of being able to see his reactions to my admissions rather than making them into the impersonal speaker of a phone.

Despite that, we hadn't really covered too much that we hadn't spoken about earlier. He once again expressed concern that Alyssa and I were perhaps moving things too fast with her moving into my house, but he countered the statement with his delight that her influence on me was so positive.

By the end of the session, we'd done little more than set a structure in place that would allow my continued visits for as little money as possible. After he'd finished laying out his plans, I almost had to take back all the cracks I'd made over the years about him being opportunistic. They were true at the time, and if I was still raking in the big bucks he probably still would have charged top dollar. But with my chips down, he showed he did care about more than just the bucks in his bank account.

I wondered what he'd have thought about my little project to paint Phoebe's room. No doubt he'd have some warning about how dangerous it was to make big life decisions in a time of crisis, but fuck him. Paint colours were hardly life-altering, and if it made Phoebe's life that little more comfortable when she returned to our house, that was all that mattered.

An hour later, I returned home with all the essentials to paint and redecorate her room, including tins of paint the precise shade of purple that Phoebe had selected on the computer, rollers, and drop sheets.

Walking past the TV I'd left on in my haste to get out the door, I saw that Morgan had claimed pole over that fucker Hunter, which put a smile on my face. Sometimes good things did happen.

The rest of the afternoon was a meld of physical labour and painting. First I stripped the bedroom out, then I laid the drop sheets. As I used the rollers to paint the walls, I discovered I had no idea what I was really doing. The paint went in every direction, coating some areas darker than others. Even though it threatened to overwhelm me, I took a deep breath and started again.

I was halfway through my second coat when I wondered whether maybe I should paint the whole house. Maybe it would get rid of the ghosts of the past. Before I could get that far, I shut down the idea. One thing was clear: I had too much time on my hands. Before long, I'd be tearing down the walls just for the sake of it.

"HEY, DEC." Alyssa's voice was a welcome change from the monotony of silence I'd been surrounded with all day. "You want to see me and Phoebe again as soon as possible, right?"

Her voice was ringing with excitement—she was planning something. "Uh, yeah."

"Are you free next weekend?"

"Unless a job miraculously falls into my lap, I'll be free for the rest of my fucking life. Why?"

"Well, Flynn came over for dinner tonight—"

I clenched my jaw at the mention of his name. Even though I'd agreed to try with him for Alyssa's sake, that didn't mean I had to like the smug arsehole, or the way he spoke to me. He always seemed so fucking happy about my misery that it wouldn't have surprised me if he was laughing it up big time after the Gossip Weekly article and subsequent online stories. Fucker probably thought it was all my just desserts or something.

"—and he had a really good idea."

"Uh huh." I couldn't manage to form any other words or I risked saying something I'd regret.

"He suggested we have a mini-break. Just you and me."

I wasn't sure I'd heard her right, but it didn't seem like she needed a response from me anyway.

"He thought it could be a good chance to get everything out in the open. You know, a weekend where nothing is off limits. Where every question we ask each other has to be answered, regardless of how bad the answer might be."

Fucker! There wasn't a doubt in my mind that he was trying to set me up for a fall. And what about Phoebe? Where the fuck was she supposed to go while we had this weekend away?

"And the more I think about it, the more I think it's a great idea."

"Where?" It wasn't what I wanted to ask, but I wasn't sure what else I could say. Even though I wanted to say no, I couldn't. If I argued against it, she'd only think I had something to hide. Even though the words, "Fuck Flynn and his fucking idea," were on the tip of my tongue, I couldn't let them go.

After all, Dr. Henrikson had made a similar, albeit less outright, suggestion. In my session, he'd advocated getting everything between Alyssa and me out in the open. Especially with the paparazzi breathing down my neck, seemingly desperate for a scandal. At least if Alyssa knew everything, anything they dug up that could threaten the happiness we had would be meaningless. Or at least, she'd be aware of it long before it could become an issue. On the doc's advice, I'd already decided I was going to share any details she wanted, but I'd hoped it would be at our own pace and not all at once. And certainly not to a timeframe dictated by her fucking friend.

Obviously my discomfort over the idea was evident in my question because when Alyssa answered, it was with less confidence than before. "We don't have to do it. I mean, if you don't want to, I'm not going to force you to. It has to be something we both agree on or it'll be pointless anyway."

"It's okay. It might be good for us." My jaw was still tightly clenched so I had to force the words out between my teeth.

"Can you pick us up at the airport on Friday and drop us back the next Monday?"

"Airport?"

"Yeah, I, uh, I've already booked a weekend up at a motel near Bondi. It was a last-minute special and I . . . well, I really think it's worth us going there for our weekend of truth. I mean, I booked it hoping you would agree, but figured the deal was worth it even if I just had to use it for some time away. I could take Mum and Phoebe for a girls' weekend or something instead, if you'd rather."

There was no way Alyssa was going to come to Sydney and not spend time with me. "No, it's okay. I can pick you up."

"Great. Mum's going to come with me to watch Phoebe for the

night. Did you want her to book a hotel?"

A weekend of letting Alyssa sort through my dirty past and having to see Ruth again for the first time since the magazine shit went down. Fucking great.

"Dec?"

A silent sigh slipped from my lips. "No, of course not. She can stay here. Hopefully Phoebe will be a little more comfortable than if she's at a hotel."

I found out all the details before disconnecting the call. The excitement that overtook her voice for the rest of the conversation almost made everything I'd agreed to worth it. Almost.

Placing my phone down on the counter, I closed my eyes and said a silent prayer for strength. And for Alyssa. There was so much I needed to tell her, and I could only hope my demons wouldn't chase her away.

As if to stave away the panic, the memory of the ring I'd purchased before our do-over date at the Suncrest Hotel flittered through my mind. Needing to have it in my hands again, to confirm that I was doing the right thing—that we were heading in the right direction—I headed straight to my bedroom. Digging through the top drawer of my dresser, I shoved aside my boxers and stray socks to find the little velvet box I'd hidden there shortly after Alyssa arrived on my doorstep.

Flicking open the black lid, I looked at the ring. The diamond was bigger than I remembered. I was fucking grateful I'd purchased it before I'd lost my job or I never would have splashed out on something so extravagant.

I gently plucked the white gold ring from the stand inside the box and held it between my fingers. It was the perfect ring for Alyssa. Slender enough to be feminine, but still packed with enough diamonds to shine like her inner beauty. The one-carat princess-cut diamond in the centre was set in a twist at a forty-five degree angle to the rest of the stones. I'd picked that setting because the rotation of the main stone represented the twists we'd faced on our way back to each other.

Cradling the ring between my fingers, the words Alyssa had

spoken the night before she'd left Sydney floated back to me. Of wanting to chase away the ghosts and exorcise the demons from my past. That's what the weekend was about. If we were strong, the weekend would purely be a continuation of that process. My cock grew hard at the thought, because it would be two days and a night of nothing but Alyssa. Besides, she knew most of the shit, and she was still there for me. Still willing to give me her trust despite the campaign Gossip Weekly seemed to be running against me.

I drew a deep breath, and forced away the negative thoughts. The positives were growing. Day by day they were gaining strength. I needed to focus on them, that was all. It was easier with Alyssa at my side, but it wasn't impossible to do it alone. After all, I'd done what I'd set out to do: I'd regained her trust. I'd earned it back despite the odds and the shit we'd faced since.

For a moment, I debated giving Alyssa the ring over the weekend, but it didn't feel right. The process was supposed to be about getting everything out into the open. Even if there was a positive outcome, the admissions I would make weren't the sort of things I wanted to associate with the day I asked her to be mine forever.

With one more glance at the ring, I put it back in its box. One day, when the time was right, I would offer it to her. In the meantime, all I could offer was my love. That would be enough; it had to be. It was all she'd asked for, after all.

As the positives that could come from the weekend solidified in my mind, I felt the stress rush from my body. Alyssa trusted me. She loved me. Those truths were all I needed. All I ever would need. I thought back to the moment Ruth had told me she'd left and wanted to laugh at myself for thinking she could be going anywhere but back to my side. How could I ever have doubted her? How could I have thought she'd leave over something as stupid as a few photos and a bunch of bullshit?

I slid the drawer shut and tried to think of something else I could do to distract myself until she came back to me.t and tried to think of something else I could do to distract myself until she came back to me.

CHAPTER ELEVEN

ON TRACK

SUNDAY, I WOKE up to an empty bed and a nightmare that everything I'd experienced had been nothing more than a dream. The thought left me hollow. Empty. My heart raced and my head throbbed as the possibility bounced around my body.

No! Fuck that.

It had to be real. It was too perfect and at the same time too fucked-up for it not to be.

I went to roll over to where Alyssa had slept, to see if the pillow still smelled like the lingering scent of her coconut skin cream, but stopped short. I couldn't move. It hurt too much. At first, it was the proof my mind needed that it'd all been a fantasy. Maybe I was really in a hospital bed in a coma after the last time I'd hit a wall in my V8.

Then it occurred to me that it was the wrong type of pain for that to be true. It wasn't the sharp agony of broken bone and torn tissue, but rather a slow, rolling ache. My whole body was stiff and sore. It ached from being overused after too many days of not enough use. I was out of shape. Sure, my muscles were as defined as ever, but clearly I hadn't used them enough. The more I woke, the more I understood the pain was proof of everything that I'd shared with Phoebe and Alyssa. It was my arms and shoulders that hurt the most, the ache of holding the roller for too long the day before.

The painting hadn't felt particularly difficult at the time, but it had obviously worked muscles I hadn't used in a while. It fuelled my desire to spend the day working out in my gym. Maybe I wasn't driving anymore, but that didn't mean I shouldn't keep myself fit, and other than the heavy bedroom sessions Alyssa and I had shared, I'd hardly been keeping up my fitness.

With nothing better to do, I climbed out of bed and headed to the treadmill. Hopefully a workout on that would loosen up my stiff muscles. There was only one way I would have preferred to work myself out, but Alysa was too far away for that.

After I'd completely exhausted myself on the gym equipment, I headed back downstairs to watch the last race in Bahrain.

It was strange watching the sport, and the team I'd been such a big part of for so long, as nothing more than a spectator again. With each lap, I shifted closer to the edge of the couch, until I was barely resting more than an arse-cheek on the suede as I watched Morgan and Hunter race practically door-to-door around most of the track. Red and blue dancing over the track, the way the fans loved it. The rivalry between them was as strong as ever.

"Are you fucking blind?" I shouted at the track officials as Hunter dived in front of Morgan, cutting him off in a barely legal move. He braked late, cut the corners too hard, and rode the chicanes. They were the actions of a lunatic, someone who gave less than zero shits about the car, the team, or the other drivers.

Along the next straight, Morgan caught him again. Sinclair had the power, even if Hunter had the crazy. My heart was in my throat as I said a thousand silent prayers for Morgan to get up. The championship was so fucking close; a win for Hunter could put him in the lead. My DNF at Bathurst had set Morgan back, but thankfully because I'd taken Hunter out too, he hadn't gained any ground. Instead, Andersen, the driver in third, had crept up on both of them. Despite everything, I wanted Morgan and Sinclair Racing to win that championship. I felt like Sinclair retaining the championship would in some small way keep me connected to the team—even if I wasn't part of that team anymore.

The rest of the race was nail-bitingly close and I watched most of it from the edge of the couch. Each time it looked like Hunter was sure to gain a position on Morgan, Morgan managed to pull out a minor miracle. When an incident further back on the track caused a safety car and the leaders came in for their final pit stop, the Sinclair team showed why they were the best on the track, beating every other team's time by a good half second. The flurry of activity around the car in the seconds Morgan was in the pits made me miss the race almost as much as watching him loop around the track did.

I counted the seconds while they were filling the fuel and worked out roughly how many litres they must have put in. It didn't seem quite enough, which meant Morgan must have had a little in reserve already. I could only hope he'd make it. Strategies that they might be running ran through my mind. The sport was part of me. The thrum of the engines echoed in the beat of my heart. Fuck, I missed being out there. How had I sat and passively watched it for so many years? How could I sit on my arse and *not* be in a V8 for the rest of my life?

I missed every aspect of racing; the camaraderie at the track, the feeling of being a part of something greater than myself. It was all stuff I'd taken for granted, stuff I'd ignored, but now I could see it all from the outside and knew just how much I'd lost. Alyssa had told me to check out some job search websites, but that wasn't what I needed in the end. All it took was a day watching what I loved to know that the job I wanted was there. I didn't care *what* I was doing, but I wanted to do something on a team. Something important. Something that meant something bigger than me. Just like I had for the last four years.

After watching Morgan claim the chequered flag, I turned off the TV and flicked Eden a text to congratulate her. Because of the time difference between Bahrain and Australia, the race wasn't broadcast live, so I figured she would probably already be half-tanked celebrating, but it didn't matter. At least she'd know I watched the race. Know I was happy for her, for Morgan, and even for Danny, despite what happened.

Five minutes later, my phone rang.

"I didn't think you'd watch us," Eden slurred down the line. She was more than half-cut. In fact, she was probably well on her way to shitfaced. The team must have retreated to one of the hotel rooms because drinking in public wasn't exactly allowed. Especially not for an unmarried woman out with a bunch of blokes.

"Of course I watched it, Edie. I wanted to see Morg wipe the floor with that fucker, Hunter."

"Except next year, that arsehole Hunter Blake will be a Sinclair man and they'll be teammates." Eden held nothing back when it came to showing her distaste for the bloke who would be driving what should have been my car.

I scoffed. "Maybe he'll have the Sinclair colours on his car, but he'll never be a Sinclair man. And Morg will still wipe the floor with his arse."

"I know. I wish it was you still on the track. You may have been a manwhore and an arse, but at least you weren't a lunatic."

I laughed. Eden always had an eloquent way of speaking the unfettered truth. "Thanks for the compliment."

"How are you going, anyway?" she asked. It was clear she meant without Alyssa.

"Well, I haven't started twisting the noose just yet."

"That's not funny, Declan. I'm worried about you."

"I know, Edie. I'm worried about me too. I have no idea what to do with myself now. I mean, 'disgraced V8 driver' hardly makes a winning resume when it's the only thing on there."

"Maybe you should take Wood's offer?"

"I don't even know if it's still on the table. Even if it is though, I told you I don't want to race for her."

"Maybe another team will want you after the shuffle Hunter's move will cause has settled down."

"Maybe." I wasn't sure if she could hear the doubt in my voice, but I didn't know that I wanted to race for another team. If I did, I'd always have the shit that went down with Danny hanging over my head. "I already know the team I really want to be with doesn't want me though."

"Well, if you're not going to drive you should at least try to get into something around the track." Alyssa had been right about Eden knowing what I could do. Not that I hadn't already thought of it, but it was nice knowing that I was at least on the right track and someone else had faith I could slip into another role.

"Maybe." But what? "Why don't you keep your ear to the ground? I know you know about these things long before they become public. Perhaps you can point me in the direction of someone willing to take a chance on someone who used to matter."

"You still matter, Dec."

"You know what I mean." I wanted to move the conversation on. Move it away from the uncomfortable topic of what I'd lost. "How's Morg? He must be pretty stoked to have those extra championship points under his belt."

The statement was enough to draw the conversation away from me, just like I knew it would. For the next twenty minutes, I heard everything about every corner of the race and had a pit-side play-by-play of the session. There was so much that I'd missed only being able to watch it on TV. One day, I'd get trackside again, even if I had to beg for Eden to issue me a pit pass for the day out of pity.

CHAPTER TWELVE

CLEAN OUT

MONDAY CAME AND went in a blur. First I had my next face-to-face appointment with Dr. Henrikson, where we started to delve into greater depths of why I had been crashing, and he offered his own version of career advice. It didn't clear anything up, but left me feeling like I could actually do anything I put my mind to. Near the end of the session, I told him about Alyssa's planned weekend, and he was supportive of her suggestion.

A weekend where no question was off limits and where we would confront our past—our demons—with no one else around to interrupt. It was going to be hard, and with each minute that drew it closer, the realisation of what we'd really be doing struck me with more intensity than ever. We'd agreed to ask anything that was on our mind and in return we would tell each other exactly what we felt. I braced myself for a weekend of agony. The bittersweet agony that only Alyssa could deliver to me. I just hoped that nothing I admitted was bad enough for her to change her mind about our life together.

"You need to work these things out together," the doc told me.

"To plan a way to deal with issues as they arise. Ideally, I'd still like you to consider couples' therapy, but for now keeping open and clear lines of communication will only help."

Despite being put out by his continued push for couples' counselling, it was the confirmation I needed that the weekend might not be a bad idea. After confirming my next appointment date—we'd decided to maximise my visits before the end of the year to get the most benefit out of the Medicare arrangements—I headed back to my car, flipping the bird to the now-familiar faces of the paparazzi as I went. I might have been trying to keep my nose clean, but that didn't mean I needed to be a goddamned saint.

In a wave of vigour after I got home, I dismantled my whole study and rearranged it according to some article I found online about feng shui. Apparently the whole area was set up in a way that made wealth and prosperity flow out of the door.

Even though it had occurred to me that there were probably better things to spend my time on, my fear of what I could expect from the weekend struck me motionless.

While I tried to keep positive, I tried to prepare myself too. It was possible that once everything was laid bare, Alyssa might choose not to move in with me. She might decide I was just too fucked-up, that I'd screwed up too often. Regardless, I owed it to her to get everything out on the table. The thoughts that spun around my head were too confusing. Too reckless and dangerous. They risked rendering me totally immobile.

It was far better to distract myself with busy work and try to keep my mind off everything until it came time to pick her up. I couldn't face the daily grind as worries about what questions Alyssa might have lurking danced around my head. What would she want to know? Would I be able to be completely honest?

Would she kick me out the instant she learned the truths buried in my past?

Fuck.

Turning back to my tasks and away from the deadly thoughts, I swung my desk around to face the door. Once more I debated whether maybe it was worthwhile to take the ring, but I talked myself out of it. Did I really want our engagement tainted with my past if she said yes? Worse, what if she said no? What if the things I said turned a yes into a no? How would I be able to pretend everything was hunky-fucking-dory if that happened?

When I finished the office, I decided I might try to redo the whole house. It was only after I'd emptied out half the contents of the linen closet that I'd decided that maybe, just maybe, I'd gone stark raving mad purely because I was alone and had nothing better to do. I shoved everything back into the cupboard and moved back to my gym to do a couple of hours on the bike.

Around three in the afternoon, my mobile phone rang. The display showed a Brisbane number, but not one I was familiar with.

"Hello?"

"Hello, son."

My teeth clenched and my lips curled up into a snarl at the sound of Dad's voice. "What do you want?"

"Is that any way to speak to your father?"

"Father?" I snorted. "You haven't been my fucking father since you decided it was more important to get your dick wet than look after your family. Your wife."

"Declan, that's not fair. You don't understand what it's like to have your dreams snatched away from you. To live with the festering regret over decisions you made."

His words turned my stomach. That was me he was talking about. I'd snatched his dreams away. Sure, he might have blamed Mum, but I was the cause of the regret that had festered until he believed he had no other choice but to cheat again and again. That thought made it hard to feel even remotely charitable toward him.

"Fuck off," I said. "I know exactly how that feels. That's been my life for the last four fucking years because of the doubt you forced into my fucking head. If you hadn't had your own fucking head up your own fucking arse so much, you might have seen how much I suffered being away from Alyssa. How good we were together. You would have fucking tried to help us find a solution to our issues and told me about the twins. You would have been a fucking parent. I've lost my fucking racing career, and I'll give you the hot tip: even though it sucks, it doesn't suck half as much as having to say goodbye to Lys did."

"I'm not going to get into an argument about this." He sounded tired, but that didn't make me feel sorry for him.

"Good, because there is no argument. There's no way I'm willing to bend. Get to your point, 'cause I've got shit to do."

"I need to know where your mother moved the money she stole from our bank account."

I scoffed. "Good luck with that."

"You'll tell me, or I'll get the police involved."

If he wasn't so pathetic, I would have laughed at the pointless threat. Mum was an authorised signatory on the account so she hadn't legally done anything wrong. "What does it matter? It's not like you don't have other money."

"That's not the point."

"Of course it is. You've spent years donating all your money to your little whore, buying her houses and financing whatever fucking lifestyle the two of you have been living, and Mum's been at home managing the rest of the finances. Anything she saved up in that account is rightfully hers."

"I need that money."

"Why? It's not like you don't earn enough at the bank."

There was silence on the other end that said more than his words ever could.

"Unless you lost your job, of course," I taunted. A smile danced on my lips at the thought that he'd been served his just desserts.

Again the silence was deafening.

"Let me guess . . . your bosses found out you were porking your secretary and weren't impressed?"

"That article you inspired has caused me nothing but grief."

"Yeah, well, that's the price you pay for letting your little whore open her mouth to try to ruin me, isn't it?" The justice in the situation settled over me like a comfortable blanket.

"If you'd just stopped and listened to me, she wouldn't have been forced to resort to those measures. I would never have allowed her to speak to that reporter."

"Allowed?" I scoffed. "I knew Hayley in school and I doubt she would have stopped just because you asked her to. She saw her chance at her fifteen minutes of fame and took it. I doubt you could have talked her out of it."

"If you hadn't attacked us, she never would have—"

"Are you fucking kidding?" I snapped to shut him up. "Stop blaming everyone else for your fuck-ups." It was something I'd done for so long, and now I could see I'd learned it from the best. Only, I was trying to get better where he just wanted to keep on fucking up. "You have to own them or you'll never be able to move on."

"Don't you dare try to give me advice! You're nothing more than a boy!"

"Yeah, well, I'm a boy who's hanging up on your arse. Don't call me again, or I'll get the police involved."

My hands shook as I pressed the End Call button. For so many years, I'd idolised my father. I'd looked up to him and wanted to fulfil my dream of racing so that he could live his dream too, albeit vicariously through me. Now I could see I'd lived in the shadow of his regret all my life, and the bastard had let me. In fact, he'd revelled it in, letting me worship him as a fucking hero.

Fuck him.

Fuck him and fuck his mistress. They could have each other. They fucking deserved each other. They could live in their twisted world where everything was everyone else's fault. Their eventual self-destruction seemed almost inevitable.

If only there was some way I could truly make them pay. Them and everyone else who was involved in the article that had cost me so much. That had stolen my job, and could have easily cost me Alyssa and Phoebe as well. At least karma was coming to get Dad and Hayley. I'd just have to give it a helping hand with Blake and Darcy Cooper, Paige Wood, and T—whoever the fuck she was.

Driven by the need to do something, I booted up my computer and loaded up the Gossip Weekly Online website. Thankfully, because I'd stayed locked away, I'd given the paps out the front of my house nothing to use, so I was no longer on the home page.

Now, the top story was about Australia's soapie princess, Katie Medler, shacking up with some fucking Yank singer. Why the public needed to know the details of her sex life was fucking beyond me. Ignoring the current stories, I searched for my name on the site.

In addition to the articles I'd expected: the one with Christina, the "attack" from the beach, the teaser to the eight-page scandal in the printed magazine, and details of the almost-threesome in the nightclub with Tillie and her girlfriend, there were at least thirty other articles. Many were from days and nights I'd rather forget. Times I'd have to tell Alyssa about on our weekend.

Forcing the memories from my mind, I focused on the latest scandals, trying to get any information I could about the elusive T who was making my life hell. The last three articles on me, from the nightclub onward, all had the same byline credit: By: Miss M. (Photos by W.T. Entertainment).

Following the lead, I searched W.T. Entertainment, but when I got to their website it was just bare bones. There were no details about who T might be, just a series of photos of various celebrities they'd hunted. Photos of me from the beginning of my career right up to date were splashed around the page together with some of Morgan, Hunter Blake, and a few of the other drivers. Intermixed with the ProV8 drivers were a number of traditional TV and radio celebrities.

One thing was clear: this W.T. Entertainment seemed to have a heavier focus on the ProV8 series than any normal paparazzi group would. There was a connection there, somewhere just out of my grasp. Once I found that connection, I'd know why T was in league with Paige Wood and how to deal with them both for trying to ruin me.

My heart leapt into my throat as a potential lead crossed my mind. There was a woman with a name starting with T who popped up far too regularly to be a mere coincidence.

My mind wandered back to the night in the club, and the magazine cover that followed. My face was clear in all of the photos, but the faces of my two female accomplices had been obscured. At the time, I'd thought nothing of it because, although they were in the VIP room, I hadn't recognised them. I'd assumed that, unlike me, their faces weren't going to sell any magazines. It had never once crossed my mind that they'd been blurred because of who they were.

Could Tillie from the club be T?

My mouth went dry at the thought. I had no idea how to even start looking to confirm my suspicion or where I could turn for more information. Hadn't she told Alyssa she was in publishing?

I was focused on the computer, scrolling through a number of websites trying to get ownership or employee information for W.T. Entertainment, when my phone rang. It yanked me from my search and sent my heart racing for a second until I placed the noise.

When Alyssa's voice greeted me, I couldn't help myself.

The possibility of T's identity came flooding from me. Before I'd thought the words through, everything spilled from my mouth. The fact that she was at the club when the photographer captured that moment. The fact that she was miraculously at the airport on my way home. Her appearance at the benefit—and the fact that she'd had plenty of opportunity to spike my drink, either over dinner or when she came to get me to sign her T-shirt. I paced around my living room as I spoke, unable to keep still with the nerves coursing through my body over the fact that I might have a lead.

For a moment, Alyssa was quiet. The silence seemed more deathly than shocked as her breathing sped.

"Lys?" I asked, wondering what the fuck could be wrong. Was it the realisation that we might have both been played?

When she finally spoke, her voice was tight. Controlled. As if she were trying to stop her tears. "She was one of the girls from the nightclub?"

Fuck! It'd completely slipped my mind that I hadn't told Alyssa the full details of the history between Tillie and me. I couldn't answer her, mostly because I didn't know what words would make it better, but I had no doubt my silence spoke volumes.

"You let me sit there and talk to her like a friend when both of you were well aware that there was stuff going on I didn't know about? Did it even cross your mind to mention it to me, considering what happened at that event?"

"How exactly was I supposed to mention it? Lys, this is Tillie. She and her girlfriend nearly shagged me rotten in a nightclub, and then she tried to suck my cock at Heathrow airport. Really? How could I have told you that? How would that have gone down at the charity event?"

"You could have found some way to let me know."

I closed my eyes while I clenched and unclenched my free hand. God, I needed a drink, but I still didn't have anything in the house. "I know. I should have. I just didn't think. She tried to crack onto me during the fundraiser too, but I told her that I was a one-woman man."

"You have to understand, Dec."

"Understand what? Help me here, Lys, because more than anything I don't want to fuck this up—fuck us up—but you need to help me." I moved and sat at the dining table. With my free hand, I spun one of the coasters on its corner.

"Photos of you around random women I can deal with. I know you're not living in some bubble where you'll only ever interact with men. But real history, actual people you've screwed or come close to screwing, that can't be swept away. I have to know about those."

I slapped my hand down on the coaster, stopping the spin. "But—"

"No, Dec. No buts. I have an issue making small talk with someone else who's seen your dick, and I don't think that's unreasonable."

It would be impossible for me to tell her all of the people I'd slept with because the list was too long. I was smart enough not to mention that fact at that precise time though. "If it comes up again, I promise I'll let you know."

"Is it likely to come up again?"

"I don't know. Maybe. God knows I wasn't a fucking saint without you in my life, Lys. You know that as well as I do. But that's changed now. I've got a case of blue balls like you wouldn't believe because of how badly I need you."

A quiet chuckle echoed down the line. It'd clearly slipped out in spite of her anger because it stopped as soon as it had started.

"That's what this weekend is about anyway, isn't it? Get it all out in the open. Although, I don't think I'll be able to give dates and times or names and addresses."

"I don't want a play-by-play, Dec. God knows I don't need that. I just need to know if the mouth forming words in a conversation with me is one that's been on your cock."

"Maybe we need a code word. Like a safe word. Something I can use whenever we're near anyone I've slept with."

"Like what?"

"How about regret?"

She was silent, but I didn't know if it was because she was upset or thinking.

"I'll work that word into the introduction and then you'll know."

"That might work."

"We'll make it work. I can't change the past, Lys, but I can change the future. And I can learn from my mistakes."

"I know that you're trying. It just caught me by surprise. I mean, she's just . . . I don't know, the complete opposite of me."

I played with the coaster in front of me again, concentrating on that rather than the words that were about to leave me. "That was kinda the point."

"Oh."

"Yeah."

There was a moment between us that was entirely awkward in a way things hadn't really been on the phone before.

"Do you know any way to do a search to see if my suspicion is right?" I asked, trying to break the silence and lead the conversation away from the specifics of past conversations with Tillie and onto more proactive focuses.

"There might be a few. Let me look into it for you."

I thanked her and then we started chatting about Phoebe's day.

It was too late to talk to my little girl, because she was already in bed, but that didn't mean I didn't want to know about the things she'd done. After a little more conversation with Alyssa, I confirmed some firmer plans for the weekend before we said our goodbyes. When we did, she dropped the bombshell that she'd be working for the rest of the week so our calls would be very limited.

CHAPTER THIRTEEN

COINCIDENCE

SOMEHOW, I MANAGED to make it through to Thursday without tearing down any walls in the house. I'd even managed to go grocery shopping at one point without completely losing my mind. My meals since Alyssa had left might have consisted of the same three dishes she'd cooked in her time in Sydney, and had shown me how to make in the process, but at least I was eating something more than just vegemite toast and takeaway for every meal.

Better yet, the number of cars parked out in front of my house waiting for the hint of a scandal had shrunk to just one lone photographer—the same one who'd baited me at the beach. I didn't know where the others had fucked off to, but I didn't really give a shit either. They were off my case, and that was enough for me. The one guy left had to have been bored out of his fucking mind considering I'd only left the house twice in almost a week.

Around two in the afternoon, while Christina was busy cleaning the messes I'd left throughout the house in my demolition phase, the phone rang. Since I'd decided to use her presence as an excuse to lock myself away in my gym, I was a little over thirty minutes into my run and more ready for a break. I hopped onto the sides of the treadmill while the mat kept spinning at a little over ten kilometres an hour. Blowing out a breath, and sucking down a drink, I took a second to recover from my workout before jabbing at the button to stop the treadmill.

The phone had stopped ringing before I got to it, but when I saw Eden's name as the missed call, I waited for her return call. She never called just once and gave up. It was more her style to try two or three times before resigning herself to the fact that she'd have to wait for a call back—usually after leaving some smart-arsed voicemail.

While I waited, I grabbed my towel and patted down my shoulders. With the summer heat setting in early and November storms, my house was like a sauna. Normally I would have run the air con to keep it cool, but with my money growing tighter and tighter every day, it felt far too indulgent to have it running for just me. Instead, I was just making my exercise routine as clothing optional as possible, and had spent most of the day in little more than a pair of gym shorts.

Barely a minute had gone by before my screen lit up as Eden rang again.

"Be ready at six, I'm taking you out for dinner." She hadn't even said hello. At least nothing had changed between us despite everything that had gone down.

"Well obviously you're home then," I said.

"Yep. Flew in last night, and now I wanna meet up. There's some stuff I need to talk to you about."

"Okay." There were some things I needed to discuss with her too, but I wasn't sure whether her statement should excite or scare me.

"See you tonight then." She hung up the phone before I could ask for more information.

Knowing the worst thing I could do was linger on the possible reasons for the call, I turned back around and jumped on the treadmill again. Maybe I was spending too much time on that and my bike in the last few days, but focusing on getting my technique right, on keeping my feet in the right place and getting the most out of my workouts was a good distraction and kept my monsters at bay. For a few moments at a time at least.

A little over two hours later, I was dressed in a button-down shirt and black slacks. I had no idea whether Eden was taking me somewhere formal or out to the local KFC, so I wanted to be ready for either. It was a little before six when she knocked on the door.

"Ready to go?" she asked. "Or do you need a few more minutes to fix your make-up?"

"Fuck off, Edie. I don't have to spend time with you, you know."

"Who else have you got to keep you company? And I don't want to hear about Mrs. Palmer and her five daughters all wrapped around your cock all night long."

"Yeah, because all I've been doing since Lys left is masturbating furiously." I held up my hand, palm facing her, before spinning it around and dropping the right fingers to flip her the bird. "Seriously, why are we friends again?"

"Because you love me?" She fluttered her eyes and made kissy noises.

"I wouldn't be too confident about that."

"Because I'm the only one who puts up with your shit?"

The amusement that had been growing with our banter released in a chuckle. "That's probably closer to the truth."

"Although Lys puts up with it too."

"Yeah, but Lys gets other benefits." I waggled my brow at her and clutched my crotch.

"Fuck off, Reede, you're a dirty manwhore."

"Only for one woman."

"Get in the car and you can tell me all about your undying love on the way."

We ended up going to Il Riscatto, a little Italian restaurant about forty minutes from my house.

When we arrived, I half expected Morgan to be there to meet us. "Where's Morg?"

Eden grimaced.

"What is it?"

"He's being a little precious about the whole thing."

"About what exactly?"

She sighed and rolled her eyes. "About you. Things are a little tense around Sinclair at the moment. There are two firm camps; those who want you back and those glad you're gone."

"So Morgan isn't going to be my friend anymore because some fuckers have said he shouldn't? What is this, the fucking third grade?"

"No. It's not like that exactly."

"Well, then what's it like *exactly*?"

"Morg's so close to claiming the championship. Even with the Bathurst crash, he's clinging on to it by the skin of his teeth. Right now, the last thing he needs is any controversy around him distracting him from the last few races."

"And I'm controversial."

She shrugged. "At the moment you are. You know Morg doesn't want this. Obviously he's hanging for a boys' night out. He just wants to wait until he can do it properly without the paparazzi hanging around and without worrying about any issues around work." She indicated out the window, where the lone pap who was still following me around stood with his camera in hand. He gave a twisted smile and little wave. The fucker didn't even bother to try to hide anymore.

"And what about you? Why are you here then?"

"Well, for starters, I don't give a shit what the press says about me. For second, I'm already tangled up in all this crap, so it doesn't make sense for me to keep my distance. It'll only make us look guilty."

"Except it could fuel rumours that we really are an item."

"Ha! If they are going to think that anyway, we should give them something to really froth at the mouth about." She grabbed my face in her hands, leaned across the table, and planted a kiss on my lips. I recoiled in shock as she fell back into her chair, laughing. "Seriously, if anyone can think there's anything going on between us, they need their head read. Besides, you, me, Alyssa, and Morgan all know the truth so fuck the rest of them."

"Fuck the rest of them? Very philosophical."

She held up her hands and gave an exaggerated shrug. "What can I say? I'm a freaking thinker."

"A regular fucking Plato."

She flipped me the bird but laughed as she did.

After we'd eaten, I was ready to leave to go home and give Alyssa a call before she headed to bed after her shift at work. Before I could make it that far though, Eden gave me a quick sideways glance and then gasped. "Danny? What are you doing here?"

"What have you done?" I mouthed to her.

A sly smile tipped up her lips and she gave a far too innocent shrug as she moved around me to greet him. "I didn't know your reservations were for tonight."

Bullshit. With my heart beating against my chest at a few thousand RPM, I spun around in the direction she was headed. He already had Eden in a warm embrace, dropping away when he saw me.

"Declan," he said with a curt nod. His voice was tight. Restrained.

My jaw ached with pressure as I shot daggers at Eden. I'd thought her impromptu dinner was a gesture of friendship, not her being an interfering cow. My tone matched his as I nodded in reply. "Danny."

Hazel, Danny's wife, gave me a polite smile that lacked all of the warmth she'd shown in the years I'd been with the team. I bit the inside of my cheeks at the sight.

It was just further evidence of how badly I'd screwed up everything with my surrogate family. As if I'd needed more.

"I need to go powder my nose," Eden announced. "Hazel, would you care to join me?"

Danny gave Eden a look of betrayal that echoed my own, but then his gaze met mine and something in his eyes softened. He nodded to Hazel, who quietly slipped away at Eden's side.

"It appears we've been set up," Danny said as his gaze followed the pair toward the restrooms at the back of the restaurant.

"So it would seem." My tone was as dead as my career. Even though I wanted nothing more than to prove that I was doing fine despite the way he'd shafted me, I couldn't infuse my voice with warmth, or life, or anything.

"Care for a drink?" he asked.

"Not really."

"I'm guessing Eden set this little stunt up to give you a chance to explain yourself. Do you really want to give up that opportunity?"

"Why should I explain myself to someone who is uninterested in listening?"

His fingers rubbed along his forehead and then he sighed. A moment later, he nodded toward the bar. "Come on. You might not want a drink, but I think I need one."

Even though I wanted to tell him to shove his drink up his fucking arse, I followed him to the bar. My gaze drifted back toward the restrooms, and I wondered how long Eden was going to keep me waiting. How long she was going to force me to make small talk with the guy who'd fired me less than two weeks earlier.

When we reached the bar, Danny waved over the bartender and ordered a drink. I just shook my head when I was offered again. My eyes were trained on the marble in front of me, following the intricate patterns and imperfections so that I had something to concentrate on other than Danny beside me.

"I heard a rumour you were offered a place at Wood," he said, without trying for any small talk first.

Lifting my gaze from the marble to meet his, I shrugged and tried to play it nonchalantly. I feared that I was failing when I had to swallow down the lump in my throat.

"I also heard you turned it down."

Not trusting myself to speak, I nodded.

He leaned forward onto the bar, resting his weight on his forearms. "Why?"

"Because I don't want to race for just anyone." *Especially not a psycho who likely coordinated this whole thing.*

He raised his eyebrow.

Spinning so that I could face the wide open space of the restaurant rather than the small corner the bar was in, I sighed before continuing. "There was always a reason I took the job with you. Why it was barely a consideration to sign the first contract you offered me. I *wanted* to race for Sinclair Racing long before you offered me a chance. As a kid, it wasn't just about being behind the wheel of a ProV8. It was about being behind the wheel of a Sinclair car." I lifted my face to the ceiling because it was hard for me to make my admission. Especially after everything that had happened since. "It was always the dream."

I glanced at him out of the corner of my eye and saw him nursing his drink, sloshing the contents around as he stared into the amber liquid. "I'm sorry for how things went down, son. It's possible I was a little rash in my decisions. Eden tells me that things haven't been easy for you in recent weeks."

I scoffed. "That's a fucking understatement."

He took a sip of his drink and then placed it back down on the bar. "She wouldn't tell me why, though."

It was clear he was fishing for more, but I didn't owe him anything. Not only that, but if I got into all the details about Emmanuel and Phoebe, about Dad and Hayley, about all the things I'd discovered and faced in the last month, I would be demanding a drink of my own before long.

Probably a bottle of the stuff.

And if I started that, it wouldn't end well. Not while I was alone.

"No offense, sir, but I don't really want to talk about any of it with you."

He twisted his hands up in a gesture that obviously meant he wasn't going to press. Then he chuckled. "You would not believe how much Eden has been in my ear about you the whole time we were in Bahrain."

"Fuck, I can't do this." I pushed away from the bar and headed out into the night. Fuck Eden and her interfering. Fuck Danny and his pretence of being friendly. I didn't need pity or an accidentally-on-purpose encounter to try to get me my job back. Or whatever the fuck this was supposed to be. When I hit the street, I paced along the footpath while I waited for Eden.

The paparazzo outside smirked at me. "That looked like an intense conversation. Wanna tell me about it? Better yet, why not go inside and tell him how you really feel? There must be something you want to say to him after the way he hung you out to dry."

Even though I tried, I couldn't ignore the fucker. "Fuck you!"

He laughed, but I just turned away from him.

As I did, all of the things I'd wanted to say to Danny since he'd given me the sack rammed against my skull. Maybe the arsehole photographer was right. Every thought smashed against my tongue and demanded to be released.

In the next second, I was back through the door and stalked straight to the bar.

"Actually, I do have some things I need to say to you." The words flew from me without thought as I got closer to Danny. "I've been Sinclair through and through since the day you hired me, but fuck if I haven't made some mistakes. There are some you know about, some you don't, but not one of them was ever done with an ounce of spite.

"What you did to me, giving me the arse over hearsay and rumours during what was in some ways the worst month of my life, was something I never in my darkest imaginings would have thought you'd do. I thought we were like a family."

He stared at me. His face was impassive, but his eyes raged. It was clear why. We were like a family, which was exactly why he'd done it.

"Fuck, I get it, okay? I didn't tell you about Wood's offer. *Offers.* Multiple. I didn't see you after Hazel saw me talking with Paige to reassure you that I wasn't planning on leaving. Maybe if I'd told you the truth then, you'd have known there was no way I would do that to you. To the team. And I fucked up by not checking with you about the fundraiser. In hindsight, I can see that I should have. Even before that, I wasn't honest with you about the issues I was having on the track, but only because I wasn't being honest with myself. I own all of that. What you have to own in return is that you didn't even give me a chance to explain myself. You didn't even pause or stop and think about it before you assumed the worst."

"You think I didn't pause? You think I didn't stop and think?" He shifted closer to me and grabbed my arm. His fingers dug into my bicep as he tugged me closer. When he spoke again, his voice was a dangerous whisper. "I was willing to turn the other cheek when I found out you were doing drugs because I knew you were getting treatment. I was willing to put you on the track, meet after meet, when you told me you were okay to drive only to watch you crash hundreds of thousands of my dollars into the fucking wall. How was I supposed to react when I saw that you were representing Wood Racing at a function? What was I supposed to think other than the fact that maybe you'd been sabotaging the team, and would continue to for the last few months you were there before jumping ship?"

I yanked my arm out of his hold. "You knew about my issues when I first started?"

"It's my team, Declan; it's my job to know everything that happens."

"Eden told you, didn't she?" My lips mashed into a hard line as I glared in the direction of the restrooms. I'd thought she was my friend, and yet she'd thrown me under the bus.

"Don't be so foolish as to think Eden and I didn't discuss it the day you decided to come in stoned. She was firmly on your side even then. Begged me to give you another chance. Promised me that she'd get you straight. I've tried so hard to be on your side too, Declan. But sometimes you make it very hard."

"Fuck!" The curse left me a little too loudly as I ran my fingers through my hair and paced away from Danny. Still, it wasn't loud enough. I wanted to scream the word at the sky. To howl at the moon until I released all the demons swirling through my body. I spun back around. "You know the most fucked-up thing in all of this is that a few more fucking months and I would've been a different man. I *am* a different man. That arsehole kid I was a few months ago is gone. He's buried under a pile of shit so big he'll never get out because I know things now that I didn't then. I can't ever let that fucked-up kid make a reappearance, or I'll lose things that are way more important than a damn fucking job. Despite all that, it's now that I get the arse."

"We all have to pay for our choices, Declan."

"And what about your choices?" I challenged.

"What's that supposed to mean?"

"You were the one who put me on that plane next to Alyssa without any regard to what the outcome might be." Even though the action had worked out well for me on a personal front, it was also the catalyst for everything that had happened since. Except the paps were apparently already on my arse before then, or they wouldn't have caught everything that they had. Still, Danny needed to accept his portion of the blame, just like I was willing to accept mine.

"I paid for that choice by losing someone who could have been a damn fine driver if he pulled his head out of his arse long enough to get around a race track."

"You didn't *lose*. You tossed away."

"I still don't know what you expect me to have done? Having a liability on the track is a danger for everyone."

I scoffed. "Yeah, well, you'll know all about that soon enough."

"What exactly is that supposed to mean?"

"It means that Hunter is a lunatic. If you think I'm a loose cannon, you have no fucking idea."

No fucking clue at all.

Then again, how could I expect him to when I'd kept the information hidden for so long?

CHAPTER FOURTEEN
ON THE PROWL

"IF YOU HAVE information about Hunter you think I should know, I'd appreciate it if you shared." Danny raised an eyebrow at me.

Despite how much I'd raged and shouted at him, he'd mostly kept his calm. I'm sure the pap outside was annoyed by that fact. He'd probably pissed his pants with excitement when we'd started arguing.

It would have been so easy to open my mouth and tell Danny the deep dark secrets I knew about Hunter, but I couldn't. Too much time had passed, and it would add dirt to the top of my already nailed-shut coffin. It was yet another secret I'd kept from the team, another thing I'd confided with the enemy. Even Eden didn't know about the night I'd met Hunter out on the town almost eighteen months earlier.

THE BEAT of the music in the club called to me like a siren song. It pounded out a rhythm that would become my heartbeat for the night, eliminating the need to listen to my own—or to the irregular beat from the piece of me that was missing. The intensity of the sound drowned out all need for thought and left me in my element.

While I scoped out the local talent, I stood to one side dancing to the music with a drink in one hand. Although bobbing was probably a more apt description for my movement, considering I didn't move any part of my body besides my chest and head. In the ten minutes I'd been there, I'd already assessed the crowd and performed my usual quick analysis. Thirteen girls had been immediately ruled out based of the colour of their hair, three girls based on the number of layers they were wearing, four scary-looking girls for their potential STD risk, and six girls because there was just no way in hell I could go there.

Of the remaining pool, I definitely had my eye on a few with talent. A couple with a *lot* of talent. Initially, I was going to go out into the room on a bit of a fishing expedition, but after a few minutes, I decided to bait the line and wait to see what came to me instead. Those ones tended to be a bit easier to hook, and tonight, I wanted easy more than the chase.

It was still early in the night. I was having a kick-arse time on my own, celebrating my win on the track and my lead in the championship series. I thought about Morgan locked away somewhere with Eden and pitied the poor bastard. Who'd want to be stuck fucking the same woman every night? Especially when, like me, he could've had his pick of the pond if he hadn't shacked up with Eden.

I watched the girls in the club closely. It was important to ensure whomever I took to my hotel room was ready, willing, and much more than able to do anything and everything I asked.

It wasn't like I wanted too much, really. Just one—or two—hot little fillies I could ride all night long. Already hard just thinking about the fun I could have, I licked my lips in anticipation. No ties meant no limits, no restrictions, and definitely no repeat performances.

With one eye still on the talent in the room, I made my way back to the bar for a refill on my whiskey. As I ordered my drink, I nodded to Hunter Blake. I barely knew him beyond the fact that he was the lead driver for Wood Racing. He was sitting at the bar licking his wounds because although he was coming third in the championship behind Morgan and me, he'd suffered a DNF in the second race of the Winton round earlier that day.

I felt for him. I couldn't even begin to imagine what a DNF would feel like. The thought alone was soul crushing.

Throwing caution, and party politics, to the wind, I decided to have a few drinks with him. It would probably cause a scandal. I could almost see the headline: Holden driver drinks with Ford driver.

I smirked, knowing it wasn't quite that bad but, other than a few drivers who had made the dreaded crossover, drivers tended to be either red or blue, through and through. We had to be because some of the fans were rabid in their distaste for the opposing manufacturer.

"Hey," I said. "Whatcha drinking?"

He grunted a response. I called the bartender over and indicated he should give us another round.

"That was shit luck today," I said, offering him one of the glasses.

He regarded it for a second and then shrugged. "I've learned there's no such thing as luck on the track. You'll learn that in time too, kid. If something is wrong with the car, it's the mech's fault. Today, the stupid pit crew fucked me over, plain and simple."

"It's not like they could have anticipated brake failure," I said in defence of the people who worked in his pits—a crew I didn't even know.

"Yeah, well, that's your opinion. Mine is that they fucked me over." He shrugged again and then said, "Fuck it, nothing I can't make up in the next few rounds."

"If you say so," I said. "I might have to stop those plans though."

He snorted. "You can try."

"Don't worry. I'll make sure I give you a run for your money at least."

"Yeah, kid, you sure got some kinda magic when you're on the track."

I nodded my appreciation of the compliment.

"What're you doing here anyway?" he asked. "It's not like you need to drown your sorrows."

As if to demonstrate his point, he knocked the rest of his drink back and called for another. He ordered a new one for me as well, so I drained the contents of my glass too.

"I'm just looking for a good time," I said, nodding in the direction of the dance floor filled with girls. "I've been wound so tight in getting ready for this race. I just really need to get some fucking relief."

"I hear ya," Hunter said, raising his glass. "Maybe that's a better way to drown my sorrows too."

"Well, it certainly never hurts," I laughed.

"That it doesn't, kid. That it doesn't." He looked around the room. "What's caught your eye so far?"

I shrugged. "There's a few around that are interesting."

He smirked. "What's your type?"

A flash of honey-gold eyes and brown hair appeared in my mind for a split second before I tuned them out. "I don't really have a type. But I'm a tits and arse man, and tonight I think I just want an easy score."

"I hear ya," he said, offering me a fist bump.

We spent a few minutes in silence, watching the girls in the room bump and grind against each other, steadfastly appearing to ignore any male presence even as their eyes darted around to ensure they were being watched. I noticed one pair, a blonde and a brunette, sitting at one of the few tables around. Both of them were shooting us regular appreciative glances. They were definitely ready to be targeted.

"Lock and load?" I asked.

"I got the blonde," he said as he stood.

I shook my head. "Nah, man, I don't do brunettes."

He gave me an odd look. After my talk of wanting an easy score, he probably assumed I wouldn't be fussy, but I had my reasons for avoiding brunettes and he didn't need to know them.

I shrugged. "I just . . . can't go there. I won't."

He made a hand signal to indicate he didn't care. "Whatever. A pussy is a pussy, I guess."

I laughed and followed his lead as he collected another round for us—beers this time—as well as two frilly, fruity-looking cocktails for the girls.

"They go wild for this shit," he whispered, before turning back to the bar. I turned away as he reached into his pocket for his wallet. He threw a couple of notes at the bartender before putting his wallet away. With a wink, he handed me my beer and one of the drinks. "They'll be putty in our hands after this."

It was strange having a Ford driver as a wingman, but good to have someone to work with again. Although Morgan had introduced me to the lifestyle, he'd quickly dumped me when he'd hooked up with Eden. I still went out with the pair of them on occasion, but Eden was very vocal, especially when it came to her opinion on my choices. When it came time to go trawling the bars and clubs, I was usually on my own.

"Ladies!" Hunter schmoozed as soon as we were close enough for them to hear us. He grinned at the brunette and offered her a drink. She took it straight away and drank deeply from the concoction.

The blonde looked at the fruity drink with all the bells and whistles, including a tiny umbrella, and shook her head. "That," she inclined her head toward my beer, "is much more my style."

I grinned. "A girl after my own heart."

She chuckled as I passed her the beer. Her tongue pressed forward and circled the tip of the bottleneck, before tipping it back and chugging it down.

I was more than slightly turned on watching her full lips tease the neck of the bottle as she drank. My mind immediately offered the image of my cock slipping into her perfect pout. I trailed my eyes down her neck and across her breasts, before she caught me looking. Lust blazed in her eyes as her gaze performed a similar, unabashed assessment of my body. She smirked and placed the empty bottle on the table. Hunter scowled at the still full cocktail on the table—not that I could blame him, because that shit was expensive. That was the risk in buying a drink for someone with unknown tastes though. I'd had my share of losses over my time in the club scene.

After promising I'd be right back, I headed for the bar for two more beers. When I returned, I pushed one of the beers toward the blonde. While I spoke to her, I tried to remember the name she'd given me when she'd introduced herself. Not that it mattered. By morning, she would be gone and her name forgotten. I only tried to use her name because in my experience chicks gave it up easier if they thought you were actually interested in who they were as a person regardless of whether it was true or not.

The four of us sat talking for a little while, sharing laughs about nothing in particular. The good thing about hooking up in clubs was that the music was loud enough that it was impossible to carry on a conversation that consisted of anything more than one-liners and small talk. It was the perfect environment for meaningless encounters.

Hunter pulled the brunette to him and started to rub her back. A moment later, he turned her in his arms and kissed her deeply. I couldn't help feeling a slight disgust in the pit of my stomach as I watched his hand run through her long chestnut locks. A memory tried to take hold in my mind, but I shook it away. There was no room for *her* in my life. I was happier now than I'd ever been back home. I turned to the blonde to try to get all thoughts of brown hair and honey-gold eyes out of my head.

The girls excused themselves to go "powder their noses" or some shit. As she stood, the brunette staggered. Her legs were like jelly beneath her. I acted instinctively, reaching out to stop her from falling. As soon as she was able to right herself, I let her go, dropping my hands quickly to my sides.

"I told you, man," Hunter said, indicating the drink in front of the brunette's seat and winking. "Putty."

He reached into his pocket and had his hand closed around something when he pulled it back out. He shifted slightly until he was in front of Blondie's drink, then he pushed his hand forward slightly, touching the top of her bottle.

My hand shot out and grabbed his wrist.

"What the fuck are you doing?"

"Making putty." He smirked at me.

I yanked his hand around and found a small white tablet resting between his thumb and palm.

"What the fuck?" I exclaimed.

"You said you wanted easy. I'm getting you easy."

"Fucking easy, man, not fucking drugged!"

He shrugged. "What's the difference?"

"Are you fucking kidding me?" I stared at him for a few seconds, waiting for him to laugh and tell me it was all some sick joke and it was actually just a sugar tablet or something.

He sneered back at me. "What's wrong? Don't have the balls to go through with it?"

I blinked at him. "You're fucking nuts!"

"You're a fucking pussy!"

"Go!" I said, hoping my tone would tell him it wasn't a request. "Get the fuck out of here before I call the cops on your fucking arse and ruin your career."

He dropped the pill into the blonde's drink. "I'm not the one whose fingerprints are on not one, but two drugged drinks."

"Fuck you!" I spat at him.

"Thanks for the offer, Reede, but I'd rather let the girls do that." He leaned back against his chair and smiled at me, daring me to do something.

What could I do though? He knew as well as I did my hands were tied unless I wanted to implicate myself too.

"Speaking of which . . .," he added.

The two girls emerged from the crowd in that instant. Hunter yanked his hand from my grip and lifted Blondie's drink, offering it to her. He watched me intently the entire time, glaring at me, as if goading me to stop her. Daring me to out him, all the while knowing I would be fucked by association if I did.

I watched in horror as the chick raised the bottle to her mouth. I knew I couldn't let her drink, but I couldn't risk my career either. It left me only one option. I stood quickly, pushing my chair back roughly as I did. Then I "accidentally" smacked into the blonde, being sure to knock the drink from her hand as I did.

"What the fuck?" she exclaimed as the cold drink spilled down her front. Her nipples puckered to attention with the icy wave.

"I apologise," Hunter snarled, not sounding sorry in the least. "My friend is one clumsy, *and stupid*, motherfucker."

The blonde turned on me. "I've got nothing to change into, you fucking prick!"

It wasn't quite a, "thank you for not letting this asshole drug and rape me," but I wasn't sure what more I could expect when she didn't know what I'd saved her from.

Hunter stood and whispered something into her ear. She seemed thoughtful for a second before nodding. He wrapped his arm around her shoulder possessively and began to lead her back through the crowd. I had no doubt he was going to have his way with her — willing or not.

"Wait," I called after them. "Please, don't go with him."

She raised her eyebrow at me. "Give me one reason why I shouldn't?"

I looked down at the table, trying to think of anything that would stop her from leaving with him.

"What about your friend?" I said. "She doesn't look well."

She took a second to regard the scene. Luckily for me — and her — her brunette friend took the opportunity to open her mouth and hurl all over the table before slumping into her chair.

"Well, isn't this the fucking perfect evening?" Blondie exclaimed.

Hunter looked at the brunette in disgust for a second. Then he glared at me. "Just bring her with us," he suggested. "The more the merrier. Or better yet, my friend here can take care of her. Let Mr. Chivalry get her home safe."

The blonde regarded him for a second before sighing. "No, I'd better take her home. If something happened to her ... Well, I'd never forgive myself."

"I'll organise a taxi," I offered. "I'll even pay for it — to make up for the shirt."

Blondie's face softened as she looked at me. "Sure," she said.

"But what am I supposed to do? Your friend there got me all revved up. Someone's got to take care of my situation." Hunter grabbed his crotch as if to prove that he was hard and ready for action.

"Why don't you go home and take care of it solo?" the blonde asked.

"Why, Hunter," I said snidely. "I do believe the lady just told you to go fuck yourself."

As the blonde collected her friend from the table, Hunter grabbed hold of my wrist. "You watch yourself, Reede. You'll get yours. When you least expect it . . . I'll be there. I'll make sure you fucking pay."

I laughed. "You don't scare me."

"Don't I?" he asked, raising his eyebrow. "You have no idea what I'm capable of."

"Oh, I think I have some idea, you sick fucker," I said, eyeing the still untouched cocktail on the table.

I yanked my arm away from him.

"Now fuck off, because I've got to help these girls into a taxi."

"You're a fool, Reede."

"I'd rather be a fool than a fuckwit," I quipped back at him as I helped Blondie juggle the brunette out of the club.

"Can your shirt wait?" I asked Blondie when we were out in the cool of the night.

"I don't know. Why?" She sounded more than a little annoyed. I imagined the night wasn't going quite as well as she'd hoped. The July air was crisp and cool, and through her wet shirt, her nipples were so hard and pointed they probably could have cut glass.

I pulled my jacket off and offered it to her. "I didn't want to make a scene in there, but I think your buddy may have been drugged."

She gasped. "What? Why? By who?"

I closed my eyes. I could man up—and risk the consequences of being labelled as guilty even though I wasn't—or I could lie. As I opened my eyes again, I sighed. "I don't know who. I just know the signs."

"Oh my God!" Blondie exclaimed. She began to pace. "Oh, fuck! What should I do?"

"Calm down," I whispered. "Panicking won't help the situation. We'll get her to the hospital. They'll be able to make sure it's nothing serious. Then you'll be able to take her home, and she can sleep it off."

I helped both girls into the taxi and asked the driver to take us to the hospital. Once there, I waited with the pair in Emergency. The brunette was practically paralytic, but kept stroking my cheek and telling me how beautiful she thought I was.

At one point, I turned to say something to her, but her almost-black eyes looking out from underneath her fringe of brown hair that was too familiar a shade, was just wrong. The words stuck in my throat as I pushed thoughts of my hands caressing a girl with similar-coloured hair so long ago.

Another lifetime ago.

After Hunter's victim had been seen and cleared by the hospital, I helped the two of them into another taxi. By then, the brunette was passed out cold and snoring loudly. I looked down at her peaceful face and was consumed by a sadness I didn't understand.

"Thank you," Blondie said. "For being so sweet back there. Most men probably would have just thanked their lucky stars and taken her home to fuck her."

I shook my head. "I couldn't do that," I said.

"Could you help me bring her upstairs?" Blondie asked, pointing to her house.

I nodded. Within half an hour, the brunette was firmly tucked up in bed, and I was firmly up inside Blondie.

I used her, every part of her, to elicit my own sweet pleasure and drive images of my past life from my mind. While I claimed her body, I relished her cries of ecstasy. Each one was proof that I was a free agent. A man able to do what I wanted, and who I wanted. It was just fucking for fun and, although her body didn't make my own sing like only one had before, I enjoyed my release anyway.

It was only afterwards that I began to feel like an arse. Not for fucking her—I would have done that a hundred times over—but because I hadn't really stopped anything. I may have saved those two girls from the night from hell, but I couldn't help but wonder how many more had suffered at Hunter's hand or how many more would.

I was all for a drunken fuck, and nights of regret, but not without consent. The thought of going as far as drugging girls horrified me—especially considering I knew all too well how easily drugs could fuck up your life. And at least my usage had been my own choice—mostly.

I crept out of the house early the next morning, unable to completely shake my feeling of guilt. For the next day, I was on edge. I worried about news of the night getting back to Danny, Eden, or Morgan. If someone made the connection between the girls and the nightclub, then it would be easy to trace the fact that I was the one who had been at the hospital. What if someone then connected the drugging with the drinks with my prints on the outside? The police might turn up and accuse me of the worst possible crimes.

I made it back to my hotel room, quickly checked out, and began my long drive back to Sydney with all of those concerns racing around in my mind.

I had to think of a way to make Hunter pay. I had to make him realise that what he was doing wasn't fun or right. But I had to do it in a way that wouldn't risk fucking up my own life.

In the end, I decided I had nothing to lose—nothing Hunter could take from me at least—so I told his boss, Paige, about the roofies. I didn't know what happened to him from there—I'd heard nothing about it in the media.

The fact that he was still on the track the very next week proved that Paige hadn't done much—if anything. In the races after that, he began to ride my arse harder. Almost to the point of dangerous driving. He'd developed a serious grudge against me, and there was nothing I could do but drive to the conditions. Even if one of those conditions was a lunatic in my rear-view mirror.

After that, I didn't see Hunter out at any clubs, so I was largely able to put my concerns about him taking advantage of women out of my mind.

CHAPTER FIFTEEN

DICK MOVE

I STARED BLANKLY ahead of me as memories of the night I'd learned just how psycho Hunter was ran through me. Knowing what I'd learned about Paige over the past few months—the measures she'd taken to get me on her team—I had no doubt she'd swept my accusations under the rug. She'd probably bought off countless other women over the years. She'd probably even covered it up in the press if she really did have the sway I thought she might. In hindsight, it was easy to see I'd been stupid and naïve to think that Paige was even remotely like Danny and cared about things greater than her own team.

"Declan?" Danny prompted.

"He—he's not Sinclair material. He's only in it for himself and—" Meeting Danny's gaze, I swallowed down the words the memory had forced into my throat. What could I say without sounding like I just had a bad case of sour grapes? It was years ago, and there was no proof by my testimony. I had nothing at all to back up my claim.

Why would he believe me? I was the dumped driver, desperate

to get my job back.

Maybe if I'd said something when it'd happened, I would have had a case. But now I had no hope of having anyone believe me. "No. Just that he's a menace on the track, but you already know that."

Even as I said the words, Danny's eyes narrowed at me. It was clear why. Hunter might have been a liability, but he'd only crashed out of one race recently—and that was only because he'd become tangled with me.

"Don't say I didn't warn you," I said, backing away. "Look, Danny, it's been solid, but I have to go. Tell Eden I'll be waiting out front."

"Wait."

The commanding tone in his voice stilled my feet.

"I was serious when I said I didn't want it to go down this way. I've had a chance to think things over, and I think I would do things a little differently if I could. It's too late to change it now, but I wanted you to know that."

I shrugged. His words were little more than platitudes really. They wouldn't get me another job. The best it might do is allow me to use him as a reference, but that still left me with the issue of trying to figure out what sort of job I was actually qualified for.

"Yeah. Me too. See you 'round I guess." I turned and walked away without shaking his hand or letting him say anything more. The whole conversation was just a reminder of my failure.

I waited outside for almost fifteen minutes before Eden came back out to greet me. She had her head dropped and didn't meet my eye.

"How could you fucking do that, Edie?" I paced toward the car as soon as she was at my side.

"Fuck, you men are so pig-headed."

"It's not pig-headed to try to have some scrap of dignity left. To not have to face the fucking man who sacked me."

"Sorry, Dec, I just thought that if the two of you were face-to-face, you might be able to work it out."

"Work out what exactly? It's not like there's a spare car

anymore."

"No, there's not. But there are other positions. I want you back on the team, Dec. It's just not the same without you."

I shook my head at her blind faith that things could just go back to how they were. "I wouldn't hold your breath if I were you."

"I won't, but you shouldn't write off the possibility either."

"Who says I want to go back?"

"I know you do, Dec. If part of you wasn't hoping for it, I think you would have taken the job with Wood Racing."

"I told you—"

"I know what you said, but I still think I'm right."

"And you say I'm pig-headed."

She laughed. "I guess we both are. Must be why we're friends."

I stopped my fast stride. She took one more before spinning to meet my gaze.

"Look, if Danny came begging for me to come back, I wouldn't say no," I admitted. "But why would he? What possible reason could he have for wanting me back when he's got that cock Hunter now? He's only got two licences, and now he's got two drivers."

"You're right. And maybe it was a bit of a dick move forcing you together like that, but we're all entitled to one of those every now and then, aren't we?"

In spite of the situation, I chuckled. "Some of us more than one."

She bumped her shoulder against mine. "Exactly. So when are you seeing Alyssa next?"

"Tomorrow. She's flying down from Brisbane so that we can have a couple's retreat weekend where she gets to grill me over everything that happened while we've been apart."

"Sounds fun."

"Oh, it gets better. Her mum's coming down to look after Phoebe while we're away."

Eden laughed. "Man, sucks to be you."

"It could be worse, I guess. Her dad could be coming too." I told Eden all about the tenuous relationship I had with Curtis, and Alyssa's brother, Josh, as well, while she drove back to my house.

After Eden had dropped me at home, I saw I'd missed a call from Alyssa while I was out to dinner. It was too late to call her back though. She had an early flight in the morning. The thought was enough to send me to bed. I was like a kid on Christmas Eve—desperate to sleep the night away but too excited to actually close my eyes.

I SLEPT late the following morning. Even though Alyssa's plane left Brisbane early, the time difference due to daylight savings meant it would be almost eleven in the morning before her plane arrived in Sydney.

When I woke, I actually felt better about the situation with Danny. I'd never admit it to Eden, but seeing him again, being able to speak my mind and apologise in my own way for not telling him about Wood's offers was actually a little cathartic. I breathed a little easier. The weight on my shoulders was just that little bit lighter. I was practically fucking buoyant by the time I climbed into the car to head to the airport.

I pulled up into the passenger pick-up loading zone and pulled out my phone to text Alyssa to let her know I was there. As I did, I saw I had a message from her already that simply read, *Sorry*.

The sweat that leapt to the skin of my palms at the sight of that word made the phone slippery in my hold. Sorry? For what exactly? My throat ached as I thought of the reasons she might send me that one-word text. My gaze lost focus on the screen. Had she changed her mind? Was she not coming?

As I tried to decipher the meaning in her one word text, the passenger door swung open.

"Wanna pop the boot?" It was Alyssa and I wanted to reach across the car and pull her lips to mine.

Instead, I nodded and, after wiping my hands on my pants, reached for the boot release. A tiny smile crossed my lips at the thought that the word sorry clearly didn't mean that Alyssa wasn't coming. Whatever it did mean was something I could work out later.

A second later, the door swung open again and Alyssa climbed into the passenger seat. Without hesitation, she leaned across the centre console and cupped my face in her hands. "God, I missed you, Dec," she murmured before pressing her lips to mine.

I put my hand to the back of her head and clasped her tightly against me. "I missed you too," I said before deepening the kiss.

The back door opened and a throat cleared. Fuck. I hadn't meant to devour Alyssa's mouth with her mother watching. Or Phoebe, for that matter.

I turned back to greet Ruth, but instead I met a pair of ice-blue eyes. Amusement danced in Ruby's irises as she helped Phoebe into her child seat.

Fucking hell.

"Hello, Ruby," I said, as politely as I could manage given the shock of seeing her in my car.

"Mum couldn't make it," Alyssa said. When I glanced at her, she mouthed the word, "Sorry."

"Luckily for you, Mum had a flexible ticket, a deal came up on flights for me, and I had nothing better going on," Ruby said as she buckled up her own seat belt. "But I do have to go back on Sunday rather than staying through to Monday with Alyssa."

As soon as she was in, I put the car in gear and headed back home.

"When Mum couldn't make it, I agreed to come with Alyssa so that you two could still have your weekend of debauchery."

Alyssa rested back into her seat with a sigh. "How many times do I have to tell you it's not that sort of weekend away?"

"Mummy, what's da-bor-tree?"

After glaring at Ruby, Alyssa rubbed Phoebe's knee. "It's an adult word, honey, it means work."

I snorted. "Yeah, like that won't come back to bite your arse."

"Declan!"

"Sorry."

"He's right, you know," Ruby said. "She'll go to day care next week and tell them all that Mummy's having a day of debauchery."

"Will you stop saying debauchery!" Alyssa's arm flailed as she snapped at Ruby. "It's an adult word, honey," she said to Phoebe. "Okay?"

"Okay, Mummy." Phoebe's smile was wide and her absolute innocence made me chuckle.

"Don't you encourage her," Alyssa said, snapping her eyes to me.

With a smile on my lips, I made a one-handed gesture of surrender. "Leave me out of this. I'm innocent, isn't that right, Pheebs?"

I met her gaze in the rear-view mirror and winked. She curled up her nose and nodded. I wasn't sure she knew what I was talking about, but it was cute that she was willing to go along with it.

"So that's how it's going to be, is it?" Alyssa asked with a chuckle. "The two of you ganging up on me?"

She reached back and tickled Phoebe's stomach.

"Oh my God, would you guys cut it out already?" Ruby laughed as she said the words. "This happy family thing is just too surreal."

"I told you, didn't I? This is us now." Alyssa reached for my thigh and cast a look over her shoulder at Ruby.

Ruby's gaze darted between me and Alyssa. "I still can't believe it. But I'm happy for you."

During the drive home, Alyssa told me about her week at home and about her mum's emergency dash to help a friend in the hospital. Ruby and Phoebe interjected from time to time. I kept my mouth shut, just revelling in the noise. It was such a difference from the near silence of the rest of my week.

For a long time, I'd filled my life with random noise. With nightclubs and the blissful moans of strangers. With V8s and the sweet purr of my Monaro. The sounds of my family in my car, of Alyssa at my side, were far more pleasant than any others. It was only as I pulled into my garage that the reality of what came next struck me.

I grabbed Phoebe's bag and Ruby's bag out of the boot, but left Alyssa's in place. As I did, I huffed out a breath—trying to release my apprehension as I exhaled.

Carrying the bags inside, I saw Phoebe and Alyssa in the living room setting up a DVD.

"I'll show you to the spare room," I said to Ruby as I passed her with her bag in my hand.

She followed me up the stairs. "Nice place."

I nodded and thanked her. It was easier than launching into a whinge about the fact that I didn't know how long I'd be able to keep it without some way to pull in the wage I'd had before. Taking a detour past Phoebe's room, I dropped off her bag.

When I turned around to leave, Ruby had one brow raised at me.

"What?"

"That's a very, um, feminine room." She waved her hand at the two pale purple walls. Tiptoes, according to the label. It was paired on the other two walls with Apple Slice at half tint. At least that's what the consultant at the hardware had told me when she'd run me through it all.

"What?" I walked away, toward my other spare room. The one that originally had only a fold-out couch, but now sported a double bed. "Phoebe wanted purple walls. So I gave her purple walls."

"And the bed? I can't imagine that was there before."

I didn't see why she was making a fuss over the fact that there was a white bed with a headboard in the shape of a tiara in the room. "The double was too big for her. It made her feel scared, so I got that one."

"And the doona?"

My brows pinched together as I looked at the new pink blanket on the bed. "I couldn't exactly leave a double-sized doona on a single bed, could I?"

"And the teddy?"

"Fuck off. I told you when we had our little chat that I was going to try, didn't I?"

"See, there's the Declan I know and love to hate." Ruby laughed. "Did you cover up the whore slide while you were making the changes to Phoebe's room?"

"The what?"

"You know, the escape hatch to kick the girls out quickly in the morning. Did you board it up or just put a temporary cover on it?"

"I would have thought it was pretty fucking clear that part of me is done."

"Is it though? Really?"

"Seriously, Ruby, I—"

"I'm sorry that I find it hard to believe that you're willing to give up the life you were living down here. How do you go from screwing a different girl every night to being a faithful daddy overnight?"

"I made mistakes. Why won't everyone let me put that behind me?"

"You were an arse to Alyssa for four years. You can't expect everyone to forget that because you've been nice to her for a few short weeks."

Dropping her bag on the floor, I shoved one hand out to stop her from walking. "I don't know how I can make you understand if you're not willing to, but I could have a thousand women in my bed—"

"You probably have."

"And," I emphasised the word as I spoke over her, forcing her to let me continue, "not one of them would come close to satisfying me the way Lys does."

When Ruby grimaced at my words—no doubt thinking about her sister-in-law and me bumping uglies—I decided to dig the knife in a little more.

"The things she does to me." I moved closer to Ruby, boxing her in against the hallway wall. "The way she makes me feel. There's nothing else like it in the world."

"I—"

"But even Lys doesn't hold my heart half as much as that little girl. In a matter of weeks, she's twisted every preconceived notion I've ever had about being a father and left me willing to do anything to make her life better. Even if Lys wasn't everything I dreamed of, I'd be willing to try to do the right thing by her just to keep a smile on Phoebe's face. She makes me want to live better. To *be* better. That's all you and any of your family needs to know. And that's why I bought the goddamned fucking teddy bear."

She held her hands up in surrender. "Okay, I'll back off. Convincing Dad and Josh might be a bit harder though. I did try after our last chat."

"But they got to you." I pushed away from the wall and ran my fingers through my hair. "They convinced you that I was going to hurt her."

"This weekend. Are you really going to be honest with her?"

"Yes."

"Even if it hurts her?"

It was my turn to wince because there was a truth in her words that maybe she didn't fully understand. Every aspect of my life in Sydney had the potential to hurt Alyssa, and yet if Alyssa wanted the details, I would tell her. I didn't want secrets between us that could risk tearing us apart. "Yes."

"Even if it means she walks away at the end?"

The steel fingers of doubt and panic clawed at my chest, tearing into the parts of me that were still fragile and shattered. Still, there was only one answer. I swallowed, trying to dislodge the icy sensation, and nodded. "Yes." My voice was almost silent as I said the word.

"I guess all I can say then is good luck. Is this my room?" She reached for her bag with one hand as she pointed in the direction of the door across from the bathroom.

I nodded.

"I'll show myself to it."

Without another word, I stalked to my bedroom and sat on the bed. My hands lifted, tearing into my hair, and I buried my face against my palms as a growl ripped from my throat. With the stress already bumping around my body, I really hadn't needed Ruby's words.

"Hey, you." Alyssa's voice pulled me from my thoughts before they could spiral into self-loathing. I glanced up to see her leaning against the doorway. "Ready to go?"

Sucking down a steeling breath, I met her eye. "Yeah."

"Just before we do, there's something I need to tell you."

"What's that?" My heart hammered as I considered the possible bad news she might need to impart.

"Apparently, the CEO of W.T. Entertainment is Talia Wood."

"Paige Wood's daughter?" I leaned forward. *That* was an interesting piece of information. It was the link I'd needed to figure out why I'd been targeted—continued to be targeted. I'd been right in thinking it couldn't have been a coincidence. I'd known someone was playing a long game with me—I'd been correct in my suspicions that Wood was involved.

Despite her denials, she'd obviously exploited her own fucking daughter, Talia, to try to ruin me. Had she recruited her daughter's redheaded lover, Tillie, too? It made sense that the three of them might all be involved. If so, they'd played me like a fucking fiddle.

I wanted to get angry and exact revenge on them, but then I looked at Alyssa and my rage burned itself out. If not for that first article, I wouldn't have them back in my life. If not for the second—more scandalous—article, I would never have known how much faith Alyssa had in me or how strong I could actually be when tested. Maybe I'd given in to the depression, but I'd resisted the lure of the bottle. It was a fucking hard trial, but I had passed it.

It wasn't that I didn't long for revenge, but the understanding gave me the patience I needed to wait for it.

Still, the vindication that settled over me at the poetic justice that had been dealt to Paige grew with the revelation. She'd worked a campaign of fuckery to try to get me on her team, and had ended up heading into the silly season without any drivers. Served her bloody right.

Of course, there was still no way for me to prove that Talia was definitely the T the paparazzo had referred to. Or that Paige had anything to do with it all. At least, not without forking out a fortune for a private investigator and a good lawyer.

I knew the truth though, and that was worth something.

"There's something else too," Alyssa said.

"What?"

"Well, I had Dad do some searches a little deeper than what I could. And it turns out Matilda—"

"Who?"

"Um, Tillie, I think you called her."

The final tumbler in the lock slammed aside in my mind, opening to reveal the full picture. "She's Miss M, the writer, isn't she?"

Alyssa's eyes widened. "How did you know?"

"I didn't. It was a lucky guess, but it makes sense. Fuck. Why didn't I see it sooner? The three of them have been fucking with me since Bathurst. Maybe longer." I thought back to the other articles I'd seen on the *Gossip Weekly Online* website. None of them had been career-ending scandals, but they possibly could have been if I hadn't had Eden and Danny on my side. Had this been Paige's plan since the first time she courted me to drive for her?

"Do you think Tillie was the one that drugged you?"

I glanced up at her. "Who else? She had the access, the opportunity, and what better way to guarantee a story than to fabricate one?"

"Fucking bitch. God, if she was here right now, I'd tear out her fucking eyeballs."

"Language." I chuckled and grabbed Alyssa's waist. "Fuck, I love you, Lys, and I have to say it's almost cute when you threaten physical violence."

She swatted my shoulder lightly. "I guess there's not much we can do about them right now." She let loose a shaky breath. "Shall we get this show on the road?"

In an instant, I was at her side and leading her out of the room. On the way past Phoebe's room, I watched Alyssa's reaction. Her head turned to take in the refurbished space. A small, satisfied smile lifted the corners of her mouth, but she didn't say anything.

"Actually, there's one thing I want to do first," I said.

Alyssa gave me a smirk, as if she guessed what it might be.

"Hey, princess," I called down the stairs. "Come upstairs, I've got something to show you."

A few seconds later, I heard Phoebe's footsteps on the stairs.

"Yes, Daddy?" she asked as her head poked over the top of the stairs.

I knelt down in front of her bedroom door and waved her over to me. "Have a look."

She turned around and squealed. "It's purple." She looked around the room again before running into it. As she neared the bed, she looked back at me and made another excited little squeal. "Mummy, see it's purple! And there's a princess hat bed."

"I saw. The tiara bed is perfect, isn't it? Did Daddy do a great job or what?"

"Is that a little bit less scary?" I asked.

"It's not scary. It's pretty." She raced back to me and threw herself into my arms.

I picked her up and slung her onto my hip to carry her back downstairs. "I'm glad you like it."

Downstairs, we said goodbye to Phoebe and Ruby, and prepared our bags. Two nights away—alone and baring all. It was either going to be the best or worst weekend of my life. I couldn't see any in-between.

CHAPTER SIXTEEN

GETAWAY

THE DRIVE TO Bondi passed without a word between us. We were both lost in our own thoughts, and I wasn't willing to break the silence in the car. I wondered whether Alyssa was mentally tabulating a list of questions for me or if her mind was somewhere else entirely. Perhaps back with Phoebe and Ruby.

Once we arrived at the motel, I left Alyssa to check us in while I unloaded our bags from the boot of the car. I cast an eye over the exterior of the motel and my lips curled up in disgust. There was nothing wrong with it, per se; it was just a standard cut-price motel.

But that was exactly the issue.

It was so different to anything I'd stayed in recently. When the team was away from home, I had stayed in nothing less than five-star hotels. Perhaps that had made me a snob, but it was easy to get used to the finer things in life with Sinclair Racing. Now, though . . . I guessed I was going to have to get used to the not-so-finer things again. Having no income would change that attitude pretty damn quick.

I was glad when Alyssa appeared with the room key in hand,

cutting off my thoughts before they could spiral down into darkness.

After following Alyssa into our room, I dropped the bags on the floor. A quick glance around confirmed my assessment of what the room might be like. The faint scent of mould filled the air. The air-conditioning hummed so loud that it had to be at least ninety decibels. Even though the bed was a double, it looked like it was at least a foot shorter than the one I had at home, and it only had a thin wool blanket over the top sheet. The kitchenette, with mustard-yellow and tan tiles patterned with little daisies, looked like it was probably new in the seventies and hadn't been touched since.

Despite all of that, when I lifted my gaze to take in the view in front of me, I realised I was better off in the small space than I ever had been at any five-star hotel I'd ever stayed at previously. It was easily going to be my most pleasant stay anywhere, even with the plaid couch that looked less comfortable than a sack of potatoes.

The reason the room was better than any other was the one thing it contained that none of them had before: Alyssa.

I reached out and grabbed her wrist, tugging lightly to drag her into my hold. Without letting myself overthink it, I picked her up so that she was completely encased in my arms and buried my nose into the hair at her nape. In that moment, I needed to feel close to her—I needed to *be* close to her. I carried her across to the bed and laid her down on top of the blankets.

She curled herself into me, and I rested my chin on the top of her head.

I closed my eyes and just relished being near her. It was ridiculous how much I'd missed her in the week and a bit we'd been apart. After just enjoying our proximity for a while, I ran my hand up and down the length of her back. Although I'd meant it as a purely comforting gesture, Alyssa hummed into my chest in response to my touch. The sound travelled all the way to my dick, making it stand instantly at attention.

Alyssa shifted slightly, and I tipped my head down. Our mouths seemed to gravitate toward one another's without conscious thought. As her tongue swept across my bottom lip, I groaned and shifted us both so that I was lying on top of her.

I still hadn't opened my eyes and part of me was concerned that perhaps I had fallen asleep and was dry-humping the air, thinking I was with Alyssa. The image made me chuckle.

"What's so funny?" Alyssa asked with a hushed voice, breaking the contact I had with her sweet, sweet mouth.

At first, I shook my head to dismiss the question. But then remembered the rules of the weekend: no unanswered questions; no withheld information. "I was worried this might all be a dream. That I might wake to find I'd been assaulting you while we slept."

She smirked a little at me. "I wouldn't complain if you were."

"I'll remember that tonight." I ducked to capture her lips again, my mouth eager and desperate. One hand trailed through her hair in soft strokes. Each movement of my fingers against her scalp elicited another small moan of desire.

The urge to be closer to her built in me. I wanted to crawl inside her and take up residence. What we were starting wasn't necessarily the intention for the weekend, at least not explicitly, but I didn't care. In that moment, I didn't need questions or answers. I needed *her*.

Judging by the way she kissed me back, and by the way her hips lurched forward to brush against mine, the feeling was completely mutual.

My fingers found the hem of her shirt as my tongue brushed against hers. In unison, we sat up so that I could slide her shirt up her chest. As one, we broke off our contact so that I could sweep the cotton tee up over her head. Our lips met again as my hands roamed her body.

Her fingers curled around the buttons on my shirt one by one, undoing them in a rhythm that matched the dance of our tongue. Her hands caressed my chest through the opening she'd created. My eyes rolled back as her fingers dropped to clasp my cock through my shorts.

Spurred on by her actions, I pushed her skirt up to reveal her panties while she yanked down the fly on my shorts. Barely minutes after I'd initiated the kiss, I was undressed and wrapped around a naked goddess. Once I had her beneath me, naked and writhing—waiting for me to make a move—I slowed down. I needed her desperately, but I didn't want to just fuck her senseless. I wanted to make love to her—slow and sweet.

It might have made me a pussy, but it was also the one thing that we alone shared. In all my experience, I'd never made love to another woman. I'd only fucked. It may have been semantics, but in my heart and head there was a big difference. I'd screwed around and I'd used women for my own benefit. My mind and heart had been absent as I'd let my dick take control.

But not with Alyssa. With Alyssa every part of me wanted to be near every part of her. I wanted to enjoy not only her pussy, but every inch of her beautiful body. All of her perfections and imperfections. Everything that made her *her*.

Working my way down her body with my hands and mouth, my fingers found her nipples. A soft growl left me. A moment later, I claimed one with my mouth. She arched her back and gave a cry of unadulterated passion. The smouldering gaze she gave me when I looked up her body to meet her eyes proved how desperate she was for me. Without breaking eye contact, I dipped one hand down between her legs and brushed my fingers across her arousal.

Fuck. She was so wet and ready for me.

Her hips bucked up to meet my touch as her eyes drifted closed. Tension coiled in her body, giving away her desires. I could read her like a book; read every inch of skin as she longed to be touched.

"Declan, please!" She half-sat and reached for my hips, the fingernails of one hand grazing over my arse. With her other hand, she reached for my head and tugged me closer to her so that she could claim my lips.

Taking her obvious hint, I lined myself up and pushed into her. The hiss of pleasure that rushed from her lips was music to my fucking ears. My movements were unhurried inside her as my mouth explored her neck, chin, and breasts.

She panted my name as her body tensed beneath me, spurring me on.

"I love you, Alyssa," I whispered as I moved back to meet her gaze.

Alyssa looked up at me with a smile beaming on her lips, and the sight made my heart clench. There was nothing I wouldn't do for this woman.

I dropped my forehead to her shoulder as my thrusts became harder and deeper. My lips found her body. My teeth gazed across her smooth skin, sinking into her shoulder as I pushed myself as far into her as our bodies would allow.

Her lips blew soft breaths across my ear as she whispered her devotion to me.

Raising myself up onto my elbows, I took a moment to revel in her subtle beauty. Desperation grew in me to drink in every feature, as if it were my last opportunity to see her like this. I tried not to linger on the fact that it could be, because the doubt would ruin the moment.

Resting my forehead against hers, I pushed my hips forward harder, getting deeper and more aggressive with each thrust. In turn, her hips bucked back against me faster and faster.

Her eyes closed as her back arched, and her mouth formed a delicious O as the muscles of her thighs began to tighten in anticipation of things to come.

I felt myself coming undone too, and I knew it wouldn't take much for me to fall.

When I kissed her lips again, Alyssa came around me. Her walls clenched and released around my length. The sensation was my undoing. I gave one last grunt as I followed.

After the last tremors of my orgasm stilled, I dropped onto the bed beside her, dragging her with me so she stayed in my arms.

Neither of us moved for the longest time. Moving would be taking that first step toward the difficult conversations we anticipated sharing this weekend.

Anticipated but feared—at least in my case.

Eventually, she sighed and shifted, indicating a desire to get up. When she climbed out of the bed, she headed straight for the bathroom and started the shower. Because she'd left the door open,

I was able to watch as she climbed under the stream, sending rivers of water flowing over her breasts and down the length of her legs. Water cascaded along her beautiful body, and the sight was too much for me.

I practically leapt out of bed to join her. Unable to suppress the desire she raised in me, I took her in my arms under the warm stream. With her in my hold, it was easy to caress her body and lavish her mouth with soft kisses.

Anxiety built in the pit of my stomach, and I wanted to get the hard part of our isolation out of the way. There was never going to be a right time, so I just took a deep breath and launched into the first question. One that had been burning at the back of my mind since the race meeting that had started my downward spiral. Since the day I'd seen her in the arms of Flynn, and the fires of jealousy were stoked deep within me.

I knew now that he was gay, but the image still gave me pause.

"How many have there been?" I asked as I kissed along her collarbone.

"What?" she asked the ceiling, her voice little more than a soft pant.

"How many ... men?" I asked, adding the last word almost silently against her skin.

"You're asking me this now?" she asked, disbelief evident in her tone.

I rubbed the tip of my nose along the curve of her neck as I whispered, "It's what this weekend was supposed to be about, right?"

"Ugh! Yes, but ... *now*?"

A soft chuckle left my lips and brushed her skin, raising a small trail of goosebumps.

"Fine." She turned off the water and stepped out of the shower. She handed me a towel before wrapping one around herself as she walked back out and sat on the end of the bed. She was quiet as she dried herself off, and I could understand why. It wasn't the sort of conversation you had dressed in nothing more than a towel. I pulled on a pair of boxers and my shorts before sitting on the bed beside her. When I did, she rested her head on my shoulder. I assumed the position was so that she didn't have to look at me while she spoke, but it left me comforted by her touch, so that was fine by me.

"You don't have to tell me if you don't want to," I murmured. Although she was the one who'd suggested no unanswered questions, I was willing to let her off the hook if she didn't want to answer it. The truth was, since asking the question I was more anxious than ever to learn the truth.

"No. We said everything on the table, right? That means for both of us." She moved her head a little, kissing my throat. I wrapped my arm around her, and she snuggled against my chest. "I didn't even try dating until after the twins. And then, well, I attempted a few times. For a while at least. Not a lot, just some nights out after uni and things like that. It was all too hard though. So many guys just wanted an easy lay and nothing else, you know?"

I flinched at her words because that was me. That was who I'd been for so long.

"Oh, Dec, I didn't mean . . ." She trailed off.

"You did." I twisted so I could gather her completely in my hold. "Remember, we promised honesty."

"Okay, maybe I did. But I never wanted that. Sex without emotion. It's just not me."

"I know, Lys. And now, I can see why." I caressed her cheek and lifted her chin so she'd meet my gaze. "It's better when it comes from here." I pressed my hand over her heart.

She clasped my hand and lifted it to her lips. When she dropped it again, she wore a small smile. "In the end, outside of a couple of sloppy end-of-date kisses, there was only really Cain."

Cain—Flynn's brother. She'd told me a little about their relationship previously.

"Did you ever . . ." I wanted to ask whether she had fucked him, but the question stuck in my throat.

She seemed to understand anyway and shook her head. "No. I mean, we weren't completely celibate, but we never—" She cut off and sighed. "You're the only one I—" She chuckled darkly. "Why is this so hard?"

It was hard watching her struggle. It was harder listening to her talk about being with other guys—even though I was the one who'd asked the question. Now that the conversation had started though, I could see the advantage behind getting everything out in the open and moving forward with no secrets. There wouldn't need to be any lingering doubts over what happened to each of us during our time apart.

As her words settled over me, relief and joy bubbled up within me. It was absolutely fucking hypocritical of me, considering how many girls I'd been with while we were apart, but I couldn't help but be glad that I was the only one who had known her carnally. It wouldn't have made me think less of her if she'd slept with a hundred guys, but I still felt a little bit of tension leave my body with the knowledge that she hadn't.

"Will you . . ." She trailed off before sucking in a deep breath. "Will you tell me what happened after you left?"

I nodded. "It's a long story though." I pulled her up the bed and lay down with her in my arms, her head tucked against my shoulder.

Before I could second-guess my words, I began my story of a dark descent into drugs, alcohol, and screwing random women. Shifting as far away from Alyssa as I could without actually letting her go, I dropped my head back and whispered my tale to the ceiling. I was unable to meet her eyes for fear of seeing the disappointment I was certain would be buried beneath the honey-gold surface. I told her the story of the nightclubs and strip clubs. I held nothing back, explaining how Eden had saved me—how she'd prevented me from going to work under the influence. In the middle of my explanation, I told her about my recent discovery that Danny knew all along.

I didn't stop there.

I launched straight into my train wreck of a life. Without pause, I told Alyssa all of my secrets. The fact that she'd haunted my dreams, making me unable to sleep. How whenever I was finally able to find rest, I was subjected to nightmares of our break-up strong enough to render me helpless. Of how I spent so many nights cowering under my blankets, hiding from her memory until I would finally throw them off and go in search of alcohol or tablets to numb the pain I felt in my chest. How I began to rely on sleeping tablets to get the bare minimum sleep I needed to function.

Without waiting for her disapproval or rejection, I moved straight on to the details of my sessions with Dr. Henrikson. The things we'd covered and what I hadn't told him. The way he'd guided me through rehab for what could have easily grown into a serious drug addiction. How we'd ended the relationship when I'd thrown a temper tantrum in his office over his refusal to listen when I'd said Alyssa was off limits. She moved closer to me after the admission, laying her head on my chest. She'd already known she was the reason I was back in contact with him, but she hadn't known she'd also been the cause of our rift.

Her silence was no doubt simply her rapt attention, but it scared the hell out of me anyway. I worried that the instant I stopped talking, she would leap from my arms in disgust at the things I admitted to doing.

So I didn't stop.

I confessed that everything I'd constructed, every lie I'd told myself to stay sane, had fallen apart when I'd seen her in Flynn's arms at Queensland Raceway. How from that day forward memories of her filled my waking hours too. How I'd seen visions of her during every race and that my regret over letting her go — giving her the chance to move on and be happy with someone else — was the reason I had crashed so often.

Holding on to her shoulders to ground me, I barely took a breath before recapping how I felt seeing her on the flight to London and how the night we'd had "sex without strings" had been one of the lowest points in my entire life. Not because of what we'd shared, just because she'd left the room — left *me* — moments after I'd finally realised how much she actually meant to me.

Trying to reassure her that it wasn't all negative, I told her about the first time I saw Phoebe. How in just a few hours, our daughter had been able to twist herself through every piece of my heart, weaving between the broken pieces to become the thread that held them all back together again. And how I'd felt when Alyssa had granted me the chance to be in their lives permanently.

Finally, when I had nothing left to say, I felt truly exorcised. I expelled a breath and waited. The demons I'd long grown used to in my mind were finally silenced. They'd had their voices heard, and Alyssa was still at my side. There were no doubts left in me. No little niggling warning telling me to run from Alyssa or worrying about what the attraction to her meant for me.

I kissed the top of her head before pulling myself from her arms and standing. With the strange peace filling me, I went into my bag and grabbed a letter I had brought with me. For the first time since I'd started my story, I met her gaze. By sharing the words I'd written, I was revealing the most vulnerable parts of myself.

Her face showed signs of concern and worry. Her eyes were slightly reddened from the tears that had been welling and quite possibly falling as I'd spoken. I wasn't sure whether the tears were the result of some pity she felt for me or whether my confessions had caused her genuine pain. Either way, I wanted them to be the last ones I caused her, even though I knew they probably wouldn't be.

I handed her the letter. "I want you to read this. I wrote it after I found out you'd left Brisbane. When I thought you'd left because you thought I'd cheated on you."

My heart pounded somewhere in my throat as I watched her eyes scan the page. A range of emotions flitted across her face as she read the words I'd wanted so desperately to tell her at the time. Words I'd worried could never convey the depth of my sorrow at the thought of losing her and Phoebe.

In the days that followed her dash to Sydney, we hadn't talked about anything more than my absolute pleasure in seeing her again and my devastation over losing my position on the Sinclair Racing team. Alyssa had stayed in Sydney for such a short amount of time that we didn't really have the opportunity to reflect on the past—only look to the future. The thought had occurred to me at the time to show her what I had written during what was without doubt the darkest period in my life, but I didn't think I could open myself up like that.

Once she'd talked about the weekend of getting it all out, I knew she had to know what I'd felt. If there was anything that could convince her how much I felt for her—how desperately I wanted her as a permanent part of my life—it was that letter.

After she had finished reading, she stared intently at the page. "Dec, it's . . . I . . ." She trailed off and took a deep breath. She looked up at me. The warmth and desire reflected in her eyes was obvious, even through her fresh tears. "I love you."

I knew then that regardless of what happened next, we would be all right.

CHAPTER SEVENTEEN

UNITED FRONT

FOR THE REST of our weekend, Alyssa and I talked a little but fucked a lot. Whenever a question popped into her head, she'd ask it, but having the cathartic start left us free to spend the time exploring each other's bodies rather than our emotions. By the time lunch rolled around on the Saturday, we were treating the motel room as clothing optional, only dressing long enough to get food to take back to the motel.

"I'm so glad you suggested this weekend," I said as I curled up behind her, cupping her arse with my hand. The instant the words were free, I nipped at her neck.

She tipped her head back so that I could explore more. "You're insatiable. You know that, right?"

I chuckled. She was only saying that because we'd only finished our last session minutes earlier—me taking her from behind over the end of the bed. It didn't matter though, my cock was already starting to stir once again. "Well, after you leave on Monday, who knows how long it'll be before I see you again. I'm getting my fill."

She rolled over in my arms, pressing her breasts against my

chest. "I don't want to think about it."

"Me either. Let's just think about this instead," I said as I kissed her neck.

"You'll have to come up for Christmas."

My lips trailed over her collarbone, peppering kisses over her skin. "That's weeks away still."

"Come up sooner then. It's not like you've got anything you need to do urgently here."

I pulled away with a grimace. "Don't remind me."

Failure. Jobless. Arsehole. The words raced each other through my brain, each jostling for position so that it could be the one to do the most damage.

She cupped her hands around my face, drawing my lips to hers and stopping the words in their tracks. "It'll work out."

"How?"

"Well, have you thought about what you want to do?"

"You?" I nuzzled my face against her neck.

"C'mon, be serious. What else can you see yourself doing?"

Reluctantly, I rolled away from her and stared at the ceiling while I contemplated my answer. "I'd like to still be at the track . . . somehow. It was the one thing that kept me going over the years. I know you probably think it's what kept me from you, but really it's what kept me sane. Or at least, as sane as I was. It just feels like home, you know?"

Instead of arguing or trying to persuade me of a different career choice, Alyssa simply asked, "Well, what other positions are there?"

"Race controller, but I don't have enough experience to do that. Then there are all the tech guys, but those positions all involve qualifications I don't have."

"What else?"

I hummed as I considered my options. "There's the pit crew."

"But?"

"Well, they're crack teams. It's not like you can just walk onto the team with no experience. Besides, there's still the issue of the scandal hanging over my head."

"Maybe we need to fight fire with fire," she said.

"What do you mean?"

"I wasn't going to say anything, because I wasn't really considering it, but I had *Woman's Idea* contact me the other day."

"What?"

"They wanted to get my side of the story, apparently. They'd done a little digging and knew about Emmanuel. They found out a little about the history and thought I'd been portrayed a little too negatively."

At the mention of our son's name, stillness settled over us. I'd been moving my lips over her body before, but in that moment, I stopped and pulled her body closer to mine to offer my comfort.

"They seemed willing to do a more balanced article. Maybe we can offer them an exclusive in exchange for final editorial approval."

I frowned. "But you didn't want to do it."

"Not alone, but, Dec, I meant what I said about presenting a united front. Maybe this is a chance to do that. I hadn't really thought about suggesting it to them until now, but how good would it be to have the truth out there? Our truth. To be able to shove the lies back in the faces of all of those bastards who were so willing to sell you out?" She sounded almost desperate to have it done.

I had to admit her plan had some merit. "It's all about the spin," I murmured. It was what Paige Wood had said to me when she'd been trying to persuade me to join her race team.

"Exactly. Maybe it'll be the start of making you into someone that the sponsors clamour to get behind. You know if you can do that, you'll have all the teams banging on your door."

"All except the one I want."

"You don't know that."

"I know Danny. His pride will stop him from getting me back on the track, even if I had a thousand corporate backers all lined up and ready."

"Why do you want back on Sinclair Racing so badly then?"

"It's hard to explain, but it's like a family. He's been more of a father to me in the last four years than my dad has. Being dumped the way I was, it fucking hurt, but you can't hate your family even when they hurt you." *Mostly.* My father was one exception.

"Have you tried explaining that to Mr. Sinclair?"

I laughed. "No. And our last conversation didn't go much better than the one where he fired me."

"Maybe you should?"

"Maybe." It was more an automated response than an agreement.

"Will you?"

"I don't know," I admitted.

"So your pride won't allow you to go back, even though you say it's the perfect workplace?"

I chuckled. "Touché."

"On Monday, I'll talk to the reporter who called me the other day. I'll see if they're still interested."

"Okay, and I'll call Danny and tell him I want back in even if it means cleaning the fucking toilets." I really hoped it wouldn't mean that. "Who knows if he'll listen though."

AROUND MIDNIGHT on Saturday night, Alyssa's phone rang. And then kept ringing. It took a moment for her to wake enough to reach for it. The ringtone shut off seconds before her groggy voice whispered, "Hello?"

A second later, she sat bolt upright and threw the covers off. Her voice grew panicked, but I was still too sleepy to understand the rushed words as she moved around the motel.

She threw some clothes at me before wiggling into her own.

"Get up, we're leaving," she said to me before turning her attention back to the phone.

I did as I was instructed, trying to figure out what the hell was going on.

While I struggled to wake up fully and get my pants back on, she dashed around the room packing everything back into our bags. Her hands moved constantly, throwing the items into haphazard piles.

After another moment, she disconnected the call and threw her mobile down onto the bed.

"What is it? What's up?" I asked, my voice deeper than usual because of the vestiges of sleep clinging to my vocal cords.

She threw my keys at me. "It's Phoebe."

CHAPTER EIGHTEEN

FULLY SICK

WITHIN TEN MINUTES of the call waking us, we were in the car heading back home. I left the motel room key in the after-hours box, together with a note to explain our speedy departure and leaving my number in case there were any dramas.

"She'll be okay." I reached across the car and placed my hand on Alyssa's knee before giving it a small, reassuring squeeze.

"I know. I just hate it when she's sick. I worry it's going to be the one thing that sets her back. I can't lose her, Dec. I just can't."

"What did Ruby say was wrong?" I hadn't been able to get that out of her yet; all she'd said was that Phoebe needed her and we had to go home.

"Phoebe's been vomiting for the last hour and her temp is close to forty."

"And forty's bad?"

"Yeah, Dec," she snapped. "Forty's pretty fucking bad."

"She'll be okay," I said again.

"You can't know that. I shouldn't have left her. I shouldn't have gone away."

It was clear Alyssa wasn't in any position to be reasonable. "We'll be home soon, okay?"

For the rest of the drive home, I whispered reassurances to Alyssa. I was sure she didn't want to hear them, but I couldn't let the time pass in silence either. Especially when she was panicking. I just wished I was enough to cut her panic in half the way she did for me.

The instant I pulled the car into my garage, before I'd even killed the ignition, she was out of the car and running for the house.

Leaving our bags where they were in the boot, I followed her inside. I found her at the top of the stairs drawing Phoebe into her embrace.

"Mummy, I don't feel good."

"I know, sweetie. Aunty Ruby called me and let me know, so I came straight home. Where do you hurt?"

Phoebe's response was to hurl over Alyssa's shoulder. Seeming to sense my gaze on her, Alyssa turned to me. "Can you get me some towels and a wet face washer?" When I didn't move instantly, she huffed out a breath. "Please?"

Not knowing what else to do in the face of an obviously sick child, I followed her instructions. I was running the face washer under the tap in the bathroom sink when Ruby found me.

"I'm sorry for cutting your weekend short," she said, with something that almost resembled a friendly smile gracing her lips.

"It's okay. You don't have kids of your own so I guess it would be hard to know how to cope." Fuck knows I didn't have a clue.

"Are you fucking kidding me?" She yanked the washer out of my hands and snarled at me. "Alyssa packs a small chemist for Phoebe everywhere she goes. Between that and what's between my ears, I have all I need to look after a sick child. But if I hadn't called and Alyssa found out Phoebe had been sick, I would never have heard the end of it. That is the *only* reason I called her."

She stalked off before I could say anything more. I wasn't sure what had caused her turnaround, but all niceties had been wiped away in an instant. "Well, fuck you very much too," I muttered as I grabbed the dry towels from the linen cupboard.

By the time I got back to Alyssa, she had Phoebe lying down in my bed with the wet face washer over her forehead. When I walked into the room, Phoebe hurled again. She sat up and aimed for the container Alyssa had, but still managed to coat the bedding and mattress in vomit. I tried not to think about how expensive the carpet in the room was, or how much the deluxe mattress had cost, and concentrated instead on the sick little girl leaning into Alyssa's embrace.

I offered the towels to Alyssa, who took them and made a little shield around herself and Phoebe.

"How are you feeling?" I asked Phoebe.

When she turned her gaze to me, the sight shattered my heart. Her doleful gaze and small pout made her appear like a completely different child from the one I knew.

"Her temp is coming down," Alyssa said. "Ruby gave her some Panadol before we got home. Hopefully her stomach will settle soon, and I've got some Hydralyte in her bag for her to sip on once it has. Ruby's making it up now."

I nodded. "Is there anything I can do?"

Alyssa shook her head. "Not at the moment."

Feeling like I was intruding, even though it was my bedroom, I stood to leave.

"Where are you going?" Alyssa asked.

"I just thought you'd want to be alone with her."

"You're not going anywhere, buddy. You can lie down with us. That'll make her feel better. Won't it, sweetheart?"

With her lip still pouted, and quivering slightly, Phoebe met my gaze and nodded. Climbing onto a bed with vomit on the sheets wasn't exactly something I wanted to do—even if it wasn't the first time I'd done it—but because Phoebe needed me, I shifted onto the bed on the other side of her, away from the towels covering the puddle that still needed to be cleaned up, leaving her sandwiched between us.

"This won't make her too hot?" I asked.

Alyssa shook her head. "Just give her space and she'll be fine."

Using the wet washer, Alyssa wiped Phoebe's brow. Phoebe

whimpered and cuddled into her a little more. Feeling useless that I couldn't do something more, I just rubbed my fingers along Phoebe's arm and whispered to her that I was there as well.

Even though it wasn't anything life-threatening—at least I hoped to God it wasn't—I felt helpless. More than anything, I wanted to have some magic cure that would make her better. I marvelled at Alyssa's strength once more. She'd dealt with Phoebe in hospital, with her practically on her deathbed. I couldn't even begin to comprehend how constantly terrifying that must have been. How would I have coped if I'd been there? I wasn't sure I would have.

Within a minute, Phoebe was dozing. Once she'd drifted off completely, Alyssa towelled her down and removed her wet clothes before slipping her into a fresh nightie. Watching her work, doing so much with only one hand because the other was still tucked around Phoebe, I was amazed. She was some sort of fucking natural at it all.

"I'll change the sheets in a minute too," Alyssa said.

All I could do was nod.

When Ruby brought in a clear sippy cup filled with an orange liquid a few minutes later, she didn't say anything. She slammed the cup onto my bedside table. With her eyes narrowed, she gave me such a glare my dick shrivelled away to protect himself from the beating promised in her ice-blue stare, before leaving the room again.

"What did you say to her?" Alyssa whispered.

"Nothing. Why?"

"Something happened when you were getting the towels to put her in the foulest mood I've seen in . . . well, in a very long time."

"And you think it's something I said?"

"I'm just going from history, Dec. She's never been your biggest fan. Although, I had thought you were winning her around."

"She just apologised for interrupting our weekend."

"And?"

"And nothing. I said it was okay because she couldn't expect to know how to deal with a sick kid when she didn't have any."

"Are you serious?" Alyssa's gaze flashed with something not entirely dissimilar to the glare Ruby had given me. My hand dropped to protect my balls because I was sure they were going to be ripped off or kicked or something based on that look. Especially with two out of the three other people in the house giving it to me.

"What?"

"You can't say things like that."

"Like what?"

"Saying that she doesn't know how to be a mother just because she doesn't have kids."

"But—"

"She's been there for Phoebe from day one. I couldn't even count the number of nights she came over to take a shift in Phoebe's room and forced me to get some sleep."

"I—I didn't know."

"And she and Josh have been trying for a baby for years. It's not by choice that she doesn't have children."

"Oh." I chewed on the inside of my cheek as I considered what Alyssa was saying, and the repercussions of my thoughtless words.

"Yeah, *oh*. It's no wonder she's so upset."

"I'll try to make it up to her."

"You can't tell her I told you about not being able to get pregnant."

"So I have to apologise for something without telling her what I'm apologising for?"

Alyssa chuckled. "Something like that. Can you take her for a moment?" She gently coaxed Phoebe to roll into my arms.

Once I had our daughter wrapped in my arms and settled again, Alyssa got up and expertly stripped the dirty sheets off most of the bed without spreading the mess that the towels had covered. With a few hand gestures and nods, she directed me to move just right so that she removed the sheets completely without having to get Phoebe out of bed. A few minutes later, she brought in another clean face washer and wiped Phoebe down once more. On her next trip, she brought up a blue-and-white box of white powder.

"It's bicarb. It's for the smell," she explained.

I wondered where the hell she pulled it from, but figured it was probably something from Christina's supplies. She sprinkled the bicarb powder over the slightly damp patches on my mattress before laying down another fresh towel and putting a fresh set of sheets down. I had to lift Phoebe out of the bed to let her spread them out, but I was able to do that without waking her.

"You still all right with her?" Alyssa asked as I laid Phoebe down again.

I nodded.

"When she wakes, have her sip on the Hydralyte." Alyssa pointed at the cup. "But just sips. We don't want to overload her stomach."

"Okay."

"I'm going to check on Ruby and then have a quick shower. Call me if you need a hand."

"Sure thing."

At some point, I must have drifted off to sleep because the next thing I knew, Phoebe was calling to me.

"Daddy." One of her hands pushed my shoulder. It wasn't enough force to shift me, but it roused me from my sleep.

I grunted, trying to figure out where I was and why she was rocking my shoulder. After a few blinks, my eyes had adjusted to the darkness. When Phoebe met my gaze, her eyes sparkled through the darkness. Instead of the pout which had been present before she'd fallen asleep, her lips were curled into a little smile.

"How are you feeling?" I asked. Sleep still strangled my voice so I cleared my throat and started again. "Better than before?"

"Little bit."

"Mummy wanted you to drink a little of this," I said as I reached for the cup, wondering where said mummy was.

Taking the handles on the cup in her hands, Phoebe took a big gulp of the drink.

"Just little sips. You don't want to get sick again, do you?"

She shook her head and offered me the drink back again.

I took the cup off her and put it back on the bedside table.

She snuggled against my chest. "I missed you, Daddy," she

murmured sleepily before settling back to sleep again.

I fell asleep again soon after and the next time I woke, the muted early-morning light crept around the barrier of the curtains. My arm was above my head with Alyssa's hand wrapped around mine. Between our bodies, Phoebe lay on her back, fast asleep with her mouth hanging open a little.

My gaze slid between my two girls. Despite the interruptions during the weekend, it had been helpful. It had helped solidify a few things for me—namely the lengths I would go to in order to keep my girls happy, safe, and healthy. I would walk to the ends of the Earth over broken glass just to make either of them smile.

I would do any job, take any role, if it meant I could provide for them the way I was supposed to.

Taking care not to wake either of them, I climbed out of the bed and grabbed clothes to change into.

After I'd showered and changed, I headed downstairs for an early breakfast. Sitting at the table, with a steaming mug of what I assumed was coffee in front of her, was Ruby. She glanced up at me as I approached, but didn't say anything.

"About last night . . ." I trailed off because I wasn't sure what to say or how to word it. "I didn't mean what I said. It was thoughtless."

With a wave of her hand, she tried to tell me it was okay, but I wouldn't be deterred.

"I mean it, Ruby. I know you've been there for both Alyssa and Phoebe when I wasn't. I won't ever be able to thank you enough for that. The entire fucking support network she had makes it a little easier to forgive myself for the shit I did to her."

"Do you really think you deserve forgiveness?"

I wasn't sure whether she meant for the unintentional hurt I'd inflicted with my words or for my misdeeds in the time after Alyssa left. Either way, my answer was the same. "I don't know, but I'm willing to do everything I can to earn it."

"Alyssa told you about Josh and me. Didn't she?"

I could have denied it, pleaded innocence and possibly avoided dumping Alyssa in the mess, but for all I knew, they'd had a deep and meaningful conversation last night and Ruby knew all the details. I was damned either way. "She mentioned something briefly, but no details."

Ruby nodded.

"Are you upset with her?" Seeing that I wasn't in any immediate danger of having my balls cut off, I moved into the kitchen to make some breakfast while we continued our conversation.

She shook her head. "No. How else could she have explained my reaction? I know it wasn't entirely rational. But . . . I don't know. It's a little hard to explain to someone who's never been in the situation. It's just something that I've wanted for the longest time. To fail month after month would be like you getting kitted up for a race, event after event, and every time you make it to the car you're called back to the pits and told that this isn't the right race for you. That maybe you'll get your chance at the next event."

A bark of laughter ripped from my lips as I pressed down the toaster.

In response to my chuckle, she frowned at me and tilted her head in confusion.

"Did you just describe bumping uglies with Josh as an event?" I asked.

She joined my laughter. "Well, it fits."

So that the image her words called to mind didn't stick, I concentrated on my memory of Alyssa in a race suit. With that picture in my head, and no more laughter on my lips, I started the conversation again. "Look, I don't know anything about making babies."

Her laughter grew into a howl and I realised what I'd inadvertently said.

"Wait, I take that back. I know plenty about what it takes to make babies, but usually I try to avoid making babies when I do it."

Her nose curled up and her lips twisted as though she'd just tasted something unpleasant. "When did we get to the stage that it was okay to discuss our sex lives?"

"Sometime between vacations and vomit, I think." A smile

grew on my lips as I buttered my newly popped toast.

A fresh chuckle slipped from between her lips. "I'll deny it if you ever tell anyone, but I actually don't mind this new you."

After spreading a thin layer of vegemite over the butter, I turned around and met Alyssa's questioning gaze. She had a sleepy but seemingly better Phoebe in her arms. I nodded to let her know everything was okay.

"You won't be able to deny it," I said to Ruby. "There are witnesses." I indicated Alyssa and Phoebe.

"Witnesses to what?" Alyssa asked, winking at Ruby.

"Oh, I see how it is. All the hens in the house ganging up on the lone cock."

"Rooster," Alyssa said the instant after the last *K* sound crossed my lips. "They're called roosters in our house."

Phoebe peeked her head out from where she was hiding against Alyssa's neck and crowed like a rooster.

"And that's why they're roosters," Alyssa said.

With things mostly squared with Ruby, I sat with Phoebe on my lap and ate my breakfast while Alyssa prepared some plain toast for Phoebe.

"Did you tell Declan about that cow?" Ruby said.

Phoebe made a mooing sound, but I didn't pay much attention because there was something in the way Ruby asked her question that made me think there was something Alyssa had intended to tell me during our weekend of truths that we either hadn't got to—or she'd chickened out and not said it.

"What cow?"

"That girl," Ruby said.

It didn't slip my notice that Alyssa hadn't said anything. When I looked at her, she was studying the light spread of butter over Phoebe's toast with attention greater than it really warranted. "What's her name?" Ruby continued. "D something. Da . . . Dar—"

"Darcy?" The name slipped from between my teeth.

The butter knife in Alyssa's hand clattered to the bench as I said the name, confirming that Darcy had done something else to hurt Alyssa.

"That's the one," Ruby said. "Nasty piece of work, she is."

I nodded, wondering if she knew the half of it. Did Ruby know that I'd had a one-night stand with Darcy? That Darcy had then lorded that over Alyssa?

"What did she do?" I wanted to get up and offer Alyssa some comfort, but it was hard with Phoebe on my lap, and I didn't want to jostle Phoebe around too much, considering the night she'd had.

Alyssa dropped the plate of toast in front of Ruby. "Phoebe, sweetheart, can you sit with Aunt Ruby while I talk to Daddy for a moment?"

Taking my cue, I carried Phoebe around the table and placed her in Ruby's lap. By the time I'd done that, Alyssa had already left the room.

"She's getting back at me for telling you she can't have kids," Alyssa said when I approached her.

"What?" I'd thought we were going to be talking about Darcy, so Alyssa's words confused me.

"Ruby. I told her last night that I'd let her situation slip to you."

A relieved sigh slipped from me that I hadn't lied to Ruby. It would have caused more trouble if she'd known the truth the whole time. The Ruby situation wasn't the one I was worried about though.

"What happened with Darcy?"

"She's just doing everything she can to make my life hell. It started when she saw me at the Grand Plaza after I got home from here. She just kept talking about how you were already bored with me and that was why I was back in Browns Plains while you were still in Sydney."

My jaw snapped shut at her words. I should have known Alyssa going home alone would fuel more rumours. "And?" I asked through clenched teeth.

"And she came into work to hunt down copies of last week's *Gossip Weekly*. I had to serve her and watch as she opened every single page of that damned article on each and every copy so she could make sure it was all there. All while discussing the article in great detail and pointing out all the reasons why you'd gotten bored with me. It meant that most of my regular customers found out about everything even if they've never picked up a gossip mag before. Worse, she comes into the shop every few days now. It's like she's decided my shop is the only one she can go to when she needs something, even though it's not the closest one to her home. Of course, I can't say anything to my boss because the customer is always right."

"Bitches like that will get their comeback," I said. "Why didn't you tell me?"

"It wasn't important. It won't be long before I'll be leaving and then I won't have to see her again."

"But that's still weeks away. Are you just going to put up with it until then?"

"A snotty bitch bent out of shape because you won't screw her again is hardly the worst thing I've had to deal with." Her gaze dropped to the floor.

"Fuck, of course it's not. But that doesn't mean you have to put up with it, either. What happened to the girl I knew, the one who dragged Darcy down onto the school oval just because she gave me a Valentine?"

Alyssa's gaze shifted up to mine as the hint of a smile graced her lips. "You know, I'd forgotten about that."

"If I hadn't already been mad about you before then, I think that would have been the moment that cemented it for me."

"Except we broke up that afternoon."

"You broke up with me, not the other way around."

She laughed. "God, we were crazy weren't we?"

I cupped her cheek and moved so my mouth was inches from hers. "I'm sure I've still got a bit of crazy in me." I claimed her lips. Even though I did crave her, I kissed her for another reason. I wanted to change the subject. It wasn't that I wanted Darcy to get away with what she was doing—in fact, I wanted to make sure she paid. I didn't want to tip Alyssa off to that fact, though, because if I did, she might tell me not to. I wouldn't go against her wishes if she asked me not to do something, but what she didn't know wouldn't hurt her. I just had to think of the perfect plan.

CHAPTER NINETEEN

SUCK IT UP

AFTER WE DROPPED Ruby off at the airport, Alyssa, Phoebe, and I went for a walk along the beach to get some fresh air. The whole time, Alyssa watched Phoebe like a hawk, looking for any sign that she was going to be sick again.

I was relieved to notice that I'd apparently lost my lone stalker photographer. Either he'd decided that I wasn't worth following anymore, or T had recalled him for some reason. I had no idea which, but I was happy for the break. Overall, it was the best fucking day I'd had in a while.

It was clear even to me what made the day so different from the others I'd faced in the last week. Life just wasn't complete without my family near me. Maybe that made me a sap, but I was the happiest fucking sap in the world.

After getting our fill of fresh air, we headed back to the car and I saw that I wasn't as lucky as I'd assumed. The pap was there, leaning against a white X-Trail and grinning at me. Knowing that what he wanted more than anything was a picture of me reacting in a negative way, I tuned him out and focused on Phoebe and Alyssa.

When I reversed the car out, he was right behind me. All I wanted to do was put my foot to the floor to try to lose him, but I knew there wasn't much point. He knew where I lived and would no doubt be camped there before long anyway. At least if I stuck to the speed limit, nothing could be reported about me driving recklessly or any other bullshit they wanted to try to invent.

"You're handling him well," Alyssa said. "I don't know if I could be quite so patient."

Even though her words hadn't been a joke, I couldn't help laughing at them. "Patience isn't exactly my strong suit. It's taking everything in me not to thump the guy every time he gets that damned camera in my face."

"And it's good that you're not doing it, for Phoebe's sake."

I glanced back at Phoebe in the car seat in the back. She was already well on her way to falling asleep again. Her little head bobbed and nodded, then she startled upright for a few seconds. A moment later, her eyes drifted closed and the routine started again. Before long, she'd nodded off completely.

To give her a proper chance for a nap, I drove the long way home, winding out through the suburbs and blasting along the highways. It was actually nice being able to stretch my legs a little in the car again. To not have to be driving to somewhere, but just in the car for the sake of it.

I drove Alyssa around Sydney Olympic Park in Homebush, and then out to Parramatta. The music was playing and Alyssa was watching out the window. It was peaceful. Relaxed in a way I'd never imagined a drive could be without it being in my ProV8.

When Phoebe started to stir, I headed home. Alyssa and I spent the rest of the afternoon and all of that night just doting on Phoebe. We played games, watched a few movies, and just spent every second we could with her before she crashed early after her late night of being sick.

My weekend alone with Alyssa might have been cut short, but I had no real complaints. Especially not when I was able to take her into my bedroom at the end of the day and claim her body on the clean sheets.

I woke before everyone else in the house on Monday. When I first opened my eyes and looked down at Alyssa's body snuggled against my chest, I thought about what I'd said to her about my love of Sinclair Racing. My heart began to race faster than the engine in my V8 at the thought of what I was going to do, but I didn't have much choice. After having some breakfast, I swallowed down my pride and rang Danny's office. Even though it was still a little before eight, I figured he'd be there. He usually was.

"To what do I owe the pleasure?" he asked after realising it was me. His tone indicated he thought the call was anything but that.

"First off, I wanted to apologise if I seemed rude the other night."

"Seemed?"

"Fuck, okay, I was an arsehole and I'm sorry. It just took me by surprise, seeing you there. I still can't believe Eden would do that."

"Really?" A small chuckle came down the line. "You can't?"

I joined his laughter. "Well, yeah, I guess you're right. It was totally in character for her. I just didn't think she'd do it to you and me."

"Apparently, she thinks there is some stuff we need to sort out."

"Evidently." As I spoke to him, I moved around, picking up some of Phoebe's toys. Some of them would be going home with her, but just as many would be staying to start the transition of her life to Sydney. Looking at the little stuffed dog that was practically falling to pieces—one of the dark brown ears had split at the seam and stuffing was poking out of the hole—I knew I had to suck up my pride and beg. It was the reminder I needed; I was calling him for Phoebe. A job somewhere close to home would only benefit her. It was what I'd promised Alyssa I'd do. Fuck if it didn't feel like I was taking a rusty razor blade to my pride though—and maybe to my balls as well. "I think she's right too."

"Is that so?"

"Yeah. See, I want to come back."

"I can't have you race for me anymore, Declan," he said. The tone he used was frank, almost confrontational. I wondered if he was trying to gauge my reaction or if it was that cut and dried for him. Either could be true.

Despite the fact that I'd known it was impossible, it still stung to have him confirm that I had no chance of driving for the team again.

"Your latest series of stunts, whether true or not, have generated too much bad press," he continued. "The sponsors that bring in the big dollars these days are the family-friendly ones and frankly, you don't have anything to offer us in that department after the latest scandal."

A scoff left me at his words. With Alyssa upstairs asleep, and Phoebe in her little tiara bed, we were practically the perfect picture of domestic fucking bliss. Very few drivers were more family-fucking-friendly than I was when my little family was with me.

Despite that, it wasn't worth having the argument and pushing Danny even further offside. That could wait until I had a steady pay cheque again. "So I won't race then. I still want back in."

"What?"

I sat on the couch with the phone cradled between my ear and my shoulder, holding the stuffed dog in my hands. "I have a family I need to support, Danny. They mean the world to me, and I'd do anything for them. Anything. I don't particularly want to, but I could take the position that Wood offered me. However, that would mean moving to Brisbane when Alyssa is due to move down here to start at Pembletons. So the thing is, even if I wanted to be part of that team, which I don't, I don't want to move away from my family. I made that choice the last time I had a contract to consider, and I fucked it up then. I'm not going to fuck it up again. I owe them better than that." *I owe me better than that.*

"I don't understand what that has to do with me."

"Sinclair is a family. You know that, man. You foster that environment. Even if I can't be out on the track, I want to be nearby. Watching the Bahrain race from home almost killed me. I was fucking counting down the seconds in the pit stops. I was holding my breath with every corner. I want to be part of that success on the fucking track. Of course I'd prefer to be out there behind the wheel, but if that's not possible, then I want to do whatever it takes to prove that I'm a team player. To prove that you fucked up by firing me."

"How do I know you're not just telling me what you think I want to hear to let you back on the track? You have to understand my hands are tied."

I gritted my teeth. "I'm not gonna lie, I want back on the track more than you could possibly imagine." Even as I said the words, I understood it was possible they weren't entirely true. He knew what the drive to be in control of the car was like; he'd been there before he'd retired almost twenty years earlier. But he'd never had the choice taken from him by someone else either. He'd simply raced until he didn't have that hunger any longer, and then he'd retired into team ownership. "Being out there, at one with the car, it's like nothing else. You know that at least. The need for that pumps through my veins like lifeblood, but I don't want that just anywhere. And I'm willing to do whatever it takes to get back there. If that means I've got to clean the fucking toilet so that I can pay the bills and be near my girls in the meantime, that's what I'll do."

"And what if it means that you never get to drive again?"

"Well, then I fucking deal with that like a big boy, don't I?"

"This is a very different attitude from you, Declan." He sounded skeptical, as though at any second I might tell him I was joking and to fuck off. It was fucking tempting. I wasn't the sort to grovel and beg. Except maybe where it came to Alyssa, but that was fucking different.

I would have my say, leave it with him, and never beg again. If he really didn't want me, well, I'd cross that bridge when I got there. "I told you. I'm a different person now. It might only be a few weeks since she crashed back into my life, but Alyssa is good for me." I'd had my say and now I just needed to let the dice fall where they may.

"I appreciate what it would have taken to make this call, Declan. Will you give me the time to consider what you've said?"

"Sure, just don't take too long or I might have to reconsider the role with Wood Racing, after all." I laughed so that he could tell I was joking. There was no way I would become indebted to the person who'd tried to destroy my family and did destroy my career. If he didn't come back to me soon though, or came back with a no, I would still be fucked. Then I'd have no pride and no fucking job. Maybe it was a mistake after all.

I took a calming breath and tried to focus on the positives.

By the time I'd ended the call, Alyssa and Phoebe were awake. Phoebe was sitting at my dining table while Alyssa danced around the kitchen singing a song to her. With a smile on my lips, I caught Alyssa on her next twirl and held her in my arms for a moment before planting a chaste kiss against her mouth. As the three of us sat and ate breakfast together, I looked around the table. I couldn't help but laugh at the perfectly domestic scene.

"What is it?" Alyssa asked.

"Just that for someone who is supposedly not 'family friendly,' this is a very Norman Rockwell moment."

Alyssa laughed in agreement.

"What's Normal Rockwall?" Phoebe asked, causing Alyssa's laughter to grow.

Alyssa patted her arm. "I'll explain when you are older, honey." She turned her gaze to me. "So I called that reporter while you were on the phone."

"Really? And?"

"And they sounded like they were still really keen for the idea. The only problem is when we might be available to do it. Obviously they want to do it sooner rather than later because in another few weeks—" She cut herself off and grimaced at me.

The rest of her sentence was obvious though. In another few weeks, no one would care. I had a big *ex* in front of my position as driver for Sinclair Racing and my stock as a person of interest to the public was falling almost by the hour. If we were going to try to get our side of the story public, it had to be while there was still some interest in the story. In me. "When are they available?"

"Whenever we are." She twirled her hair around her fingers.

"What is it?"

"Well, they actually said my call was perfect timing because they had a hair and make-up artist, and a photographer set up in a hotel in town for a shoot with Katie Medler, but apparently she had to cancel because of some filming commitment."

"Shit." I glanced at Phoebe even as the swear word escaped me. I shot Alyssa an apologetic look and continued, "Uh, I mean, really? You wanna do it today?"

Alyssa shrugged. "We don't have to, but if we don't we'll have to arrange for you to come home, or me to come back here. I'm not sure when we can do that."

Despite the fact that my palms were getting sweaty and my heart was pounding in my chest at the thought, I nodded. "Today is probably doable. Are you sure?"

"I'm sure," she said, giving me a smile which somehow both showed her confidence and her fear.

"You never know what they might ask," I warned. My fear was that they'd ask about Phoebe and Emmanuel. "It might be difficult."

She swallowed hard but nodded. "I know. No one said our life was going to be easy, but it's ours. I want to tell our side. If we don't, those little—" She huffed and cut herself off. "Darcy and Hayley just get away with it all. Publicly, at least. People will believe the lies they've told, because it's uncontested."

Even though I didn't want to talk about the bitches who'd been heavily involved in my downfall, possible plans for revenge started to form in my mind. Karma was going to bite both their arses anyway. Even if I had to force its hand.

Instead of focusing on that part of Alyssa's words, I asked what was my greatest fear about the situation. "How do we know that the magazine isn't going to twist the events and make it worse though?"

"I've already told them that we'll only agree to it if we get ultimate copy approval and veto if they don't agree to our suggestions. I've also instructed them that Phoebe isn't to be included in any photos, and discussed a sizable donation to the children's hospital foundation rather than cash remuneration."

All I could do was blink at her.

Fuck, she was efficient.

And damn sexy when she spoke all professional. If she wasn't going into corporate law, I had no doubt she'd rule any fucking courtroom that she stepped foot in. Between her ability to argue, her way with words, and her looks, she'd be a deadly opponent regardless of the guilt or innocence of her client.

The things she'd already had the magazine agree to were things that probably wouldn't have even crossed my mind to ask.

"Is that okay? I know you're not working and we could probably use the money, but I figured it would help the whole positive-PR spin if you donated the story proceeds."

God, she was fucking smart. And beautiful. And sexy. I pushed away from the table and stalked toward her. "Of course it's okay. I'm just wondering how the hell someone as sexy, smart, and beautiful as you ever fell for such a dumb fuck as me."

"Well, it wasn't for your vocabulary, that's for sure." She nodded toward Phoebe.

Her subtle hint to watch my mouth raised another question. "If someone's not going to be involved in the photoshoot, what are we going to do for a babysitter?"

Alyssa's slight smile twisted downward, no doubt at the reminder that getting a babysitter wouldn't be as easy for her when she moved to Sydney. "Who do you know?"

"Only Eden. She'll probably have to work though. They'll be prepping for the Tassie race this weekend."

"Maybe it'll be easier to tell the magazine that we'll do it another time."

"No, it makes sense to do it sooner rather than later. I'll call her and see what she says. It'll only be a few hours right?"

"Yeah. I'm not sure when though. This afternoon sometime. Then I have to be at the airport by seven, too."

I pressed my fingers to her lips. "No talking about airports. It doesn't exist until at least six tonight, okay?"

"Sure thing, Dec." She sounded as reluctant to discuss it as I was anyway.

"Okay, I'll give Eden a call. You call the magazine and work out a time."

"What 'bout me, Daddy?"

"You sit there and look cute." I winked at her.

"That's hardly going to give her the confidence to rely on her intelligence rather than her looks."

I raised a you've-got-to-be-kidding-me eyebrow at Alyssa, but she just shrugged. "Well, shit, okay then, you sit there and do some maths."

"I don't know what's maths," Phoebe spluttered with her mouth full of toast.

Giving Alyssa a look that was supposed to convey the thought, "See, my way was better," I quickly hunted down a piece of paper and pencil. "Well, then, why don't you draw?"

"Draw what?"

"Something that makes you happy."

"Okay."

With her satisfied and the plan sorted, I pulled out my phone and called Eden. As soon as I told her the reason why we needed a babysitter, she wouldn't let me tell her it was okay if she couldn't.

"I was leaving at lunchtime anyway."

I wasn't entirely sure I believed her statement. It would have been just like Eden to tell me that even if it was utter bullshit, just so that she'd get her way.

"Besides, it sounds like Alyssa has organised a kick-arse deal with them. It'd be stupid to have to give up something like this, something that could be a positive, just because you can't find a babysitter. Just let me know when you want to drop her off."

"Thanks, Edie, you are a lifesaver."

"I actually thought you were calling about something else," she said.

"Like?"

"Like a certain phone call this morning."

A lump rose in my throat. Should I deny it or admit I'd basically tried to trade my balls for a job?

Eden didn't let me do either. "I think it was a step in the right direction. Even if it doesn't mean anything happens with Sinclair Racing, at least Danny will be more likely to help you find your feet somewhere else."

Her words sent any hopes that had been building in me plummeting to the floor. It seemed the best I could wish for was a driver role at a team that wasn't completely terrible. All of the top teams had their drivers stitched up tight. Except Wood Racing.

My silence must have warned her of my shifting mood.

"It'll work out for the best, Dec. Just trust me."

I wasn't sure I could, but it was just easier to say, "Sure thing, Edie. I'll text once I know what time we'll need you."

Alyssa was still on the phone when I headed back out of my office. Phoebe was colouring in her drawing, but she held up what she'd done so far. On the page was a picture with three blobs, each with hands and faces, and a small square, standing next to a big square filled with a pattern of circular shapes.

"That's nice," I said. I had no idea what it was, but I figured telling her that in such a harsh fashion wouldn't be good for her confidence. "What's that bit there?" I pointed to a circle inside the square, hoping if I could weed out some clues, I could guess the scene.

"Silly, that's da window."

Fuck, well, that gave me some frame of reference at least. "It's a lovely house with all those windows."

"It's your castle, Daddy."

"And that's us, is it?"

She gave an exaggerated nod and pointed to each of the blobs with hands in turn. "That's you. And that's Mummy. And that's me."

There was one part of the picture I still didn't understand.

"And what's this down here?" I pointed to the square right next to the person she'd said was her.

She sighed. "Daddy, you're silly. That's Emmie's stone."

My stomach twisted. I was glad that Alyssa had never hidden the truth from Phoebe, and that Phoebe understood as much as she could about the situation considering her age, but I hadn't considered that she might have the expectation that we could somehow bring him with us when we moved. Alyssa had explained to me how they went to visit him every couple of weeks, so it shouldn't have been a surprise that Phoebe expected that to somehow continue. How did we explain to her that Emmanuel's grave had to stay in Brisbane?

Because I didn't want to ruin Alyssa's mood before the photo shoot with questions that were so depressing, I stuck the picture to my fridge with a magnet, and then distracted Phoebe with something else. When Alyssa got off the phone, she nodded and told me it was all set up.

Within half an hour, we had everything lined up for the photo shoot.

Just as we were getting into the car, my mobile rang. Seeing the name that flashed up on the screen, I told Alyssa who it was and asked her to get Phoebe sorted in the car. I headed just outside the garage door so I could talk without risking Phoebe trying to chatter over me.

"Danny," I said in greeting.

"I hear you're having a photo shoot with *Woman's Idea* this afternoon."

Fucking Eden. Does she ever keep her mouth shut?

"Yeah." *What's it got to do with you?*

"I think it's a great idea. Getting your image into a more positive light will only help your case in the longer term."

I don't remember asking your fucking position on the matter. I sighed. I'd all but begged him for a job just that morning. The mere thought of the way my effort was basically dismissed had put me in a foul mood, and I needed to shake it or I would just cause myself more trouble. Despite the fact that I knew I needed to fix it, my tone was still a little snippy when I said, "I'm in a hurry, Danny, was there something you wanted?"

"Yes, actually there was. I was wondering if you can come in to the offices to see me tomorrow?"

I blinked. Swallowed. Wondered whether I'd misheard. "Tomorrow?"

"Yes. Around nine if you can make it?"

"Um, yeah, sure."

"Excellent. I'll see you then."

Unable to think of anything else to say, I repeated my last line again.

Alyssa was practically jumping out of her skin with anticipation when I approached the car. "What did he want?"

"He, uh, he wants to see me. Tomorrow."

"Well, that's good, right?"

"Maybe." Despite the fact that I was trying so hard not to get excited, I couldn't help the little bubble of hope that grew in my chest. He wouldn't want to speak to me if he didn't have something to tell me, right? For good, or for bad.

"Let's get to Eden's," Alyssa said, drawing me from my thoughts.

When I turned on the ignition, I took a second to put things in perspective. I had a great family and awesome friends that I'd never really appreciated before. Regardless of what Danny said, none of those things could change.

I'd already hit rock bottom, and now the only way to go was up.

CHAPTER TWENTY

GOOD MORGAN

A LITTLE BEFORE one, I pulled up in front of the block of flats that housed Eden's swanky little inner-city Sydney apartment. Of course, despite it being so expensive, there was no off-street visitor parking. Although it meant arriving in the city during the lunch rush, and having to fight to find a place to park, I'd wanted to make sure we had plenty of time for Alyssa to get comfortable before we'd have to leave Phoebe there.

So that they wouldn't have to be in the car while I drove around to find a park—or listen to the swearing that would no doubt occur when I couldn't find one—I pulled into a loading zone in front of the building so that Alyssa could unload Phoebe and take her ahead while I found a spot.

After lucking out and finding a park just up the road, I walked back to Eden's building. When I got there, I found Alyssa out front—with Phoebe perched on her hip—looking flustered and more than a little frustrated.

"What number apartment was it again?" she asked when I was close enough.

"Seventeen," I said, confused because she'd double-checked it with me before climbing out of the car.

"That can't be right," she said. "There was a man there . . . And before he opened the door, he grumbled something about not being allowed to have any afternoon delight, and didn't people respect the concept of privacy anymore. He opened the door wearing black silk boxers, Dec. Not to mention that he was . . ." She glanced at Phoebe to make sure she wasn't paying too much attention before nodding down toward her crotch. "You know." Her eyes widened, as if she was trying to psychically force the information into my mind. "He was excited."

Eden had said she was planning on having the afternoon off. Surely she couldn't . . . She wasn't . . . I was sure Morgan would still be at work but maybe . . .

Oh shit. I realised that in the excitement of picking outfits, packing so I could take them straight to the airport, getting some entertainment organised for Phoebe, I'd completely forgotten to text Eden the time we'd be at her house.

"Was he blond?" I dreaded the answer. God, if I'd interrupted Morgan's chance for afternoon delight before he needed to go away with the team, I'd never hear the end of it.

Alyssa nodded.

My suspicions confirmed, I chuckled. *Great.* "Well, that'd be the wonderful Morgan McGuire."

"Morgan McGuire? You mean your teammate?"

"Yeah, I'd say so," I said. "They must have decided to have some time alone before the team goes on the road again. And it looks like we coc—uh, interrupted them. Honestly, I'm surprised you didn't recognise him from the promotional posters."

A pink stain crept up her cheeks. "I never paid much attention to anyone else on the posters," she admitted.

Despite the knowledge that she was mine, I couldn't deny the rush of desire her admission caused within me.

"Morgan!" Phoebe said over Alyssa, obviously trying out the name.

"Are he and Eden . . .?" Alyssa asked.

I nodded. "For a few years now."

"Wow . . ." Alyssa said. "Nothing like keeping it in the team."

"Yeah." I chuckled. "They never really let it affect their race-day performance though, so I think Danny just lets it slide."

Holding Alyssa's hand, I led her back to Eden's door. Once again, Morgan answered it and, not noticing me, gave Alyssa a curious glance. At least he was wearing pants and a shirt this time.

"You again?" he asked, the corners of his mouth turning up into a slightly worried smile. It was a look I recognised—one reserved for crazy-arse stalker fans.

"Yes, you arse," I said, earning a kick to the shin from Alyssa for my language. "Now are you going to let us in, or do we have to stand in the hallway all day."

"Squirt?" he said, his gaze spinning to me with surprise evident on his features. Then realisation dawned on his face, "Oh, then this must be the little woman and the munchkin."

"Who's a munchkin?" Phoebe asked.

"You are, munchkin," Morgan replied, tousling Phoebe's hair before cupping her cheek.

I could sense Alyssa bristle beside me and instantly understood why. Unfortunately, I couldn't warn Morgan that she didn't like unknown people being touchy-feely with Phoebe. Ruth, Alyssa's mum, had explained it to me, how Alyssa still viewed Phoebe as the broken little girl who needed a new kidney to survive.

Morgan was just being Morgan though. He didn't mean any harm and probably hadn't even thought through the movement before he'd acted. He always exuded an air of confidence and people generally liked him; it was one of the reasons he was regarded as being a gold mine to the family-friendly sponsors, despite his past being almost as chequered as mine.

"I'm *not* a munkchin," Phoebe declared. "I'm Phoebe Castor Dawson!"

"You tell him, missy," I said, laughing. Then I pushed my way past the still slightly dazed Morgan into Eden's living room, ready as I would ever be for the first real collision of my two worlds. Eden might have been there to help Alyssa when they were worried about me, but that was different. Then, circumstances had forced them to at least be cordial. Now, there was nothing binding them besides their mutual friendships with me.

Eden flittered out from the bedroom at that moment and grinned at me. Her jeans-clad legs poked out from the bottom of an oversized short-sleeved flannelette shirt that looked at least three sizes too big. She was doing up the button on her jeans as she moved.

"You could have at least got dressed before we showed up," I teased.

"Well, you were supposed to text before you showed up, buddy, so you're lucky I'm not standing here in my birthday suit."

"Sorry, I got a little distracted. So did you, evidently." All of the buttons on her blouse were buttoned through the wrong holes.

She looked down at her shirt, adjusted the belt holding it tight around her waist, and then grinned at me. "Morgan hasn't been formally introduced yet?"

I shook my head.

"Allow me," she said, as if I could have stopped Cyclone Eden if I'd wanted to. "Morgan, this is Alyssa, Declan's . . ." She seemed to struggle over the word. I wondered how I would have filled it. Love, life, future—any one of those words fit. Eden settled for "Partner. And this," she pointed to Phoebe, "is—"

"Phoebe Castor Dawson," Morgan said. "That introduction, I did get."

Alyssa put Phoebe down on the floor. Ignoring Morgan's disbelieving expression, I pulled the colouring books and crayons out of the backpack I had on. In no time at all, Phoebe was sitting at Eden's coffee table colouring in a book of princesses.

Eden led Alyssa away to chat about something or other, no doubt trying to ensure the list of instructions for Phoebe's care was set in stone. I watched with a goofy smile on my lips as they talked like old friends. It made my life easier that Alyssa and Eden had fallen into such an easy friendship. If nothing else, it meant Alyssa would have one more person in Sydney she could rely on.

"Boy, are you ever whipped," Morgan said to me after pulling me away and offering me a beer. "Who'd have thought it? Declan Reede, the eternal bachelor, having a photo shoot that will all but declare him off limits."

"What can I say? London changed me." The grin on my lips wouldn't be shaken, not even for his negativity.

"And playing daddy."

"I'm not playing, man."

"You know what I mean. It's just a shock to see you being, I don't know, Mr. Mum or something."

"Shut the fuck up, bro," I said. "You'd do the same."

"Yeah, well, I might have to one day soon. No thanks to you, I should add."

"What?" I asked, glancing over at Eden. Was this his way of announcing a new arrival? "She's not . . ." I couldn't even bring myself to say the word.

"Nah, man, but she's clucky as hell, thanks to your little munchkin."

"Uh, uh, uh, remember, she's not a munchkin," I said, laughing.

"Yeah, yeah, whatever, man," he said. Before I could say anything more, he continued, "So the little girl . . ."

"Phoebe."

"Yeah, Phoebe, is she . . . really yours? I mean, are you sure? Have you been tested?"

"Are you kidding me, dude? Tested? She's not some fucking disease. Besides, I don't need to have DNA work done to know. I mean, did you see her eyes? She's mine. There's no doubt about that."

"Sorry, man, it's just, well, you know as well as I do what some of these fangirls can be like."

His words made me think of my father's assertions that Alyssa had been trying to trap me or some shit. I sighed. "Yeah, I get it. If the roles were reversed, I'd probably ask the same thing. But trust me when I say it's all legit, and that I'm actually happy about it."

"That's all I need to know, bro. How the heck have you been about the rest of the shit? It's been odd not having you on the track.

Especially after all the prep for Bahrain. It was so weird not having to worry about overtaking your arse."

I shrugged. "It just makes it that much easier for you," I teased, ignoring the first part of the question because I was still working it out myself. "Less *real* competition."

"Yeah, right. As if you offered any competition." He must have seen the brief pain that crossed my features, because he quickly changed the subject. "So what happened with you and . . .," he trailed off and looked over in Alyssa's direction, "anyway? Edie hasn't really told me much. Says it's your story to tell."

With a sigh, I started to formulate an answer that would satisfy him without giving him all of the dark details. It was a story I was going to have to tell repeatedly over the next few months, but that didn't make it any easier.

"Basically, I left Alyssa behind when I left Brisbane," I said. "What can I say, we were together in high school, had the cliché after-formal moment, and weren't careful enough." Even as soon as the words were out, I wanted to reel them back. I had basically called Phoebe an accident, which was exactly what my father had thought of me. I wouldn't be him. She might not have been planned for, but I didn't ever want her to think she was resented or loved less than completely.

"Oh shit," Morgan whispered, pulling me from my worry. He glanced at Alyssa again. "That's *the* girl?"

I nodded.

"You were tapping that before you left?" he asked. His gaze trailed her body once again, this time with a more appraising eye.

I clenched my jaw and bit back the harsh words in my head. It wouldn't pay to piss off Eden's boyfriend in her apartment, or to alienate one of my few friends in Sydney.

"And you still left?"

I nodded. "I was a fucking idiot."

"You're not wrong," he whispered again with a grin, his gaze roaming up Alyssa's legs to her arse.

I punched his shoulder to draw his eyes off her. "I'll tell Eden you were perving on her," I threatened.

"Yeah," he said, his eyebrow raised as if daring me to say a single word. "Well, I'll tell your little woman about your life down here."

"No point."

For a moment, a victorious smile twisted the edges of his mouth.

"I've told her everything."

"Everything?" He raised an eyebrow at me.

I nodded.

"That's—"

"Brave?" I finished for him, cutting him off.

"I was going to say stupid."

I shrugged. "It's the only way I know to earn back all of her trust. I don't want some bullshit I didn't tell her coming back to bite us in the arse later, you know? That almost happened with that damned magazine, and I won't let it happen again. I've only just found her again after so long apart. I'm not willing to throw that away over a past mistake—or a future one."

"God, man, you left with a frank and beans and came back with an empty plate."

"Fuck you," I said, laughing. It barely registered with me that the words were a little louder than the rest of our conversation.

"Declan," Alyssa called out, before inclining her head in Phoebe's direction.

I nodded sheepishly. It was easy to fall back into old habits talking with Morgan. I turned back toward Morgan to continue our conversation but stopped when I saw he'd paled until he was as white as a sheet.

"Holy fuck," Morgan whispered almost silently. "That's the girl. From Brisbane. The girl you left behind."

"Yes, Morgan," I said, speaking slowly, as if trying to explain a very fucking difficult concept to a child. "That's Alyssa."

"Wait, I didn't think you ever wanted to talk to her again? Didn't she do something to make you hate her?"

I shrugged. "I know that's what I said, but I've never stopped loving her. At least on some level. I know that now."

"Holy fuck," Morgan repeated. His face was growing paler, yet somehow greener, by the second.

"What is it?" I asked. "You look like you're gonna barf."

"I swear, I didn't know," he rambled, his eyes flicking between Alyssa and me in rapid succession. "Fuck, how was I supposed to know? When you said . . ." His hands came up to scrub his face. "Fuck!"

"Eden, you're going to have to come over here and decipher for your boyfriend again," I called out jokingly, trying to draw something solid from him, even if it was just a "fuck you."

Eden and Alyssa both turned back toward us.

I saw Morgan's eyes roam to Alyssa's face, and she offered him a small smile. I smiled at my girl, so willing to give him a chance just because he was my friend and Eden's boyfriend.

Morgan exhaled heavily beside me.

"Seriously, dude, what the fuck's wrong?" I asked.

Morgan didn't turn away from Alyssa's face as he spoke. "I didn't mean anything by it. I just wanted to help you out, squirt. You said you didn't want to talk to her anymore and . . . I . . . when I heard the message . . . Then on your computer . . . I just thought . . . well, I . . . Fuck. I never knew she was pregnant. I didn't think before . . . I wasn't thinking. Well, I wouldn't have been would I . . . with everything we were taking that night."

Something clicked for Alyssa with his incoherent rambling. "It was you!"

Morgan finally stopped staring, dropping his eyes to the floor instead.

I looked to Eden to see if she could enlighten me to what was happening, but she looked as confused as I felt.

"You fucking arsehole!" Alyssa screeched before launching herself at him.

Eden quickly spun around and grabbed Phoebe, pulling her swiftly from the room.

I wrapped my arms around Alyssa, pulling her away, but not before she threw a couple of punches in Morgan's direction. Judging by the soft thud, at least one connected. We could deal with the fallout from that after she was calm. More important was figuring out exactly what those two had worked out about each other. Eden seemed as out of the loop as I felt. I held Alyssa tightly in my arms as she fought against me.

"Calm down, baby," I murmured into her hair.

"You don't understand," she screamed. "It was him."

I spun her in my arms so that she was facing me instead of Morgan. Hopefully if he was out of her sight, it would allow her to calm a little. I took the risk of loosening my grip and used one hand to brush her hair off her face. "What was him?"

"The email, Dec," she seethed even as tears filled her voice. "He sent the email. That's why you don't remember. It's because you were right. You didn't do it."

Her words sunk in. Morgan had been the one who sent her an email of me in an orgy with cheerleaders, in an attempt to have her stop contacting me. Somehow, despite that information, I couldn't find it in myself to blame him as much as she obviously did. I wasn't thrilled about the fact that he'd taken that choice into his hands, but ultimately I was still to blame. He may have pushed the send button on the email, but he hadn't coerced me into the middle of the girls; he hadn't set up the camera. He hadn't kept the recording. The timing of the email—before he hooked up with Eden—meant he was likely as off his face on whatever I'd procured as I'd been. The footage was already there and *that* was my fault.

Plus, I'd also been the one who told him, repeatedly, that I never wanted to speak to, or about, Alyssa. In the haze I had of my memories from that time, I could remember some of the things I'd called her and I deserved to have her hate me for them all.

I pulled her tighter to me and whispered to her, "It's in the past. We're making a new start now. One where I'll never hurt you, and Morgan wouldn't dare."

She shook her head. "Don't you see? It hurt so much to see that. Of everything that you ever did to me, that was one of the most painful."

I saw Morgan turn and leave the room, his hands clenched into tight fists by his sides.

I tipped her chin back lightly with my finger, drawing her gaze to my face. "Baby, I'm sorry that I ever did anything so stupid and allowed it to hurt you. I will never again do anything that will hurt you." I dipped my head and pressed my lips to hers.

"You did what?" Eden's voice screeched from the bedroom. "So help me, Morgan John McGuire, I cannot believe you would deliberately try to hurt a young girl like that."

Phoebe started to wail, no doubt as a result of all the raised voices.

"Come to Mummy," Alyssa called to her. She ran across the room and practically flew into Alyssa's arms.

Eden came out from the bedroom with an apologetic look on her face.

"I'm sorry, Eden," Alyssa said. "I think it would be best if I took Phoebe with me."

Her pronouns worried me. The use of I instead of we, and me instead of us wasn't a good sign. Wondering just how much Morgan's stuttering confession had set me back, I sighed.

Alyssa turned to me, obviously misunderstanding the reason behind my sigh. "I'm sorry, I know he's your teammate and friend, but I just . . . I can't deal with this." She shook her head and raised her free hand in a dismissive wave. "Not today."

"Forget Morgan," I said, shooting Eden a remorseful smile. "We'll just get the photographer to work around Phoebe, okay?"

Alyssa nodded.

Eden grabbed her keys. "Let me come with you to the shoot. I can watch her there."

Alyssa went to argue.

"Please? It'll just be me, and it'll mean you can relax and enjoy the process."

With the corners of her eyes still pinched, Alyssa relented. "Okay, but I don't know if I'll be able to relax anyway."

"Look, I know he can be an arse, but he usually means well."

"That sounds like someone else we all know," I joked. It didn't bode well for me if Alyssa and Morgan didn't get along, not when Morgan had always been such a big part of my life in Sydney.

Instead of a laugh, my joke earned an if-looks-could-kill-I'd-be-dead type glare from Alyssa.

"Thanks for changing your plans to come with us, Eden," Alyssa said, clearly ready to leave the apartment entirely. "Are you sure you don't mind? Like Dec said, we can probably ask the photographer just to shoot around Phoebe if he needs to."

"It's fine. I need some time away from the bozo in there anyway, before I do something he'll regret." She indicated the bedroom where Morgan was still hiding from Alyssa's rage. "Ready to go?"

I couldn't help but feel a little sorry for Morgan; not only had we interrupted his afternoon delight, but he'd also become public enemy number one where Alyssa was concerned.

CHAPTER TWENTY-ONE
SNAP HAPPY

WHEN WE REACHED the hotel, I'd thought it would be a fairly easy afternoon. I was so fucking wrong, it wasn't funny. While Phoebe sat and watched, under Eden's supervision, the make-up team transformed both Alyssa and me.

For a little over an hour Alyssa was primped and preened to within an inch of her real appearance. For almost half of that, the two person make-up team slathered all sorts of crap on my face too. The feeling of an extra layer of stuff over my skin wasn't something I could get used to. Although I'd had to do it in the past, for promotional shoots and the like, it was never something I enjoyed.

After the gunk was on my face, and my hair was styled into a slightly longer version of my trademark spikes, the photographer called me over to help block the lighting and get a few solo shots.

"The camera loves you two," he called.

The remote flashes linked to the photographer's camera lit up the room again.

I resisted the urge to roll my eyes at him. After the first thirty minutes of his over-the-top enthusiasm, I was definitely done. And that had been over an hour earlier. I wondered how much longer it would take, just so I could escape his constant chatter. I didn't really have too much cause to complain about any other part of the shoot. In fact, as photo shoots went, it was relatively pain free. The fact that I'd been able to spend 90 percent of the time kissing and snuggling with Alyssa was a definite advantage.

When Alyssa had finally joined me, we were put into a range of poses that weren't entirely natural, but that we were assured would look awesome in print. Even though the positions were awkward, they drew a smile from my lips because in each one, I was entwined around Alyssa—in poses designed to show off our obvious love.

Better still, Phoebe was in our line of sight the whole time, playing with Eden off to the other side of the room. Once we were done with the photo session, we'd just have the interview, and Phoebe could join us for that. Just like we'd agreed with the magazine, she was off limits to the photographer and they'd kept to their word so far which gave me some confidence for the overall article.

It was good that they didn't press the issue because neither Alyssa nor I would allow our daughter's photo to be splashed all over a national magazine. Not if we could help it, and definitely not for an article we were doing to try to salvage my career. Even though I needed to be family friendly to get sponsors back onside, I wasn't going to allow photos of Phoebe to be the catalyst for the turning point in my future. I wouldn't use her in that way, as a pawn in some fucked-up game of someone else's design.

Ultimately, although Alyssa had stood by my side for the photoshoot and would join me for the interview, it had been her choice to do so. I wouldn't make that decision for Phoebe or force her into the spotlight. It was too much of a burden for my little girl.

I wasn't stupid though. I understood that even though Talia's paparazzi campaign seemed to be targeted at me for the moment, it was still possible, likely even, that Phoebe would be papped at some stage. Especially after the *Woman's Idea* article went to print and brought her into the public's attention, at least in print. How long would it be before another magazine included photos? Then people would know what she looked like, and regardless of whether I was able to salvage something of the shit my career had descended into, she would be known as my daughter.

That was already more than any three-year-old should have to deal with.

"Just a few more shots," the photographer called. "Let's have you here." He grabbed my arm and dragged me so that I was sitting on the couch, close to the armrest. With a little twirl of his fingers, he silently instructed me to twist so that my body faced down the couch, with one leg hanging off the front and the other resting up against the backrest. "And you here," he added as he helped Alyssa into position.

I swallowed heavily as she settled into the pose that he was after, lying between my legs with her chest facing mine. Most of her body rested between my legs—her hip pressing against my cock— and her head was curled against my shoulder so that I could feel every breath she took blowing against my ear. Even though I was trying to be professional, the pose put her in the right spot to send thoughts of her shifting slightly to a reverse cowboy position into my head.

I glanced down at Alyssa's face and saw her stifling a smile. She had to have been able to feel my ever increasing hard-on. God, I wanted to kiss her, to toss her against the back of the couch and fuck her hard.

"Now, caress her face." The photographer's voice reminded me where I was, and who else was present.

Taking care not to twist in a way that my body would be blocking hers, I lifted my hand and cupped her cheek.

"Perfect."

The shutter whirled a couple of times and then the flash exploded twice.

"Now, lean in as if you are going to kiss her."

Taking my time, and waiting for him to call stop, I moved my lips closer to Alyssa's.

"A little closer."

My lips barely grazed Alyssa's when he said to stop. It took everything in me to stop myself and not continue on to the kiss. I did though. Instead of claiming her mouth, devouring her the way that my whole body longed to, I hovered my lips over hers so that each whispered breath she took brushed over my skin. It was agony. The sweetest torture I could imagine. I met her gaze, and the hunger coursing through my body was echoed within their honey-gold depths.

Fuck.

The shoot was a bad fucking idea for one reason and one reason alone—she was going straight to the airport and I'd be left in Sydney with nothing but my hand to satisfy the fires she'd stoked within me.

The camera clicked a few more times. A couple of times the flash accompanied it, a couple of times it didn't. He was obviously playing with the lighting.

"And now let's get an actual kiss."

I didn't even wait for any further instructions; I was so desperate for her. My lips crashed against hers and my tongue darted straight into her mouth. Her replying kiss was just as needful.

The photos forgotten, I moved my hand from her cheek to her hair, drawing her closer to me. A sigh slipped from her into the space between us. For a few blissful seconds, I forgot about everyone else in the room. The kiss was so all-consuming. My body twisted so that Alyssa and I were chest to chest, and then I rolled slightly to pin her beneath me. I rubbed my cock against her pussy and drew a small moan from her lips.

It was only when I pulled away and watched Alyssa panting for air that I remembered where we were and what we were doing.

Shit.

I only hoped Eden had the good sense to keep Phoebe occupied while I'd practically dry-humped Alyssa in front of everyone.

The photographer cleared his throat. "I, uh, I think we've got everything we need."

"Brilliant," I said. "Can I get this shit off my face now?"

He laughed. "Sure. I think they left some make-up removal wipes in the bathroom. Sara will be here in about ten minutes for your interview."

Without letting her argue, I grabbed Alyssa's hand and dragged her into the bathroom. The second she was in the room, I shut and locked the door behind us.

"Dec, what are you—"

I silenced her by clasping her face between my palms and drawing her lips to mine again.

"We've only got ten minutes," she said as she pulled away.

"Fuck, Lys, with how much I want you right now, I won't even need that."

"There are people right outside the door." Despite her arguments, when I guided her hand to my crotch, her fingers caressed my cock over the material of my shorts.

My lips formed a familiar smirk. "We'll have to be quiet then, won't we?" I raised one brow at her as I ran my hand up her thigh and over her panties. With one stroke of my fingers along her pussy, I confirmed she was as wet and ready for me as I was hard and aching for her.

I pushed my shorts down just far enough to pull my cock out, guided her to turn around so she was leaning against the vanity, and slid her panties down to her ankles. Meeting her gaze in the mirror, I entered her from behind.

When the sexiest little moan left her lips, I clamped my hand over her mouth. I used the hold to guide her backward to lean against me.

"Remember, you have to be quiet," I whispered against the shell of her ear.

She nodded, but I didn't move my hand. Twisting her head slightly to the side, she moved her mouth to my fingers and drew one between her lips. Her eyes closed as she sucked my finger as far into her perfect mouth as she could. In a matching rhythm, she rocked her hips back against mine.

"Fuck," I groaned against her throat. The way she was going, I'd be lucky to last a couple of minutes.

Because I didn't want her lasting memory of me to be someone who two-pump chumped her in the bathroom, leaving her unsatisfied hours before she got back on a plane, I used my free hand to reach for her clit. My fingers danced around that magic button, causing her to suck harder on my other hand.

"Fuck." The word left my lips louder than before, but still quiet enough to be captured by the walls around us.

Needing more of her, I slammed into her, pushing her hips against the vanity and capturing my hand in the process. I opened my eyes and met her burning gaze in the mirror. The position left everything exposed and it was a damn shame I didn't have more time to fully appreciate it. My mind ran rampant with imaginings of what the position would be like if she'd been completely nude. The way her breasts bounced in time with the thrusts of my hips was such a fucking turn-on.

Craving her lips, I pulled away from her, twisted her around so that her arse was perched on the marble counter, and then lined myself up before slamming into her again. The new position allowed me to capture her mouth, and I took full advantage, letting my tongue mimic the rhythm of my cock.

It was fast and hard, but I didn't feel I had much choice. I needed her too much to walk out of the room without us both being satisfied.

Because the bathroom wasn't as cool as the rest of the hotel room, a sheen of sweat broke out across her brow and my own felt damp too. It wasn't long before she tumbled over the edge, dragging me along with her.

After taking a quick second to clean up, Alyssa pulled her panties back on and set about cleaning off her make-up. Not quite ready to face the interview, I stepped into the space behind her and nestled my cock between her arse cheeks. "You know that shade of lipstick looks great on your lips," I murmured as I kissed her. "But do you know where I think it would really look awesome."

"Where?"

"Wrapped around my cock," I said.

She met my gaze in the mirror again. Her mouth formed a little O, as if anything I could say could still shock her despite the time we'd spent together. She spun around to face me before leaning against me so that her boobs pressed against my chest. "I'll try to find a matching shade, and we can test that theory next time I see you."

"Fuck, Lys, you make it hard to let you go."

"I know the feeling. Now, we need to get this stuff off our faces and go talk about ourselves for the next half hour or so." She sounded as enthusiastic about it as I felt.

After getting off most of the crud on my face—and getting her to help me with the rest—I made sure I was decent, that I didn't have jizz on my shorts or anything like that, and we both headed out.

The reporter hadn't arrived yet, but when I caught Eden's gaze it was clear she knew, or had guessed, what had transpired in the bathroom. To fuck with her a little, I fixed a smirk on my lips and adjusted my crotch as I walked.

She raised an eyebrow and I waggled my brows at her in return. Even though she'd missed her afternoon delight, I'd had mine, which was what mattered.

"Mummy, you looked beautiful," Phoebe said. "Like a princess."

"Thank you, sweetie. Didn't you think Daddy looked very handsome too?"

Phoebe nodded.

"The camera really does love you two," Eden said. "I saw a couple of the photos as they came onto his screen. They look great, and that's *before* the Photoshopping." She laughed.

"Thanks again for being here to look after Phoebe," Alyssa said. "It definitely made it easier."

"No problems at all. It was too easy. She's a sweet kid. I can stay right up until your flight, Alyssa," Eden said. "I've got plans for dinner with Morgan a little later tonight though. And then who knows?" She winked at the implications.

"I do *not* need to know about your sex life with Morgan," I said.

"Well, you seemed so willing to share yours with me a minute ago. It seemed only fair to reciprocate. Especially considering your lack of a warning left us thoroughly, shall we say, interrupted."

I shook my head at her as Alyssa laughed. God, I fucking loved the sound of that laugh. It spurred me into action. I reached down and grabbed her again, pulling her to me and kissing her sweet lips.

Seconds later, the door opened and gave us our cue to break apart.

A young woman, probably no older than Alyssa and me, bounced through the doorway. Her platinum-blonde hair was swept up into a haphazard bun, with bits sticking out everywhere. Her legs were wrapped in a pair of jeans so faded and torn it was surprising they were still holding together. The soft blue blouse she wore over the top helped to restore some of the professionalism that her jeans wiped away.

"Hi, you must be Declan and Alyssa." The way she introduced herself reminded me of an overly excited puppy. In another life, her orange-painted lips, blackened eyes, and obvious stamina probably would have been a target for my heat-seeking dick, but now I could just chuckle at her exuberant personality. She stuck her hand out as an introduction. "I'm Sara."

Alyssa and I both said, "Hi," and then Alyssa introduced Eden and Phoebe.

After nodding in greeting to Eden, Sara crouched down in front of Phoebe. "Lovely to meet you, Phoebe."

With a shy smile, Phoebe glanced up from her colouring and said, "Hello."

Sara asked a couple of questions to Phoebe, just simple things like what she was colouring. Things clearly designed to make Phoebe more comfortable. Despite the fact that the questions were all directed down at our daughter, it was clearly working on Alyssa as well. Out of the corner of my eye, I saw her stance relax, her smile grow, and the mask she put on so often with strangers slowly fade away.

After a few minutes chatting with Phoebe, Sara rested her hands on her knees and looked up at me. "Are you ready to do this?"

Swallowing down my fear over the possible questions she might ask, I nodded. "I am. Lys?"

Alyssa gave me a smile that suggested her worries were at least as deep as mine. Maybe deeper, because she'd never had to deal with the press before. I'd been grilled before in interviews, with questions that covered everything from my meteoric rise to my spectacular crashes. It was easier knowing that we had control over what would go to print.

When Alyssa nodded as well, Sara pointed to the couch.

Flashes of the photo shoot, and the resulting bathroom session, flooded through my mind. I tried to hide my smile as I sat, but was sure I failed when I met Alyssa's questioning gaze.

"You don't mind if I record, do you?" Sara put a tablet on the desk. It was already recording, but I figured she was just getting our permission on record.

Both Alyssa and I told her we didn't.

"Now, Declan, I know you'll be familiar with this process, but Alyssa, just pretend it's the three of us and you've invited me around to chat, okay? Try not to think of the recording. I know you've managed to get final copy approval, so nothing that you want off the record will go to print anyway. Okay?"

"Yeah," Alyssa said.

"Awesome. Let's start with the easy stuff first, shall we?"

CHAPTER TWENTY-TWO

INTERVIEW WITH AN EX-DRIVER

SARA PULLED OUT a notepad and flicked through it, clearly having a specific page in mind. Her eyes scanned the page, and then she obviously found the list of questions she must have organised. "Declan, until recently, you've had a reputation as a ladies' man. You're even on record multiple times stating that you didn't think there was a woman out there for you. It's, uh, quite the turnaround to now be revealing that you are in a committed relationship with the mother of your three-year-old daughter, isn't it?"

That was the easy stuff? *Fuck.* A nervous chuckle slipped from me as I tried to work out the best way to explain the shift that had happened for me in the last month. "What can I say other than denial isn't just a river in Egypt? I've always loved Alyssa. On some level, I think I knew that. I fought so hard against it because I didn't know how to cope with it. The last month, having her in my life again, has reminded me of all the good and bad we shared back in high school. Everything that makes us who we are, both as individuals and as a couple."

"So you were high school sweethearts?"

Both Alyssa and I said "yes" at the same time.

"And why did that end?"

A loaded glance passed between Alyssa and me. She was silently asking me to answer, but I would have anyway because ultimately the decision to leave had been mine. After all, she'd tried to reconcile even before she knew about her pregnancy.

"I was offered a chance to race, and at the time I thought that was the most important thing."

"And now?"

"Now, well, I wish I knew then what I've learned in the last month. I think the choices I made would have been a little different."

"How so?"

"Even though the thought was terrifying at seventeen, I actually think that Lys and I could have made a go of things in Sydney. There were universities down here she could have gone to. At the very least, we could have tried to make it work long distance."

"With that being the case, do you regret the choices you made while you were apart?"

I cast my gaze in Alyssa's direction and she wrapped her hand around my arm. We'd touched on this between us in so many little ways, but I wanted to frame my answer in a way that wouldn't hurt her. "Yes and no. All of those things hurt people, hurt Alyssa, but they also ultimately led me back to her. They forced me to hit rock bottom and now I know that the only way is up. When I rebuild, I'll be building on a stronger foundation than I've ever had before. Plus, I'll be doing it with Alyssa at my side. And Phoebe."

"Your daughter?" It was clear it was a question purely for the recording.

As if she thought I'd called her, Phoebe wandered over. We'd told Eden that it was fine for her to be around us during the interview if she was getting unsettled.

"Look, Daddy." She held up the colouring book to show me the now purple-skinned princess she'd been working on.

"Very nice! That one deserves a high five," I said, holding my hand up. She smacked her palm against mine and then ran back over to Eden. "She's, uh . . ." My gaze followed her, and I trailed off while I tried to think of the appropriate words. When I moved my focus back to Sara, I was certain a smile a mile wide crossed my lips. "Well, she's the light of my life. God, that sounds so clichéd, doesn't it? But it's true. She gives me a reason to be better, in a way that even Alyssa could never provide." I reached for Alyssa's hand and clasped it in my lap, letting her know I hadn't meant the words in a malicious way. She gave my fingers a gentle squeeze, reassuring me that she hadn't taken offense. "Just a few months ago, anyone who knows me would have said I wasn't exactly the daddy type."

Alyssa chuckled. "You would have said that about yourself."

I couldn't help laughing because it was true. "Probably. Now though. Well, I can't imagine a life without her in it."

"He's so good with her too." Alyssa's smile made my heart melt. "A natural."

My grin matched hers. Fuck, I was growing into a sappy wanker being around her—the worst part was that I couldn't even find it in myself to care. "I wouldn't say a complete natural. The first time I was alone with her, man she had me by my—" I cut myself off before I finished my sentence by naming parts of my anatomy best not discussed with a national magazine. "Let's just say she had me wrapped around her little finger the whole time."

We talked a little more about Phoebe, and about the mistakes I'd made in the past. Alyssa chipped in where she could. Before long, the conversation turned to the article in *Gossip Weekly*. We were careful with what we said, because they could easily sue us for libel if we said anything too derogatory about them, but by the same token, we didn't want to let anyone think that we were happy with the bullshit they'd printed.

Sara was a complete professional, touching on subjects just deeply enough to be interesting to readers, without delving too deeply into the story about how I left Brisbane in the first place and why Alyssa and I hadn't had any contact in the intervening years. She even skirted around her knowledge of Emmanuel expertly, leaving his history off the record completely.

Although we had no real clues what they'd ask before we started, we didn't have any complaints by the end. We'd been certain they wouldn't bother to ask anything that we would veto anyway, because it would be pointless and a waste of everyone's time. Especially when we just wouldn't answer the question. In the end, because Sara had avoided the worst topics for us, neither of us had shied away from any of her questions.

The interview had become a study in reflection of things that had happened over the past few months—years really—of my life. Sara's frank questions had forced me to consider some things that I'd been happier to ignore, and reminded me of some things I never wanted to forget.

When we finished the interview, Sara told us we were welcome to use the hotel room for the night if we wanted, as it was paid for until the following morning, but I refused, explaining that Alyssa and Phoebe were due on a plane. And I sure as shit didn't need, or want, a hotel room on my own.

"The issue is due to the printer at the end of the week, so I'll courier a copy to you tomorrow afternoon for final copy approval. I have no idea how you managed to wrangle that. You must have one hell of a negotiator on your side."

Alyssa looked to the floor as Sara said the words.

I wrapped my arm around her waist. "The best."

And after almost an hour reminiscing about what my life had been like before, I couldn't be happier that she was at my side. In a little over a month's time, she'd be down in Sydney permanently, and our life could truly begin.

Before that, though, I needed to ensure that the ones who'd almost cost us our happiness paid for their interference.

Whatever the price.

CHAPTER TWENTY-THREE
SECOND CHANCES

AT EIGHT THIRTY the following morning, I was parked in front of a familiar building trying to stave off a panic attack. I was breathing through my nose, repeating my mantra over and over, and trying to think of Phoebe and Alyssa. It was all failing.

All of it was useless.

I was fucking useless.

The impression of the steering wheel was probably branded across my forehead because I'd pressed my face hard against it to hide from prying eyes. My heart sputtered and raced, pounding so hard that I could almost taste each beat. Sweat coated my palms no matter how many times I rubbed them against my pants. My fists were clenched so tight around the leather that my short fingernails were digging into the flesh of my palms. I was a bundle of nerves strung together with a pile of contradictions. Saliva flooded my mouth, but my throat was too dry. I couldn't breathe. My was heart too big in my chest; my lungs too small. A churning rocked my stomach as it both twisted around the quickie breakfast I'd had, and yet felt empty at the same time.

Why was I even bothering to turn up for the meeting with Danny? From the moment I'd awoken, every possible outcome of Danny's request had assaulted me. None of them were great.

It wasn't like he was going to do a one-eighty and give me my fucking job back. He'd said as much in every conversation we'd had so far. He was probably just going to rub my nose in his decision one more time. Remind me of all the reasons he didn't want me on his fucking team.

Why am I here?

Would anyone even notice if I drove home and never showed? It was a thought I'd had at least ten times on the drive over. Twice, I'd even got to the point of pulling over and bringing up Danny's number on my phone, ready to tell him I wasn't coming in.

Despite that, I was cleaned and pressed, and ready for the meeting. At least on the outside. Inside, I was a quivering mess. It was only made harder by the fact that I'd had to fend for myself all morning. I'd awoken alone. Had breakfast alone. Showered alone.

Just like last time they were in Sydney, the precious few days I'd spent with Alyssa and Phoebe had spoiled me, and crashing back to reality was fucking hard.

Fuck, Morgan was right. At some point I'd definitely traded my cock for a vagina. Not only that, I'd done it willingly. I'd fucking do it again to see the awe in Phoebe's turquoise eyes as she looked at me when we told her the truth about me. To taste Alyssa's lips over and over. To spend mornings having breakfast together and making jokes over our Weet-Bix.

Fuck, I missed them.

A chuckle escaped me as I lifted my gaze to the rear-view mirror. "You've had a night where you thought you lost them," I chastised my reflection. "You made it through that. Is going for a meeting with Danny really worse than that?"

Letting my feet carry me from the car before the doubts could settle back in, I headed into the office. At the security desk, I greeted the guard. He didn't seem surprised to see me, but I didn't think he would be. Even though it wouldn't be news that was shared with everyone in the building, Danny would have told key staff that I was coming.

What did surprise me was that after getting me to sign in and giving me a guest pass, the guard left me to find my own way to

Danny's office. Generally guests would only be allowed past reception with supervision. It could only have been on Danny's instruction. None of the security staff would have risked their jobs doing something so reckless just because they knew me.

Was Danny trying to give me some sense of normalcy? But why?

I walked down the hallway of Sinclair Racing's headquarters, thankful I was alone for a moment as the memories of the last time I walked through the corridor flashed through me. The last time I'd tread the path, it had led to one of the darkest moments of my life. Now, it seemed to offer a ray of hope, however miniscule that might be.

When I reached Danny's office, I paused in front of the door. My heart was in my throat and my hands shook slightly. I tried to tell myself there was nothing that could happen that would be worse than what already had, but it didn't help the nerves that had come back in force, racing laps around my body and dragging my sanity away in their wake.

I tried not to think of what came next and reminded myself that regardless of the outcome, I would be seeing Alyssa and Phoebe again in person in four weeks—for Christmas—at the longest.

Sooner if I could.

And after that, they'd be moving in and everything would be the way it was supposed to be.

Still, the questions looped. Questions that would be answered as soon as I opened the damned door, but it felt like too much effort. Was Danny going to offer me another chance like Eden thought? Would I take it if he did? Alyssa seemed cautiously optimistic when I'd told her.

Even after time to think on it—to stress over every implication that might come from going back—I still wanted to be back with Sinclair Racing. Despite his knee-jerk reaction to the magazine, Danny had always been understanding—especially considering he'd known the worst of my drug use and had been willing to overlook it because I'd gotten clean. He genuinely gave a damn about his staff, and that was worth something to me. If my hope wasn't misplaced, then maybe he was big enough to swallow his pride, admit he'd made a mistake in sacking me, and offer me a role on the team. Any role. If he did, didn't I owe it to myself and my family to accept?

If I had a job lined up before Phoebe and Alyssa moved to Sydney, it would only make our lives easier. I couldn't get ahead of myself, though. Knowing my luck, there was probably just some paperwork he needed me to sign to formalise everything with my sacking.

Sucking down a deep breath, and pushing all hope from my mind lest it let me down, I knocked on his office door.

"Come in," his voice called.

When I pushed through the door, I was greeted by Danny stationed behind his desk. He regarded me sternly as I entered before standing and moving around the small space to shake my hand.

"Thank you for coming today, Declan."

"Of course." My words coated my tongue so that I had to give a small cough to clear my throat.

"Sit," he said, waving his hand toward the chair across the desk from him.

I didn't wait to be asked again, taking the seat he'd indicated.

"I'm sure you're wondering why I asked you to come by."

Worried that if I tried to speak through my stress, my voice would come out high and scratchy, I nodded and gestured for him to continue.

His fingers formed a steeple in front of his nose. "Your phone call yesterday certainly gave me cause to stop and think."

Drawing in a calming breath, I waited for him to continue.

"I meant what I said though, Declan. I can't have you race for me anymore. Even if I had a spare car, there are simply too many factors that would make it a bad business decision."

"The magazines?"

He parted his hands, giving a half shrug before clasping them back together in front of him again. "Among other things."

"But?" I knew there was one. Otherwise I wouldn't have been

sitting across from him in his office just days before the team was due to race in Tasmania. The behind-the-scenes prep would have well and truly started. In fact, Danny was probably due in Tassie later that day or early the next. If it was just a friendly chat, it would have waited until after the season had broken in two weeks.

"Well, despite the difficult days you have endured recently, including some undoubtedly caused by losing your position here, you have shown fierce loyalty to Sinclair Racing. Loyalty like that is rare indeed, and I believe it should be rewarded."

My heart started to stutter, but I tried to remain outwardly calm. I leaned back into the chair, attempting desperately to give off an air of indifference even though all I wanted to do was lean forward, slam my hands against the desk, and demand he tell me more.

"I believe we might be able to find you a position here. However, it's unlikely to be the one you want."

Fuck. He probably was planning to have me scrub the toilets or some shit, just like I'd joked. I forced my jaw closed, clenching my teeth. My cheeks and jawline probably showed the telltale signs, but if Danny noticed he didn't say anything.

"After our phone call, I talked at length with Liam, and he's agreed to take you on as an apprentice mechanic. If you're interested, that is. I believe you have some talent in that area."

Despite my offer to come back to any position, and Danny's repeated confirmation that I wouldn't drive for him again, part of me had obviously still clung desperately to the hope that he'd backflip on the issue. Even though it had been battered and wounded almost beyond recognition lately, my pride had me wanting to push out of my chair and leave, telling Danny to shove his offer up his fucking arse on the way. What a fucking long way to fall. From driver to apprentice grease monkey. I would be the laughing stock of the team.

It was so fucking tempting to tell him to piss off.

Only, I had Alyssa and Phoebe to support now. Being an apprentice *would* give me a trade. Something to fall back on—or move on to, as it were. I stared impassively at Danny as the two sides waged war in my head.

"I still think you have a lot of potential as a driver, young man. It's unfortunate a lack of sponsorships make that impossible right now. I'm sure you understand that I have to think of what is in the best interest of the whole team, not any one individual within it. But I do feel that it would be pertinent at this juncture to remind you that you're still young. You have a lot of life left to make up for certain mistakes. Right now, the most important ally you have is time." His gaze was stern. Steady. It held me captive as I tried to decipher the message he was trying to portray, hidden within his words. Something he couldn't say outright lest it bite him on the arse, but something he wanted me to know regardless. "If enough time passes, some controversies can be forgotten by the public. And by the sponsors. Especially if no new ones come to light."

I nodded. My heart was in my throat as I pieced together his cryptic clues. Despite everything he'd said so far, there was hope. A huge fucking hope. If I interpreted him correctly, he was telling me that not only was there a position for me at Sinclair Racing as an apprentice, but that perhaps another position—maybe even my old position—would open up if I could avoid being in the spotlight for the wrong reasons for long enough.

There was a possibility I could be back on the track before too long. It might be small, but it was there. In the meantime, I could learn a fall-back trade and support my new family. My heart was in my throat as I considered it. It was as close to a win/win as I could ever expect to be offered under the circumstances.

I could have told him to shove it and waited for another driving role, but there was no guarantee another one would be offered to me. Especially if sponsors were using their money to keep me out after the scandals. Not all teams would be willing to make the gamble that Paige was willing to make, and I was certain she was only making it because of her connections to the media.

Even if I were offered another driver role, there was no guarantee it would be in Sydney. Or with a team that valued each member as much as Sinclair Racing always had.

"So, Declan, what do you think of my offer? Obviously it will mean a reduction in your salary, but you could start back on Monday. That is, if you'd like."

It wasn't until he'd spoken again that I realised I'd been sitting, staring at him like a tosser as the possibilities ran through my mind.

Swallowing hard on the mixture of fear and shattered pride that had risen in my gullet, I glanced at the hand extended to me across the desk. The metaphoric olive branch that might one day see me back in the seat of a V8 without having to sacrifice Alyssa, move, or work for an insane cougar.

Meeting his gaze across the desk, I considered my options. The thing was, I truly didn't blame him for the decision he'd made to kick me off the team. He'd felt hurt and betrayed. I could easily understand those emotions—it was how I'd felt after Josh's attack years earlier. The decisions I'd made then, with a knee-jerk reaction, hadn't been all that dissimilar to Danny's. I'd cut Alyssa from my life because I'd assumed something that wasn't entirely true. I hadn't trusted her or myself enough to believe we'd be able to work it out.

Besides, all the evidence presented to Danny had pointed in the direction of the conclusion he'd reached. It was likely I would've thought the same thing if the article had been about anyone else.

The fact that he was even admitting he was at least partly wrong showed his integrity. It would be difficult to swallow my pride each day and deal with the shit that was sure to result from my choice, but to make up for it, I would be back at my dream team.

After everything we'd been through, I knew beyond a shadow of a doubt that Alyssa would be by my side through it all. She wouldn't look down on me for accepting the role. She'd just want me to be happy.

It wasn't a difficult decision, but I wrestled over something internally for a few more seconds before stating, "I accept. On one condition."

The hand wavered and dropped just a little.

"What's that?" Danny asked sceptically, as if shocked by my unwillingness to accept the offer point-blank. No doubt my words to him over the phone were playing through his mind.

Was he wondering whether I'd lied to him?

"Can I start after the Christmas break?" I asked, offering my hand in response. "I have a few issues to deal with at home first and I'd like to finish what I started when you put me on that plane to London. I want to come back without the shit of the past hanging over my head. I'll also need time off to visit my psychiatrist. I don't want to turn my back on the progress we're making."

"I'm sure we can manage both of those, especially if it will help with some longer-term goals." Danny smiled broadly at me as he grasped tightly to my hand with both of his own. "Welcome back to the team, son. It's time to start fresh."

As I shook his hand and we worked out the basic details, I felt like I was planning my trip home. I couldn't wait to tell Alyssa the good news.

CHAPTER TWENTY-FOUR

TRIPPING OUT

I WAS ON the phone to Alyssa before I'd even reached the car, bursting at the fucking seams to tell her the news.

"So?" she prompted. I climbed into my car but didn't start it. I wanted to finish the call before I went anywhere. Not that I really had anywhere to go.

"So, I miss you already."

"Funny, Dec. How'd it go?"

I couldn't help teasing her a little. "I wasn't trying to be funny. I miss you."

"I miss you too." The impatience crept into her voice even though I was sure she was trying to hide it. "Now, how'd it—" There was a bang in the background and Alyssa swore under her breath. "Damn, I've gotta go, Dec."

She hung up before I could finish my sentence or say goodbye.

I blew out a breath, wondering what could have been so vital that she'd had to cut our conversation so damned short. With my mind turning over the various possibilities, I dropped my phone on the centre console. Dropping my head back against the headrest, I closed my eyes.

A second later, the passenger door popped open.

"What the fuck?" My eyes were open and my hand was on my phone in a heartbeat.

Morgan had stuck his head into the car and laughed at my reaction. "Hey, shithead."

"What do you want, Morg?" I asked, unable to force any emotion into my voice.

"Geez, curb your enthusiasm next time, would you?" He slid into the seat beside me.

"Sorry, I just . . ." I trailed off before I could admit to him just how big a pussy I now was by saying I missed my girls. Or that I was desperate for Alyssa to call me back already. It was less than a minute since she'd hung up, but that felt too long. After rubbing my face with my free hand, I blew out a frustrated breath. "What can I do you for?"

"So, you had a meeting with Danny today?"

"Well, that would explain why I'm in front of the fucking building now, wouldn't it?"

"I hear you're coming back." The excitement in his voice as the words slipped from him was almost contagious. In different circumstances, it would have been. Knowing Morgan, though, he was probably building me up for some practical joke.

If I were coming back as a driver, I might have been unable to resist responding in kind, but because the situation wasn't that ideal, I just blew out another breath. "Apparently good news travels fast."

"Fuck, what bug crawled up your arse and died today? Do you know how big this is? Sinclair doesn't give second chances. Not once you're out."

"If you're just stopping by to congratulate me, save it. I'm not interested in hearing it right now." I wanted someone else's congratulations.

"God, you're an arsehole."

I shrugged. In some ways, he was right. On a personal level, it was something to celebrate—at the very least it would mean that we could have food on the table—but professionally, it was anything but. "What can I say, Morg, being in the pits is a long way from being out on track."

"Still, I think it's worth a celebration. What are you doing tonight? Or are you so pussy-whipped by that wildcat of yours that you can't go for a few drinks?"

His statement actually drew a half-smile from me. "She'd kill you if she heard you calling her that."

He chuckled. "I don't doubt that. But c'mon, what d'ya say? Let's hit the town. It's been too long and I'm off to Tassie tomorrow."

"I won't be good company."

"Well, yeah, I know that, but when have you ever been?" he teased.

His words, an attempt at the banter we'd always had, managed to draw a slight chuckle and something of a smile from me. "Fuck off, McGuire."

"Seriously though, I feel like I haven't spoken to you in months."

I didn't feel like reminding him that was because he'd spent the entire lead-up to Bathurst walking around making threats that included bringing rusty tools near *my* tool. Instead, I just said, "I don't think it's a great idea to be heading out when that bullshit article is still so fresh."

"Okay. I'll be at yours at seven then."

"Wait, what? Why?"

"'Cause you need a boys' night so that your cock doesn't fully retract. From what I've seen, it's at least halfway there."

"My cock is perfectly fine. Thank you for your concern though. It's been noted and reported to management."

"Please? Eden's informed me she needs me out of the apartment tonight. She's got some girly shit to do or something."

Knowing I wouldn't be able to resist them tag teaming me if I continued to refuse, I relented. It was easier than waiting for Eden to be involved. "Fine. If you're that in love with me that you can't resist coming to see me, at least bring dinner. I'm not that easy that I'll put out without a meal."

He punched my shoulder. "Sure thing. I'll see you then."

Once he was out of the car, I started it up and left. I was halfway home when Alyssa called back.

"Sorry about that," she said. "Phoebe got into the cupboards and was dismantling the house to help me start packing."

Picturing it, I laughed. "It's okay."

"So?" she prompted.

"It wasn't what we expected. He confirmed that I definitely won't be coming back as a driver."

"Oh." The disappointment in her voice was too fucking cute. Even though me having a driving career had once seemed impossible to her, she was actually upset that I hadn't got my position back.

"But he did offer me a different position."

"Oh?"

"An apprenticeship." I blew out a breath, hoping she wouldn't think less of me because I was going from prime position in the team to bottom of the fucking ladder. "As a grease monkey."

"Really? And what did you say?"

"I told him I'd take it. What other choice do I have?"

"You could hang out for another team."

"But that might never happen."

She hummed in agreement. "Are you happy?"

"Baby, it's a job. With everything else going on, I don't think I can be picky. Besides, Danny seemed to suggest that if I keep my nose clean, I might even get back on the track one day."

"That's great news. So when do you start?" Alyssa asked.

"After Christmas break. It all works out perfectly. There's only one thing missing in my life now."

"What's that?"

"My family."

"You're cute, Dec, but there's only a month or so to go. In fact, I had a meeting today with the real estate agent about breaking my lease. They've got someone who's able to move in a few days before Christmas."

My smile widened. Without a doubt it was the best fucking day I'd had in a long time. After so many shitty things piling up on me, it was overdue. "So, you'll be coming down here for Christmas?"

"Oh. Um, no. I've already planned to stay with Mum and Dad for Christmas and then come down before New Year's."

And there was the sting in the fucking tail. I could just picture myself sitting around my house in my underwear and socks, alone on Christmas fucking day like a pathetic loser even though it should have been my first with my family. "Oh, okay."

"I still need to figure out all the details for the move, but seeing as though your house is pretty much furnished, I'll get rid of anything that I don't have a sentimental attachment to, and then hire a truck or something to bring down the rest."

"Uh-huh." I wasn't really listening to her. Instead, I was imagining what my solo Christmas would be like. It was supposed to be my first as a father, and now it looked like it'd be the first where I would be alone. Before Alyssa, it would have been an excuse to get wasted and have my fill of lonely women desperate for companionship. That option was out, but apparently so was spending the time with my family.

"So, when do you think you can get here?"

"Huh?" I'd obviously missed something.

"Well, you are coming up for Christmas, aren't you?" The way she said it, it was like it was a given.

"Didn't you say you're staying with your parents?"

"Yeah. So?"

"So, I hardly think I'm your dad's idea of a great Christmas guest."

She chuckled. "Dec, it'll only be for a few days. Besides, he's got to get used to you before long anyway."

"I guess. You really want me to come up?"

"Do you think you're the only one who misses what we have when we're together?"

The sorrow in her voice made me long to be at her side, to smooth it away with a kiss. "Of course not."

"Besides, you said you would. Phoebe has been asking about you already. Wanting me to remind you of your promise."

It took me a moment to remember what promise. "She

remembered that?"

Alyssa chuckled. "She's like an elephant when it comes to things she wants."

Even though I was physically sitting in my car in the middle of traffic, my mind was already halfway back to Brisbane. Then it struck me that there was no reason for me not to go. Things were falling into place for the following year already, and there was nothing more I could do to speed it along anyway. There was nothing I needed to be in Sydney for. In fact, some things would be easier from Brisbane. Like my plan for revenge.

"Tell her I'll be there tomorrow," I said.

"What?" Her shocked voice echoed through the speaker.

"If it's okay with you, that is."

"What?" The surprise had morphed into something a little closer to excitement. "Are you kidding?"

"Why not? I've got nothing I need to be here for until after Christmas. And I've got every reason in the world to be up there with you two."

"Are you telling me that you're going to stay up here for a month?" I wondered whether butterflies were racing through her stomach as she asked the question. It certainly sounded like it.

"If you'll have me that long."

"God, Dec, of course. Of course, I will. I know I hesitated when you first asked me to move in with you, but that was only because I was scared. I was so scared that I'd let my hopes rise to the point where I'd never recover from the heartbreak that followed. But, now . . . What can I say, Dec, my hope is so sky-high right now. You've raised it there and now it—" She cut herself off. "Sorry, I'm rambling and that probably sounded really pathetic."

If she could see me, she'd be able to tell from the smirk on my face that her words were anything but pathetic. If she found her words embarrassing though, I didn't want to linger on them and prolong her pain. "If I leave first thing in the morning, I should be able to make it there by the time you finish work."

"Okay, Dec."

"And Lys?"

"Yeah?"

"I'll be counting the minutes till then."

"Me too."

"Actually, maybe you should keep it from Phoebe for now. We'll surprise her tomorrow night."

She chuckled. "Yeah, I think she'd like that. I'll see you tomorrow, Dec."

When I got home, there was a parcel sitting on the front doorstep. Bending down, I saw it was from *Woman's Idea*. A moment later, I pulled the advance copy of the article from the envelope and read through it to ensure I was happy with the overall portrayal of both Alyssa and me.

I smiled at the photos that accompanied the article. Eden was right; they were fucking hot. The thought even crossed my mind to ring and see if I could get copies of some of them. When I was still in my ProV8, I'd endured many photo shoots, but none had ever made me want copies of the prints before.

Happy with the article, I took it inside and scanned it into my computer. I emailed a copy to Alyssa, and another to Danny. Maybe getting Danny to look it over was brown-nosing, but now that I had a job hanging in the balance again, I would do what I could to keep it. If I had him cast his eyes over the article before I gave it my final approval, he couldn't argue later that it wasn't positive enough or caused more problems. Besides, if it took a little bit of arse-kissing to get another step closer to being back behind the wheel of a ProV8, it was worth it.

While I waited for a response from Alyssa and Danny, I slid the copy back into the envelope and went to start packing.

HOURS LATER, nursing a beer that was well on its way to being warm, I tried to quell the heat of the jealousy racing through my veins as I listened to Morgan's glowing endorsement of the Bahrain track. With no chance of getting back behind the wheel in the foreseeable future, it was extra maddening to hear him wax lyrical about the performance of his car and give a fresh driver's-eye play-by-play.

It was almost a relief when my phone rang and interrupted the evening. When I saw Alyssa's number, I thought maybe she was calling to talk about the magazine article, even though she'd already emailed the magazine with a few minor changes.

"Dec, I don't know if it's a great idea for you to come up anymore."

My heart stopped beating and dropped to my stomach. "What?" I could barely find the volume to say the word. Part of me wondered whether there was some chance she'd changed her mind after our conversation. Had something happened to shift what had seemed to be unshakable faith? I moved away from Morgan into my study, because if she really was trying to get me to stay away I wanted to be able to argue my case without him thinking I was pussy-whipped. Or more than he already did at least.

"There's just . . . some stuff happening, and I think it would be better if you stayed away for a while. Maybe just come up before we need to move."

"What is it?"

"It's hard to expl—"

"No, Lys, don't give me excuses. Tell me what it is, or I'm getting in my fucking car right now and I'll be on your doorstep before you know it."

"It's that pap who was following you around."

I clenched my fist as I tried to recall whether I'd seen the guy or his white X-Trail that day, but I couldn't recall that I had. Was it because he was now in Brisbane? "What about him?"

"He was at Emmie's grave when I took Phoebe there today." Her voice was quiet, filled with tears that I was sure had been falling since whatever altercation she'd had. "He knows. He knows all about Emmie, and . . . and he said that Emmie's death would be a great focus for the next article. He—he took photos of Phoebe and me, and I just . . . I'm just glad that Flynn was there. But the guy threatened to make me look like some sort of monster for trying to hide the details. He accused me of lying to you. If you're here too, it's only going to give him more ammunition. It's better if we stay apart, at least for now."

"No."

"What do you mean, no?"

"I mean, no, Lys. I'm not going to let them dictate our lives. United front, remember? Like you said. Besides, if he's there causing you trouble, I want to be the one to shove his fucking camera down his throat."

"This is why I don't think it would be a good idea for you to be here. He's trying to goad us. As it is, he got photos of Flynn and me together with Phoebe. I can't even imagine what will go to print next. It's only going to make everything you're facing harder if you're mixed up in it too."

"I don't give a shit, Lys. You and me."

"But—"

"You and me, Lys. Okay?"

"Okay."

"And when our article comes out, it'll prove the truth, okay?"

"You know some people won't believe it. Darcy isn't going to back off just because of an article. There will be people who think there's something going on with Flynn and me. They'll think I'm some sort of gold-digging liar."

"All the more reason for me to be up there. Fuck, if it helps I'll get the paps to photograph me and Flynn together." The thought wasn't one I welcomed, but I wasn't going to live my life running scared from them anymore. I refused.

"What if no one believes the truth though?"

"I don't give a shit who believes it at first. It just means that we have to prove it. Day by day, we show everyone how fucking happy we are. By being together and being there for each other."

Alyssa gave a sad little chuckle. "That sounds almost easy."

"Yeah, well, loving you is easy."

Her laughter grew. "You think you're such a sweet-talker, don't you? Think your mouth can help you get away with anything."

"Oh, baby, you don't even know everything my mouth can

253

do."

"That's the cheesiest line I've ever heard."

"But did it work? Did it make you picture my mouth on your body? My tongue licking your pussy?"

She didn't respond, which I took as a yes.

"Are you now imagining all the things I could do to you, Lys? Because I sure as fuck am, and it's making me hard as a fucking stone."

I heard her swallowing even as her breathing sped up.

"Did you still want me to stay away for another month?"

Once more, she didn't say anything in response, but it didn't matter. I knew the answer by the sound of her shallow, needy breaths.

"Or do you want me to come up there and show you the things my mouth can do?"

"Yes." She breathed the word.

It was issued with such need that it bypassed my ear and went straight to my cock. "Good. You can't get rid of me that easily. I'll see you tomorrow night, okay?"

After reassuring her again that it would all be okay, I disconnected the call. I headed back into the living room and skulled the last of my beer. I was certain a scowl crossed my lips, and I didn't say anything to Morgan.

"Trouble in paradise?" he asked, looking genuinely concerned.

A frown tugged at the corners of my mouth. "Maybe."

After grabbing another beer for each of us out of the carton he'd brought, I opened up. Taking him in as a true confidant, just like I had with Eden, I told him the whole story of Alyssa and me, ending with my desire to pay Darcy, Hayley, Paige, Tillie, and Talia back for their roles in my downfall.

Whatever else happened, I would make them pay.

And Morgan might be the perfect ally in that.

CHAPTER TWENTY-FIVE
COMING HOME

THE ALARM ON my phone blared.

The high-pitched beeping pierced straight into my skull and pulled me from my dream.

Fuck, how much had I had to drink? I dropped my head back against my pillow and tried to piece together reality from dream.

What a fucking dream too.

It was all about Alyssa. For a half a second, I smiled as I recalled the girl I'd left behind when I'd moved to Sydney. To retain the images of the dream, which had featured her in full, living colour like so many had in the past, I screwed my eyes shut. I was desperate to cling to the memory my mind had offered up of her body.

My hungover brain ticked over with the reasons why it was a bad idea to be thinking about her. For so long, I'd turned to sleeping tablets whenever I'd woken from similar dreams.

Only, this one wasn't exactly like the others. This one was a dream where we'd been together again. Happy. Where I'd met her on the way to London and followed her to Brisbane after I'd learned of our child. Where I'd lost the job I loved, but was somehow okay with it because I had her.

Where I was travelling to Brisbane to meet her again soon.

In the dark of night, alone and hungover, it seemed too impossible to be true.

Glancing through the darkness, I tried to make out the ceiling with my tired eyes. Tried to work out why my alarm was set for such a stupid-arse time of the morning. Tried to work out how the fuck to get it to shut the fuck up without me having to move a fucking muscle.

The blaring surrounded me, smashing against my skull.

"Fuck off!" I croaked as I threw my pillow at my phone.

When all it did was change the angle the sound was coming from, I finally dragged myself out of bed. As I did, I pressed my lips together. They were dry and my mouth tasted like stale beer. I'd definitely had too much to drink.

What the fuck would Alyssa think if she knew how drunk I'd let myself get?

As soon as the thought struck me, I laughed at the absurdity of thinking it was all just a dream. As if my mind had the imagination needed to dream up Alyssa's new curves and full chest. The thought of being at her side again by the time I went to bed that night brought a smile to my lips, despite the pounding in my head.

I had a quick shower, which left me feeling halfway human again, and then dressed in something comfortable for a day of driving. When I'd finished, a memory of the previous night struck me, and I chuckled.

Morgan had been too drunk to drive home. When he'd called Eden to come get him, she'd chewed him out for letting himself get to that stage and refused to come. He'd ended up having to stay with me like he had in the past.

I left my room and headed straight for the spare bedroom at the end of the hall, where Ruby had stayed when she'd been there. Morgan's name was on my lips as I pulled the door open, but he wasn't in the bed there.

Either he'd passed out where he'd been sitting on my couch, or . . .

The door to Phoebe's room stood slightly ajar and I pushed it open silently. I had to bite my lip to stop my laughter when I saw Morgan's tall form draped over Phoebe's white princess bed. He was lying on his back, with his head dangling off the side and his blonde waves extending in all directions, like he'd just stuck his finger in a socket. One arm was lifted up over the back of the tiara-shaped headboard.

Before I woke him, I pulled out my phone and snapped a handful of images from different angles. You never knew when a little bribery image might come in handy. God knows he had a few of me from over the years.

After I was satisfied I'd got the photos I wanted—and texted one to Eden for good measure—I tried to wake him. Always a hard task after a night on the piss.

"Morning, princess," I said, kicking his foot.

He groaned and rolled over, dragging his head back onto the bed and drooling on the pillow.

I kicked his other leg. "Fucker, are you seriously going to drool on my little girl's pillow?"

"Fuck off, squirt, what fucking time is it? The sun's not even up."

"It's five in the morning, and you need to get your arse out of my house because I've got a hot date in Brisbane tonight."

"Can't drive. Still drunk."

"Well, at least drag your arse out of bed and get started on some breakfast."

"Five more minutes." He buried his head under the pillow.

"Two minutes, or your new nickname at work will be princess." I wiggled the phone in my hand.

"What the fuck are you talking about?" He lifted his head and took in the bed. "Fucker, what happened to the bed?" He glanced around with bloodshot eyes. "What happened to the room?"

"It's Phoebe's room now."

"God, it's worse than I thought. Not only are you pussy-whipped by your pseudo-wife, you're wrapped around the finger of a little girl too. We need some serious man counselling."

"Ha ha, now fuck off out of her bed. Your two minutes are up."

He held up his hand in surrender, but got up.

"You smell like a brewery," I said. "You should have a shower."

"Yes, Mum."

I was already halfway out of the room by the time the words left his mouth. Nothing he could say could bring me down. After all, I was going to Brisbane and when I came back home again, I'd be bringing my family with me.

While Morgan pottered around getting food and coffee, and trying to work out when he might be safe to drive, I packed the stuff I was taking with me into my Prado and wrote a note for Christina explaining I would be away and letting her know how to get in touch if she needed to finish up early. True, I probably shouldn't have trusted her; for all I knew she could plot to steal all my shit for firing her, but she'd been privy to so much shit over the years that if she were a dishonest person, she probably would have sold a stack of stories to the gossip rags. Call me a sap, but I trusted her.

"You're not taking the Monaro?" he asked, standing at the door to my garage with a bowl of Cornflakes cradled in one hand.

"I figured we might need to tow something back."

"You're leaving your baby here for a month? Alone?"

I shrugged. "She'll be fine."

"God, what happened to you, man?"

"I got my priorities straightened out by a three-year-old. Maybe you should try it sometime."

"Got no immediate plans to hand over my balls to anyone just yet, thank you very much."

"I'm sure Eden will be thrilled that you said that."

A look of genuine fear crossed his face. "You wouldn't tell her."

"Nah, not yet. I'll wait until I need something first." I smacked his shoulder as I passed him to grab some food for the trip.

"Fucker." He chuckled.

After I'd finished packing the car and grabbing enough snacks to get me most of the way, I placed the keys for my Monaro in Morgan's hand. "Check on her every few days, won't you?"

"I knew you couldn't leave her completely alone."

"And make sure the house doesn't burn down or some shit, hey? Christina will still be coming by to clean up like normal, at least until Christmas, but there's a house key on that key ring if you need to get in." I might have trusted Christina, but I wasn't a complete idiot to give free run of my house unchecked to someone I had effectively fired.

"Sure thing."

"It also means you can let yourself out."

"Anyone would think you're in a hurry to go."

"Hey, I got a hot woman with a wet and ready pussy waiting for me at the end of my trip. Who wouldn't be eager to start?" I climbed in the car.

"Don't let me stop you."

"And you're still okay, for that other thing?"

He flashed me an evil grin. "Looking forward to it. I'll text you the details once I get them sorted."

"Awesome. Catch you on the flip side." I stuck my key in the ignition and started to reverse out before realising I'd forgotten the most important thing. Something I wanted to give Alyssa before we came back home. "Shit!"

I leapt from the car and raced into the house. Less than a minute later, I had what I needed and was back at the car.

"Is that what I think it is?" he asked. His eyes widened to the size of saucers as he glanced at the velvet box in my hand.

I lifted one shoulder in response. "You know me. Pussy-whipped. And what a fine fucking pussy it is."

"Whatever, it's your dick that's going to suffer from disuse once you slip that ring on her finger."

"You underestimate the quality of my dick." I started the car.

"I really don't want to think about your dick."

"Sure you don't. Now it'll be all you can think of until I get back."

I laughed as he flipped me the bird.

THE DRIVE up to Brisbane wasn't as comfortable or as fast in my Prado as it had been in my Monaro. True, then I'd been driven by the ghosts of the past, whipping me into a frenzied state where I couldn't stop unless I had to, and now it was just my own desire compelling me onward.

By the time I hit the Gold Coast, the sky was stained with pinks and purples. The big black clouds and increasing humidity hinted that a storm would roll in before long. I could only hope to make it to Alyssa's before that happened.

As I continued north, the clouds overhead grew thicker and darker in the fading light of the day, casting an almost apocalyptic shadow over the world. When I turned onto the motorway just fifteen minutes later, the clouds had opened up. Even through the heavy rain on the roof, I could still hear the near-constant rumble of thunder. In the distance, lightning flashed, illuminating the area around me for fractions of a second at a time. It wasn't the sort of weather that was good for driving. In fact, visibility was down to almost nothing, but that was typical of a November storm.

It slowed me down as I drove to match the conditions. All I wanted was to be back at Alyssa's side. Between her telling me not to come and the weather delaying my arrival, it felt ominous.

I shoved aside the worry that it was a sign of things to come. Instead, I worked to convince myself that none of the shitty things really mattered. Alyssa's family would either come around or they wouldn't. The lingering threat of the paparazzi and gossip columns would ease if we didn't give them anything to focus on.

Almost an hour later, long after I'd promised I would show, I pulled up in front of Alyssa's house. After I'd stopped the car, I hid the ring box in the back of the glovebox, but left all my other bags where they were in the boot. Unpacking could wait until after I'd said hello.

Fuck, it could all wait until the morning if it needed to.

I practically ripped the door off its hinges to get to my family. The first breath I took outside the car was filled with the still air, heavy with the heat of the day trapped by the clouds overhead.

The rain had paused momentarily but was gearing up to fall

again. Hopefully it would bring release from the cloying humidity.

Glancing through a small gap in the curtain, I saw Alyssa sitting on the end of the couch chewing on her thumbnail. I wondered if she knew I was there and was just restraining herself, or if she was still unaware of my arrival. As if feeling the weight of my stare, she glanced up and met my gaze. The grin that crossed her mouth was fucking worth every kilometre I'd driven.

She was at the door and pulling it open before I could knock. With a gentle tug on her arm, I pulled her outside for a moment of alone time. I didn't even say hello before taking her face between my hands and guiding her lips to mine. The sheen of sweat that had burst across the back of my neck in the warmth didn't deter her as she gripped my hair and pulled me close in response to my kiss. My lips melded with hers, and my eyes sank closed as I fell into her.

Knowing that there was someone else I needed to say hello to, someone who was likely needing to head to bed soon, I pulled away from Alyssa.

"Hi," I murmured before resting my forehead on hers and planting one more open-mouthed kiss against her lips.

"I'm glad you ignored me when I said not to come."

I slid one hand down to her arse and pulled her hips against mine. "I'll be coming all right, and so will you, just as soon as Phoebe is asleep."

She flushed red and gave me a playful shove, but the need in her gaze told me that it was a false protest.

"Speaking of . . . I should probably say hi to her too."

"She doesn't know you're here yet."

"Okay." After one more kiss with Alyssa, I headed in through the open door.

Phoebe looked up as I came into view. Almost instantly, her gaze dropped back to the book in front of her, but then lifted to mine again.

"Daddy!" She squealed the word and the sound of it made my heart explode with joy.

I knelt down to her level and opened my arms for her. She was across the room and in my embrace in a heartbeat. The force of her flying-leap hug was almost enough to knock me on my arse.

"Hey, baby. I promised I'd come up as soon as I could, didn't I?"

After she'd finished hugging me, she stepped back and fixed on a frown that could have melted even the coldest heart. "We should stay together."

"We will, baby. I'm here until you guys are ready to move into my castle."

"Good, 'cause Mummy is sad when you're not here. And I don't like it when Mummy's sad."

"I'll let you in on a secret," I said, moving closer to her ear while looking up at Alyssa. "I don't either. Mummy has spent enough time being sad, hasn't she? From now on, I only want to make her smile. And I want to make her laugh. Is that a deal?"

Phoebe nodded and then squeezed my neck again. "I liked it when Mummy laughs."

"Me too, princess. Me too."

CHAPTER TWENTY-SIX

FAILURE AND FATIGUE

THE FOLLOWING DAY Alyssa contacted Phoebe's day care to give them notice that her last day would be the following Friday. Her name was already down on a waiting list at a couple of highly recommended centres in Sydney, but because I was in town until the move, Alyssa and I agreed to take her out of care. It had the double benefit of letting me spend some time with her while also saving Alyssa some money in the short term.

Because Phoebe was still booked in for care the next day, and Alyssa still had to work, I had some free time. I spent the day alone reminiscing about our reunion as I followed the directions Alyssa had left, helping her to start sorting and packing one of the rooms.

Even though she said thank you at the end of the day, I was certain I'd fucked up more than I actually helped. Some of the stuff I'd packed in one of the boxes was discreetly rewrapped and moved into a different box. Regardless, it was all pushing us closer to the day when she'd be in my house.

Our house.

Each time I peeked out the window, the paparazzo was hanging around out front. At one point, he caught me looking and waved. I gave him the finger in return. Unfortunately for him, he was too busy gloating that he wasn't quite quick enough to catch it on film.

Two days later, Alyssa and I were up to our elbows in boxes after Phoebe had gone to bed. While we were going over our plans and timeline again, she broke some slightly unwanted news to me.

"I'm not having the garage sale like we talked about," she said over a pile of boxes in what was once Flynn's room. Instead of the usual two piles—stuff coming with us and stuff going—she was creating three. The third was all the stuff to go back to him.

"Why not?"

"Because we've got another option now. A better one. Well, an easier one at least. We just need to hire a truck and take it over to Mum and Dad's. Dad wants to put the stuff in storage."

"Really? Why?"

She grimaced and looked away.

"Why?" I asked again, my tone making it clear that I wouldn't take silence as an answer.

"Dad wants me to store everything. Just in case."

"Just in case?"

"You know, just in case I need it again later."

"Just in case I screw things up, you mean?"

She gave me a sad smile and a shrug.

"And you agreed to go along with it?" I stared at her impassive expression, which confirmed my words without any need to speak. "Because you think I'm going to screw things up too."

She zipped the tape across the top of the box she was working on. "Dec, it's . . . it's not like that. Not really. I told you I trusted you, and I do. But Dad didn't give me much choice." When she looked up at me, her expression called to me, begging me to understand.

"Here I was thinking that we were past this bullshit, Lys." I shoved the trinket I'd just finished wrapping in newspaper into the box a little harder than was probably advisable, but I couldn't shake my irritation.

She sighed and rolled her eyes. "We are. But Dad is going to buy the furniture for double the price I'd ask for it at the garage sale and then pay to store it. And we don't have to put aside a whole day to have people rummaging through all my stuff. Plus, there's no guarantee that what I have would even sell. With the cost of day care and the fact that I wouldn't start work for a week after we get to Sydney, we need the money."

Even though her words were meant to reassure me, all they did was dig the knife in further. Everyone thought I was going to fail her, and I already was because I couldn't afford to tell Curtis to shove his offer up his arse. The fact was that the wage I would be bringing home would barely cover my mortgage payments and Alyssa's would barely cover the day care and other expenses. That meant we'd need every extra cent we could get. I hated it. I'd failed them both before we'd even left Brisbane.

As the money issue swirled anew through me, it occurred to me that by taking the lower-paying job as an apprentice mechanic, I'd probably signed the sales notice on at least a couple of my precious cars that were stored in the back shed. My decent collection of classics, the one I'd added to over the years whenever a beauty I couldn't resist came along, would soon be decimated. Between rego and insurance, it cost a significant sum each year to maintain them. I couldn't even begin to consider which ones to get rid of first, though. That was like asking me which limb I wanted to lose the least.

I taped up the box I was filling, and noticed the writing on the outside— "going."

Or fucking not, apparently.

With a growl, I shoved the box to the side and pushed myself up off the ground. Alyssa gave me a look that was halfway between a question and an apology. It made me feel worse. More than anything else, I just wanted to leave. I wanted to climb in the car and drive, but I had the wrong fucking car. I needed my Monaro or one of the classics in the back of my shed for thinking. Regardless, I left the room without another word.

My jaw was clenched tight so I didn't let loose the stream of curses that was on the tip of my tongue. Alyssa didn't deserve the harsh words, but they danced on my lips regardless. I didn't stop until I'd found my way to the kitchen. With my fingers curled around the laminate of the counter, I leaned heavily against the bench, took a handful of breaths, and tried to force out my frustration without making any sound.

Alyssa followed me. "I worried you'd react like this."

I twisted my head to cast her a look, but I couldn't look at her for long without all the emotions bubbling in me again. "Like what, Lys? Like the fucking failure I am."

She stepped back in shock. "Failure? What?"

"What else would you call it? You feel like you have to do a special deal with your father just to put food on the table. Six months ago, I had a contract worth more money than you could imagine, and now I've got Jack and Shit and even they're thinking of leaving."

"That's not true, Dec." She moved closer to me before running her fingers up along my spine. "You've got a house."

"And the fucking mortgage to go with it."

"You've got a job."

"A low-paying, shitty job."

"You don't know that. You might love it."

"You don't get it, Lys. I'm the man. I'm supposed to provide for you guys, and I'm failing."

She wrapped her arm around me and rested her head on my shoulder. "Says who?"

"What?"

"Who says you have to provide for us? Because you know what I think? I think that's patriarchal bullshit." She ducked under my arm and I moved back to allow her to come between me and the bench. Her arms wrapped around my neck, and she smiled the sweetest, most heartbreaking smile I'd ever seen her wear. "*We* need to provide for *her*. That's what's important. And in that respect, we're not failing. She doesn't need a fancy house, or a pile of expensive junk, she just needs our love. She needs food and clothes, and the rest doesn't matter."

"But what about—"

She placed her fingers over my lips. "It doesn't matter. We'll find a way. We'll manage."

Instead of responding with words, I moved my hands from the counter and wrapped them around her waist. "When did you get so wise?"

She flinched away from my words.

Fuck. My stomach twisted as I saw the flash of heartbreak over her face. What a stupid fucking question. *She got wise when she fucking had to, arsehole.*

With a deep breath, she wrapped her arms around me. She hadn't slid the mask she sometimes wore back into place, which I was glad of. If I was being an arsehole, I wanted her to call me on it, not mask her feelings and pretend everything was okay.

"About Dad, I just thought it would be easier," she said. "It'll make him happy if he thinks I have a backup plan. It's easier for us if he's happy."

"I don't plan on fucking this up, Lys. You have to know that. I need you both too much."

"I know, Dec."

She'd stopped a panic spiral dead in its tracks with nothing more than her presence and a few key words. I didn't think she fully appreciated that. But I wasn't going to argue with her anymore. "C'mon, let's give packing a rest for the night. I've got something I want to unwrap instead." I grabbed her hips and lifted her legs around my waist and carried her to the bedroom.

AROUND SPENDING time with Phoebe and Alyssa, I managed to watch most of the Tasmanian race. Alyssa even sat with me when Phoebe had her nap. Seeing Morgan rip up the track made me almost excited to be in the pits the next year. Almost.

"Are you looking forward to being there next year?" Alyssa asked as I shifted forward on the couch when Morgan went into the pits.

I shrugged. "It's not exactly the dream. But it's good enough for now."

Not long after Sinclair Racing had won the event—and almost secured the championship—Morgan called my mobile.

"I'm all set for next weekend, and have sorted those things you wanted. Do you think you can arrange your part?" he asked after some preamble and my congratulations.

"I'm pretty sure it'll be a cakewalk, but I'll let you know if I've got any problems. Where are you going to be staying?"

"Edie's booked a room for us at the Suncrest."

Eden and her fucking Suncrest Hotel obsession. "Okay. Keep in touch, and I'll let you know how I go."

When I saw Alyssa coming closer, I ended the call.

"What are you planning?" she asked.

"Boys' night with Morgan to celebrate his win."

She rolled her eyes. "Ugh. I know he's your friend and all, but I just don't get the appeal."

"He was looking out for me. We've both had to deal with crazed stalkers in the past, and he didn't know the truth about us." Even as I said the words I tensed, ready for the fight.

Right or wrong, she was still pissed about his interference with the email. It seemed unlikely that she'd ever find a way to get past it. On one hand, I could understand that it had hurt her. On the other though, I'd agreed to try when it came to her friend, and I didn't see why she couldn't extend me the same courtesy. It wasn't like he knew our history and wanted to deliberately hurt her.

"That doesn't change what he did."

"No, it doesn't, but I can't turn my back on him for trying to help either. It doesn't have to be a boys' night," I said, deciding to make a bluff and hope she didn't call me on it. She couldn't come because I didn't want her involved in the plan for the moment. She might tell me not to do it. "We could leave Phoebe with your mum, or Ruby, and go to see him together."

"I'd rather gouge out my eyes with a rusty spoon." She glanced up at me and must have seen the frown that tugged on my brow. "But you go, have fun. I don't want to stop you from being friends; I just don't want to be in the same room as him."

"He'll be here next Saturday."

"Fine. I'll call Flynn to see if he wants to come around for pizza, just like old times."

I clenched my jaw and glared at her. She was playing a game: she'd see the friend I didn't like if I saw the one she didn't. Two could play at that game though. "Fine. I'm sure you'll have a great time."

"I'm sure we will. Phoebe loves spending time with Flynn." Something behind me caught her gaze and her eyes widened in shock.

I understood a second later when Phoebe's excited voice cried, "Flynn's here? Yay!"

Hearing her enthusiasm at seeing the fucker who, for all legal purposes, was still regarded as her father was too much. I stormed from the room. Even if it hadn't been intentional, it pissed me off that Alyssa used Phoebe to hurt me just because I wanted to spend some time with someone from my other life. I intended to go straight to Alyssa's room to get some space and cool off, but when I passed Phoebe's open door, I stopped in my tracks. Remembering our conversation in Sydney, I knew she'd likely assume any anger I showed was her fault.

With two deep breaths to centre myself, I turned back to head to the kitchen again. A fake smile was on my lips as I watched Alyssa explaining that Flynn wasn't there now, but they'd invite him around for dinner on Saturday.

Alyssa glanced up at me, an apology in her gaze. My smile became more genuine and I mouthed the word, "Sorry," back at her.

"Phoebe, what do you say we go to the park this afternoon?" I asked. "We need to get out of the house for a while, don't you think?"

Seeing her enthusiasm over something so simple made me glad I'd made the suggestion. After Alyssa ordered her to find some shoes, Phoebe disappeared from the room.

"Do you think there'll ever be a day where we don't argue about something?" I asked.

"Who was arguing?" Alyssa asked with a chuckle.

"You know what I mean."

"I do. And probably not. But that's what life is about. It's not about agreeing about everything, it's how we act after each disagreement that's going to make a difference. "

"Are you sure you don't mind me hanging with Morg next weekend?"

"I guess I don't. I mean, if you can deal with me hanging with Flynn, I can extend the same courtesy, right?"

I nodded, but used the opportunity to redirect to another issue I'd been meaning to raise with her but hadn't. "You know what burns me the most there?"

"What?"

"That it's still Flynn's name on the certificates."

"Shit, we were going to fix that, weren't we? Sorry, Dec, there's just been so much going on. I hadn't even thought—"

"I understand, Lys. I really do, but now . . . I don't know. I guess I want the world to know she's mine. To celebrate that fact."

"The world hardly looks at birth certificates."

"You know what I mean. How do we do it?"

She nodded. "It'll probably be best if we have DNA tests done to make sure there are no hiccups in the process. That'll be undeniable proof that there was a mistake on the original certificates."

"Won't that paint you as some sort of hussy who slept with more than one man and didn't know the real father?"

A laugh slipped past her lips. "Hussy? Really, does anyone even use that word anymore, Dec?"

Ignoring her remark, I pressed my question. "But you're okay with people thinking that?" If she was hesitant or worried about it, she didn't show it.

"It's better if the world thinks that, considering the alternative is that I falsified a legal document, which is much worse, especially when I'm supposed to be getting into law soon."

"There were extenuating circumstances though."

"I know. It's stupid. I would've preferred to keep it blank, but there was just too much paperwork for me to cope with on my own. I was drowning and all I wanted to do was sink under it all. If it hadn't been for Phoebe needing me and Flynn supporting me however he could, I don't think I would've kept afloat."

My heart broke listening to her and once again, I wondered whether I'd ever fully understand just how hard that time was for her. All of my pain—all of the agony that had torn through me after learning the truth—was removed from the heartbreaking events by time and distance.

"Can we play soccer 'gain, Daddy?" Phoebe asked as she came running back into the room with a pair of pink sandals with Velcro straps on her feet.

Alyssa swiped her fingers under her eyes, wiping tears that I hadn't even seen fall. A smile lifted her lips and the mask was back in place. I wrapped my hand around hers and led them both out to the car. We could have walked, but it would have been well after dark before we got home, and I for one didn't plan on fighting away the mozzies and midges. Plus, it was easier hiding from the pap in a car.

Later that night, Alyssa jumped online and booked to have DNA testing done and also started the process of amending the birth certificates. I had no idea how we'd get to the facility without the paparazzo following us, but we'd deal with that when it came.

Slowly, but surely, the pieces were coming together.

WHEN WE woke Monday, it was with a little trepidation, because the *Woman's Idea* article was due to hit the stands within twenty-four hours. It could only go three ways. Either it'd go over well with the sponsors and public, and things would start to turn away from the constant negative press, it would be slammed as nothing more than a publicity stunt, or it would be ignored completely by everyone. As much as I hoped for the former, I thought it was much more likely to be the latter. People just didn't seem to buy the magazines for the happy stories, only the fucked-up ones.

I just hoped that the bastards who'd set me up so far didn't take it as an excuse for a renewed attack, but there was little I could do about it.

Around lunchtime, the calls started.

For me, it was Eden first, calling to congratulate me. There was no doubt in my mind that she'd already seen the article when I'd emailed it to Danny. When I confronted her about it she just laughed and said that it looked better in the full-gloss magazine.

Then it was a few other drivers I'd been on the track with. Each one told me that their wives or girlfriends had purchased the magazine and shown them—even the ones that I was certain had neither a wife nor a girlfriend—and that they wanted to offer me their support.

For Alyssa, it started with her mother. Ruth called and gushed over the article, spouting about how happy she was to see us so happy. So in love. She demanded we investigate the possibility of getting some of the photos for her too.

Around four, my phone rang again with a Brisbane number. The first person that sprang to mind was my cockhead father. Considering his little bit on the side—if they were even still together—was so heavily into the gossip magazines, I had no doubt she'd have seen the cover with Alyssa and me staring into each other's eyes with a hunger and need that was unmistakable. I wondered what he would have thought about the proceeds being donated to charity. He was probably having conniptions over the fact that we'd never see a cent.

Good.

With the expectation that he was the one calling, I moved away from Alyssa and Phoebe and answered the phone with a, "What do you want?"

"Declan, wonderful article in *Woman's Idea*. Absolutely darling!" The voice wasn't the one I was expecting. Instead, the smooth tones of a female voice filled my ear.

"Ms. Wood." Even though she wasn't exactly top of my list to talk to, it would at least give me a chance to put my plan in place.

"I don't suppose you've reconsidered your position on the

driver role I have here for you? It's ripe and ready for the plucking if you want it."

I glanced through the window at my family. Fuck, Alyssa would be pissed if she knew what I was about to do, but I didn't have much choice. I had to do what I could to look out for my family. And that meant finding a way to show the haters and the doubters, the ones who'd try to hurt us and pull us apart, that we were as solid as a fucking rock and that they would be better off backing the fuck off rather than push me. "Yeah, actually I have. And I'm definitely considering it."

"You are?" It was the reason she'd called, and yet she sounded surprised as fuck at my answer.

"Yeah. It's just, well, I was wondering whether you might be able to do something for me before we talked more about it."

"Anything." She was almost too eager. Something told me things weren't as rosy at Wood Racing as she'd have everyone believe.

"Have you got tickets to the New Year's Masquerade Ball?" I figured she would; they usually went to all the local charity events, and even Sinclair Racing came up to Brisbane every year for the event. It was the reason I'd even been there, and how I'd hooked up with Darcy. Even if they didn't, I figured if things were so bad that she needed star power enough to launch the dirty campaign against me, she'd do whatever it took to get the tickets I wanted.

"We have a table."

"I'd like to come along and discuss my options with you there, if you're attending. I think it's fitting, don't you? Considering that we might be unmasking my future in the sport and all that."

"Of course, and I assume you will need more than one ticket?"

"Yeah, one other. Can, uh, can you send it out for me though? I have a different woman in mind and don't want to have to explain that to anyone else."

"Trouble in paradise already, young Declan? Is your girl not woman enough for you?"

I forced a laugh. "You know how it is. There's only so much you can drink from the same well without craving a different taste.

And what my family doesn't know won't hurt them, right?" Even saying the words made me feel sick. I was trying so damn hard to implicate myself without saying anything that would be regarded as concrete evidence if she were recording the conversation—I wouldn't put it past her—but I had to give her enough to be convincing.

"I can appreciate that. Why do you think I've never stayed married for long?" She gave her throaty, I'm-so-sexy laugh that probably would have made old me's dick stand on end. Instead, my cock hung flaccid between my thighs, waiting to come alive at Alyssa's command. "So where can I send the other ticket?"

I gave her Darcy's address. "And can you send a note with it?"

"Of course. Anything for my new star driver."

It was almost too fucking easy. "Okay, I want it to read, 'It might not be New Year's but I'm humbly requesting a do-over. DR.' Have you got that?"

"Every word. I don't suppose I can tempt you to come in to see me earlier and start on some of the negotiations?"

"Sorry, Paige," I said her name with as much honey in my voice as I could muster. "Alyssa has been watching me like a hawk while she plans her move to Sydney. She's agreed to let me find out more about this ball because it's for charity. Besides, it's not that far away anyway."

"Can I take it that this, Alyssa was it? That she's moving to Sydney regardless of where you drive?"

"That's right. But I've gotta have my own priorities sorted, right? I'd be an idiot to throw away something so important over something so insignificant." Not one word was a lie. It was hardly my fault that Paige would interpret it to mean that I wouldn't leave a job for a relationship and not the other way around.

"I think that's very reasonable. I'm sure if it's needed, I can find you some accommodation near headquarters until you're back on your feet."

I could imagine. The room would probably come with an all-you-can-eat Paige Wood buffet. A shudder ran down my spine at the thought. How could I have ever had the slightest interest in her when I had someone like Alyssa waiting for me the whole time?

After we'd said goodbye, I headed inside. Phase one of getting revenge on those who'd tried to ruin my life was set. Morgan would help with the planning of phase two on the weekend. Then all I had to do was wait for the pieces to fall into place. In the meantime, there was little more I could do but keep organising our move and doing what I could to look out for my family.

"Everything okay?" Alyssa asked around Phoebe, who was curled against her chest, fast asleep.

"Perfect," I said.

CHAPTER TWENTY-SEVEN
TESTING

THE DAYS SLIPPED away like laps at Bathurst, each one passing in a blur as a set-up for the next big one. The move, the ball—*Christmas*—everything was so close, and barrelling down the straight far too fast.

It was amazing just how quickly time went with them at my side. More amazing was how fast I'd settled into the whole domestic scene that I'd once avoided like the plague. Existing on a diet of takeout and booze had been fine when I was single, but it wasn't like Alyssa or Phoebe could, or should, live the same way. While Alyssa cooked most nights, there were some nights I had to. The ones where she was at work, it was step up to the plate or risk a super-tantrum from a hungry toddler. Given a choice between the stove and Phoebe, I knew which one I was more willing to fight.

Because Alyssa only worked a few nights a week, Phoebe didn't need to go to day care anymore, and I had no other place I needed to be, we spent most of our time together. We went to the park as often as we could, and tried to ensure Phoebe had as much quality time with both of us as she could, considering we had no idea what to expect when our lives started over again in Sydney.

I was so determined to make the most of our time in Brisbane that I arranged playdates for Phoebe with Ben and his kids. We even managed a dual family outing to the movies one day. It ended up as a disaster because none of the kids would sit still long enough to get through the movie, but it was a good day anyway.

Outside of that though, Alyssa and I mostly cleaned and packed her house. I had no idea there was so much involved. When I'd moved to Sydney, I had a suitcase full of clothes, and that was about it. Everything else stayed with Mum and Dad.

As the days had gone by, Alyssa's place had become less and less a home, and more and more just a house, as every bit of personality was stripped away and boxed up. We were constantly busy, but it still felt like there was a pause button over our lives, as if they wouldn't truly begin until the new year. Until we were all settled into our new life in Sydney.

The closer it got to the day Alyssa and Phoebe would be moving in with me permanently, the air between Alyssa and me seemed to grow thicker. Or maybe I just imagined it because of the blanket of guilt I'd wrapped myself in ever since the phone call with Paige.

Even though I probably should have told Alyssa of my plan, I didn't. I was certain she'd only tell me to stop. Only because she didn't understand. She'd already moved on, and had said she was happy it was all behind us now. That she was ready to move on with the next part of our life.

As much as I wanted what she said to be true, it wasn't for me. Mostly because she didn't need revenge like I did. She was too forgiving, but I couldn't be. Not when our future happiness could be attacked. I needed everyone who'd hurt her—who'd tried to hurt me—to burn. I needed to look in the eyes of every person who'd tried to bring me down—and very damn near succeeded—and show them all how happy I was. How happy we both were.

If I didn't make them pay, how could I ever really be free? When the tables finally turned, and I had them crushed and disappointed at my feet, maybe then I could let it go and move on in peace. Even though I couldn't bring Alyssa in on the plan, I was certain she'd thank me once it had all gone down. She'd be just as happy as me to rub their noses in the fact that they'd not only failed to bring us down but had given us the chance to be stronger than anyone could have imagined.

After all, if Tillie and Talia hadn't run that first article, Alyssa and I might have never been forced together on the plane to London. I would never have learned the truth about Phoebe and Emmanuel, and we certainly wouldn't be planning to move all of her shit into my house.

In just a few more weeks.

Around the family stuff, my night out with Morgan had come and gone in a flash. Just like he'd promised, he'd played his part perfectly, getting me a pair of tickets to the New Year's Masquerade Ball, and booking a room at the Suncrest, where the ball was being held this year.

He'd had another surprise for me too. Tickets to the last race of the season. "I can't exactly celebrate stealing the championship from you without you there, can I?" he'd said as he'd given me the details and insisted I attend. It was close to my house, so at least I wouldn't have to worry about accommodation.

Telling Alyssa about the trip was a dance around our feelings. A part of her obviously wanted me to go because I wanted it so badly, but it was also clear she didn't want me to go. Because of that, there was a part of me that wanted to stay, even though I really wanted to be back at the track again. Neither of us wanted to disappoint the other, but she'd ended up winning—and losing at the same time. As much as I wanted to stay for her, I couldn't say no to her when she told me to go.

Because I was going to be away for three days, and we still had to arrange the changes to the birth certificates, we'd planned a day in the city with just the two of us. Only the day before, we'd got the DNA results—which came back exactly as expected. I was Phoebe's father, not that there'd ever been even the tiniest doubt.

"She'll be fine," I said reassuringly as Alyssa stared out the Prado window at her parents' house. We'd just dropped Phoebe off to spend the day with them while we went into the city to organise all the shit we needed to do to lodge the forms to update Phoebe's birth certificate.

Alyssa had agreed when I suggested I should wait in the car while she got Phoebe settled. The last time I'd been at the house was the disastrous reunion that had resulted in Josh and Curtis cornering me against the side of their house and trying to run me out of town, Wild West style. Considering it had almost worked, I understood Alyssa's ready approval of my request.

"Think of it as an opportunity for them to spend some time together before we take her away," I added. "We've only got a handful of weeks left in Brisbane now."

"I know she'll be fine." Alyssa sighed. "Just dropping her off here, it's a reminder that I won't be able to do that soon. That we're moving. It's an adjustment, that's all. This place is all I've ever really known, you know?"

My chest tightened as I wondered whether she was starting to regret her decision. I knew she trusted me. I knew she loved me. But in that moment, I wondered if it was enough. Was I being selfish asking her to move in with me so soon?

"Did you want to stay?"

She shook her head, and her hand came to rest on my thigh. "No. I'm happy about where I'm going . . . where *we're* going," she added with a smile. "And the job is what I've been working toward. I just can't help feel a little sad about having to leave all this behind too. I guess in a perfect world, we could have it all. But if it was a perfect world—" She cut off and looked down at her hands. I didn't have to ask what she was going to say because I already knew.

I picked up her hand and placed it against my lips, kissing it softly. I didn't have words to comfort her, because they would just be trite and meaningless anyway.

"Do you think we can do a bit of Christmas shopping while we're in the city?" she asked, clearly trying to change the subject.

"Of course." The mention of the C-word was another sharp reminder that I'd soon be facing my first Christmas as a father. More than that, we'd be doing Christmas with Alyssa's family, and staying through until New Year's for the ball. So many challenges all lined up to greet me. All I could do was grin and bear each one as they came.

The positives were that ever since my phone call with Paige, our friendly neighbourhood pap had fucked off to whatever assignment his bitch of a boss had for him next. Which left us free to just be a family without being goaded into reacting negatively to bullshit, and also confirmed my suspicions that he'd only been following me to dig up more dirt.

It was good that he was off our back before we went to the clinic clearly marked as a DNA testing facility. And before we hit our itinerary for our city trip. DNA tests and trips to Births, Deaths, and Marriages weren't exactly the sort of things you wanted random photographers following you to.

A little over an hour later, we'd completed all of the paperwork that would facilitate new birth certificates. The office had been a little cold, clinical, and the process had been free of emotion, and yet I was still a bundle of nerves by the time we left. It was like I was on my way to becoming official.

"So this ball, is it really fancy? Can I still wear that same dress? I'm not sure I can afford a new one." Alyssa's stream of questions was obviously a way to fill the space between us as we walked back up to the Queen Street Mall.

After Morgan's visit, I'd given Alyssa one of the tickets for the masquerade ball—at the Sinclair Racing table. Although she'd been reluctant at first, it wasn't hard to convince her that we needed one last hurrah in Brisbane. A night out alone, without Phoebe, before moving into what would be our new life. After all, we'd barely spent much time alone, and when we arrived in Sydney we wouldn't have much opportunity. Our only ready babysitter would be Eden, but that would mean leaving Phoebe with Morgan as well, which Alyssa wasn't keen on.

"It's a proper ball. You'll need a proper gown, and I'll have to wear my tux." I'd packed it the last time I'd gone to Sydney in preparation for the night.

"Do you know how much ball gowns cost?"

"Surely there's a way we can hire one or something?"

"Maybe . . ." She sighed. "And it's here at the Suncrest isn't it?"

"Yeah, in the same room we had our date."

A dreamy look glazed her eyes for a moment. "It won't be as good as that date."

"Oh, I don't know. It might be better." After all, what better way to get my revenge on everyone who tried to break us apart than to propose to her in front of them all?

With a nod, she dragged me up the mall. She moved with such purpose I knew she had a destination in mind.

"Well, I guess if I have to hire something fancy, it makes sense to hire it from here. The place I got my formal dress is just around the corner here."

Even though I would rather race for Paige than go spend time in a dress shop, I sucked it up and followed willingly behind her.

"ARE YOU sure about your plan of action?"

I sighed when Dr. Henrikson started up his psychobabble. Because I'd gone back up to Brisbane, he'd agreed to another phone session in place of my scheduled face-to-face visit.

During the call, after we'd celebrated my job at Sinclair Racing, I'd told him my plan to get my revenge and the girl all in one fell swoop. His reaction was less enthusiastic than I'd hoped. "Why wouldn't I be?"

"Let's put aside the most obvious issue, about how unhealthy your need for revenge actually is, and deal with the next one. Are you sure marriage is a good idea after being reconciled for only a few months?"

"Of course I'm sure. I mean, getting engaged is hardly the same thing as being married. We can set a date a year away if she wants. Two. But we fucking love each other, and there's Phoebe to consider. Her parents should be married."

"Why?"

"Because parents should be married."

"That's quite an old-fashioned notion coming from someone with your past, Declan."

"For an ex-manwhore, you mean?"

"That's putting it in a slightly less eloquent way than I would have."

I paced around Alyssa's backyard as I spoke to him. "Fuck you. I'm full of old-fashioned fucking values. I just got a little lost along the way. I'm finding my way back now, thanks to her. I'd have thought you'd be fucking happy about my progress."

"I am delighted with your progress. I just don't want you to make any rash decisions while you are still in a transitional phase of your life."

I gave a non-committal grunt in response.

"Putting that issue aside for the moment, there's the bigger one to consider."

I stopped midstride. "Which is what exactly?"

"How will Alyssa feel having her engagement linked with your desperation for revenge?"

"She . . ." I trailed off. "She'll be . . . I don't fucking know." The truth was, I did know.

She was sentimental about shit like that. I'd probably have my balls cut off if I even tried it. But it would be the best revenge I could imagine and why shouldn't I kill two birds with one stone? She'd understand.

"I would suspect she'd much rather the moment be meaningful just because of its significance for you as a couple, rather than because of some perceived justice you inferred from the event."

"You don't know that. You've never even spoken to her."

"I know. Although as I've explained in the past, I would like to change that when you are comfortable —"

"We're not doing fucking couples' therapy. We don't need that shit. We're perfect. Better than fucking perfect. We're so peachy-fucking-keen we may as well live in a fucking orchard."

"If you say so, Declan."

"I do."

"Will you at least consider what I've said?"

I didn't answer him. Even though I tried to resist it, his words had crept under my skin and were writhing like insects. Perhaps it was worth thinking things over after all. Regardless, I would still make everyone who'd hurt me, who'd hurt Alyssa, pay. He spent the rest of our call going over what he thought was the greater concern as he pleaded with me to reconsider getting revenge at all. His words mirrored Alyssa's—be thankful it's over. But neither of them understood just how ruthless Paige could be. As soon as my return to Sinclair became public, I'd probably have a team of reporters on my arse all over again.

No. It was much better to make a stand and show them exactly why they should never have fucked with Declan Reede in the first place.

CHAPTER TWENTY-EIGHT

SET UP

BEING BACK IN Sydney, at Homebush to watch Morgan race live, was un-fucking-believable. I hadn't been trackside at an event without the intention to race since I was sixteen, and I'd almost forgotten the thrill of standing near the barriers as the cars roared past. Of course, just like it had then, the noise and smell made me yearn with everything in me to be out there in one of the cars.

The urge was almost strong enough to force me to hunt down Paige and tell her that I would do whatever it took to be back in the driver seat. The only thing that stopped me was the knowledge that if I played my cards right, I could be back in the seat at Sinclair.

Of course, because I'd been in my own little bubble of it being just Alyssa, Phoebe, and me for so long, I didn't even consider what attention my visit to the track might garner. Especially considering I'd had Morgan swing by my house so I could grab my Sinclair Racing team shirt. Most of the morning, I'd been approached by fan after fan, getting autographs on everything from shirts to posters.

It was strange feeling like someone noteworthy again, especially considering the track was my domain. Most of the people who'd approached me weren't just autograph hounds desperate for any squiggle. They were genuine fans. Some of them expressed their disappointment that I wouldn't be back the next season. A few seemed to think I had something big buried up my sleeve. They were right, but not the way they expected.

Of course, one out of every dozen seemed to want to approach me for an entirely different purpose. I'd been propositioned multiple times—each one promising me that they would give me an experience that would change my new monogamous ways—and I'd also been screamed at for my "disgusting" past. One girl even went as far as slapping me for being a deadbeat dad. Luckily the roaming security guards saw her and escorted her out before it could become a worse situation for me. Why she thought my business was any of her concern was beyond me, but I guess that was the price of fame.

Once the initial shock of my appearance among the crowd had died down a little, I walked around the venue. Each step was one I'd taken before, but only as a driver. I'd never been to Homebush just as a spectator. A tangible excitement seemed to buzz in the air that was thick with the scent of hot asphalt and burned rubber. It was something I'd never fully noticed or appreciated during race preparations.

Then, every thought had been on the car, on the track and its corners, and on finishing first. It had been stressful, and had turned what I loved into a job. A job that I still loved, but a job nonetheless.

I'd missed just being able to breathe in the atmosphere. More than I cared to admit to myself. Without the worries about whether the next time I was on the track would end in a DNF, I could watch the other categories and just enjoy them. At one point, the Micro series raced past with their tiny four cylinder engines buzzing like mosquitos. Then an hour later, the trucks had their turn—tonnes and tonnes of chrome and gleaming paint travelling at such speeds it seemed almost suicidal.

Although Morgan had offered to lean on Danny for a pit pass, I was happier without one. It meant I could wander around without the expectation of talking to those people I'd be working with next year. It gave me an excuse for not having to tell my story over and over.

It also occurred to me that Danny would probably prefer me to stay away until my agreed-upon start. After all, he didn't want my plans spilling over into the new race season. He'd said as much when he gave me his tacit, if uncertain, approval for my plan, just so long as he didn't know what it was.

If Paige said something more to Danny, he'd likely dismiss it. After all, he had something she didn't—my signature on a piece of paper outlining the details of my new employment contract. It had come when I'd dropped by the Sinclair Racing headquarters late on Friday night when I arrived in Sydney. It was only when we were finishing up our conversation, just before I actually signed the document, that he mentioned hearing about a fresh offer from Paige, and of my potential signing with her.

There was no doubt that the information had been passed straight from the horse's mouth, but it didn't really bother me. I admitted to the conversation and started to explain.

He held up his hand. "Have you ever heard of plausible deniability, Declan?"

I grinned at him. Of course I had, because it was exactly what I was giving Alyssa by keeping her out of the plans.

"Just keep whatever you're planning out of the papers, try not to get into too much trouble, and turn up on time on your first day and we won't have any issues."

Agreeing readily, I asked just two favours—his short-term silence on my hiring and his agreement to announce my return at the New Year's masquerade ball. True to his keep-me-out–of-it policy, he didn't ask any questions as he agreed. Without a second thought, I thanked him again for the offer—which was actually a little more generous than what I'd expected after our first meeting— signed the contract, and then left to find Morgan again.

Once it was all set, I had nothing left to do but wait and make sure I'd executed my plans before I started so that they didn't blow up in my face later on.

DURING ONE of the production car races, I caught sight of Paige madly dashing around, and thought I'd bait the hook a little more.

Racing after her, I managed to corner her away from everyone at the back of the grandstand.

The instant she spotted me, she turned around with the smile of a predator adorning her cherry-red lips. Her smile fell for a fraction of a second when she took in the shirt I was wearing, but it lifted again when I moved closer to her with a smile of my own. I indicated I wanted her to follow me. She complied beautifully, coming with me until we were around the corner and out of view.

"Declan, I didn't expect to see you here this weekend."

"I'm here to watch Morg take the championship. Hand off the reins, you know. Even though I'm not out there now, I'm still the reigning champ." As I'd said the word, designed to remind her what a fucking prize I was, I'd moved even closer to her, invaded her personal space the way she'd done so often to me. "And Danny wanted to see me about something too."

When I had her backed firmly against the grandstand, I pressed a hand against the wall on either side of her head, trapping her between my arms. The position felt almost too intimate, but that was kinda the point. I was trying to flood her with just enough false hope that the fall would be spectacular, while also giving her a reason to give me the proof I needed that she was behind everything.

Her cougaresque smile pulled at her thin lips. "I don't suppose I can tempt you to come cheer him on from my office?"

The thought of going anywhere near the Wood Racing pits or truck wasn't appealing, especially when I was wearing a Sinclair Racing shirt. I'd be booed by the crew and fans alike.

"Nah, sorry, Paige," I leaned in closer as I spoke. "I'm just here as a spectator. Wanted to see how the other half lives, you know? It's been so long since I was at a race just for the fun of it."

"And where's your little family?" Her gaze was focused on my eyes, and even though I was the one cornering her, it felt like some power had just shifted back into her court. Maybe it was because my family was the reason I was doing this. Was I pushing things too far though? Was the doc right?

My stomach twisted into knots, but I let my smile grow. "Not here. I didn't want them to spoil my fun."

"Ah, so it's one of *those* weekends, is it?"

The fact that she was openly approving, perhaps even encouraging, the thought that I would ever betray Alyssa was enough to cement my decision to make her fall. She'd spent too long allowing her drivers to get away with far too much. How bad would things have to be before she'd intervene? The questions over what exactly she'd done about Hunter's habit of drugging girls leapt to my tongue, but I swallowed them down. I couldn't tip her off, or she'd be suspicious and might find a way out of it. I couldn't allow that. She had to suffer—and she deserved everything that was coming to her.

"Yeah, I'll be hunting down some sport a little later."

"I'm sure you'll have no issue finding some. A young man of your—" Her tongue pushed forward to slick across her lips and her gaze dropped down to trail over my body before landing squarely on my crotch. "—reputation."

"I don't think I'll have too much trouble at all," I said. "In fact, I was thinking about hitting Firebird again. Maybe those two hotties I almost scored with last time will be there." Letting memories of Alyssa fill my mind, I pretended that the thought of meeting with Talia and Tillie again turned me on. I waited for half a second before tipping my head to the side as if some thought struck me with my words. "Actually, did you know that one of them knows you?"

The shock that flooded across her face was priceless.

"Yeah, that, um, what was her name again? T. T something . . ."

Paige was almost white as a ghost. If that wasn't enough, the fear that flickered through her eyes proved she knew all about Talia's role as T. It didn't surprise me, but it was nice to know for a fact.

"Tillie!" I exclaimed, as if I'd just remembered. "That's her name. She went to the fundraiser in Brisbane with your son."

The relief that sagged through Paige was almost palpable, and yet it was clear she'd hoped I wouldn't make even that association.

"Fuck, it's hard to remember names sometimes. Not that it

matters really, right? Just so long as it's my name they're screaming at the end of the night." I winked at her. "It's a damn shame I didn't get to finish what I started with her and her friend after Bathurst. Something tells me those two would be wildcats in the sack."

I was trying to push all the right buttons to stoke the fires of jealousy toward her own daughter.

"You know, I think Felix might have her phone number," Paige said. "I'm sure I can help arrange a rendezvous."

I'm sure you can. And I'm sure you can ensure there are cameras there to capture every fucking second so that you have some collateral over me. "That would be," I licked my lips, "a fucking delight. You should definitely tell her to invite her friend."

She grinned. No doubt thinking she was gathering more shit on me. My earlier mention of Sinclair Racing courting me and the fact I was wearing their shirt were surely playing havoc in her mind. I'd have a pap on my arse before the day was through, and all the proof I needed to feel vindicated in making her fall.

"Actually, she said something to me at the charity do. What was that again?" I narrowed eyes and pretended to wrack my brain. "Oh, that's right, that she was actually in love with his sister. But that must mean . . . Oh, wow! Is Blondie your daughter?" Without waiting for an answer, I moved so that my lips were right against her cheek. "What can I say? The apple certainly doesn't fall far from the tree."

I pushed away from the wall, and took a backward step to put some distance between us again.

A devious glint lit her eyes; it might have been lust or it might have been some new, crazed plan for blackmail. Who could tell with her? "I don't suppose I could tempt you to come out to dinner to discuss your future with me beforehand?"

Fuck, she was desperate and it was too easy.

Taking another step back from her, I shrugged and flashed her a panty-dropper smile. "Sorry, I have a dinner planned with Sinclair Racing already. How about a rain check for next time though?"

Her smile morphed into a snarl for a fraction of a second before she fixed it back in place. I was playing a dangerous game and would have to be damn careful that I didn't step even a toe out of line or I'd be headlining in *Gossip Weekly* again, but it would be worth it. I hoped.

After giving her a little wave, I disappeared into the crowd before she could press me further. I didn't want to have to string together too many lies, because the more I told, the more things would stack up and risk falling over.

I spent the better part of the day trying to avoid the pits and Paige. Morgan and Eden hunted me down during one of his breaks, and we had a quiet lunch together—at least as quiet as possible with autograph seekers coming up to us at regular intervals.

It was a little after four before I received a text from an unknown number.

Looking for some fun tonight?

Paige had obviously lived up to her promise to try to arrange a meeting with Tillie and Talia. Not that I'd doubted she would. She was like some sort of fucking pimp, and even her own daughter wasn't off limits. If Hunter expected the same sort of treatment when he started at Sinclair Racing he'd be in for a rude-arse shock.

I had my phone in front of me as I walked back toward the track, trying to frame a text reply that wouldn't incriminate me if it was publicly released. Halfway through my reply, someone shoulder checked me.

"Watch where you're walking, arsehole." Hunter Blake's voice was practically a growl. Even though less than a second had passed, I could see the exact moment when he realised it was me. The fire of anger in his eyes grew more intense, but his mouth formed a self-righteous smirk. "Well, well, I didn't expect to see your face within a hundred miles of a racetrack again."

It was hard to hold back my own smirk, knowing that I'd soon be at every single race again. Maybe not in the same capacity as before, but that didn't matter. "You might be surprised to see just where I turn up in the future, Blake."

"Funny, 'cause the way I hear it, you were too pussy to take the job with Wood, and there's no other positions coming up, so I don't think I have too much to worry about."

I shrugged. "Guess not."

"Why the fuck are you here, Reede?"

"Just enjoying the event. Here to support Morg, you know, as he claims the championship."

"It's not his yet."

I chuckled. "But it will be."

"Like fuck. I can still win it."

"You'd have to come first, and Morg would have to finish mid-pack. I can't see it happening."

"He could always DNF."

The way he said it made me stop. The menace in his voice made it seem more like a threat than an idle statement. "I don't think so. Morg's got his game face on this weekend. He's not racing for the win, just the points."

"Well, then, he's a pussy isn't he?"

"No, he just knows that you're more likely to win a championship when you're not tangled with other cars." My words hit their target, and I watched as Hunter's mouth curled into a menacing snarl.

"And you'd know all about that, wouldn't you? You know the championship could have easily been mine if you hadn't fucked me up at Bathurst." Hunter was practically seething.

"You're an idiot. If that hadn't happened, Morgan and I would probably have won."

"Whatever, loser, it doesn't really make any difference to me, does it? It's not like I give a crap if Wood gets the trophy. Next year, I'll be in Sinclair colours, and you can bet your arse there'll be a new pecking order. McGuire is going down. And you . . . Well, it doesn't get much lower than where you are already. It's pathetic really."

"Have you always been an arrogant wanker or is that something you're just trying on for size?"

"Fuck off, Reede." He snapped the words at me loud enough that three families nearby all turned to stare wide-eyed in shock.

I resisted the urge to laugh. When needed, I could hold back the curse words that were always dancing near the tip of my tongue. Days at the track were usually one of those times. Of course now that I wasn't there in any official capacity, it didn't matter. For me. Hunter was just lucky that he wasn't near any race officials, or he could have been facing a reprimand. It was fine in the pits, or places where it wouldn't be heard or accidentally broadcast.

He glared at me. "Stay the hell away from me."

"Gladly." I didn't worry about telling him that we'd be seeing each other soon enough at Sinclair Racing. What was sure to be a priceless look on his face wasn't worth the risk of him telling Paige or someone else at Wood Racing before I could spring the trap.

Without waiting for him to reply again, I walked away. Within a second, I'd finished the text he'd interrupted. I'd decided in the end that simple was better, so just sent Tillie or Talia, whichever it was, a text that read, *Sorry, booked for tonight after all.*

A second later, another message popped up on my phone. *Can't we tempt you to change your plans?*

With the text came a photo. Even though I was worried what exactly it might be, I clicked to open it. If nothing else, it could be good for blackmail. The image was relatively PG, just an image of a woman with red curls and one with blonde hair tangled together in a kiss. Neither face could be made out because they were blurred and out of focus. It was obviously a selfie that hadn't been taken properly because of the locked lips.

Sorry, plans are immovable. What about New Year's?
What about it?
Suncrest. Brisbane. Ball. Going?
Yeah.
I'll slip you key and room number at dinner. Come by after ten, I'll have company until then.

A second later, another message popped up on my phone. *Family?*

No. Fun.

If she spoke to Paige about the night, I was certain Paige would tell her I had indeed invited someone other than Alyssa. Paige just didn't know that I'd actually donated my ticket at her table to another party. Or at least, Eden had on my behalf. A second later, my phone pinged again.

Game on.

A smile crossed my lips as I put my phone back in my pocket. Game on, indeed. If I was right, there would be some hell to pay on New Year's. God, I could be a prick sometimes but fuck if those bitches didn't deserve it.

CHAPTER TWENTY-NINE

ROLL ON

"HELLO?" RUTH CALLED from the front door.

My heart began to stutter as I considered the reason Ruth was there, and the fact that Curtis and Josh would be with her. Even though I'd offered to do two trips to get the truck over to their house, and had considering trying to lug the fridge all on my own just to avoid them, Alyssa had insisted. Something about not wanting to see me pancaked by white goods.

"In the kitchen," Alyssa answered in invitation. We hadn't worried about locking the front door because we'd been in and out of the house so much lugging the boxes. Even Phoebe escaping wasn't a concern because she'd been hovering around our feet, being extra clingy as the house was torn apart and the boxes and furniture were packed up.

With the exception of three items, everything was packed and sorted into either the rental truck, the back of my Prado, or Alyssa's Swift. Two of the three items that were still to be packed were both from Phoebe's room: a small chest of drawers and a dressing table. They were the only big items coming with us. The third item was the fridge.

Each trip outside was done under the watchful eye of our

friendly neighbourhood paparazzo, who'd made a miraculous reappearance after I'd mentioned the possibility of a Sinclair Racing return to Paige Wood. It was exactly the confirmation I needed that Paige was doing what I'd thought she would: trying to gather dirt in case another smear campaign was needed. It had been easy enough to ignore him this time though, especially considering his life watching us would have been boring as bat shit, because the three of us had been the picture of domestic fucking bliss, and his boss didn't want photos of that. At least, not yet. I was certain that aspect was the spin Paige had mentioned the first time she'd called to offer me the role with her team.

Ruth walked into the kitchen with a smile on her face, and Phoebe squealed, "Nana!" throwing herself at her. It was only as Ruth bobbed down to catch her that I saw Curtis standing behind her. Although I knew he and Josh were coming with Ruth to move the fridge and then drive the truck to their house, I'd expected him to wait in the car. Especially considering the reason they were even taking the spare furniture was because he'd refused to let Alyssa sell it: just in case.

Just in case I broke her heart again. Fucker!

"Declan," he murmured when he saw me staring.

"Sir," I said. My voice squeaked as I choked back my fear. I'd offered to do a return trip to take the trailer over, so that he didn't have to come around, but Alyssa had refused.

He raised his eyebrow at me. I'd never called him sir before. He had always just been Curtis to me. Curtis, who had been like a second father to me. Curtis, who, in hindsight, was probably a better role model, and father, than my own had ever been.

Curtis, who'd tried to drive me out of town barely a month earlier.

"Are you ready to go, pumpkin?" he asked Alyssa.

I was trying very hard not to be reminded of the fact that "going" meant leaving the relative sanctuary of Alyssa's three-bedroom rented house and the three of us moving into one bedroom at Ruth and Curtis's house. Alyssa's old bedroom, in fact.

"Is Josh here?" she replied.

Curtis glared at me for a moment before answering. "No. He wanted to wait in the car until it was time."

"I'll go make myself scarce then, shall I?" I muttered.

Even though I hadn't intended anyone to hear me, Alyssa's gaze moved to me. "No, Dec, this has been your house too for the last few weeks. You're in my life for good now, and Josh has to learn to be a big boy about these things."

"Yeah, so far in your life you need a just-in-case escape plan." The words left me as I headed out of the room. Louder, I added, "It's okay, I'll just be down in the bedroom."

I didn't wait for any further argument, but none was exactly forthcoming either. Heading straight down the hall, I went into the master bedroom and started working, double-checking the bathroom cupboards and in the top of the built-in wardrobe just in case something had been missed while we were packing. Nothing had been, and I knew that because I'd performed the exact same checks before, but it gave me something to focus on.

"Hey, Declan, are you okay?" It was Ruth's voice that sounded from the bedroom door.

"Peachy keen," I snapped. "Why wouldn't I be?"

"I know it's not easy, but they'll come around eventually when they see how much you two mean to each other. You just have to keep doing what you've been doing."

"Yeah, 'cause that's worked so damn well for me so far."

"They're men. They're stubborn. The best way to show them that you really won't hurt Alyssa and Phoebe is to be there for her."

"I am. Always. I'd rather shove my hand into a meat grinder than hurt her again."

Ruth chuckled. "Let's hope it doesn't come down to that."

I smiled in spite of myself. "It won't."

"So, have you got everything ready in Sydney? It's got to be a big adjustment, right? I mean, are you sure you're ready for living with a three-year-old full time?"

Ruth's expression and laughter made it clear that she'd intended the statement as a joke. Except Alyssa had made similar statements in the past. Was I ready? Did I know what I was really getting myself in for? I'd barely lived with her for a handful of weeks. Plus, I'd had my own house, my own space, that I could retreat to when I'd needed it. Okay, so I hadn't used it, but it had been there. Was I ready to lose that space? Could a few weeks living with Alyssa as a guest in her house really prepare me for what I would face next?

Before I answered, Ruth nodded toward the doorway. "They should be out of the house by now if you want to resurface?"

"I think I might just take a minute." Although I didn't want to say anything to Ruth, and I'd tried to hide it during our conversation, I wasn't okay. In fact, with every second that had passed since Curtis and Josh had arrived, I'd become less okay than ever. The truth was my heart was beating faster and faster with every passing minute. It was so rapid that the beats melded one into another so that it was an almost constant hum in my chest. It must have been too fast. Fast enough to kill me.

The reality of what was happening was closing in on me. The fucking walls were closing in on me.

The instant Ruth walked out of the room, I leaned against the wall. At least that way, I could ensure that the walls were never closer than an arm's length away. In an attempt to quiet my heart—which was still thumping a rapid tune against my ribcage like a crazed pianist—I closed my eyes and let my head fall between my outstretched arms.

The room was too quiet, the silence causing a buzz in my ears. Having my eyes closed was a mistake because vertigo struck me almost instantly. Despite the dizziness though, I couldn't force myself to open my eyes and look at the empty room.

There were too many changes all happening at once, too much to cope with. I'd been so obsessed with having Alyssa by my side that I hadn't stopped to consider what it meant. She was moving in with me.

The words were heaven. And yet, they were hell. I was tearing my chest open and letting her waltz on in. All the fears I'd had as a teen came rushing back to me. All of the doctor's words of caution flooded my mind.

What the fuck was I doing? Of course I was going to hurt her. It was fucking inevitable. It was what I did. And when that happened—when I fucked up—and she left, my entire being would be torn to pieces. Wouldn't it have been better to keep my distance and not go skipping merrily down Heartbreak Lane?

Why was I moving so fast? How had I let that happen?

What the fuck was I thinking?

"Dec?" Alyssa's voice came to me through the tunnel of darkness I'd been spinning down. It was like she was throwing a rope into the void and hoping I'd catch hold.

Her hand came to rest on my shoulder and I jolted. My eyes sprang open and I met her worried gaze.

"Are you all right?" she asked.

I turned and leaned against the wall. "Are we doing the right thing here, Lys?"

"What do you mean?"

"This. Moving in together." I rubbed my hands over my face. "Don't you think it's too soon?"

A chuckle left her lips before her face fell. "Are you being serious?"

"Yes. No. I don't fucking know, Lys. It's just, well, you've arranged for the stuff to go into storage in case I fuck up, and it's because I will, isn't it? We both know it. I'll do something stupid and you'll leave, and then what? I don't know that I can survive that."

Instead of the anger I expected, a tender expression came over her face. She moved closer to me and brushed her hand through the hair over my ear. "Did you want me to find my own house in Sydney?"

"Fuck no." The words were out before I could stop them, an instinctive need to have her near me. I frowned as the reality of what her living so close but so far from me would be like. Only seeing her and Phoebe for a few hours a day, or maybe even less. Maybe as little as once a week. "No, definitely not. I—I—"

"It's just a little case of cold feet. You're letting yourself panic."

No, that wasn't it. I had a reason. A logical reason. It was . . . it was . . .

Fuck, what was it?

"It's okay to be scared, Dec. I am."

"I'm not scared. I—wait, you are?" I wasn't sure I liked the sound of that. I wanted her to feel safe. Protected. I'd thought I'd been able to shake the fear she felt toward me.

She laughed again, a nervous little chuckle. "Are you kidding? I'm terrified. I'll be away from my family, away from Flynn, away from everyone that's ever made up my support network. Away from everything except for you."

"But that's my point," I said, feeling the weight of expectation crushing me. On one side, I had all of her hopes, on the other, her dad's doubt, and I was sandwiched in the middle as it grew tighter and tighter. "What happens when I screw it up?"

"The fact that you're worried about that is exactly the reason I trust that you won't."

I wrapped my arms around her waist and pulled her against me. "I'm sorry I freaked out."

"Honestly, I was kinda waiting for it," she admitted as she nuzzled against my neck. "This is a huge step, and we've barely found each other again."

"So you don't think I'm stupid?"

"I think you're cute."

I laughed, loudly. "Cute is hardly what I work for."

"Hmm, how about manly then?" She worked her way along my jaw with a series of small kisses as she spoke. "Sexy? Virile? Perf—"

The door swung open and Curtis glared at us. "We're ready to go," he said.

"Haven't you ever heard of knocking?" I snapped.

"There's something I can think of knocking," he muttered as he turned away.

The next week and a bit was going to be just fucking awesome. Alyssa's family always spent most of the Christmas period together. That meant staying with Ruth and Curtis would mean a lot of face-to-face time with not only them, but also Ruby and Josh. Fuck.

CHAPTER THIRTY

NOT SO SILENT NIGHT

DESPITE MY TREPIDATION, life with Ruth and Curtis wasn't as bad as I'd expected. Probably because I just stayed in the room until after Curtis had got up and left for work. And knowing that it was only for a few days before the full Christmas craziness started, and then a matter of holding tight until New Year's, made it easier to cope too.

We treated it as something of a retreat for the three of us. The only complaint I had was that Phoebe was in the room with us, which I wouldn't have minded except for the case of blue balls I was developing, sleeping next to Alyssa every night but being unable to touch her and take her the way I wanted. The luckiest I got was when I snuck across to the bathroom to shower with her, but we'd had to be so quick and so quiet that it barely counted.

Christmas Eve saw us rise early and head off to Ben and Jade's house to catch up with them again. It would be the last time before we left, because they were heading to Fraser Island for a camping trip. It had been fucking fantastic to watch Alyssa fall back into an easy friendship with Jade on our few family outings, and I hoped it would survive us moving to Sydney.

While the girls clucked around after the kids, Ben and I snuck down to his man cave at the back of his shed to spend some time catching up and have a couple of drinks. We chatted easily about his job and my upcoming apprenticeship. Although I'd told him all the details, he was sworn to secrecy, along with all of my other co-conspirators. I'd signed the contract, but as per my request, Danny hadn't made the announcement yet.

The best part about catching up with the two of them was that it was less time I had to spend dealing with the awkwardness of being at Alyssa's parents' house while Curtis wasn't at work. Even though we'd only spent three nights there, that was three nights too many, and because of my plans, we'd still be there for another week.

Fuck my life.

We spent a number of hours with Ben and Jade before finally saying farewell. We left with promises to keep in touch, and offers to stay at their house the next time we were in town. We offered the same in response, but I think everyone silently knew—with the three kids screaming and giggling around our feet—that it was likely neither would happen. The best we could hope for was catching up online and maybe coffee when we were next in town.

After we returned to Alyssa's parents' house, Alyssa and Phoebe set off for Flynn's in her Swift so they could have their Christmas with him. Even though Alyssa had said I'd be more than welcome, I didn't accept the invitation. Alyssa had been missing Flynn in the time that I'd been in Brisbane. It came out in tiny, obvious ways almost every day that I'd lived with her. She'd even said his name a few times when asking me to help with something—only to catch herself at the last second. Although I was a little more comfortable with the idea of their friendship than I had been, I couldn't deal with the twinge of remorse that hit me each time I had to watch her or Phoebe run to him and give him the pieces of themselves that he'd captured in my absence. The pieces that would have been mine but for my own fucked-up response to her calls when I'd left Brisbane the first time.

Even if interrupting their quality time hadn't felt uncomfortable, I couldn't have gone. I had a few things of my own to sort out both for Christmas and New Year's Eve.

After Alyssa had climbed out of the Prado, I retrieved my prize from the bottom of the glovebox.

When she'd driven off with Phoebe, I headed inside to arrange a few things. First, I pulled Ruth aside and asked her to arrange a small picnic for Alyssa and me to take on a walk after Christmas lunch.

"What for?" she asked, with a glint of suspicion in her eyes.

"Nothing," I said, trying to stop the knowing smile crossing my face. "I just thought Alyssa would like a little bit of time alone with me as her Christmas present. After all, when we get to Sydney, we won't have much of it."

"Sure." She winked at me, and I chuckled. "I'll get it organised," she promised. "Are the leftovers from lunch going to be okay?"

"They'll be perfect." I thanked her and then retreated to the door of the room I was calling home until we left for Sydney. "Would you mind watching Phoebe for a few hours tomorrow evening while Alyssa and I have some alone time?"

She looked like she was about to choke on her happiness. "Of course not."

Pushing closed the door for some privacy, I sat on the bed and plucked the engagement ring from the velvet box in my hand. I twirled the ring in my fingers, gazing at it vaguely while my mind alternated between nervousness and elation.

Since my freak out about her moving in with me, I'd been thinking more and more about the ring. About the way I'd felt when I'd bought it, and how stupid I'd been. It may have been less than a month earlier, but I somehow felt more mature now. Despite the certainty that it had been a mistake buying the ring so soon, when so much was still uncertain between us, I was more determined than ever to find a way to give it to her. Only, I didn't want to do it as a plan for revenge. It had to be special.

Which was why it would be her Christmas present.

I'd spent a lot of time over the past month trying to figure out exactly what to get her, before realising I already had the perfect gift. And when I asked her, it would be without any doubt in my body that it was what we both wanted. My freak-out, and her calm, measured response, had been enough to prove to me that we were stronger together. We didn't need to be married to have that strength, but just like with the name on the birth certificates, I wanted to have something to show the world how I felt. Something more than trite words and a magazine photo shoot.

Since my decision, I hadn't doubted it once. Just her response. Would she really want to marry a fuck-up like me? Yes, she'd accepted me back into her life. She'd even gone so far as to agree to move in with me. But marriage? That was a whole other step.

Still, it was a step I was ready to take with her.

A knock on the door startled me and had me racing to hide the ring back in my pocket.

"Come in," I squeaked.

"Is there something going on, Declan?" Curtis asked, crossing his arms and leaning against the doorjamb.

I shook my head quickly. "No—" I couldn't talk, my voice was strained and pitched too high. I stopped and cleared my throat before continuing. "I just wanted to give Alyssa some space at Flynn's."

"Bullshit."

I closed my eyes. "Why is that bullshit?"

"Because it is. You know it is, and I know it is. What're you up to?"

"I just want to make our first Christmas as a family special. What's so wrong with that?" I asked, feeling my hackles rising by the second. I wouldn't back down though. Not this time. He needed to learn to back the fuck off.

"It depends on exactly what you are planning on doing to make it special."

I sighed. "You liked me once," I murmured. "Remember how much easier it was then."

He raised his eyebrow. "And then you hurt my baby. I won't allow it again."

"I'm not going to hurt her. I'm never leaving her again. The only reason we'll ever be apart is if she leaves me, and even then I'll fight tooth and nail for her. I know what life is like without her, and I'm not going to do it again."

"You know she could break your heart, the way that you broke hers." He sounded a little too pleased by the thought.

I winced. Wasn't that exactly why I'd freaked out just days earlier? I couldn't take losing her. It would kill me. And yet, my action was as much for the thought of Alyssa's pain when I left than any concern for myself.

He narrowed his eyes at me, obviously not missing the small gesture. His face softened slightly in response. Not that he'd ever admit it.

I decided my shoes were very interesting, turning my head in that direction. I didn't really want to be having this conversation with Killer Curtis. Not now—not ever.

He cleared his throat to draw my attention back to his face. Once he knew he had my full attention, he said, "Just promise me that you are looking after my daughter and granddaughter."

I nodded.

"And that you aren't going to do anything stupid."

"Like?" I gulped.

"Like rush into marriage."

I choked. "I'm not going to promise that."

"Thought so," he said, any trace of the softness from moments earlier wiped away to become hard edges and hate-filled eyes.

I sighed, growing confused. "You thought what exactly?"

"Are you going to ask Alyssa—"

I cut him off. "I don't see how that's your concern."

He scoffed. "No matter how old she gets, or what happens, she will always be my concern." He eyed me off for a second before starting again. "You know, traditionally men asked their prospective father-in-law for permission before asking a woman for her hand in marriage."

"Why would I give a fuck what's done 'traditionally'?" I asked.

"Because it's a way of showing respect."

"You've got to give respect to earn it," I told him. He looked as though he was ready to smack me in the mouth. I almost dared him to. It wouldn't change the way I felt though. After all, he'd done nothing but show contempt and disgust for me since the day I'd shown up in Brisbane. Why should I show him a modicum of respect in return? I owed him thanks for letting me crash in his house each night, but I wasn't stupid enough to think that was his decision. I had no doubt Ruth had overruled any objection he'd had.

"Maybe you should follow that advice yourself, smart-mouth," he muttered.

"Besides," I continued quickly. "What about showing some respect for the one person who has suffered the most at *both* our hands? How about Alyssa being given the opportunity to decide what she does and doesn't want? When the time is right, of course."

He blinked and all the anger dissolved from his features. He stared at me blankly for a minute.

I went in for the kill. "I am not going to ask for your permission, but when I'm ready, I will ask for hers. I'm not even going to ask for your blessing, because quite frankly if you love your daughter you will honour *her* choice."

He swallowed and was silent for a beat. Then he quirked his eyebrow. "But will you?" he asked.

"Always," I replied without a hint of doubt or deception.

He rolled his eyes but didn't reply. I took it as a chance to make my exit.

About ten minutes later, my phone rang. The display showed Alyssa's number. Thinking there must have been something wrong, I was half-panicked when I answered it.

"You know how we talked about selling my car because I wouldn't need it in Sydney? That our works are close enough that we'll probably carpool, and you've got plenty of cars for the days that we don't?"

"Yeah." It was something we'd discussed in passing. I also didn't want her to drive to Sydney in a separate car because I wanted her beside me, but that was another issue.

"Well, it turns out Flynn was looking for another four-cylinder car for a rental at his work."

"Was he just?" It seemed like a pretty huge coincidence to me, but I didn't say anything that might get me in trouble.

"Yeah, he's offered me a good deal so I figured, why not? I mean it's easier than trying to have Mum and Dad sell it for me later on, right?"

"I guess."

"So Flynn's going to drop us back to Mum and Dad's and keep the car."

"Makes sense, I guess." It still seemed a little odd that he'd randomly need exactly the car she was selling. "So what did he offer you?" I wondered whether he'd lowballed her.

When she told me the figure, my jaw dropped open. It was at least twice the private sale market value of the car. With that piece of the puzzle, his desire to buy the car made sense. There was no doubt in my mind that it was his way of helping her out with the cost of moving without giving her a handout—which she'd never accept anyway. It was probably his way of contributing now that I'd taken away her need for him to move to Sydney with her.

"So, do you think that's a fair price?" she asked. I wondered whether she suspected what he was doing.

Even though I wanted to out his plan to her, I felt I owed him something for shaking up his plans and taking away a chunk of the time he'd been able to spend with Alyssa and Phoebe lately. Even though he'd only gotten as close to them as he had because of my absence, the fact was he had been close to them and I'd torn them out of his life. With those thoughts in my head, I said, "Yeah, that sounds about right for the age."

She thanked me and said she'd be home soon before hanging up, as if that had been the primary purpose of her call. After she'd disconnected, I realised she probably figured I would be the one person who would tell her if Flynn's offer wasn't reasonable. Too bad the guy had found a way to worm under my skin without even being around.

WHEN CHRISTMAS morning dawned, I was almost as excited as Phoebe. Only almost though, because it would be impossible for any adult to be *that* excited without suffering a heart attack.

My own joy had little to do with my surroundings or the presents, or even what I had planned for the afternoon, and everything to do with the fact that it was my first Christmas as a father. I was still coming to terms with it on one level, but on another, I just couldn't imagine my life ever returning to the way it was.

My existence would be hollow and meaningless without Phoebe in it. Her little smile and chatty mouth were a constant source of amusement. If I'd thought I'd loved her when the prospect of losing her had felt so real when the *Gossip Weekly* magazine hit the shelves, it was nothing compared to how I felt after being with her almost full-time for close to a month.

The fact was, I had a hell of a lot to be thankful for.

Ruby and Josh came around early for the usual gift exchange. From the moment they arrived on the doorstep before I was even fully awake, I knew the day would be a fucking barrel of laughs. What was already an awkward situation—having to sit around and make pleasantries with a man who beyond any shadow of a doubt hated me—was made even worse by the addition of a second man who would kick my arse if given even half an opportunity. I sucked it up though, for Alyssa and for Phoebe. They were the important ones.

The time came for the pre-lunch gift giving. I knew all about Alyssa's family's tradition; I'd even participated in it a few times when we were still in high school. They played an almost rotational game. One person would select a gift and read out the name on it. That person would open their gift and then select the next present before reading out the name on the card. It would continue in that vein until all the gifts had been opened.

Alyssa helped Phoebe out whenever it was her turn, which was often because Phoebe had been spoiled rotten by all and sundry. In addition to the few small items Alyssa and I had purchased, Ruby and Josh seemed to have bought her four or five gifts each, then there were the ones Ben and Jade had given us, and the one Mum sent over from wherever the hell she currently was. Surprisingly, there was even a gift from Dad that he'd apparently mailed directly to Ruth and Curtis. The only tense moment of the morning was when I had opened my present from Alyssa and had selected a present to hand out in return, only to realise it was for Curtis. I walked over to him and passed him the gift. As I read out the tag, he watched his hands, rather than me, no doubt mulling over everything that had happened between us lately.

When it came time for lunch, I found a spot at the far end of the table, and then positioned Alyssa on one side of me and Phoebe on the other. There was nothing I wanted more than to just ignore everyone else at the table, so being needed to cut Phoebe's food, to help her feed herself, and to keep her entertained, gave me the perfect excuse to be a little antisocial. It also gave Alyssa the opportunity to relax and enjoy herself with her family during what was probably the last time they'd all be together before we moved to Sydney.

When Phoebe started to get fussy, I was the one who took her into our room to help her sleep.

It was a little after five before I'd finally managed to break Alyssa free from the pack. When I did, I took the hamper Ruth had prepared in one hand, and wrapped the other around Alyssa. We walked slowly through the quiet streets until we arrived at our park. I had everything else I needed tucked safely away in the backpack I was carrying. Even though she clearly wondered what we were doing, I didn't want to ruin her Christmas surprise.

It was almost twilight when the park finally came into view. The day had been so hot that after the short walk, a light sheen of sweat clung to our bodies. The sky was filled with a haze of light grey clouds, holding the promise of an evening shower to cool things down.

My nerves were on edge, and my hand shook as it held Alyssa's when we walked closer to our tree.

"What's wrong, Declan?" Alyssa asked.

My behaviour must have been concerning her. I shook my

head. "Nothing's *wrong*."

"Then what is it?" she asked, chewing her bottom lip.

"I just wanted to spend a little time alone with you," I said. "Is that so bad?"

"Of course not, I just . . ." She gave me an odd look. "Well, you're acting a little strange."

I tried to laugh at her words, but it came out sounding a little choked even to my own ears. Deciding to stop trying to be casual because it was giving me away faster than showing my nerves, I turned to her. "Close your eyes," I whispered.

She obliged, and I quickly wrapped a blindfold around her eyes.

"Declan? What's—"

I cut her off with a kiss. Her mouth moved of its own accord against mine, needing no guidance from her sight. I stepped back when we both began to get a little breathless. Her lips were full and plump, begging to be kissed again.

I turned away and quickly began setting things up for our date. First, I set up the pop-up tent. It wasn't big, but was closed in and would block us from prying eyes if things went the way I hoped—I needed some time alone with Alyssa. To add to the privacy, I'd set up our little picnic in the corner of the park that farthest from the houses, hidden away between the long grass around the edge of the park and the giant tree that had seen so much of the relationship Alyssa and I had shared. I laid out the picnic blanket, and set up the tea light candles. The dinner I'd organised wasn't anything fancy— just leftovers from the massive Christmas spread as Ruth had promised.

As far as co-conspirators went, Ruth was pretty perfect. I had no doubts she knew what I was planning, and I was certain she knew that I guessed her suspicions, but we didn't mention it—each pretending we had the other fooled.

All I'd done though was ask her to pack something small for us, but she'd gone one step further and got a few of Alyssa's favourite foods, and then packed them all away in her nicest Tupperware. Then she began throwing together everything I would need for some privacy—especially with the photographer still hanging around. Not that I'd seen him on our walk.

Once the picnic was all set up, I guided Alyssa to her place. I helped her to the ground before dropping the blindfold away from her eyes.

"Ta-da," I said, immensely proud of the feast I had laid out for both the senses and the stomach.

"Wow," she breathed before smiling widely. "What's this for?"

"It's your Christmas present," I said. "Some time alone, just the two of us. Unless you want me to leave, of course? It is your present, after all."

She laughed. "Oh, well in that case, you most definitely should . . ." She paused for a beat too long for my comfort. "Stay."

She leaned forward across the mat, kissing my lips softly before turning to the food. "Although, I really don't think I can eat another thing after the lunch Mum put on today."

I smiled, not upset in the least by the turn of events. If she wasn't hungry, it gave us more time to enjoy being alone together.

"I can fix that," I said, putting the lids back onto the containers and packing them into the hamper.

"You sure you don't mind?" she asked. "You went to all this effort."

"The effort wasn't about the food, Lys," I said.

I hoped she didn't notice the fact that my voice wavered at the end. Even if I didn't care about the food, it meant that things were speeding hastily toward the part of the evening I was dreading and anticipating in equal measures.

She raised her eyebrow at me, obviously not missing the quiver in my voice. A small smile crossed her face as she watched me fumble with the last of the containers.

I turned back toward her—nerves now wracking my body and causing my fingers to shake. She wrapped her hands around mine, and I watched our intertwined fingers for a moment, trying to settle my stomach.

"There was something else," I whispered finally, not willing to meet her eyes for fear of turning chicken. I tried to continue, but the words stuck in my throat.

After a moment's silence, Alyssa released my hands. "What is it?"

"I have something else," I repeated. "For your Christmas present." I reached my hand into my pocket. "Actually, now that I think of it, it's a selfish gift. Very selfish, in fact. I hope you'll forgive me for that."

Her brow furrowed in confusion.

I pulled the little velvet box from my pocket and opened the lid to reveal the contents to her. A few drops of rain started to fall, but I barely noticed them. It was time. It was perfect. It was happening.

My heart was pounding as I spoke. "I want you, Alyssa. I want only you, forever. Will you be mine? Not just for Christmas, but for the rest of our lives?" I held out the diamond ring to her, once again feeling relief that I'd purchased it when funds were less restricted.

She stared at me and didn't breathe for the longest time. The rain was coming down heavier, but the night air was warm, so I didn't mind. Her eyes lingered on the ring for a moment, before moving to my face. She regarded me for a second before nodding.

"Yes," she whispered.

I couldn't help my wide grin or my sigh of relief. I didn't know what to say, knowing nothing—not all the words in the world—could ever be as beautiful as the little affirmation she'd just issued. I let my fingers do the talking instead. I closed my eyes and leaned toward her, cupping her face softly with my hand and pulling her lips against mine. I kissed her softly at first, becoming more hungry as the seconds passed. The whole time, a new mantra ran on a loop through my head. *She said yes, she wants to be mine.*

She moaned against me in encouragement as my fingers found her hand and gently slid the ring onto her finger while keeping her lips busy. She didn't even glance at the way the ring looked against her skin before moving her hands into my hair to pull my mouth harder against hers.

It really had been too long, for both of us. I was ecstatic that she seemed to want me as much as I wanted her.

She hummed as she released my lips. Both of us were oblivious to the rain as it poured down and soaked through our clothes.

My hands caressed her arms before reaching for the buttons on her shirt. I made short work of them as I let my desire overtake reason and control. I pushed lightly against her, and she complied, falling back onto the blanket. My lips caressed the skin on her neck and collarbone as I pushed her shirt up out of my way.

The rain moistened her skin and raised small goosebumps over her stomach. Needing to have her naked beneath me—or on top of me, I wasn't fussy—I offered her my hand and we moved into the relative privacy of the small tent, dragging the blanket with us.

I sucked one of her nipples into my mouth and ran it softly between my teeth. I trailed my mouth lower as she ran her fingers through my now wet hair, pushing it back off my face. Her skin was flushed and warm with desire, but the rain had cooled it as it landed. I worked on the button of her shorts, quickly pulling them off with a flourish. I didn't care that we were—for all intents and purposes—still in a public place. We were hidden enough, and I needed her so badly. I hadn't been able to taste her properly in the longest time. The sex we'd had in recent weeks was always rushed, as we hurried to finish before Phoebe woke or so that we could get a precious few moments of sleep.

Now that I had Alyssa alone, and we weren't due back for at least another couple of hours, I was going to enjoy every second with her—and every inch of her.

My tongue circled her belly button before trailing small kisses along her stomach. I pressed my cheek against her thigh as I adjusted myself lower. I ran my nose along her inner thigh and down to her knee, before tracing the same line back with my tongue.

She muttered indecipherably as she writhed in pleasure—the sound and movement heading straight through my body to my already hard dick. It twitched against its material cage, begging to be released and allowed to return to its home between Alyssa's legs. It would have to wait though; I wanted to taste her first. I wanted her to scream my name as I kissed her deeply. I grazed my teeth lightly along her clit, and she moaned throatily. Needing to do more, I planted a small kiss where my teeth had been seconds earlier, and her legs closed around my shoulders, wrapping me in heaven.

I ran my tongue up the length of one of her lips, circling around and running it down the other. Alyssa shuddered beneath me and clenched the picnic blanket tightly in her fists.

I pulled back from her. "Alyssa," I whispered softly. "Can you show me how you fuck yourself?"

Her head rose off the blanket, a look of shock on her features. I wanted her to feel comfortable, but I also wanted to see her own fingers dance across her skin. It was something I hadn't been treated to yet.

"Please," I begged, before adding, "But only if you want to."

She regarded me for a minute, before nodding minutely and running her hand across her stomach and over the apex of her thigh. Her finger dipped to her pussy, and then she ran it lightly across the surface. After following her movements with a hungry stare, I dipped my head and followed the trail of her finger, eliciting a sweet groan.

I raised my head slightly and watched as her finger trailed back to her clit. When it did, I licked her fingertip where it met her sweet spot. She pulled her hand back a little, permitting my tongue to take the lead, but I couldn't allow that. Instead, I held on her hand and guided her fingers toward her entrance. A moan of delight left me as I watched her digits move in and out, slowly at first, but faster and more fluidly with every passing second. Sitting back on my haunches, I watched her pleasure herself. My cock was screaming at me to stop the madness already and bring him into the game, but I couldn't. At least, not just yet.

A pink tinge ran up the length of Alyssa's body as she saw my eyes appraising her. Her hand stilled and her bottom lip was captured by her teeth.

I smiled at her, trying to make her see how fucking beautiful I thought she was. Then, reaching out, I grabbed her hand, pressing her fingers softly into my mouth and rolling my tongue around the tips. Without missing a beat, I replaced her fingers with my own, enjoying the warmth surrounding my fingertips as they entered her. She was so wet and ready. Moving my fingers in a slow circle, I grinned when Alyssa bucked her hips toward me. I leaned over her again and dipped my head to press my mouth against her skin again.

Her left hand grabbed my hair, pulling me even closer to her. I could feel the band of the ring there grazing against my skull and couldn't help smiling. She'd agreed to be mine—I could think of nothing I wanted more in the world. The thought made me kiss her more deeply, wrapping my tongue around her clit until she cried out my name repeatedly in blissful elation.

As soon as her walls began to tighten around my fingers, I slid them out and stripped off my shorts. My cock crowed with delight as I positioned myself between Alyssa's thighs. Her legs wrapped around me and guided me home. I slammed into her again and again, harder and harder, as she came around me. The rain had eased off and was little more than a light mist against the tent when I twisted us around so that Alyssa could ride me.

She turned her face up to the ceiling and cried out in delight.

My hands caught her breasts as they danced in time to her rhythm. My fingers grazed her nipples as I tried desperately to stop myself from coming too soon and ruining the little time we had together. I bit my lip and moved my hands to her hips, pulling them tightly against mine to still her movements, relishing the feel of my full length within her. I pulled myself upright, keeping Alyssa in position, and she wrapped her legs around me in response, mirroring the action with her arms around my neck. I softly kissed her neck before allowing my lips to slowly graze a tender trail from her breast to her hair.

"I love you, soon-to-be Alyssa Reede," I whispered against the smooth column of her throat.

I silenced any argument she might have had to the name by pulling her hips against me, pushing my length deeper into her.

Her response was a throaty groan, and I knew I couldn't last any longer. Yanking her hips roughly against me again, I spilled into her.

Desiring to be even closer to her, knowing all the while that I could never be close enough, I wrapped her securely in my arms. As my breathing slowly returned to normal, I rested my cheek against her heart and listened to it slow to a steady beat while her fingertips brushed lightly through my hair.

We sat like that for an unknown time before she began to extract herself from our tangle. I grabbed her hand and pulled her back toward me. "I'm not finished with you yet," I growled softly.

She laughed and swatted my hand away playfully. I moved quickly before she could put too much distance between us, and pulled her back into me.

"You think I'm joking?" I asked, before nipping her neck. I ran my hand along her thigh. "I am so not finished with you yet."

"Declan, we can't," she argued with zero conviction. "We have to get back."

"Why?" I asked, ducking down to suck one of her breasts into my mouth.

"Phoebe—" she started.

"Is with your mum and is perfectly fine," I countered.

"Umm, Ruby and Josh—" she continued.

"Will still be there when we get back."

When I saw that she would be compliant despite her debate, I released her. I reached outside the tent to pick up the blindfold that I'd discarded earlier and wrapped it around her eyes before she realised what I was doing.

"Declan?" she questioned, obviously uncertain about the turn of events.

"Trust me," I whispered.

She nodded.

"We've had the main course," I told her. "Now it's time for dessert."

CHAPTER THIRTY-ONE

A BLESSING AND A CURSE

I LIFTED MY head off Alyssa's chest, surveying the scene, before freeing one hand from its hold around her and lightly brushing the remnants of crushed strawberries out of her hair. I grabbed the blindfold that had recently been discarded and gently wiped the last few smears of chocolate sauce from her chest. I stared down at her, marvelling at her beauty. Her brown hair lay fanned out around her face, and her eyes were loosely shut as she rested. Goosebumps littered her body as the night air cooled her skin. She was stunning, but most importantly she had agreed to be mine.

Thinking back on the evening we'd just shared, I smiled. If someone had asked me what my favourite dessert was when I was younger, I probably would have said pavlova, or maybe cheesecake. But after my evening with Alyssa, a new favourite topped the list. Who would have thought that simple strawberries with chocolate dipping sauce could be quite so . . . appetising? Even then, though wholly and completely satiated, the thought of her plump lips closing around the red flesh of the berry as her teeth broke through the skin made me hard. I imagined her tongue darting out to catch the juices or lick a little of the chocolate that had dripped onto her lips, and groaned.

How had I got so lucky? Not only was she stunningly beautiful, and wholly in love with me, she was a willing participant in all things I introduced to her.

Like the blindfold.

Knowing she couldn't see me as I moved around her, touching and caressing her, was surreal. She made new noises that I'd never heard before. By the end, I'd had her gasping for breath as she came hard. Even as the moments played on repeat in my mind, I wondered whether she would still taste of the strawberries and chocolate if I kissed her.

I trailed my eyes down the length of her body, lifting myself up further, so that I was kneeling above her. My attention roamed around the soft peaks and valleys of her body before landing on the ring that had adorned her left hand for a little less than two hours, but would stay there forever.

When I kissed her again, I felt relieved that our pap stalker hadn't been spotted once. Maybe he'd been given Christmas off. Even if he was skulking about somewhere hidden, it was too dark for him to have snapped any photos of us naked in the very public park without a night-vision camera with the ability to see through the walls of the tent.

"What're you smiling at?" Alyssa asked sweetly. Her voice startled me; I'd thought she was dozing. I looked back at her face, but her eyes were still shut.

I leaned into her neck, kissing it softly, and murmured, "How do you know I'm smiling?" I closed my own eyes as I renewed my ministrations on her skin.

"I always know when you are smiling," she said simply. "It's my job."

"Hmmm," I mused. "Is it your job just to know, or to put a smile there?"

"Both." She grinned.

"I know a way you could make my smile wider," I said suggestively. "And maybe yours too."

She remained silent, but her hips rolled a little in my direction, telling me to go for gold. I nudged her thighs a little wider with my knee before sliding straight into her. I knew I needed to get my fill of her before heading back to her family, and eventually to real life. At least I could do that absolutely secure in the knowledge that she was mine.

Holding her tightly, I pushed deep inside of her. I wanted something more than just sex—more than fucking. I wanted to communicate to her all the joy I felt from her "yes." If it meant I had to give her a third orgasm in as many hours, well, that was a price I was more than willing to pay. I stared into her eyes as I took her over the edge and back into oblivion.

Eventually, we untangled ourselves and pulled on our clothes. They were wet from the rain, and the night air was cooler, so it was going to be a very uncomfortable walk back to her parents' house. Entering looking like we did was not going to be any picnic either, but it was worth it for the "yes" and our time alone.

Alyssa tightened her grip on my hand as we neared the house. She turned to me and shot me a quick smile. I beamed in response. The truth was, I'd never been happier. Still, I wondered if she was thinking about what came next. Walking through the door to her parents' house would be opening a huge can of worms. We would need to give her family the awesome news in a way that they would accept. Ruth would be over the moon, but I honestly wasn't sure how it would go over for everyone else. I knew Curtis wouldn't be happy, but screw him.

We walked past the front window, but the curtains were drawn, so I couldn't see what everyone was doing. There was a lot of noise and laughter coming from inside.

"I don't want to hear that about the father of my grandchild!" Ruth shrieked with laughter.

I froze, wondering who had said what about me. Alyssa coaxed me forward gently with a tug at my hand.

"Well, you asked." Ruby's laughter joined the mix.

"I didn't mean I needed all the intimate details of my son's sex life. There are some things a mother just doesn't need to know."

It was Alyssa's turn to freeze. Her mind was obviously five

steps ahead of mine. While I struggled to catch up with the conversation, she quickly turned, pulling me back down the drive and away from the house. Once we were a short distance away from the house, she shook her head in disbelief before smiling at me. She glanced down at her ring, twisting it in a circle around her finger, and then she shook her head again, before finally settling on chewing the inside of her lip.

"What is it?" I asked.

"We can't tell them," she murmured, looking back up toward the house. "At least, not tonight."

I followed her gaze, then back at her, and then back at the house again as if it would reveal whatever information Alyssa had worked out from the conversation we'd overheard. "What? Why not?"

"Ruby's pregnant," she said, as if it were obvious. The huge-arse grin crossing her features again told me she was happy about the information.

"And?"

"And I'm not going to take away from her news."

I scrunched my eyebrows together in confusion. "So?"

"Dec, I told you. She and Josh have been trying for . . . well, for forever. If it's worked. It's . . . wow . . . it's . . . great! I'm not going to take any of her joy away from her. Not tonight. I can't do it."

I looked back up toward the house again. "But how is us announcing our engagement going to take away from her news?"

Alyssa sighed in exasperation. "It just will."

"I think your parents know anyway," I coaxed. "Or at least your mum suspects, and your dad is dreading that it might be the case."

"Let them speculate," she said. "Just for tonight?" She slid the ring off her finger and, after realising her outfit had no pockets, slipped it into mine. "Please? For me?"

I closed my eyes so she wouldn't see the hurt there. I tried to tell myself it was just a ring, just a symbol. She wasn't telling me no—she'd already said yes—but part of me felt like she'd just ripped out my heart and handed it back to me, before it had even stopped beating.

"Fine. If that's what you want," I muttered.

"Thank you," she said, placing her hands on my face and gently stroking my cheek. "For everything." She planted a light kiss on my cheek. "Today was perfect. Everything I could have hoped for and more."

I nodded, unwilling to try to get any more words past the lump in my throat.

Alyssa led us back to the house, planting another quick kiss on my cheek before unlocking the door and walking into what could only be described as a shitstorm of estrogen.

Ruth screamed as we walked in. "It's finally happened," she shrieked. "My baby boy is giving me more grandbabies!"

"Congratulations," Alyssa said. I stood back and ignored everything. At least until I saw Ruth's eyes fall to Alyssa's left hand, taking in its bareness, then to my face.

Disappointment crossed her features, but after taking in whatever emotion was currently on my face, it turned to pity. She obviously thought I'd asked and been turned down.

Worse than the look of pity on Ruth's face was the smug look of derision Curtis wore. I wanted to rip the ring from my pocket and force it on Alyssa's finger. The next time it went on, I would make sure it would stay there forever.

"Congrats, guys," I said, to distract myself from my own horrid thoughts. I waited for what felt like the appropriate length of time, listening to bizarre conversations about things that didn't seem polite to discuss outside of the bedroom, before whispering to Alyssa, "I'm heading for a shower."

She nodded. "I'll go next," she said, before starting up a conversation with Ruby about weeks or due date or some shit that I didn't want to hear about.

I grabbed a change of clothes and gently stepped around the trundle that held Phoebe's sleeping form safe. I showered quickly, and then headed straight back to the bedroom. I couldn't listen to anything more. The last thing I did before going to sleep was to lay Alyssa's ring on her bedside table. She would put it back on in the morning. I was sure of it.

Wouldn't she?

Lying in the bed, trying to sleep, my heart was doing so many erratic laps of my chest that I felt like I'd run a marathon. With each passing second, the "yes" Alyssa had given me seemed less and less real. By the time I fell asleep, I was convinced it was nothing but a dream.

WHEN I woke, it was dark and a strange sound filled the air. I took a second to shake the sleep from my head to figure out what it was. When I did, I realised the noise was a soft sobbing. I turned over and felt Alyssa shaking with tears beside me.

"Hey, what is it?" I whispered.

She shook her head and nestled into me.

I brushed her hair back with my hand and held her against me. "Please, tell me."

"It's just seeing how well Mum and Dad took Josh and Ruby's news." She sobbed a little harder. "I never had that. I mean, they came around eventually of course, but their first reaction was anger and disappointment. I guess I just feel . . . I don't know. It just makes me sad that my pregnancy is so different to Ruby's."

"I'm sorry I wasn't there for you." I felt like I was always apologising for leaving her, but I would apologise every day for the rest of forever if that was what it took to wipe away her pain. "But do you know what? I'm not sorry it happened. I can't image my life without her. Without both of you."

Alyssa nodded. "I sound stupid, don't I? I mean, I wouldn't change a thing if it meant I'd lose her, but I guess I never understood how much I really wanted that approval."

"It's only as stupid as me telling you that I really didn't like you giving your ring back to me tonight. It made me feel like you were rejecting me."

"I'm sorry." She sobbed harder. "I didn't mean . . . I didn't know . . . I'm sorry."

I shushed her and held her tighter. "It's okay, baby," I whispered. "I know you didn't mean to hurt me. Just like Ruby and Josh, and your parents for that matter, didn't mean to hurt you."

She nodded against me.

"Sleep now," I told her softly.

"Dec?" she whispered.

"Yeah?"

"I didn't like the feeling of it being off either." She pressed her hand against mine, and I could feel the band of her engagement ring. "Thanks for leaving it out for me."

I hummed. It was about the most I could manage as emotion clogged up my throat.

"Can we tell them in the morning?" she asked.

I smiled. "I'd like that."

"Me too," she murmured sleepily.

THE NEXT morning was interesting. Alyssa and I were up early with Phoebe—too fucking early after the night we'd had. We stumbled sleepily from the bedroom while Phoebe bounced down the hallway. I slipped my hand onto Alyssa's arse and gave it a gentle squeeze. When she slapped my shoulder, I captured her hand and kissed it gently. Then I slipped off to the toilet, while Alyssa led Phoebe off to the kitchen for some breakfast.

The squealing that echoed from their direction carried all the way in the bathroom, and I buried my head in my hands. Honestly, how many times could those chicks squeal over a baby? I briefly debated going back to hide in the bedroom for the next week. But then I remembered Alyssa's sleepy promise the night before and practically skipped down the hallway.

I was immediately wrapped in a huge hug by Ruth. "It's about time you joined the family properly."

"Thanks for the support," I said. "I have a feeling we might need it."

"Don't worry about Curtis. He'll be fine. Trust me . . . he just wants what is best for Alyssa."

"That's all I want too."

She smiled. "See, you do see eye to eye on something."

I chuckled. "I guess so."

"So," Ruth started, turning back toward Alyssa. "When's the wedding?"

Alyssa buried her head in her hands and mumbled something that sounded suspiciously like, "Oh, God."

I walked over to her before wrapping my arms around her waist and lifting her slightly so that I could plant a row of kisses along her neck. "What's the matter?" I asked.

She turned back toward me. "We have to have a wedding." She wrinkled her nose in disgust.

I laughed. "Isn't that every little girl's dream?"

"You knew me as a little girl, Dec," she said, rolling her eyes. "When did I *ever* indicate that was my dream?"

It was true. Whenever she'd mentioned the future, it was almost more in regards to *being* married rather than *getting* married. If I could have Alyssa beside me forever, without all the white wedding bullshit, I had no complaints. "That's fine, a quickie down at the courthouse suits me." I chuckled.

She smiled at me. "Sounds perfect."

"Don't you dare!" Ruth gave me a look that easily rivalled any of the evil glares I'd received from Curtis.

Alyssa rolled her eyes again, and I stifled a chuckle.

"You can't take that away from your father, Alyssa. You know he's been chomping at the bit to walk you down the aisle."

It was my turn to roll my eyes. I knew the last thing Curtis wanted was to walk Alyssa down the aisle and hand her off to me.

I pulled Alyssa into me, kissing her cheek softly. "You get what you want—don't worry about anyone else." I was already planning just how quickly we could get married and get all the nonsense over with. Information that had actually been posted publicly in the Births, Deaths, and Marriages offices. A month and a day, and she could be mine officially.

She nodded and turned her face to kiss my lips. "Thank you;

but Mum's right. We should do this properly."

I sighed but didn't argue. I couldn't because Killer Curtis seemed to take that as his cue to enter. "Do what properly, pumpkin?" he said lazily, from somewhere behind me.

I watched Alyssa's face carefully. She flinched a little as he spoke, and I realised it wasn't going to be pretty. I didn't want Alyssa to have to say anything she would regret later, so I decided to man up and take the pressure off her.

"Our wedding," I said boldly, turning to face him. I was glad that neither Alyssa nor Ruth could see my face because it gave me the opportunity to sneer at him just a little. I returned his smug smile from the previous night, more than willing to rub Alyssa's acceptance in his face.

He choked and his face turned pink, then red, then an odd shade of purple. His eyes shot to Ruth.

"But I thought—" He started.

He was obviously cut off by a look on her face or something, because he stopped short. He stood, mouth gaping, staring between Alyssa and Ruth, not even sparing another glance in my direction.

I took this as my opportunity to score some Alyssa brownie points. "I'm sorry I didn't get to ask your permission first, but the decision was made so quickly. I guess I'll just have to ask for your blessing instead."

He finally looked at me—although glared was probably the better word. The look made my lips twitch upward. I didn't doubt that murder was crossing his mind at that point in time. Alyssa, misinterpreting his glower as an objection to our plans, walked closer to me, and wrapped her hands around my arm. Score one for Declan.

"It's what I want, Daddy," she said. I could hear the defiance in her voice. "He's all that I ever wanted. You know that. Please, can't you just be happy for us?"

Ruth, who'd obviously seen the anger coming, sat a plate of food down on the table for Curtis at that exact second. He regarded it for a moment before deciding that Alyssa and I could wait.

He chewed his food and seemed to be deep in thought before

he finally spoke—when he did, he drew each word out.

"I'll support you," he said. "I'll even give you my blessing." He shot me a dark look. "I'll walk the prettiest bride in the world down the aisle. But I *don't* have to like the person at the end."

"Dad!" Alyssa exclaimed.

"Fine by me," I said at the exact same time without a word of a lie.

Now I just had to survive until New Year's Eve without him killing me in my sleep, and we'd be fine.

CHAPTER THIRTY-TWO

CATCHING ON

EACH MORNING I woke, I was thankful.

There were so many things I was thankful for. First, I was alive. That meant Curtis hadn't found a way to sneak past Alyssa and murder me while I'd slept. Second, the fact that the prison didn't close for the holidays, meant Curtis was still required to leave the house every day. Third, my ring still adorned Alyssa's hand—a promise from me to do the best I could, and a promise from her to love me even when I fucked up. And fourth, that it was one day closer to an escape from living with the soon-to-be in-laws.

During the days since Christmas, there had been a rotating front door of friends and relatives of Ruth and Curtis coming and going, almost at whim. After living alone for so long, the constant presence of so many other people was driving me insane. But during the brief lulls, when no one else was home and Phoebe was asleep, the silence was just as unbearable.

The need for constant noise, but not constant chatter, was one of the reasons I always felt so Zen in my ProV8. It was easy to focus on the drone of the engine, on the hum of the rubber on the track, on the telemetry information and feedback from the team, rather than on everything else. Other than the brief moments where

Alyssa's memory had haunted me, I'd never felt more focused than when I was on the track. Which was why I'd insisted on heading out to the kart track the morning of New Year's Eve. I needed clarity before all the shit was supposed to go down that night. All the things I'd kept hidden from Alyssa were buzzing around my head like a swarm that I needed to escape.

Throwing the kart deep into the corners, feeling the arse slide out as the drift took over, being so low to the ground—low enough that I felt like it was just me and the track—wasn't quite the same as being in a car, but it was close enough to be a much-needed salve to balance everything else I'd been doing.

While I tore up the track, Alyssa and Phoebe just watched from the stands. Even though it felt a little selfish doing something that I needed—something only I would truly enjoy—neither of them complained as they watched me run lap after lap. One day soon, that would change. In a little under two years, Phoebe would be able to go on a tandem kart, and damned if I wasn't going to try to make a little revhead out of her. My little girl could be a princess and kick arse on the track. And Alyssa could choose to join us or wait in the café.

When I came back in from the hour-long session on the track, Alyssa was waiting with Phoebe perched on her lap.

"Feeling better?" she asked.

"Much." It was amazing how much a few laps could make a world of difference. It had clarified some things for me, and thrown other things into sharp focus. In a little under twelve hours, I'd have shown Paige and her lackeys that I wasn't someone to be trifled with. Then in the morning, Alyssa and I would be picking Phoebe up from Ruth and Curtis and starting the journey home.

But first, we had to get ready for the night.

When we left the kart track, we headed for Alyssa's parents' first, dropping off Phoebe and grabbing my tux, before driving straight into the city.

Alyssa's expression during the drive was enigmatic. I had no idea what she was thinking, and part of me didn't want to ask. I didn't want to start any conversation that might lead back to the evening's plans.

We were almost into the city when Alyssa turned to me, curling up in the passenger seat and staring at me with such a reverent look that I couldn't help but reach for her and brush a strand of hair off her face.

"It's funny how quickly life can change, isn't it?" she asked. Her voice was wistful and full of wonder.

Unsure what she was getting at, and what she expected me to say in return, I simply nodded. Obviously, she'd been thinking something over and it was dangerous for me to try to guess at what. A second later, her gaze dropped to her engagement ring and she started to play with it, using the diamond to twist it around her finger.

A gentle sigh left her lips. "I mean, this time last year, I was panicking about how hard the last year of uni would be, trying to get over the fact that things would never work with Cain, worrying about what I'd do for work when I graduated, because I had no prospects lined up. Being at the end of the uni year just seemed so far away."

I tried to ignore her mention of Cain, but it surprised me that it had been so recent. The way she'd talked about him made it sound like it was ancient history—not something that had happened a year ago.

"God, New Year's always makes me so sappy." She laughed. "I guess I'm just trying to say that this time last year, I was terrified of what might come next for me. It was all so unknown. And it's still unknown, but knowing that I'm heading there with you at my side, Dec, that's . . . I don't know. Amazing. I never allowed myself to believe we'd be here, but I never stopped loving you. Never."

"Me either, Lys."

"And now, well, the BS with the paps is all behind us. I won't have to pretend to be nice to Darcy to keep my job ever again. We can finally just look to the future, and we've got the rest of our lives ahead of us."

"Lys, I—" The details of my plan were right on my tongue. It would have been easy to warn her, but I needed her reactions to be real so that no one implicated her. If the plans didn't go the way I wanted, she needed to have plausible deniability—just like Danny. After a gulp of air, I swallowed down the words, along with the rising tide of guilt that washed up from within me. "I can't wait."

Ten minutes later, we arrived at the Suncrest Hotel car park. We'd already planned for what came next. I'd go to our hotel room and get dressed with Morgan, while Alyssa and Eden went off to have all sorts of shit done. Words I didn't even know the meaning of had been discussed: mani-pedis, blow-waves, up-dos, and a whole range of other things. I was happy enough to leave the two of them to get that sorted. It gave me time to sort some other stuff.

Almost as soon as Alyssa had left, I texted the random number in my phone.

Room 607. Room key will be at your table.

The reply came back almost instantly. *Looking forward to it.*

After an hour of messing around in the room, throwing back a few beers, Morgan and I decided it was probably time to get ready. He slipped across the hall to his room while I dressed in mine. We'd already agreed to meet the girls downstairs, because they'd be cutting it close to the start time.

So much of the night felt reminiscent of the formal. Even though I'd had the do-over date with Alyssa and had exorcised most of the demons from that night, a nervous energy built in me. When I met Morgan at the lifts, he was practically buoyant. For him, the night was just going to be a fun-filled night of pranks and mischief—exactly his type of thing—but the revenge I'd planned felt so much more important than that to me.

"Are you 'right?" he asked, staring at me as I paced back and forth in front of the elevator.

"Yeah. I just, well, I can't help wondering if this is the right thing to do. Maybe I should have just left it."

"Dude, it's too late to back out now," Morgan said when we got into the lift. "It's time to strap those balls of yours back on for one night and get this done."

"I guess."

"No guessing. The time to back out was last week. Now, there's nothing left for you to do but hold on for the ride."

And hope that I don't lose anything important along the way.

It didn't take long to find Alyssa and Eden in the crowd. In fact, the instant my gaze slid to Alyssa, it stuck. Although I'd seen her silver-and-turquoise dress before, during her shopping trip when she'd said she wanted to get it because it matched my eyes, it didn't seem like the same outfit.

Maybe it was the way her hair was styled, the make-up, or the lingerie beneath, or maybe it was the way the soft lighting in the foyer seemed to backlight her body, but the outfit had gone from pretty to downright illegal. The way the strapless dress hugged her breasts, and slipped down to accentuate her waist and hips, left my mouth dry and my pants tight. The silvery lace overlay that curled around the curves of her breast highlighted the delights hidden by the satin underlay.

My lips curled as I thought about what Phoebe would say if she saw Alyssa just then. She'd no doubt think her mother had become the living embodiment of a Disney princess. Although there was nothing Disney about the things I wanted to do to Alyssa. Especially with the turquoise mask she wore over her face that just made her look like sex in disguise.

God, the things I would do to her while she wore that mask, if given half a chance. The colour made her eyes gleam almost gold, and when she focused them on me, they shone like stars in the night. Despite how shit-hot she was, she looked at me like I was the centre of the fucking universe or something. I wondered if my own simple black mask did the same things to her imagination as hers turquoise one did for me.

Almost as soon as I met her gaze, every thought of what the night might hold, disappeared. I wanted nothing more than to drag her back to the elevators, up to our hotel room, and have her fuck me every way she wanted to—so long as it was with that mask in place.

When she saw me devouring her with my gaze, she grinned and smoothed down imaginary wrinkles in the dress. My body moved closer to her long before my brain had caught up after it's appraisal of her fuck-hot look.

"You like?"

"God, that dress looks fantastic on you."

"But let me guess, it'd look better on the floor?" She laughed as she teased me.

"Fuck, you stole my best line."

"I find it amazing that you were able to charm anyone with your cheesy lines."

Even though I had a retort, I bit down on it. With everything that was lined up for the night, I didn't want to give Alyssa any extra reminders of what had happened at the New Year's Ball the year before. Especially when she would soon face a pretty major one. Maybe it was time to warn her. At least she wouldn't be totally blindsided by what she was walking into.

"Lys, can we talk for a moment?" My voice was as sombre as I felt, but I'd decided in that moment that I needed to warn her. Plausible deniability be damned, it was more important to ensure she didn't assume the worst when everything came out.

"Is everything okay?"

"No, it's—"

Morgan came up behind me and elbowed me in the back. "You're up."

Alyssa's gaze flicked to him and she grimaced. It was clear she still wasn't comfortable with Morgan's presence, but that was the least of my problems. Time was up, and I'd missed my chance to warn Alyssa. *Fuck!* "It's fine, Lys. Shall we go in?"

When I walked into the ballroom with Alyssa on my arm, I had no doubt I was the proudest guy in the room. She looked like a million dollars, maybe more, and turned so many heads. Including the one I wanted to notice her.

"Declan? What's going on?" Darcy's voice cut through my pride, and reminded me of the reason I'd had Paige invite her for me.

"What do you mean, Darcy?" I afflicted the most innocent tone I could muster. "I'm here to celebrate the coming of the New Year with my future." I gave Alyssa a reassuring smile.

"But why is *she* here when you invited me?"

Alyssa gasped and turned to me. *Fuckity fuck!*

Ignoring the pain radiating off Alyssa, I spoke directly to Darcy. "I thought I made myself clear in my note," I said. "I want a do-over of last New Year's. More than anything."

Darcy puffed out her chest and wore a victorious smile. I wanted to shake my head at her stupidity. Even if there were a chance in hell I wanted to go anywhere near her—which there wasn't—I wouldn't exactly be telling her I wanted to fuck her while Alyssa was at my side.

Alyssa tried to pull from my hold, but I held her waist tighter, curling my fingers around her stomach, and refused to let her go.

"I think you misunderstand, Darcy," I said, ensuring my air of innocence was unaffected by the tightening of my throat at Alyssa's reaction. "If I could have the do-over I want so badly, I wouldn't let this," I grabbed my crotch, "come within a thousand Ks of your poisonous pussy. In fact, I would never have left Alyssa, because I'm hers and hers alone. Utterly and completely, and no amount of smear campaigns will ever change that. All it will do is make me rain fury down on anyone who says a single bad word about her."

"What?"

"That's why I invited you here tonight, so that you can see just how in love we are." When I saw the person who'd just slipped in the door pass us, I smirked. Timing couldn't have been better if I'd planned it—which I kinda had. After all, Morgan had been watching for Darcy so I could ensure she was inside the ballroom before I led Alyssa in, and I'd had Eden keep Blake Cooper amused for a few minutes outside. "Oh, I probably should have told you too." I pretended to grimace. "I gave the other ticket I had at Paige's table to Blake. You know, your husband. I thought that couples should be together on a night like this. Although, to be honest, I'm a little surprised that neither of you mentioned it to one another."

Darcy fumed. I could almost see the smoke curling from the top of her perfectly coiffed head. And she hadn't even noticed her husband was right behind her yet.

"Of course, he might not have mentioned it because he thought he'd been invited to a date with the leggy strategist from Sinclair Racing. I hope he's not too disappointed to find out who his date really is."

"Fuck you, Declan!"

I chuckled. "I thought I'd just explained that, Darcy. Never. Again." In the next breath, I called out, "Hey, Blake! Over here."

Darcy went from a red so deep she'd almost gone purple to a white that would rival the finest china. She'd clearly thought I was bluffing about inviting Blake.

"Declan? What—" He cut off when he saw Darcy standing with Alyssa and me. "Darce? What are you doing here?"

"I could ask you the same question, Blake!" The words were spat with such disdain, I almost felt sorry for him. But only until I remembered the things he'd said about Alyssa in the pub when I'd first arrived back in Browns Plains.

"God, you're both as bad as each other," I muttered and then led Alyssa away as the two of them started a shouting match that soon filled the entire room with their voices.

When I was far enough away from them, I turned to Alyssa. I almost didn't want to look at her, because she'd fallen suspiciously quiet and her back was ramrod straight as she'd walked at my side.

"What the fuck was that about?" she asked. Her mouth was tight, mashed into a line that showed her clear displeasure.

Fuck. I'd hoped she'd see the funny side of it. "Exactly what I said it was about. I wanted to be sure Darcy got the message loud and clear that we're together and to back off."

"So you tricked her into coming into the city, spending a fortune on a dress, getting made-up, just to prove a point."

Across the room, the sound of a slap echoed around the hall and Darcy stormed off, out of the ballroom. Despite Alyssa's unease, I chuckled at the sight because honestly, I was feeling pretty damn proud of the reaction I'd got. It was no less than either of them deserved.

"Are you kidding me right now?" Alyssa's gaze was wild as she turned back to me.

The laughter died on my lips. "What?"

For a moment, all Alyssa did was stare at me. She barely even blinked. Then she turned away. "We should probably find our table." Her voice sounded like something had defeated her—as if she'd been the one on the receiving end of the payback I'd dished to Darcy. She walked off without waiting for me to escort her.

It took me a moment for my thoughts to catch up with what had happened. "Lys?"

I started after her, but Paige's hand caught me instead. Her talon-like nails dug into my forearm. "I didn't think you were bringing, um, what was her name again." She waved her hand in Alyssa's direction as if to dismiss her as unimportant. "Oh well, I'm sure we can squeeze her onto our table."

"I don't have a seat at your table."

"Don't be silly, Declan, of course you do."

"No. I don't. Sorry, Paige, I was given a better offer for tonight, so I gave my ticket away." I nodded over to where Blake was sitting in the seat that should have been mine, looking like someone had just run over his puppy. "He's an old school friend. I didn't think you'd mind."

I tugged my arm free of her hold and started toward Sinclair's table, where Alyssa was just finding a seat.

"You're sitting at Sinclair's table?" Paige's voice pitched higher than I would have thought possible.

"Yeah. See, Morg and Edie invited me. They were so excited about seeing me again that I didn't have the heart to tell them no."

"What about our little chat?"

"Yeah, about that. Can we rain check it again for a couple of hours? I have some entertaining to do soon, while Alyssa is otherwise occupied." I winked at her, certain that she would have been in the loop about the hotel room date I had with Tillie and Talia. "I should be back down around eleven if you want to chat then?"

"Maybe we can chat in your room?"

I chuckled. "Sorry, Paige, I'm hoping that will be occupied most of the night. I'll meet you at your table, and then we can go somewhere private. Although, I probably should tell you that

Sinclair Racing have made me an offer too. One I'm very tempted to accept."

The corners of her eyes pinched as she glared at me. "I thought you were set on coming to race for me, darling." The way she said the word darling made it sound more like she wanted to choke the shit out of me than anything else.

I shrugged. "Nothing's set until it's in print, right?"

After assessing me carefully, she nodded.

"Oh, and Paige." I slid my hand into the right-hand pocket of my pants, where I had one hotel room key. Being as inconspicuous as I could, I placed it into her hand. "Can you pass this to Tillie for me?"

She nodded and slipped the card into her bag.

I headed over to the Sinclair Racing table, and took my seat next to a very frosty Alyssa, who was deep in conversation with Danny's wife, Hazel.

Danny welcomed me with a nod before giving me a questioning look, no doubt in response to Alyssa's refusal to even acknowledge I'd sat down. I just waved off his curiosity and concern. She'd come around once she realised what having Darcy and the others off our backs meant for the longer term.

Before long, the first course was dropped to the table. All throughout the meal, Alyssa barely said a word to me. Even once dessert had come and gone, I was still facing the cold shoulder. Although it didn't seem arctic as much as bottled-up and ready to burst.

Not for the first time, I cursed the fact that I hadn't warned her what the night was really about. There was still one more stage too, and after her reaction to the first part, I was more determined than ever to keep her out of it. Not only would she have plausible deniability, but it would also mean she'd have less reason to be pissed at me.

Around eight thirty, I excused myself from the room. In some ways, having Alyssa not talking to me was easier for this part. At least she didn't demand to come with me.

When I was near the door, and close enough to Wood Racing's

table that Tillie could see me, I walked up to Sophie, one of the women who worked in promotions at Sinclair Racing. She was partially in on the scheme, so she knew I'd be interrupting her evening for a little while. With a nod, a smile, and a touch to her arm, I led her out of the room and toward the hotel elevator.

While I was waiting, I caught sight of Tillie watching me from the door to the ballroom.

Turning my back on Sophie, I tapped my watch and mouthed, "See you later," to Tillie.

The risk of course was that she'd go straight to Alyssa and let her know where I'd disappeared to, but Eden and Morgan were on hand for that, at least for the next ten minutes before they moved into position.

CHAPTER THIRTY-THREE
CAUGHT OUT

A LITTLE BEFORE nine, I was waiting alone in room 608 of the Suncrest Hotel with the door ajar, listening for movement outside. Sophie had headed down to her hotel room with instructions to keep herself amused for around an hour before heading back to the ball if she wished. Her part in the night was done, and now there was nothing to do but wait.

Wait for the trap to spring. For the concrete evidence that Tillie and Talia were trying to ruin me, with Paige pushing them from behind the scenes. The fact that from the time I'd agreed to discuss the position at Wood Racing I'd been paparazzi-free until I'd mentioned Sinclair again, and had the paps back on my arse, made me almost positive about my assumptions. If I was right, and she had been running some sort of smear campaign, the news that Sinclair Racing had made me an offer would be sure to send her into a frenzy.

After that would come a fresh round of scandal. Or at least, an attempt for it. The scandal she'd end up with, though, might not be the one she was hoping for.

Just as I suspected, around ten past nine—almost an hour before the time the girls were supposed to arrive for our rendezvous—there was movement in the hallway. Moving with so much care that I was barely even drawing a breath, I crept toward the door with my camera in hand.

Through the crack in the door, I spotted the two women—one a mess of red curls and the other with sleek blonde hair pulled back into a ponytail. The key card that I'd given Paige was in Talia's hand as they crept up to room 607—the one directly across the hall from mine.

Following in their wake was the young pap who'd baited me at Bondi and had followed me for so long since then. I slunk back into the shadows a little as he passed, rushing to catch up with the other two. Then I pushed the door open a little wider and stuck my camera through the gap to follow them.

Without a word between them, the three of them set themselves up in a row in front of the door. Tillie held up her hand and Talia poised the key card near the door. With a silent count of one-two-three using her fingers, Tillie counted them down. On the three, Talia slid the card into the reader on the door and shoved it open.

When they did, I crept out of my room and followed them with the camera.

"Declan, sorry we're early, we—" Tillie's voice grew quieter as she moved into the room before cutting off completely, no doubt as she spotted the actual guests. "What the hell! You're not Declan!"

She swung around and spotted me. I couldn't stop laughing when I came up behind the trio and saw that Morgan and Eden had obviously decided to take our plan a little bit too literally—they were both in a state of undress. The only thing left on the pair was his boxer-briefs, which were doing nothing to hide anything because of the way his dick made them tent out, and Edie's bra and panties.

Morgan grinned and waved for my camera. Fucker never was a shy one.

"What the fuck is this?" Tillie practically screeched. "I thought we were supposed to be hooking up for some fun?"

"I don't know what sort of kinky shit you're into, bringing him with you." I nodded toward the photographer. "Or maybe you just thought that you could catch a few photos of me in action if you got here early enough. Isn't that right, T?"

Talia's lip curled upward in disgust. If I'd been paying more attention to her face in the club rather than her boobs and her body, I might have seen just how similar her eyes were to Paige's. They were a different colour, a slate grey rather than blue, but the same shape.

"I guess you might have got a scoop, even if it wasn't the one you wanted. Sorry guys." I winked at Morgan and Eden. "It really was time you two came out into the open with your relationship. Although, I didn't expect you to get quite so . . . carried away."

Morgan grinned at me. He was enjoying himself way too much—not that I could blame him because I was feeling pretty damn jubilant myself. Especially knowing that Alyssa was downstairs, unaware of what was happening. Hopefully that meant it wouldn't make her madder at me. She'd come around about the Darcy thing before too long, I was sure of it.

"What can I say?" Morgan said. "This woman makes me insane."

He wrapped his arm around Eden's shoulders as she shot me a death stare that told me she hadn't entirely been expecting visitors so early. I shrugged, but I didn't think Morgan and I would be in too much trouble. We were still alive, for one thing.

"But the texts," Tillie said, as if she genuinely believed she had something over me because of half a dozen completely innocent texts between us.

"What about them?"

"You promised me a good time."

"What is this? A fucking men's bathroom? 'For a good time, call.' Plus, I offered nothing. All I gave in my text was a time and a place. How was I supposed to know you meant you wanted to meet up for sex? All you asked is for some fun. For all I knew from your texts, you just wanted a game of checkers."

Morgan sniggered into his hand before Eden—who'd slipped her dress back on—slapped his bare chest with the back of her hand to silence him.

"You'll pay for embarrassing us like this." Talia looped her hand through Tillie's arm and started to pull her back toward the door.

"How? Another article in *Gossip Weekly*? Is that supposed to scare me? At this point, you'd just be flogging a dead horse. It's not like the public gives a shit about me."

Tillie started to argue, but I held up my hand to silence her.

"However, they might be interested in a scandal involving a team owner running a smear campaign against an opposition driver just to get him to change teams. And about how she used nepotism and family favours to pull the strings to do it."

Talia's eyes widened a little. I could see the genuine fear flash across them for a fraction of a second. Her business probably meant the world to her; I wondered what her mother had on her that she'd agreed despite it all. Although looking at the way she looked at Tillie, I wondered whether maybe Paige had less influence than someone else.

"You can't prove that," Tillie said.

"Just like I can't prove that it was you who drugged me at the benefit in November."

Her smile was victorious.

"But," I added before she could celebrate too much. "Gossip magazines don't really need *proof,* do they? They just need enough evidence to make it not be libel. Say a recording of a trio of people entering a private hotel room looking for a scandal."

"You can't prove that's what we were doing."

"Maybe you're right. Maybe we should let the public decide? I've got people ready to send the feed to the Internet." I was bluffing, but it wouldn't take long to upload the footage. "All it will take is a one-word signal from me and it's up for the world to judge. What do you think?"

Talia grabbed Tillie's hand again. "Can we just go, please?"

"You should listen to your girlfriend, Tillie. Or should I say, Miss M?"

She snarled at me.

"I know all about your little scam that you've been running.

Chasing me all over town with your tits out and your tongue hanging from your head, pretending to be interested in me just so you could implicate me in scandal after scandal. And yeah, I probably did a pretty damn good job of helping you out, considering the shit that's been going on in my life lately, but you crossed some pretty big lines."

She glared at me.

"Sending anyone after Alyssa was the biggest. I can deal with anything anyone wants to say about me, I'll take it all day every day, but bring her into it, and you can bet your bottom fucking dollar I will burn down every motherfucker who tries to hurt her."

"You've only got yourself to blame there. She's a two-bit nobody. No one would even give a shit about her if you hadn't been involved."

"Til, let's just go," Talia said, tugging at her arm.

I ignored her pleading and focused on Tillie. "She's worth ten thousand of you."

"You wouldn't even know a good thing if it hit you."

"And you're a good thing are you? 'Cause from what I've seen, you're just desperate for a story—any story—and if you get laid along the way it's just a bonus. Admit it, it was all a set-up. Even when you were at the airport on your knees wanting to suck me off, it was all part of this game wasn't it?"

Talia flinched away as I said the words. "What?"

I glanced between the girls and saw that there were secrets between them. "Oh! She didn't tell you? How she got under the table at the fucking airport cafe, on her knees, begging me to let her suck my cock. How she kissed me in the cloakroom at the benefit, and probably would have done so much more if I'd let her? How she told me that she needs a bit of dick from time to time. Don't tell me you're keeping secrets from each other?" Each statement I said drew a new reaction out of Talia. Tillie looked like she was about ready to launch at me, claws bared.

"It was supposed to be together or not at all." I didn't know if Talia actually realised she was talking aloud. Her voice was quiet, almost pathetic, and her words were laced with agony. In the space of less than a minute, her face had paled to the point where I was surprised she was still upright. The sight was almost enough to make me feel guilty, but then a quick glance at Tillie wiped the guilt away.

Her face grew redder and redder, until I could almost see the blood vessels swelling beneath her skin. "How dare you!"

I scoffed. "How dare I? God, you're pathetic. Just admit defeat and move on."

"I'll make your life a living hell."

"No, you won't." It was Talia who'd spoken. "I won't have you and Mum using my reputation this way anymore. Let's go, Brad."

The pap snapped to attention at her words.

Tillie snarled at me before moving to stop Talia. "But, baby, it was all for the story, I promise."

"For the story," Talia scoffed. "Then why wasn't it on the list of things to include?"

I grinned at the fact that I'd just captured her admission on camera. It wasn't enough to do anything legally, but I didn't give a shit about legal. I just wanted them to back the fuck off and stay away. If I did something newsworthy, I deserved to be in the papers, but the muckraking had to stop.

"It didn't feel like it was 'for the story' when you were clamouring to get under the table," I said, to dig the knife in a little deeper. I couldn't deny I was enjoying myself immensely.

Talia left the room, with Tillie close behind.

"Or when you were clutching at my cock through my pants," I added as I rounded the corner to follow them with my taunts.

I practically collided with Alyssa. The hurt, the pain, and the heartbreak that shone in her eyes stopped me dead in my tracks. Fuck. How long had she been standing there?

How much had she heard?

"What the fuck is going on?" Her tone was deadly.

I was fucked.

"Lys, I can explain," I said as I led her back into our hotel room. The last thing I needed was Tillie coming back and witnessing the fight.

"You just can't leave it, can you?" she asked as soon as we were through the door.

"Don't you get it, Lys? We won," I said.

"Won?"

"They're going to back off. They're not going to keep trying to dig up shit about me to get me kicked out of Sinclair again."

"You could have done that yourself by not having anything for them to report on. There's been nothing new despite the photographer being back."

"They were just waiting for an opportunity because they thought I was actually going to change to Wood Racing. Now I've got something on them in return. Something that could threaten W. T. Entertainment's reputation."

Her frown deepened. "What about your reputation?"

"It was fucked anyway."

"And mine?"

"They're not going to come after us, Lys. We've got them by the balls now."

"God, you're nothing more than a man-child who's so obsessed with revenge and proving something that he doesn't give a shit about anyone else's feelings in the matter."

"Whose feelings? Darcy's? Talia's? Tillie's? Paige's? As if any of them don't deserve a bit of heartache after everything they've done to me. To us."

"No. Mine, Dec. You didn't give a shit about me. Or Phoebe. I asked you to leave it, because it was finally settling. Because I'm supposed to be starting work at a professional law firm, one of the biggest in the world—a firm that could give me access to so much if I work hard enough—and just days before I'm supposed to start, you drag me back into these games. Do you think any of them are going to leave it be now?"

"Lys, I'm—"

"Don't 'Lys' me, Declan. I can't believe you'd do this. Worse, is the fact that you'd deliberately sneak around behind my back to set it all up. If you're capable of lying to me about that, what else are you capable of lying about?"

A quiver raced through my body and my blood pounded in my ears as what I'd thought would be my moment of victory quickly became a disaster greater than any I'd faced. Even when I'd thought she'd left after the article, I didn't have to face her anger or her obvious hurt. "I—I didn't lie to you, Lys, I—"

"God help me, Declan, if you finish that sentence with 'I just didn't tell you,' I won't be held responsible for what I say next. Even Phoebe knows that lying by omission is still lying, and she's three!"

Shit. Shit. Shit! I could see her pulling away, closing off. The blank mask that had slipped back over her eyes, covering the hurt and the agony, was more effective at blocking her off to me than the one she wore over her face. I'd thought I'd lost her after the magazine, but that had been because I didn't understand how deep her love actually ran. Love that had been stitched back together with trust as the thread—a thread I'd picked at, until now the whole thing threatened to unravel. "Tell me how to fix this."

"Just leave."

My heart hammered and my breathing sped. "No. I can't, Lys. I can't leave it like this."

"I have nothing to say to you right now. I need some space."

I reached for her, grabbing her wrist. "Please, let me fix this. You have to let me try."

She tugged her wrist free of my hold. "No. I can't do this. Not now. Go!"

"No."

A growl of frustration tore from her lips. "Fine. Then I will."

Unwilling to touch her against her will, even though every part of me screamed to just pull her into my arms and kiss her until the pain went away, I stood by and watched as she walked past me and out of the room. Just before the door swung closed, my vision blurred and my eyes burned. She hadn't even looked back once.

"Wait, Lys!" I pulled open the door. Memories of the day after the formal flooded through my mind, threatening to send me to my knees.

Even though barely a second had passed, by the time I reached the hallway, she was gone. I had no idea whether she'd disappeared into one of the bathrooms on the level, into the elevator, or where. I raced up to the end of the corridor, watching for any sign of her. Too many bad memories flooded me. She couldn't walk out on me again. I had to find her.

"Fuck!" Twisting around, I sat on the steps and buried my head in my hands. How could I be so stupid? I'd ignored everyone who'd warned me that she might not understand. Dr. Henrikson. Eden. Even Danny had been cryptically cautious.

I'd thought I knew better than all of them, though. I'd thought I knew Alyssa better than they did. What a fucking joke. It was clear I didn't know her at all. Not enough. In my need for revenge, I'd lost the second-most important thing in my world. Thankfully, I was sure that no matter how badly I'd screwed up, she wouldn't take Phoebe from my life unless she thought there was some danger. Even though that was a relief, it wasn't enough. I didn't just want Phoebe part-time. I wanted our family. Together.

Needing to speak to her, to apologise and explain, I turned around and headed back to the room, intending to carry on past the hotel room to search down the other end of the hallway, but stopped when I saw the turquoise-and-gold mask she'd picked for the night. The one she'd picked because it matched my eyes.

Was discarding it her way of telling me she was done with me for good? Had the "just in case" her dad had made her plan for eventuated already before we'd even left Brisbane? Reaching behind my head, I untied the ribbon on my own mask, and slipped it off. I held both of the masks in my hand as I looked around again with her name on my lips.

The door to room 607 cracked open. A second later, Morgan came out.

"Perfect plan, squirt! Couldn't have gone better," he said, holding his hand up for a high five. When I didn't respond or slap my palm against his, he waved his fingers in my face. "Don't leave me hanging." He stared at me for a moment, no doubt trying to figure out why I wasn't celebrating. "Shit, what is it?"

Not trusting myself to talk without sounding like a total wimp,

I just shook my head and held up one finger to tell him to wait. I swallowed down on the ball of emotions in my chest and then uttered just one word. "Alyssa."

"Oh, shit. Did she hear that?"

I nodded.

"I take it she didn't appreciate the shove you gave karma's arse?"

"Something like that. You didn't see her, did you?"

"No. I haven't seen anyone else up here."

"I have to find her."

"You go downstairs, I'll look around up here."

I headed back for the elevators and hit the call button. As soon as it came, I mashed the button marked for the ballroom. Instead of going into the party though, I headed into the quieter areas. Here and there couples were taking some quiet time together—some talking, some practically dry-humping in the low light.

Almost twenty minutes had passed since I'd last seen Alyssa, when the sound of soft sobs caught my ears. With my heart in my mouth, I followed them.

"Lys, look, I—" My words died on my tongue when I saw Darcy sitting on the floor with her arms wrapped around her legs, and her head resting against her knees.

She glanced up at the sound of my voice and her lips curled into a snarl. "I hope you're fucking pleased with yourself. Blake's going to leave me. It would have been okay if that tramp reporter Miss M. hadn't come over and told him about your fucking do-over note."

As much as I wanted to say that I was happy, seeing her in tears was a hollow fucking victory. Sure, she was a grade-A bitch, and had made Alyssa's life more difficult than it had needed to be, but wasn't plotting her downfall just as bad? I'd fought fire with fire, and everyone had gotten burned. Maybe she deserved what had happened, but was it really my place to decide that?

"Actually, I'm not," I said, kneeling in front of her and resting my hand on her knee. "In fact, there's something I need to say to you. Something I should have said a long time ago. I'm sorry,

Darcy."

Her eyes widened as she recoiled from my touch. "What?"

"I've made a lot of mistakes over the years, and I know you'll deny it, but at least a couple of them hurt you. So I just want you to know that I'm sorry."

"You're a freak." She shoved at me, pushing me off balance.

"Whatever. I really don't give a shit what you think about me, but I'm done thinking about you. I'm done letting you have any sway over me or Alyssa."

"You shouldn't have fucked with me. I'm going to call up *Gossip Weekly* and tell them all about this. They'll know the truth."

I shrugged. "You know what? Try it. I don't even care anymore."

Climbing back to my feet, I moved away. I'd said everything I needed to, and I hadn't been lying. She wouldn't even be a blip on my radar anymore. I had more important things to focus on. If it cost me Alyssa or Phoebe, revenge wasn't worth the price.

I continued looking around the floor, asking everyone who wasn't glued to another if they'd seen her. Each second that passed, I was more certain I'd lost her for good. My body shook, quivers to rival the worst tyre shake. My knees threatened to buckle. The last time she'd left that way, she'd gone straight home. Then Josh had been waiting for me.

Fuck.

Needing to see whether she'd perhaps returned to the room to pack up her things, I headed back for the elevator.

I slipped the key card into the door, fearing the worst—a room that contained only my bag. When I pushed open the door, I saw something that made me forget all about the key card and the lock—everything but her.

Sitting on the edge of the bed, she looked up at me when the door opened.

Her eyes were brimming with tears, the rich honey colour glistening as she stared at me. Her body sagged and a small smile lifted her lips as she looked at me. I could have been wrong, but it looked like a small sigh left her too. It was almost as if she were relieved to see me. Fucked if I knew why after what had happened.

"Thank goodness," she said.

"Please don't leave," I begged at exactly the same time.

She rushed over to me. For a moment, I thought she'd throw her arms around me, but she slowed as she came closer. The doubt and anger were still there, even if the relief had temporarily overridden it.

"Hi." The word was almost inaudible and I only caught it because of how closely I was paying attention to her.

"Fuck, Lys, I thought you'd left." I clamped my mouth shut before I could add the "me" to the sentence. "You were so mad."

"Am."

My eyes narrowed and I frowned as I struggled with my confusion over the word.

"I'm still mad," she said.

I gave her the most winning grin I could muster and dared to take another step closer to her. "And I'm still sorry."

She sighed as she turned away. "I know. That's why I came back here. I worried what you might do if you thought me needing space was a permanent thing."

Even as she said the word, I felt the tension leave my body, sinking through the floor and draining away. "It's not?"

She gave a soft laugh and shook her head. "No. Trust me. You'll know if we're off for good. I don't want to lose you, Dec. No one else will ever be able to make me as mad as you can sometimes, but that won't stop me loving you."

I stepped closer to her again, needing to look in her eyes as she spoke to me.

Before I could reach her, she wheeled around on the spot. "But I won't blindly accept you lying to me either."

"I won't lie to you ever again," I promised. "Not even a white one."

"Not even if I ask if my butt looks too big?"

I chuckled and reached for her. "Baby, your arse is always perfect to me and that's the God's honest truth."

She melted into my arms. All of the bullshit I'd clung so tightly to, the need for revenge, the twisted desire to be right, all of it meant nothing in that moment. The tension I'd been feeling every time I thought of her move to Sydney was gone. Clearly it was my own guilt—my own subconscious—trying to force me to reconsider my plans.

Just as I pressed my lips to hers to whisper all of that to her without words, Morgan burst into the room. For a second, I wondered how, but then I recalled that I'd left the key card in the door.

"Oh, you found her." It was hard not to hear the irritation in his voice.

With a frown furrowing my brow, I turned to him. "What the fuck, dude?"

"You didn't think to text me to tell me you'd found her?"

I shook my head. "Actually, no, I had slightly more important things on my mind. Is there a problem?"

"No, it's okay. No problem. I just spent the last fifteen minutes completely embarrassing myself by 'accidentally' going into every ladies' room in this damn place to find her while you're in here making out, but it's okay. It's all good."

I chuckled, and even Alyssa smiled in spite of her dislike for him—or maybe because of it.

"Sorry, dude," I said through a fresh peal of laughter. "I was too busy grovelling and demanding she take me back."

"It's true," Alyssa said, meeting my eyes. "He's been on his knees practically begging me to take him back the whole time."

"Anyway, it's almost eleven. Danny is about to make the big announcement. You need to get back in there."

"No."

"What the fuck do you mean, no?"

I pulled Alyssa against me again. "I mean, I'm exactly where I want to be for New Year's. After all, what you're doing tonight is supposed to be what you do for the rest of the year, right?" I planted a small kiss against her cheek before letting her go and turning back to Morgan. "And if that's the case, there's definitely something I need to be doing right now."

Picking up what I was putting down, he smirked at me and backed out of the room, leaving the key on the floor and letting the door shut behind him. Releasing my hold on her waist, I moved to pick up the masks I'd dropped in my haste to get to her.

"I'm looking for the girl who was in this mask. Have you seen her? I think I might have hurt her, and now I want to kiss it better."

"I'm not sure if I've seen her," Alyssa said. "Maybe you should try the mask on every girl in the land and see who it fits."

I snorted. "This ain't fucking Cinderella, and my girl won't be going at midnight, she'll be coming."

A genuine laugh left her. "You are so goddamned cheesy."

"If it makes you laugh like that, you can call me King *Fromage*."

"As much as I'd love to stay here all night, we probably should get back for Danny's announcement." She nodded at the masks in my hands. "I think one of the ribbons broke before, though."

"You can wear mine if you like?"

Shaking her head as she moved, she grabbed both of the masks and threw them onto the bed. "I think we've had enough hidden agendas for one night. Let's remove the mystery for now, shall we?"

"Okay, but do you think that your mask is repairable?"

She tilted her head in confusion as she said. "Maybe. Why?"

"Because you cannot believe how many fantasies I've had of looking down at you wearing it while you suck my cock."

"Declan!" She flushed red and playfully swatted my shoulder. "You only saw it for the first time a few hours ago."

I captured her hip and pulled her side against my front. My cock was hard and aching for her, had been ever since our almost kiss. Kissing along her neck, I whispered against her skin, "Baby, you would not believe half the fantasies I've had about you or how quickly they can form. And I intend to make them all come true."

She shivered in my hold as I ran my hand over her arse and brushed my fingers as far between her thighs as I could with her dress in the way.

"Fuck, baby, I can't wait to apologise to you properly." I stepped away from her. It took everything in me, but I managed it. "But if you're really intent on getting back to the party, we should probably go, because I don't know how much longer I can resist you."

"Just until midnight. Then maybe we can come back up here and I'll see if I can fix the mask," she breathed.

Fuck yes!

We made it as far as the ballroom lobby before Paige came storming out of the room. Her eyes were wild and when her gaze fell on me, she snarled at me like the cougar she was.

"You signed with Sinclair as a goddamned grease monkey? Don't you know what I could have offered you? You'll burn for this. I'll make you pay."

Rather than stopping to talk, I smiled and pressed my hand against the small of Alyssa's back to encourage her to keep moving. "It's been an insightful evening, hasn't it, Ms. Wood?"

Before she could respond, I led Alyssa into the ballroom. Danny was standing up at the podium still, talking about the year ahead for Sinclair.

"Aren't you worried about what she might do?" Alyssa whispered.

"No. I don't think her daughter will be her willing lapdog anymore. Not with the evidence I have against them."

"And here's the man of the hour," Danny said, lifting his hands to point to me when he noticed I'd arrived. "And his beautiful bride-to-be."

Alyssa flushed and I could almost see her itching to rush upstairs and fix the mask sooner so that she could cover her face.

Moving as one, we circled the room until we arrived at Sinclair Racing's table. Across the room, Blake and Darcy Cooper were in the middle of a heavy make-out session. I only hoped her embarrassment would lead to some changes there. I doubted it, but at least it wouldn't affect my life anymore.

"We're very happy that Declan will be joining us during his break from racing. And for those of you disappointed that he won't be on the track next year, all I can say is you never know what might happen, and I firmly believe he will be racing again when the time is right."

Alyssa squeezed my hand, and my stomach flip-flopped at his words. Every other time he'd hinted at a possible comeback, it'd always been coded and hidden. It wasn't an announcement that I'd be back in the driver seat any time soon, but it was also a very clear message for anyone in the room—including race journalists and representatives from major sponsors not only for Sinclair but for ProV8 in general—that I had his support when the time was right.

I just had to wonder when the fuck that might be.

One thing was certain, whatever came next, I was going to deal with it with my girls at my side.

DECLAN'S STORY CONCLUDES IN

DECLAN REEDE: THE UNTOLD STORY #4

ABOUT THE AUTHOR

Michelle Irwin has been many things in her life: a hobbit taking a precious item to a fiery mountain; a young child stepping through the back of a wardrobe into another land; the last human stranded not-quite-alone in space three million years in the future; a young girl willing to fight for the love of a vampire; and a time-travelling madman in a box. She achieved all of these feats and many more through her voracious reading habit. Eventually, so much reading had to have an effect and the cast of characters inside her mind took over and spilled out onto the page.

Michelle lives in sunny Queensland in the land down under with her surprisingly patient husband and ever-intriguing daughter, carving out precious moments of writing and reading time around her accounts-based day job. A lover of love and overcoming the odds, she primarily writes paranormal and fantasy romance.

Comments, questions, and suggestions for improvements are always welcome. You can reach me at writeonshell@outlook.com or through my website www.michelle-irwin.com. Thanks in advance for your correspondence.

You can also connect with me online via
Facebook**: www.facebook.com/MichelleIrwinAuthor**
Twitter**: www.twitter.com/writeonshell**

Printed in Great Britain
by Amazon